W9-CPJ-384

My Notorious
Gentleman

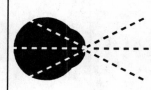

This Large Print Book carries the
Seal of Approval of N.A.V.H.

MY NOTORIOUS GENTLEMAN

GAELEN FOLEY

THORNDIKE PRESS
A part of Gale, Cengage Learning

GALE
CENGAGE Learning®

Detroit • New York • San Francisco • New Haven, Conn • Waterville, Maine • London

GALE
CENGAGE Learning®

Copyright © 2013 by Gaelen Foley.
Thorndike Press, a part of Gale, Cengage Learning.

ALL RIGHTS RESERVED
This is a work of fiction. Names, characters, places, and incidents either are the product of the author's imagination or are used fictitiously and are not to be construed as real. Any resemblance to actual events, locales, organizations, or persons, living or dead, is entirely coincidental.

Thorndike Press® Large Print Romance.
The text of this Large Print edition is unabridged.
Other aspects of the book may vary from the original edition.
Set in 16 pt. Plantin.

LIBRARY OF CONGRESS CATALOGING-IN-PUBLICATION DATA

Foley, Gaelen.
    My Notorious Gentleman / by Gaelen Foley.
       pages cm. -- (Thorndike Press Large Print Romance)
    ISBN-13: 978-1-4104-6198-8 (hardcover)
    ISBN-10: 1-4104-6198-X (hardcover)
    1. Aristocracy (Social class)—England—Fiction. 2. Regency fiction. 3. Love stories. 4. Large type books. I. Title.
    PS3556.O3913M88 2013
    813'.54—dc23   2013024072

Published in 2013 by arrangement with Avon, an imprint of HarperCollins Publishers

Printed in the United States of America
1 2 3 4 5 6 7 17 16 15 14 13

To everything there is a season . . .
A time to kill and a time to heal,
a time to tear down and a time
to build . . .
A time to love and a time to hate,
a time for war and a time for peace.

Ecclesiastes

CHAPTER 1

London, 1816

George was foxed, but that, Grace supposed, was to be expected. The carefree young dandy plopped down beside her onto the bench at the perimeter of the ballroom, and declared: "Miss Kenwood, I adore you!"

"Ah, that's very nice, George."

"I mean it, I worship you!"

"Worship God and use your head, dear lad," she answered, surveying the ballroom.

He laughed as though she had said something charming. "Spoken like a true preacher's daughter! I daresay you could save even *my* soul, Miss Kenwood. But 'tis true," he slurred, lifting his glass to her. "You are my ideal woman in all things." He glanced down innocently at her gown. "What you lack in fashion, you make up for with substance!"

She turned to him, startled. "Er, thank you, my lord."

7

Perfect. Just what she needed to hear. Confirmation from their host's own son that she *looked* as out of place as she felt in the Marquess of Lievedon's opulent Town palace.

Miss Grace Kenwood, firmly on the shelf at the advanced age of five-and-twenty, was not accustomed to aristocratic ballrooms.

Everyone raved about the worldly delights of London, but the sprawling metropolis made her miss her garden. The air in the crowded capital made her skin feel dirty compared to the fresh breezes and sunshine of the countryside.

And the people . . . well, one was not to judge, but suffice it to say these were decadent times.

"What are you doing hiding in the shadows like a wallflower, anyway?" her wayward young friend demanded, bumping her shoulder with his own, like an overgrown schoolboy flirting with his governess.

At twenty-one, George, Lord Baron Brentford, or Bratford, as she preferred to call him, was four years her junior. He enjoyed putting her up on this silly pedestal because he knew full well that nothing would ever come of it. He was heir to the Lievedon marquisate while she was but the daughter of the easygoing minister who was continually called in to help steer the young rake-hell off the path of self-destruction.

Through an odd series of events, the Reverend Richard Kenwood had become the one moral authority on earth who seemed to have any influence over the fashionable young buck.

Lord Lievedon's prodigal son still strayed on a regular basis, but at least the scoundrel was willing to listen to Papa's wise counsel now and then. Heaven knew George's own father couldn't get through to him; but then, the grand old marquess only knew how to speak in cold, clipped commands.

At any rate, Papa's taming influence over His Lordship's firstborn was what had moved the marquess to give Papa his living. With the understanding, of course, that the Reverend Kenwood would make himself available to his patron's family whenever he was needed.

In short, when the marquess summoned them to Town, the Kenwoods went.

George tossed back the last of his brandy and signaled to a nearby footman to bring him another.

"Don't you think you've had enough?" she murmured gently.

"Just one more!" he deflected with a grin, then hastened to change the subject. "So,

9

my dear, how's everyone back at the village?"

The parsonage was just a stone's throw from the marquess's ancestral pile in Leicestershire.

There was always a buzz in their tiny village of Thistleton when any of His Lordship's family came down from Town. To be sure, George certainly brought his own brand of excitement out to the country. Especially last time.

"Are they all still scandalized by my little spot of mischief with the tavern wench?" Though he had the decency to look at least a little sheepish, the merry sparkle in his eyes betrayed the fact that he still thought it was funny.

Grace did not smile. "Marianne is not with child, if that's what you're asking," she answered coolly. "So at least there's that."

"Ah! What a relief."

She clenched her teeth, shocked by his nonchalance. The spoiled lordling had no idea of the harsh scrabble for existence that poor, hard-edged Marianne had left behind in London, trying, with the Kenwoods' help, to make a new life for herself in the peaceful haven of their country village.

George wasn't even aware of the damage he had so casually done to all Marianne's progress, waving more money under her nose than an ex–soiled dove could resist.

"And, er, what about Miss Windlesham?" he asked gingerly after a moment's hesitation. "Does she still hate me? As you can see, she refused the invitation to our ball tonight."

"Can you blame her?" Grace countered in surprise.

Back home, the Honorable Miss Calpurnia Windlesham was the ruling belle of the county and had all but branded George for her future husband.

He scowled. "Callie doesn't own me, you know! Nor her mother, neither," he said hotly. "Tell them I said so, Grace! Especially Lady Windlesham. That blasted woman's practically picked out the curtains already for when her daughter's the lady of Lievedon Hall."

Grace shook her head and leaned back against the wall. "I am staying out of it."

One trifled with Lady Windlesham at one's own peril.

"But Grace, you can't abandon me! You know I'm hopeless left to my own devices."

"Why don't you speak to Papa?"

"Talk to a priest about my dalliance with a demirep?" he whispered. "Hardly! What will he think of me?"

"Ex-demirep," she corrected.

"You are my only hope, Grace. You are my guiding angel —"

"Are you drunk?" she asked, merely to test his honesty.

He ignored the question. "You have to help me with Calpurnia. You fix other people's problems, Grace! Come, you know you do. That is your designated role in life and the village, and everybody knows it! Rev wouldn't be able to find his sermon notes if it weren't for you. Why, the crops would probably forget to grow if you didn't remind them, too!"

"They're not growing this year, actually, if you haven't noticed," she said dryly. "You should see my poor little garden."

The explosion of some massive volcano on the other side of the globe had robbed the earth of summer this year, and the cold was wrecking the crops. Frosts and flurries during the Season, odd-shaped hail, weird yellow skies.

Instead of the loveliness of a balmy British spring, it was gray and wet, cold and dreary.

Some people were starting to wonder if the end of the world was at hand.

The strange turn in the weather seemed all the crueler, with the war finally over. Instead of enjoying peace, now they faced the haunting specter of starvation, at least among the common folk.

There were reports of riots due to food shortages throughout England, and indeed, all of Europe. Such hardship seemed a world away from Lord Lievedon's ballroom, but as the daughter of a pastor who also served as Overseer of the Poor for their local village, the ills of the land had become her and her father's personal problem.

Grace didn't even want to think about what corn prices were going to be like this winter. Not with all the mouths the parish had to feed.

"Well, I'm fairly sure the bloody volcano wasn't my fault, at least," George muttered.

"Language, George, please."

"Sorry."

Grace gave him a stern look but relented. "Very well. I will tell Calpurnia you asked after her."

He grabbed her hand and kissed it. "You see? You *are* an angel!" But then he continued, for he'd never been one to know when to quit. "As for Callie, well, if you want my opinion, that girl needs to learn to control her temper."

"Is that so?"

"To go into such a fury over a bit of fun with a tavern wench? Her vanity, that's the problem. Too proud! Calpurnia Windlesham thinks she is God's gift to man, but she's got bats in the belfry if she thinks she can tell *me* what to do. We're not even engaged yet!"

Grace gazed at him in calm silence while he ranted on.

"She's pretty enough, I grant you that, but the chit's ridiculously spoiled — and yes, I do see the irony of my saying so. You needn't point it out."

"Wouldn't dream of it, dear lad."

"You should warn her if she keeps this up — holding a grudge, going out of her way to try to hurt me with all her little cruel retaliations — she's going to lose her chance," he warned. "I could snap my fingers and have ten better than her by the end of the night."

"Yet here you are wasting your time talking to old, unfashionable me," Grace teased in a low tone. "What happened to all your usual admirers, anyway?"

"They've found a new idol."

"Oh, you poor, neglected thing."

"Not at all. Look at 'im, poor bleeder." George nodded across the ballroom in amusement. Following his gaze, Grace saw a crowd of women hemming in some fellow on the other side of the room. "Up to his

14

eyeballs in matchmaking mamas — and bored Society wives on the hunt for a bit of the rough, I wager."

"George! You mustn't say such things in front of me."

He snorted. "It's the truth."

Only the top of the man's head, a shock of dark hair, could be seen above the feathered plumes adorning the ladies' jeweled coifs. "Who's that they've got cornered?"

"Lord Trevor Montgomery," George replied with a wry, knowing lift of his eyebrows. "Yes, we've got no less celebrities than the Order agents here tonight in our humble home. Are you impressed?"

Grace furrowed her brow and looked at him in question.

He saw she did not recognize the term and burst out in surprise, "Oh, by Jove's braces — my little country cousin! Don't you read the papers?"

"No. It's all too depressing. Well, enlighten me!" she exclaimed.

"Right. So it came out last month that the men we all thought were merely the depraved members of the Inferno Club were actually spies or warriors or assassins or something."

"Assassins?" she retorted, sure he was teasing her again.

"I'm deadly serious, Grace! Apparently they're part of this clandestine, hereditary order of chivalry called the Order of St. Michael the Archangel."

"You and your cock-and-bull tales."

"I'm telling you the truth!" he said, laughing merrily. "You should really open a paper now and then. They're like some remnant of the Knights Templar or something, I swear. Handpicked for it as boys and trained for years until they're lethal, then unleashed upon the world to fight for England. You're still not impressed?"

She shrugged, eyeing him dubiously.

Even if he was not making sport of her country naïveté, she did not like violence and was not at all sure she wished to be in the same room with a government assassin.

"Apparently the Order's been around since the Crusades," he said. "They've been working for the Crown throughout the war. Bunch o' bloody heroes —"

"George, language." She sighed.

"Sorry. They were assigned all over Europe during the war, and just a month ago, they uncovered a plot right here in London to kill the Prime Minister."

"Oh, yes . . . I did hear something about that."

"I should hope so!" Then he nodded again

16

toward the gentleman hidden by the mob of adoring females. "That chap right over there personally helped to stop the dastardly business. Once the press caught wind of it all, and the Order was exposed, the Regent saw fit to honor them in Westminster Abbey, medals and all. Ever since, the ladies won't leave poor Montgomery alone. He's one of the last bachelors left in their set. But don't bother asking him about his service. He won't discuss it — though I'm sure he has some wild tales to tell."

"Spies, you say?" she echoed skeptically, intrigued but still not quite convinced he wasn't bamming her.

"Well, ex-spies now. They can hardly do that sort of thing anymore, now that they've been lionized before the world, can they? Fame has robbed them of their vocations."

She furrowed her brow, peered again in the ex-spy's direction, but he was still hidden. She turned to George again uncertainly. "If what you say is true, are you sure they aren't dangerous?"

"Well, of course they're dangerous, but not to *us*, you little cake-head!" he said, laughing. "That's the whole point of the Crown having men like that, isn't it? From what I hear, they're trained in all types of combat and codes and ciphers, and how to make explosives." George bumped her again with his shoulder, amused at her uneasiness. "Shall I introduce you?"

"No!"

"C'mon. I'll bet he knows nine different ways to kill you with his bare hands," George declared, grinning at her alarm.

"Then perhaps those ladies should be a bit more careful not to crowd him so," she retorted, her cheeks reddening.

He relented. "Ah, personally, I'm just glad they've found someone else to bother."

At that moment, the glittering crowd around Lord Trevor Montgomery parted, and Grace caught her first unobstructed glimpse of the visiting Order agent.

She went very still, staring in surprise. *Good heavens.* She had never seen a bona fide hero before, but Lord Trevor Montgomery certainly looked the part, dark and dashing.

He was easily over six feet tall and powerfully built, with broad shoulders that seemed to shrug off danger. He exuded virile confidence, as if there was little on earth he would not dare undertake.

He had a hard, rugged face stamped with wary cynicism that remained even when he flashed a dangerous smile at the ladies fawning on him.

At first glance, he seemed to be eating up all the attention. Though he was not a pretty fellow like some of the dandyish London peacocks strutting about tonight, he looked . . . strong.

Proud, she thought. And physically rather mighty.

She recalled what George had said about modern-day Knights Templar, and thought this man would have looked as natural in chain mail as he did in his impeccably tailored evening clothes of formal black and white.

In contrast to the gentlemanly elegance of his garb, he had long dark hair like a barbarian. Pulled back in a queue, it accented the hard angles of his square jaw and tanned skin and made him look a little, she thought, like a pirate.

Which was rather silly of her, she supposed. Odd. She was not normally one given to flights of fancy.

More distressing still were the odd tinglings in her body and daft flutterings of her heart. She dropped her gaze, startled and annoyed by her own intemperate reaction.

But unable to help herself, she stole another secret glance at him — and it was then that her gift for noticing people in pain drew her attention to the guarded, angry lines around his eyes.

The bitter intensity behind his practiced smile.

And it dawned on her that he wasn't paying the slightest bit of attention to all those women around him.

Not really.

In fact, he kept drawing away subtly from their efforts to touch him; Grace followed the line of his gaze and realized that he was constantly watching the door.

As if he was waiting for someone to arrive.

Hmm. Studying him a little more closely, she furrowed her brow and began to suspect that the "famous hero" did not want to be here any more than she did.

Of course, she might be wrong, but that smile seemed little more than a thin veneer over a vortex of churning emotion, most of it rather dark.

This was not a happy man, she mused as she gazed at him standing there like a lost soul, alone in the crowd.

George interrupted her fascinated study of the stranger as he rose. "Well, my dear Polaris, it's always a pleasure talking to you, but if you'll excuse me, I must not neglect our other guests. And . . . I believe I shall go peek in on the card games —"

"Oh George, that is not a good idea for you," she protested softly, taking his hand at once, as if she could stop him.

"Not to play! I'm only going to watch," he assured her with a smile.

Grace stared at him. "Promise?"

"If you promise to dance with me," he retorted, withdrawing his hand to fold his arms across his chest with a knowing look.

She frowned. *Stubborn pup.*

"Oh, come, one dance. I'll suffer if you will."

"Fine," she muttered, but inwardly, she shrank from the thought of parading herself across the dance floor, a spinster in a plain, provincial gown, sporting a toe in front of the ton.

She didn't even know anyone here except for George, Papa, and, to a lesser extent, Lord Lievedon himself. It was easy to picture all these glamorous aristocrats taking one look at her, wrinkling their haughty noses, and asking each other: *Who is that and what is she doing here?"*

But if that was what it took to keep George on the straight and narrow, then so be it. She'd sacrifice her dignity in front of Society if she must — and even in front of *him.* That disconcerting gentleman-assassin on the other side of the room.

Not that a man like that was ever going to notice her.

In any case, the way he watched the door made her think he was already waiting for a particular lady to arrive.

"Excellent, then!" her rakish friend declared. "I'll be back soon to claim you for our dance."

Grace nodded. *Be strong, George,* she thought, as he bowed to her, then walked away. Nevertheless, she couldn't help wishing that Callie were here.

The bubbly young belle, with her constant demand for attention, might have kept her beau distracted from his gambling habit. Then Grace could have comfortably fallen into her usual, safe role as the respectable chaperone, quietly standing behind the vivacious, golden flirt and keeping both young people in line.

She supposed she had better go check her appearance and do what she could with herself before George came back, provided his demons did not suck him down into their familiar snare.

Rising from the bench, she withdrew from the ballroom. Nobody noticed her exit.

Gliding through the marble hallways, she passed the noisy music room, full of laughter and song. Everyone here seemed to be such great friends.

She lowered her gaze and turned away, seeking a quiet room away from the crowd where she might find a mirror.

As the sounds of the ball receded, at last she peered into an empty sitting room at the end of a marble corridor. This would suit. Stepping into the dimly lit chamber, she pulled the door closed behind her with a low sigh and finally let her guard down.

There was nothing like being a stranger in the middle of a loud, lavish party to make one feel unutterably alone.

Lord Trevor Montgomery kept an eye on the doorway of the ballroom, but feeling more restless with every passing moment, he was starting to think that dragging himself here tonight had been a bloody waste.

Still no sign of Laura.

Faithless bitch.

Maybe she was hiding from him. Maybe she feared if she showed up here tonight, he'd start something with her new fiancé.

As if he couldn't kill one idiot dragoon with his eyes closed.

Well, she needn't have flattered herself.

He was already over Laura Bayne.

That was all that she or anyone else in London needed to know.

Hell, it wasn't as though he had been waiting the past few years to marry the feckless beauty or anything stupid like that. It wasn't as though he had been building her a bloody fucking dream house for them to live in once his service to his stupid bloody country was finally done.

But what the hell. He'd have probably hated being married to her, anyway, he told himself. He barely even knew her. He had wanted it that way, had purposely kept her at arm's length.

Still, being jilted, even by mistake, was more humiliation than he intended to stand for. So as much as he did not want to be there tonight, he had no choice.

What was left of his pride demanded he make an appearance and show the world he did not give one damn about how all his future plans had crashed and burned.

The whole ton knew how he had been written off for dead by his gorgeous fiancée while he'd been away at the war. In his own mind, Trevor had been jilted.

Thus, it was a matter of male pride. If she had had any faith in him at all, she should have known that he always came home alive. She should have believed in him.

She should have at least waited for confirmation he was dead. But she had not. She had washed her hands of him and moved on with her life.

In a way, he supposed he couldn't blame her. But he was too furious that at last, after years of faithful service, just when victory was in sight, his long-hoped-for reward had slipped through his fingers.

He felt like naught but the butt of a grand joke. Not that he was laughing.

All he knew was that there was no way in hell he would countenance anyone's pity. And so he had put on an evening coat and, he hoped, a not-too-cynical smile, and had come to show the world that he was perfectly fine.

Easy come, easy go.

All he really wanted was to be left alone, but since his horrible, newfound fame made it clear that *that* wasn't going to happen, he did the proper British thing and went about keeping up appearances.

He had come out tonight to show Laura most of all that he could move on with his life just as easily as she had.

Indeed, there were far too many women around him even now who could barely wait to comfort him in his, ahem, heartbreak.

Trevor rather hated them all at the moment.

All women. It was nothing personal. They were merely the spawn of Satan, the devil's own, every last one of 'em.

He smiled at the bloodsucking harpies, disinterested, detached, only half-listening to their idiotic prattle and wondering which of them might be any good in bed.

What pretty fools.

The three on his left were trying to get him to play a childish parlor game as their means of flirting.

"If Lord Trevor were an animal, what would he be?" they teased.

"A bear, I think," her brunette friend teased.

"Thanks a lot," he muttered.

"A wolf!"

"No, a hunting dog."

He arched a bored eyebrow.

Meanwhile, the three in the center were planning his social calendar for him. He was exhausted just listening to all the activities they were lining up for him. There was no way he was going to some stupid flower show, let alone the opera. No. He'd heard enough shrieking in Italian during that nasty business he and Nick had taken care of on the outskirts of Rome, thank you very much.

But, his eyes glazing over, he just nodded politely.

The two sultry adventuresses on his right, meanwhile, were a little more direct about what they had in mind.

Damn, they were sending him messages with their big, smoky eyes that had usually been reserved for his handsomer teammates.

But Beau was married, and Nick had gone to jail, so it seemed they were prepared to make do with boring, sane, reliable Montgomery.

He looked askance at the decadent pair, wondering if he should be worried. *Carnivores.* One licked her lips at him; the other smiled like she was thinking of tackling him to the ballroom floor and ripping his clothes off him.

There had been times in his past, of course, hundreds of miles from Laura, that he'd have been happy to comply, but this wasn't one of them.

They could all go to hell for all he cared.

Newly converted to a misanthrope, he looked away with a wave of coldness washing through him. When the clock tolled eleven, he was suddenly done with all this. This night. This petty exercise was pointless.

Obviously, Laura and the major weren't coming.

He had rather liked the notion of her walking in and seeing him surrounded by amorous women, but he had been here for two bloody hours and just didn't care that much.

She wasn't worth the aggravation.

He was going home.

It took some finesse, but he finally managed to extricate himself from the knot of rouged, vivacious lovelies. Shrugging off light, caressing holds designed to snare him; ignoring vapid questions meant to delay him; and impatiently lying through his teeth that of course he'd come back soon and dance with all of them, he retreated until he had gained his liberty, and fled.

As he marched off, he heard the ladies whispering to each other that he must be forgiven for his rudeness on account of his recent heartbreak.

Trevor gritted his teeth and strode out into the adjoining marble corridor, where more guests loitered. Out of habit, he glanced into the pier glass on the wall to check behind him and nearly paused mid-stride to find he was being followed.

The two little hussies in silk and diamonds did not intend to let him get away so easily, it seemed. He growled under his breath and walked faster, determined to escape them. When he picked up his pace, the whispers behind him turned to giggles, and they walked faster, too.

Did they think this was a game?

Apparently, they hadn't heard that the depraved Inferno Club had been merely a front for the Order, that its members weren't all as bad as they'd let the world believe. Especially not him.

Trevor was happy to consider himself the boring one. Responsible. Reliable. You had to be when you came from a scandalous ducal family, then were assigned for the next decade to serve on a three-man Order team with the likes of Beauchamp (flashy) and Nick bloody Forrester (bastard).

Somebody had to be the adult.

The amorous ladies hunting him obviously thought he was playing with them. He restrained the urge to turn and curtly cut them down to size.

But he couldn't have done it even if he had wanted to. Flawless manners and an inbred sense of chivalry were the bane of his existence. Like an idiot, he had even told Laura that he understood, and he had wished her happy.

What a sot.

He could hear those hussies still following him, and it wasn't difficult to guess what they desired. *Maybe I should,* he mused. Then at least he'd have the satisfaction of knowing the gossip would soon get back to Laura.

She didn't love him, but she was vain enough to be gnawed with jealousy. It was one, admittedly feeble way to get back at a woman who had publicly humiliated him.

But, no. The thought of using those harlots for his own selfish pleasure sickened him. No, he was done having sex for ulterior motives. It was bad enough to have done that sort of thing for England during his spy days. He was not about to resort to male harlotry now.

He wasn't Nick, after all.

It was time to disappear. He took a circuitous course through the marquess's excellent house to lose them. A bit of an amateur architect, he resisted the temptation to stop and study the floating spiral staircase as he passed. Adam's handiwork, no doubt.

He ducked into the music room, only to find a countess with a marriageable daughter who pinned him with a determined stare from over by the pianoforte. He'd barely extracted himself from her clutches last week.

Ah, shite. Ever so casually, Trevor pivoted and headed out the nearest door.

A nonchalant glance over his shoulder revealed Her Ladyship pushing her way through the crowd toward him. Blazes, they were closing in on him from both directions now.

Never in his shy, pimply youth, cast in the shadow of his better-looking, louder-bragging friends had he ever dreamed he might have this sort of problem.

He headed for a nearby servant door, but a stream of footmen spilled out, cutting him off; trapped, he glanced about, seeking another escape, then slipped around the corner and sped down the hall. He could hear the pursuing ladies just around the corner.

"Oh, Lord Trevor, darling, where are you?"

"We want to ask you something, handsome!"

He scowled.

"Oh, Lord Trevor? Where have you gone, my dear?"

"We have a wonderful notion of how to cheer you up!"

Their giggling grew louder.

"Perdition," he whispered under his breath. Laying hold of the nearest doorknob, he whisked into a dimly lit parlor, pulled the door shut silently behind him, and locked it. Immediately touching his fingertips to his tongue, he reached over and pinched out the flames on the nearby candle sconce.

Then he held perfectly still in the darkness, waiting for them to pass.

He held his breath as the ladies tried the door.

"No, Cecily, this one's locked."

"Come, he must've gone upstairs."

"Oooh! Yes! What a wicked tease! Maybe he's already found a bed for us . . ."

He rolled his eyes, but finally, he heard them moving off. He let out a weary exhalation and leaned his forehead against the door. *That was close.*

"Um, excuse me," a feminine voice spoke up from the darkness.

Trevor nearly jumped out of his skin. *Not another one!* He whirled around, taken more off guard than any ex-spy should ever be and irked in the extreme by that fact.

It just went to show how out of sorts he still was over, well, everything these days.

But as he focused on an hourglass figure silhouetted in the moonlight streaming through the French doors to the little balcony, he could not believe his eyes.

You have got to be joking, he thought. Another blasted woman waiting for him?

What the hell?

His eyes narrowed. *Is that what these wenches think of me? That they can do whatever they want with me? Take advantage of me? Use me?*

Well, then. Maybe Nick was right. He had always warned Trevor about being too nice to people. This was what nice, respectable gentlemen got: walked on.

No more, he vowed, suddenly full-on furious at this ambush and fed up with these games.

How this little predatory female had known to lie in wait for him here, he was too outraged to wonder. He truly could not be bothered to care.

Pushed past the point of chivalry, he decided it was bloody well time to fight fire with fire. Teach these huntresses a lesson they'd never forget. He didn't know which one had trapped him this time, but she was about to get more than she had bargained for.

"Well, my dear," he purred, stalking slowly toward the shapely outline of the woman. "Here we are," he said coldly. "Alone at last."

"What? Oh — I — um — I'm sorry — I
—"

"Don't lose your nerve now, *chérie,*" he
taunted her in a low, silken voice. "You've
got me all to yourself. I'm at your service, I
assure you. Such persistence deserves to be
rewarded." He moved closer. "I'm here to
give you what you want. So let's get started,
shall we?"

Grace stood there tongue-tied as Lord
Trevor Montgomery stepped out of the
shadows, looming before her like a mighty
fallen angel with merciless hatred in his
eyes. There was not even time to scream as
he swept her roughly into his arms; he
clamped her against his iron chest and
claimed her mouth in an angry, insolent
kiss.

CHAPTER 2

So this is what goes on in London. Grace feared she was in shock.

Fortunately, she was not the fainting sort. Who knew what this assassin-spy-pirate might do to a lady if she lost consciousness?

As it was, she barely knew what hit her. One moment, she was minding her own business, checking her teeth in the mirror, smoothing her hair before George dragged her onto the dance floor; the next, *he* had invaded her solitude, slipping into the room, all stealth and effortlessly smoldering seduction.

Silent as a marauding wolf.

At least she knew now her assessment of him back in the ballroom was right.

Something was definitely wrong with this man. An oversized ego, to start, paired with a nonexistent moral conscience. A gentleman did not go around grabbing random women and jamming his tongue down their throats.

On the other hand, half-swooning, Grace had to admit he was rather good at this.

His touch was a little more forceful than necessary as he stroked her body and held her. He seemed to be trying to scare her with the fierceness of his ardor.

He obviously did not know her very well. It was a point of pride with her that she did not scare easily (other than her general terror of Lady Windlesham).

Indeed, after the initial shock, she was more curious about this kissing business than anything.

Which was rather bad of her, she supposed. But after all, it *was* her first kiss.

Might as well enjoy it . . .

Trevor liked the way she tasted. Which annoyed him, considering his deliberately rude intent was to put the little harlot in her place.

Holding her more tightly, he plundered her mouth, driving her lips farther apart with his kisses while he stroked her silken neck. Her startled squirming against his body, combined with the sweetness of her tongue, lit a fire in his blood that had long fallen into cold, dead ashes. With a needy moan, he clutched her harder by her waist, petting her everywhere, cupping her delicate jaw in his other palm. His heart thundering, he was shocked and a little appalled at his own response, considering that he was usually a perfect gentleman.

But to his surprise, in this moment, giving in to raw lust felt glorious after going so long without.

He hadn't had a woman in months, since well before he had been taken hostage, and before that, he'd lived like a monk, saving himself for Laura. *What a fool.*

It was bloody well time to break his fast, he decided.

He wasn't usually this spontaneous, but then again, it wasn't usually autumn in the middle of June.

The whole world was out of sorts, including him. Nothing made sense anymore, so why should he follow his usual rules?

Longingly, he cupped the luscious stranger's breast, soft, generous, and round. Yes, tonight maybe all he needed was warm human contact, some kind of connection.

Whoever she was, he would take the release she was offering. Then, maybe once he'd cleared his head, he could finally start to get on with his life. Begin to let go of his anger, though anger sometimes seemed like all that he had left . . .

Grace honestly did not know what was wrong with her. Her body was now willfully ignoring clear orders from her brain. He was just too delicious.

Push him away! That's quite enough! her usual prim side yelled at her. Who did he think he was, anyway? This man had no right to grope her, kiss her, treat her like a toy made for his amusement. Not her, of all people!

A preacher's daughter. A Sunday school teacher!

But her long-starved flesh seemed to have other ideas about who she was, secretly, deep down.

Maybe in some shadowed corner of her heart, she wasn't so different from the ex–soiled dove, Marianne.

Well, she might be the soul of respectability, but in his arms, she learned for certain — if there had been any doubt — that she really *wasn't* an angel, as George and so many others liked to believe.

Oddly enough, she was glad of the reminder as this stranger showed her another, wilder side of herself. Her flesh thrilled to his fevered stroking. Her skin glowed, awakened by him; her lips swelled like blossoming roses beneath his masterful seduction; her toes curled in complete insubordination.

But while her nerve endings tingled with forbidden pleasure, her conscience was at a loss.

This had to stop. *Had* to.

She was not a hussy like some of those women in the ballroom. She was a lady, a good influence on others, and she most assuredly did not go around sharing torrid kisses in dark rooms with tall, dashing spies.

All right, that's quite enough, big fellow. Panting, she flattened her hands against his chest but forgot again to protest, marveling at the wall of muscle in front of her. Fortunately, he seemed to get the message anyway and let her up for air with a low rumble of velvety laughter.

"My, my, you don't know what you want, do you, sweet? You'd better figure it out fast, or I'm going to make the decision for you." He tilted his head to come in for another kiss.

"No — we can't!" she panted with an air of desperation.

"We already are."

"But I don't even know you!" she whispered, her chest heaving.

"So? I like your eyes," he answered, studying her with a roguish little smile made to devastate the female heart.

"Sir! This is most improper!"

"Indeed," he agreed in a hearty murmur.

"You mustn't —"

She couldn't talk with her mouth full as he swooped lower, his warm, clever, questing tongue dancing with hers.

Grace felt faint with the unbearable temptation.

But when his fingertips skimmed her neckline, something about the expert tug at her clothing thankfully brought her out of this decadent enchantment.

What was she doing? This was insanity.

He was still kissing her as she flicked her eyes open wide. "Floor or the couch, *chérie*?"

Such a question! She stopped and looked at him in shock.

"You're right," he breathed, "who cares? Just make love to me."

She quivered violently.

And just when she thought she was going to have to resort to kneeing him in the groin — a ploy she'd heard worked well, but had never tried — he reached under her backside and lifted her up off the floor, setting her gently on the scrolled, padded arm of the sofa.

"There we are, nice and cozy," he ground out as he slipped the hem of her gown upward over her knee and stepped between her legs.

Dear God! She started to panic in earnest. This had got entirely out of hand.

Now that she was pinned on the arm of the couch unable to kick him, the only weapon that came to mind was the pearl-tipped hairpin buried in her chignon.

With a gulp, she reached up and slid it out of her hair, and as it brought her long tresses tumbling down about her shoulders, she braced herself.

And did what she had to do.

She jabbed him in the arm with it.

"Ow!" The famous hero released her abruptly and stepped back, clapping his hand to his opposite biceps. "What the — ?" He looked at her in astonishment.

Grace held perfectly still, her eyes wide, her heart pounding. She dearly hoped he wasn't the most soulless sort of assassin, but then, he worked for the Crown, so he had to obey the law like anyone else did.

Right?

She continued to brandish the five-inch hairpin like a miniature sword while he checked to see if his arm was bleeding.

"What did you do that for?" he exclaimed.

"I told you to stop."

"No, you didn't!"

"Well, I *thought* it!"

He looked at her in exasperation. "Well, I apologize for failing to read your mind, dear lady." He shook his head in bewildered indignation. "Excuse me, but I thought this was what you wanted. You're the one who was in here waiting for *me.*"

Her jaw dropped. "I was not!" She gasped, her cheeks turning scarlet. "Is that what you think?"

"Weren't you?" he exclaimed.

Egotistical brute!

"Of course not!" she cried. "I was minding my own business! I-I had to fix my hair!"

He considered this, then flashed a knowing grin. "Right," he drawled.

And she lost her temper. The one that nobody back in Thistleton even knew she had. "Oh, how can anyone be so arrogant?" she uttered as grandly as Lady Windlesham herself. "*What,* sir, do you take me for?"

"I'm not exactly sure," he replied, scanning her person from head to toe, but his eyes danced.

She noticed as the moonlight sparkled in them that they were wolf-gray and altogether shrewd.

"Humph!" Unwilling to honor his cocky response with an answer, she hopped off the arm of the sofa and was relieved when he allowed her to walk past him unmolested.

In high dudgeon, she paced a few steps away to put him at a safer distance, then she pivoted in a sweeping turn and folded her arms across her chest. With a lift of her chin, she fixed him with her sternest look of Sunday-schoolmarm disapproval.

It usually worked on the nine-year-olds, anyway.

"I am no liar," she informed him. "I certainly did not *ask* you to close the door and douse the candles. That was your own doing. But then, I expect men like you go around grabbing ladies and kissing them whenever you fancy!"

He quirked a brow. "Funny, I thought you were enjoying that as much as I was."

She narrowed her eyes. "Please leave. Now."

He glanced toward the door. "Afraid I can't."

"What?"

"Don't make me go out there. Carnivores. They're after me."

"Well, you can't stay in here!" she declared though it took her a moment to figure out what he meant. Then the whole, sordid picture crystallized in her lust-besotted brain. "Oh, Lud," she said under her breath.

He had mistaken her for one of those shameless hussies who had been thronging him in the ballroom.

He frowned as he, too, finally began to realize his mistake. "Well." He turned away scratching his cheek. "This is all very awkward."

"I daresay — !"

"My apologies, Miss, er — might I ask your name?"

"*Now* you wish to know who I am?"

"Better late than never," he said with a shrug.

"I think not." She shook her head decisively, though it went against everything in her to be rude. "I'm afraid it's best if we just part ways without further introduction. Then perhaps we can both forget this unfortunate debacle ever happened."

"Is that what this was?" he murmured, while Grace ignored a twinge of guilt at her own white lie, for in actuality, she already knew who he was. No introduction was required, at least not on her end of things.

As for him, it was just as well if he never learned her name. It was safer that way for her reputation.

"Very well," Lord Trevor replied, and

though he looked a little nonplussed by the contrast of her cold treatment after such a fiery kiss, he managed a taut bow. "As you wish. My deepest apologies, madam, for this regrettable mistake." He hesitated, as though he might say more, but then he thought better of it. "Well — that is all." Pivoting, he headed for the door.

Grace watched him warily, her heart pounding. But when she heard voices in the hallway, she gasped and zoomed after him, grabbing him by the arm. "Wait!" she whispered.

He looked askance at her with a devilish smile. "Change your mind?"

She shushed him in exasperation. "Listen! There are people in the hallway!" she whispered, raising a finger to her lips.

"So?"

"If you step out there now, and someone sees me in here — alone with you, in a darkened room — my reputation will be ruined! To say nothing of my family's. You are not allowed to ruin me," she whispered angrily.

"Well, there goes the whole aim and purpose of my life," he drawled under his breath. "Very well. Don't look so terrified. I'm sure I can find another way out of here." Giving her a sardonic look of reproach, he turned away and crossed to the French doors, opening them to step out onto the small balcony overlooking the garden.

Grace followed him uncertainly.

He peered over the edge to assess its distance from the ground below. Then, gripping the railing with a lackadaisical air, he swung one long leg over the side.

"Be careful!" she warned in a whisper, which earned her another long-suffering look.

"Thank you for your concern, Miss — ?"

She shook her head again.

"Stubborn," he taunted, then lowered himself deftly off the outer ledge of the balcony. From there, he took a long step sideways onto a cast-iron rose trellis affixed to the exterior wall of the mansion.

Down this makeshift ladder the ex-spy proceeded to climb as nonchalantly as if he did this sort of thing every day.

Which perhaps he did, for all she knew.

Except for one small snag.

"Ow!" she heard him mutter as she leaned over the railing, following his progress in begrudging admiration.

"What's wrong?" she called down in a loud whisper.

"Thorn! Not that you care. You won't even tell me your name. I'll live," he assured her in a grumpy tone.

Grace refused to smile.

Upon reaching the flowerbed below, Lord Trevor stepped off the trellis and briefly lifted the middle joint of his finger to his mouth to ease the little wound.

She could not deny that she was somewhat amused.

"Good-bye," she called as loudly as she dared.

"Good-bye yourself," he shot back.

She frowned. *Well, nice meeting you, too.* Then she watched him go marching off into the shadows.

Glad he was gone, she supposed that was the last that she would probably see him. After he'd taken such pains to flee the "carnivores," it seemed unlikely he would return to the ballroom.

She, on the other hand, had better get back down there in short order, or someone might eventually notice she was gone. *You're dreaming,* she thought, recalling her apparent invisibility to others downstairs.

Oddly enough, however, she wasn't feeling so lonely anymore. The prospect of returning to the ball seemed even duller now, knowing that Lord Trevor would not be there. Nevertheless, she realized George might be looking for her even now to claim his dance. *Better fix my hair.* She could still practically feel his clever fingers running through her hair, his sensual touch on her skin . . .

Scandalized by her own thoughts, she scrabbled about to find a candle and tinder in the room. Laying hold of one at last, she struck the flint with hands that still trembled, but finally managed to bring back a flicker of light.

Then came the task of remaking her chignon. In short order, she had twisted her long, light brown hair into a smooth rope. She looped it around her hand to form a neat bun, then tucked the edges under and inserted the long hairpin she had poked him with to hold it all in place.

There. Now she looked like the Reverend Kenwood's virtuous daughter again.

In the glass, however, her cheeks still glowed coral pink. Nervously pulling up her neckline again, she frowned at her reflection.

What a barbarian he was, grabbing at her so! No one had ever touched her body like that before in her life. She still felt foolish and overwarm, guilty and unsure. *It wasn't my fault,* she assured herself, smoothing one last stray hair into place. *He's the one who started it.*

In any case, he hadn't even meant to do it. She understood that now. He had thought she was one of those awful women stalking him and had reacted accordingly.

He had only kissed her to be rude. Of course, he had apologized. Egads, there was no point in dwelling on it. Forgive and forget. The man had made a mistake.

A rather startling mistake, one they had both enjoyed . . . Indeed, every woman ought to be kissed like that just once in her life, Grace thought, as another sigh escaped her. The main thing was, it wouldn't happen again.

Her heart sank. *Back to being a spinster.*

But she wasted no time in sneaking out of the parlor. She opened the door a crack, glanced to the right and left, and finding the hallway empty, headed back to the ball.

Awkward. So, so very awkward.

Comically so — even though the humor was at his own expense.

Trevor could not believe he had made such a mortifying blunder, but it just went to show how out of sorts he was, and besides, as mistakes went, this was one he had thoroughly enjoyed.

It had also made one thing very clear: Perhaps it was time he started paying attention to life again, get his bloody head on straight, and come out of his dark fog of angry, bitter brooding.

Whoever she was, the little minx had certainly jarred him out of his disillusioned rut.

Half-amused, fully chagrined, and still smoldering from head to toe with thwarted lust, he headed for his carriage, hands in pockets.

Still, the question would not leave him alone. Who was she?

A little terror, that's who. He could not believe she had jabbed him with her hairpin — all to escape his kiss, which he had doled out as if he were doing her a favor.

Tickled by the irony, even though he himself was the butt of the joke, Trevor paused reluctantly and glanced back over his shoulder at Lievedon House, all its windows warmly aglow.

Hang it, he was torn about whether to go home now as planned or venture back inside and stay a little longer.

Try to find out who she was . . .

He shook his head to himself, well aware that his apology had been inadequate. What she must think of him!

He *knew* how a gentleman ought to treat the fair sex: Unlike his Order teammates, he had sisters, after all. He had never been a serial seducer like Beauchamp, nor took twisted pleasure in the kind of stormy, hot-and-cold affairs with dangerous females that were Nick's Achilles heel.

But now he felt like a villain, for it was obvious in hindsight that the lady he had groped like a drunken libertine was a genuine nice girl.

A nice girl! *Imagine that.* He had lost faith that they existed. It made him all the more intrigued. And all the less willing to accept her refusal to tell her name.

He could learn it easily enough, of course. He did have some experience in gathering information.

But maybe she was right. Maybe it was better to leave it alone, as she had said — a secret kiss with an intoxicating stranger. God knew he'd had his share of those, he thought, letting out a wistful sigh.

Somehow, this felt different. He looked at the house again. Then a fleeting memory of her clinging to him in a dizzied swoon of very virginal passion flashed through his mind and made his nether regions pulsate with long-starved need. *Right.* All of a sudden, his mind was made up.

This would not do. Honor had its demands. He had misused a lady: He, of all

51

people, could not possibly leave it at that. He had to go back and tell her again — properly, without sarcasm — that he was sorry and that she needn't fear at all for her good name.

Which he fully intended to learn.

At the very least, he owed it to himself to find out who she was. For the first time in ages, he felt a stirring of hope. Whoever she was, she symbolized, well, something. He wasn't quite sure what. It was enough to have seen there were still good women out there in the world.

While all the others fawned on him — exactly what he didn't need — she, with that little pinprick, had neatly popped the bubble of his own dark focus on himself.

Aye, she had done him a favor, he thought wryly. He owed the girl his thanks. And why not?

He had nothing else to do tonight, nowhere else to go.

And nothing left to lose.

Laura and her new beau obviously weren't coming, so maybe now he could finally relax. Go back in, have another drink, he mused, and at least *try* to enjoy himself like a human being again.

With the taste of that beguiling girl's innocent kiss still lingering on his tongue,

Trevor surrendered to his curiosity, drawn back toward the light.

The iron chandelier glowed, hung from the mansion's airy, half-round portico. He crossed beneath it, walking back into Lievedon House.

Rejoining the fray, he made a mental note to try to steer clear of those vexing hussies and keep to the company of men while he made his inquiries.

One way or the other, he was determined to find out who the devil he had just kissed.

CHAPTER 3

Oh, no. Grace's heart sank. Upon returning discreetly to the ball, she had arrived in the doorway of the card room only to find that George had either forgotten about their promised dance or had forfeited the bargain.

She looked on in worry from a safe distance as the marquess's son plunged himself into his fatal passion at the gaming tables. It appeared to be whist that they were playing, and if it was the long form, she would not be seeing him again for the rest of the night.

Unless I tell Papa.

Yes, that was the best solution. Not so much time had passed; George could not yet be too far gone in the grip of his vice. If anyone could still pull him back from the brink, it was the kind and unflappable Reverend Kenwood.

Frankly, she could not believe the brat would even *do* this with Papa here — but

Heaven only knew what might happen if his own father found him first. Lord Lievedon had forbidden his son from these perilous amusements. But here was George, doing as he pleased right under his father's nose. Lord Bratford, indeed. Maybe this was his way of trying to get his father's attention . . .

She shook her head uneasily, then left the doorway and went looking for her sire. Along the way, she lifted a glass of wine from a footman's tray and took a large sip to steady her nerves, for she was still a little shaken by her deliciously sinful rendezvous.

As she hurried through the glittering crowd, she was shocked at herself for feeling a trifle smug as she passed the glamorous, highborn ladies who had been thronging the Order hero. It was wrong of her to gloat that she was the one who had secretly won his kiss — and secret it had better stay. She had worked hard to earn her reputation as a paragon, and she intended to keep it.

Shaking off a shiver of remembered pleasure, she put the ex-spy forcefully out of her mind.

There's Papa. Standing on her tiptoes, she spotted her father near one of the refreshment tables before the shifting crowd hid him from view again.

She began weaving her way toward him,

sipping her wine again to keep from slosh-ing it on herself or others in the noisy throng.

When she reached the edge of the group where the amiable minister was deep in conversation with several other gentlemen, she envied his ability to make friends wher-ever they went.

It was not as easy for her, with her shy streak.

She was still on the outside of the male gathering when she heard him at it again, an excellent conversationalist on any num-ber of topics.

"If you are handy with such things, my lord, I know the perfect property you should consider," he was saying. "Back in our own home village in Leicestershire near Lord Lievedon's country seat, there's a fine old farmhouse called the Grange. It's fallen into a state of disuse since the previous owner's death and could use a skillful hand to bring it back to life. I've been inside the place," Papa continued. "Excellent linen-fold panel-ing. Brickwork 'round the hearth that dates back to the Tudor age, if it can be pre-served."

"And what is the name of your village, Reverend?" another man nearby asked.

"Thistleton. The Grange has some of the

most fertile acreage still to be had in the Midlands." He took a drink and continued. "The house sits on the brow of a hill, northward facing, a very agreeable location. The fields have long lain fallow, which would ensure abundant crop yields for years to come. The pastures are suitable for cattle, horses, sheep. It has an orchard, well established, and a fine brook full with fish. The old colonel was very fond of his fishing stream."

"You sound like you'd rather buy the Grange yourself, Reverend."

He chuckled with a mild wave of his hand. "I'm just a humble minister to my flock, gentlemen. Besides, at my age, all that work sounds exhausting. But you may be just the man for the task, Montgomery."

Grace gasped as her father stepped across the open circle of the dozen or so men who had gathered around, and handed a small piece of paper to none other than Lord Trevor Montgomery.

She only just managed to duck out of sight again behind some portly fellow taking a pinch of snuff.

Oh, God. What is he doing back here? I thought he left!

"The food at the Gaggle Goose Inn isn't half-bad — that's Thistleton's only coaching inn," her father was explaining. "But if you do decide to come out and see the Grange, by all means, call on us at the parsonage. My daughter and I would be pleased to invite you to supper."

"You're very kind, sir, thank you." Lord Trevor tucked the card into his breast pocket.

"Ah," her father said, turning and spying her, but missing her look of panic, "here's my daughter now."

Grace froze as he beckoned her over with a smile.

Lord Trevor's eyebrow arched high when he saw her.

"Grace, my dear, where have you been? I was missing you," her father said affectionately.

She turned a guilty shade of red at the question, but thankfully, Papa didn't pursue it.

"I have been talking to the most congenial fellow," the reverend continued, as cordial as ever, gesturing at the ex-spy with his glass of brandy. "He is interested in Colonel Avery's old farm."

"Oh?" she choked out.

Egads, it was only a short walk through two pastures and a grove of trees between her home at the lovely stone parsonage and the rambling old gentlemanly farmhouse known as the Grange. Of all the neighbors who might have dreamed of moving in next door — !

She managed not to choke and summoned up a polite smile instead. "Oh, but, Papa, the Grange is just a ruin. It's scarcely livable," she assured Lord Trevor with a nervous smile.

"Nonsense!" her father objected. "It just needs a few intelligent repairs, but my young friend here was just telling us he's a bit of an amateur architect — among his many other talents, so I hear."

"To be sure," Grace whispered guiltily, while Papa raised his glass to the Order agent in a discreet acknowledgment of his service to their country.

She'd had a taste of certain other talents he possessed, thank you.

Then Papa set out to do the introductions in a more official manner. "Grace, allow me to present Lord Trevor Montgomery," he said, turning to the national hero. "Lord Trevor, this is my greatest treasure on the earth, and my all-essential help since her mother passed. My daughter, Grace."

Lord Trevor Montgomery bowed to her without giving away the slightest sign of their mutual misdeeds. He was, after all, trained to lie, she supposed. "Miss Kenwood. An honor."

So much for her anonymity.

Heart racing, she bowed her head and sketched a curtsy, praying that her father did not question too much why her cheeks were scarlet. Most ladies' cheeks no doubt went as red as beets upon meeting such a man.

"Um, Papa, may I speak to you for a moment?" she mumbled, turning away with her father.

"Of course, my dear. Is something wrong?"

Meanwhile, she saw Lord Trevor gloating beyond her father's shoulder; he sent her a pointed look that seemed to ask in amusement, *"You thought this was over?"*

She took her father's elbow and pulled him another two steps away. "George is in the card room playing whist," she murmured.

His silver eyebrows shot upward. "Oh dear. I'm on my way."

"Shall I come with you?"

"No, I'll make better headway if I go and speak to him man-to-man. Why don't you stay and have a chat with this Montgomery fellow, what? You seemed to spark his interest."

"What, me? Don't be absurd! I can't imagine why you'd say such a thing!" she answered rather more hotly than his passing comment warranted.

Her father gave her a curious stare, then shrugged. "Probably because you're the only woman here who's not throwing herself at him." Then he elbowed her discreetly. "Tell him more about the Grange. We should get him in there if we can. He enjoys architecture as a hobby and was just saying he's on the hunt for a new project. He just finished having a house built and sold it, and Heaven knows the Grange needs a new tenant. Perhaps he'll even buy the old place if he likes it well enough."

"Papa, I'm sure he would never enjoy our dull country village. He's a man of action, adventure — that is, from what I hear. A warrior. He'll be bored silly out there in the sticks with us 'hayseeds.' "

"Whether he's bored or not, it hardly signifies," Papa informed her under his breath. "We need the tithe to help the village. If he could get the farm operational again, we could better afford to feed all those strays you bring to the parish."

She scowled at his pointed reminder that her charity work did not come cheap. It was true.

Because of her efforts, poor people for miles around heard about the generosity of their village and flocked to their almshouse for help in these hard times.

She realized it wasn't fair to put any more of a burden on their parish members when they already gave as much as they could, especially since so many of them were widows from the war.

Things were not going to get any easier this winter, either, with this year's crops already blighted by the disruption in the weather. But perhaps by next year, with a wealthy tenant or even an owner living at the Grange, there could be new life in the village, new crops and harvests — and more than enough for everyone to eat.

She had to admit it sounded like a reasonable idea . . .

"Besides," her father added, "every knight-errant has to settle down at some point. There's no place more peaceful than Thistleton. It would probably do him good."

"Papa."

"Trust me, daughter," he whispered low enough that only she could hear, "nobody hates war more than a man who's fought one. He's lived its horrors firsthand. You can see it in his eyes."

Grace melted at this comment. Blast him,

he always knew just what to say — but then, her father *had* been an army chaplain for a time before Lord Lievedon had bestowed his living on him. He knew what he was talking about.

Papa gave her a knowing wink, then nodded farewell to the others with a murmured, "Excuse me, gentlemen." With that, the Reverend hurried off to go and save His Lordship's scapegrace son from himself once more.

Abandoned where she stood, Grace could feel a certain individual nearby watching her with some degree of amusement. She turned slowly and met Lord Trevor's twinkling gaze. Papa was right. Even when he smiled, a perceptive soul could almost see the drifting clouds of black smoke pass behind his eyes, could almost hear the cannons boom. As for the secret missions he'd gone on and what ghastly deeds they might have entailed, Grace did not really wish to know, any more than the ex-spy wanted to tell it, according to what George had said.

All she could think was that it wasn't fair for one person to suffer so much for the rest. In a sudden flood of compassion, any resistance she might have felt about his moving in next door gave way. Her father was probably right: He usually was.

Maybe Lord Trevor needed Thistleton just as much as Thistleton needed him.

So she set aside her nervousness around him, gave him an arch look, and murmured in mock severity: "You again."

Trevor flashed a rare grin. "It's no good whispering in front of an ex-spy, Miss Kenwood. I'm afraid we have extensive training for that sort of thing." He sauntered toward her, pleased with what he had found, now that he was better able to see her in the light.

Indeed, he'd have enjoyed their stolen moments in the parlor even more lustily if he had known that his partner in the dark was this enchanting.

She was taller than he had noticed before, decisively made, statuesque, and curvy, with an air of capable self-sufficiency. Even her body seemed to suggest that there was little in life that could shake her, and after years of Laura's moods and tempers, Grace Kenwood put him instantly at ease, like taking a deep breath of clean, fresh air.

The top of her head came up almost to his chin, which was also different for him in a woman because he had always tended to go for the delicate little dolls. Their petite size brought out the protector in him, he supposed.

Grace's height made it easy for her to look him in the eye like an equal. And the eyes looking into his were lovely — clear, warm blue.

Her thick, wavy hair was a rather ordinary brown. Then he noticed the sweep of her long golden brown lashes and the milky skin that he was sure had never been cheapened with powder and rouge.

She had no trickery in her, and that in itself made him tremble like a horse that had been galloped too long finally led back to the barn.

Maybe he was more exhausted than he had realized, running too long on anger and restless energy.

Yet he managed another cordial smile.

She smiled back, and he thought her very slight overbite was possibly the most adorable thing he had ever seen. It gave her just the smallest hint of a childlike quality. Other than that, by God, she was every inch a woman.

"How much did you hear?" she inquired, folding her arms across her ample bosom.

"Enough to confirm what you already know — that I am no knight-errant."

"Mmm, not exactly." Her fingers tapped her arm as she tried not to smile. "I suppose you think you're very clever."

"But I am." His smile widened. "That is why, Miss Kenwood, I deem it only fair to tell you that withholding information from your humble servant doesn't usually work," he said with the politest of bows. "You might as well know that now. If we are going to be neighbors."

"Are we?" Her eyes sparkled with intrigue. "Were you just humoring an old man, my lord, or are you really interested in the Grange?"

"If it means living next door to you, I could be interested, indeed." He studied her for a moment, biting back a groan of inexplicable hunger for her that seemed to come out of nowhere.

Obviously, it was futile to want her so much when it was quite clear that he was dealing with a Tower of Virtue.

Ah, well. Inspired to claim her in perhaps some smaller way, he captured her hand without warning. "Dance with me, Grace!" he ordered. "Let's see if you live up to your name."

Without waiting for her reply, he set out merrily toward the dance floor, tugging her along after him. He strode through the crowd without a backwards glance.

"Lord Trevor!" she protested.

"Come, come, it'll be fun." He did not

intend to give her a chance to refuse.

Grace was nearly ready to have an apoplectic fit as she hastened to keep up, trying not to trip.

"Lord Trevor!" she insisted, while his broad-shouldered frame plowed a straight path through the throng.

He ignored her halfhearted protests.

The man had all but kidnapped her! And the *women* who had been watching him all night certainly took notice. She hid her cringe as quizzing glasses were aimed at her from all directions.

"Ignore them," he suggested as if he'd read her mind.

She let out a long-suffering grumble of a sigh. At least the jealous ladies' scrutiny gave her a taste of the constant and clearly unwanted attention he'd been subject to all night.

No wonder he had sought a hiding place.

Then he guided her to her mark, steering her gently by the shoulders. "Stand," he ordered. "There."

She obeyed, her heart pounding.

Her cheeks burned, and her stays felt too tightly laced as she found herself in the midst of one of the most exclusive ballrooms in London, waiting across from a national hero for a country dance to start.

It had to be a dream. This sort of thing just didn't happen to her.

Glancing around self-consciously, Grace felt both hot and cold, and slightly dizzy. She was sure she was going to make a fool of herself, forget the steps.

Then he smiled reassuringly at her, and somehow she could breathe again.

The music started, and Lord Trevor bowed to her on the beat, looking mischievously pleased with himself for this second coup, after learning her name.

Strangely willing to indulge him, Grace responded with a creditable curtsy.

"I'm glad your father isn't the strict sort of churchman. The kind who don't believe in dancing."

His choice of subjects helped relax her. She smiled ruefully. "Oh, Papa's a sprightly dancer. He never misses the quadrille in particular."

His roguish smile widened; it made her feel like the only woman in the room. Then their dance began in earnest.

They were far enough away from the musicians that they were able to chat each time the movements of the dance brought them together in the center before parting again to their separate lines.

Grace was nervous. Lord Trevor's full attention was fixed on her, while her own was split between her partner and the master of ceremonies. This august personage stood at the head of the room calling each new figure to be performed. She soon found it was easier simply to keep an eye on the other couples to follow what to do. *In:* They linked fingers up high and turned sedately.

Her partner looked altogether dashing with his other hand fisted behind his back. "So, your father is young Lord Brentford's mentor," he remarked discreetly.

Out again: They retreated to their respective sides.

She hesitated, but answered the question when they returned for a similar turn in the other direction. "Lord Brentford ought not to gamble," she admitted.

"The lad likes deep play from what I hear. Some people never learn their lesson."

Out again. As they parted, returning to stand across from each other, Grace could see that he had tensed. She looked at him in question from across the empty space.

He shook his head with a troubled smile, a veiled look in his eyes.

In: "What is it?" she persisted when the third figure brought them back together for a sensual turn, his palms to hers.

"Ah, nothing."

"Something," she ventured.

He shrugged, then conceded, avoiding her gaze. "I had a friend like that, too. A gambling fiend."

She noticed the taut look around his gray eyes. "I take it he ran into trouble."

"He sold me down the river, more or less, trying to recoup his losses. Nearly got us all killed."

"What happened to him?"

"Ended up in prison, and there he remains." He shook his head in regret. "I hope your father can help that lad more than I could my unfortunate friend."

Out once more: They parted again and gazed at each other intently. Grace felt sorry for him and said so when they brushed close on the next figure, passing back to back.

"It doesn't signify. I learned an important lesson."

"What's that?"

"You can't trust anyone," he said idly. "Even a friend, half the time."

She frowned. "Nonsense, there are people you can trust."

"Oh? Like who?"

"My father. Me. Plenty of people," she assured him.

He smiled at her in amusement when they

70

parted once more, as if she were some innocent child who had just said something adorably naïve.

She furrowed her brow, irked by his patronizing little smile, so knowing, so world-weary.

Still, the man was too handsome by half.

She forgot her annoyance in seconds as she moved with him. Athletically built, he was an excellent dancer, smooth and effortless. With his arm around her waist and his hand supporting hers in the next figure, he made her glide. Gazing up into his gray eyes, she felt dainty and beautiful with the way he watched her, the hint of a smile on his lips.

"I rather like you, whoever you are," he murmured in a low, silken tone that echoed the one he had used upstairs when they had been alone. "I desire to know you better, Grace Kenwood."

She blushed at his frank enticement. "Whoever I am? But you learned my name. Did you already forget it?"

"No, of course not, silly girl. It's just that I find you a bit of a mystery. You're not like anybody else here."

She snorted at what she was sure was a charmer's line. "There is nothing mysterious about me, I can assure you."

"That's precisely what intrigues me. You are exactly what you seem. You don't seem to know how rare that is."

And he released her.

As she stepped back to her side of the floor, she was trembling, struggling to wake up from this silken dream.

The wistful desire to know what it would be like for him to make love to her shocked her when she noticed the drift of her own musings.

Egads! What was wrong with her.

The lines switched as the figures moved along; he went to dance with the lady next to her, while she took a turn with the other woman's partner. Who held no such appeal though he was young and good-looking and dressed in the first stare.

Grace barely noticed him, going through the motions.

All her awareness was fixed on Lord Trevor. Her heart pounded when they returned to each other.

"Have I upset you again? Was I too forward?" he breathed, ducking his lips closer to her ear.

She was half-seduced already and feared he knew it. "Don't be silly. It's just — I wasn't expecting you to come back to the ball."

"I had to apologize to you."

"Nonsense, you already did."

" 'Twas insufficient, Miss Kenwood. I behaved like a marauding Hun with you. You deserve much better," he whispered. "And I want you to know I truly am sorry. Not just words."

She lowered her gaze, smiling, her body tingling all over. "Well, I *did* jab you with a hairpin."

"Yes," he breathed, smiling as his lips grazed her ear. "You are rather violent for a preacher's daughter, aren't you?"

She shot him a merry look. "You brought it on yourself."

"Hmmm." His eyes glowed.

She has no idea how beautiful she is. Trevor found himself all the more deeply enchanted.

Miss Kenwood's loveliness was beyond the physical. She was kind, modest, soft in all the ways that a man who had been too often cut by the world's jagged edges could desire. But his recent betrayal was not so easy to forget, let alone escape.

Just as he finished the dance with Grace, bowed over her hand, and kissed it in respectful thanks, he turned with her to applaud the musicians, and spotted a familiar flash of golden hair on the other side of the ballroom.

Instantly, he tensed.

His smile faltering just for a heartbeat, he lowered his gaze, engulfed once more by the bitterness that had further hardened his already cold heart.

Laura and her idiot dragoon. Well, well. Grace's charm must have, shockingly, got him to lower his guard a bit, but one look at Laura, and the cold fury, the stab in the back, the sense of abandonment . . . it all came flooding back.

Even more than he despised that feckless beauty, the truth was he blamed himself for ever relying on anything as weak as a woman in the first place.

No matter, he promised himself coldly. It would never happen again.

Unwilling to put Miss Kenwood in the middle of his silly Society dramatics or subject her to Laura's haughty smirk, he chose to make his exit for the night.

Grace was still applauding the musicians when he took her gently by the elbow to say farewell.

If ever he needed reminding that women weren't worth it, it was now. He made a mental note of it.

Grace Kenwood was more agreeable than

most, a calm, steady presence peacefully content in who she was, she did not need to draw attention to herself. But whatever her appeal, he was not getting lured back in, ever, to the female trap.

This one, he feared, could make a slave of him — precisely because it would never enter her head to do so.

She was quintessentially *safe*.

At least that was his assessment of her nature so far, professionally speaking. If he were still in the spy game, she'd be the perfect kind of mark, wide-eyed, naïvely unsuspecting. Devoid of cynicism, lacking vanity, obviously quick to forgive. The type who saw the best in everyone.

She should marry a country farmer, he thought dryly, who would never break her wholesome heart.

But it was true. She had a realness about her that threw him off his stride. Her lack of guile itself became a strange and foreign threat, at least to a man who had been betrayed twice by people close to him.

When Grace turned to him in question, Trevor bent closer to her ear. "Thank you for your company this evening, Miss Kenwood." He chose his words carefully, wanting both to honor her and yet, to push her away. For both their sakes. "It was a welcome distraction. But I'm afraid that I must go."

"Oh!" She looked at him in surprise, scanning his face. "Is something wrong, my lord?"

He gave her a formal smile and a middling lie, one not so much intended to deceive her, but a veiled and more courteous way of saying, *It's none of your affair.*

"Not at all," he replied. "I just remembered something I have to do at home. I'm so sorry, but it's an urgent matter of business that requires my attention before morning."

"Oh, I-I am sorry to hear it. Very well." She smiled brightly, but he saw doubts flickering in her eyes.

He saw that *she* saw he was lying, but God bless her, she chose not to press him.

She offered her hand for him to shake, another oddly genuine gesture. "It was a pleasure meeting you, Lord Trevor."

"The pleasure's mine." He shook her hand gently. "Give my best to your father, Miss Kenwood. Good night."

"Good night," she echoed.

He took leave of her with a nod, ignoring the confusion in her fine blue eyes. Then he strode off without a backwards glance toward the opposite door through which the happy couple had arrived. By now, he had shrugged off his earlier petty scheme of making Laura jealous.

It was beneath him, and besides, at heart, he didn't really give a damn.

He was beginning to think he had never really loved her. He had tried for a while, more or less. He'd told his friends many times over the years that he did, indeed, insisted on it, usually when he was drunk in some distant country, with a whore on his knee.

He had thought for a long time that they laughed at him simply because they were scoundrels who scoffed at love and used women freely — at least until most had wound up married and changed their tune. But he was beginning to understand now.

His brother agents had known that he was only fooling himself when it came to Laura; a planner, a dreamer, maybe it was only the vision in his head that he had been in love with.

An illusion that had never quite fooled his heart.

That being the case, why should he be surprised that the woman had finally jilted him? To be sure, the lack of feeling between them was mutual, if only he had cared to admit it before now. If only he had cared to quit denying that the two of them saw each other as a trophy, a prize.

They looked good together; their families approved of each other as excellent breeding stock, and any red-blooded man in his right mind would have loved to breed with Laura. Frankly, it was a wonder she had waited for him as long as she had.

But deep down, he supposed he had always known there was nothing really *there* between them.

Emptiness, he thought. Perfect.

That was what he'd built his future on, and for that, he had no one to blame but himself.

A distraction . . . So that's what I was tonight, Grace mused, a little stung by this callous revelation.

But off he went. Another mysterious exit.

Oh, well. At least he had bothered to say good-bye to her. He did not even acknowledge several other guests who hailed him as he marched off through the crowd and disappeared.

Something had obviously upset him. She hoped it wasn't her; she was fairly sure she had not committed any blunders. No, it was more like he had seen something — or someone — across the room that he didn't like.

She stood on her tiptoes, trying to get a look around at what it might have been, but just then, her father found her.

"Here she is! Look, Grace, I've found you a partner to dance with at last. My daughter's been waiting to dance with you all evening, George, just as I said. Poor thing, don't let her be a wallflower."

"Papa!" she said indignantly.

"Yes, sir." George gave Grace a sheepish smile, while she frowned at her father.

Wallflower, indeed! He obviously hadn't seen her dance with the gentleman-spy. Which, on second thought, might be just as well, considering the wicked impulses that mysterious gentleman aroused in her.

A lady's father might not approve — especially when one's father was a priest.

Well, it was he who had ordered her to charm the man in the first place! she reminded herself.

"I'm next, mind you," the Reverend Kenwood added fondly, wagging a finger at her. "Don't you go promising the next one to some young buck. A young lady ought to save at least one dance for her old dad."

"Yes, sir," Grace said archly.

His blue eyes twinkled behind his round

spectacles, for he knew full well how she felt about putting herself on display. It did not seem so intimidating now that she had done it once with Lord Trevor.

"Sorry I left you in the lurch," George mumbled after her father walked away.

Grace took his arm and gave it a forgiving pat. "I'm just glad you're back."

"I was winning, you know."

"Always best to end on a high note. George?" she pressed him since the musicians were taking a short break. "Tell me more about that Order agent fellow you pointed out before."

"Don't tell me you've gone and fallen in love with him, too, while my back was turned?" he exclaimed.

"No, of course not! I've just been watching all the guests, and I noticed he went storming out a moment ago. I cannot figure why."

"I'll bet I know," he said dryly, then he looked around. "Righty-ho. There she is."

"Who?"

"She'd be the reason he left. Lady Laura Bayne." He shook his head. "I *told* Father's secretary that inviting them both was a terrible idea. Nobody ever listens to me."

"Why is that?"

"They think I'm a nitwit."

"No, why didn't you want them both to be invited?"

George shrugged. "The two of them were to be married, but he disappeared for months nearing the end of the war; she took him for dead and gave up waiting. Got engaged to somebody new."

Grace's eyes widened. "Are you serious? How awful!"

"Not for her. That's her new beau there, Major Lord Dewhurst, of the cavalry. He'll be an earl in his own right when his father dies, while our spy friend is only the younger son of a duke."

"Only?" Grace murmured.

"I'm sure she jumped at the chance to improve her situation. Bird in the hand is worth two in the bush, as they say, and she's already your age."

Grace looked askance at him. "Practically ancient."

"That's not what I meant. She's not like you. She's a Society girl. Vain and rather mercenary. Montgomery might be a hero and all, but there was a good chance he'd never return alive," George explained. "Meanwhile, Lady Laura had a future earl down on one knee before her. What would any female do?"

Grace was sure she couldn't say. "Show

her to me."

He glanced around. "She should be easy enough to find. God knows, she's usually the most ravishing creature in any room she enters. Half the men in the ton are in love with her, or at least in lust."

"George."

"There." He nodded to the left; Grace followed his glance until she discovered the lady in question.

Oh, she thought, taken aback by her impossible beauty. *Oh . . . I see.*

Lady Laura Bayne was a smiling blond goddess with diamonds in her hair and a white silk gown skimming a perfect figure.

Grace felt her heart sink a little in dismay.

So that's the sort of woman it took to snare a man like Lord Trevor, she mused with a quiet sigh. Oh, well.

It had been fun while it lasted.

George also sighed, gazing at Lady Laura. "Montgomery was a fool not to marry her before he went off to war, if you ask me."

"Why didn't he?" Grace turned away from the depressingly radiant vision of exquisite female beauty.

"Don't know. It's shocking, really — I mean that a woman like that couldn't compel him. If it were me, she could make me do anything. But I suppose she's surrounded by people who leap to give her whatever she wants."

"Maybe that's why she chose him," Grace murmured. The man she had met had too much strength to let himself be ruled by a pretty face.

George shrugged. "I couldn't say, but if it was a battle of wills or something, she won. She quit waiting and moved on, as you can see."

"But you said that she thought Lord Trevor was dead."

"Yes, everyone did, though his family refused to believe it," he added. "Everyone felt rather sorry for them, refusing to put black crape on the door. Turns out they were right."

"Where was he, then?"

"That, my dear, is a closely guarded secret. No idea."

"Hmm." Grace looked back wistfully at Lady Laura, with her gloved hand resting in the crook of her new fiance's arm. "One wonders how she feels now that her former beau is back from the grave."

"Feels?" George laughed cynically. "You and your quaint country notions, poppet."

"What do you mean?"

"Well, it's not as though they were in love."

"Why do you say that?"

"If he really loved her, he'd have married her long ago. Instead, he made excuses. Trust me," George muttered, "I would know something about that."

Grace pondered this. "Then why did he go stomping off like that when she arrived?"

"Pride, I daresay," George said with a shrug. "Never forget, Gracie girl. The man's a trained assassin. He's hardly going to play the role of a brokenhearted sot — except for the benefits it gains him with the ladies, I should think."

"What?"

"Sympathy!" He winked at her. "That's why they all throng him so — offering their tender care to heal his poor, broken heart. Smart man. Sympathy always does bring out an interesting reaction in you females. I should try it myself sometime. Concoct a tale of woe . . ."

Grace scowled at him.

"In any case, the ladies of the ton had all but written him off years ago as spoken for, the property of our jealous goddess over there. But now he's free again. They've got another chance. You can't blame them for trying —" George shuddered all of a sudden. "God, I hope my Callie never meets him!"

Grace looked at him abruptly. The moment he said the words to her, it almost seemed like fate.

Beautiful, lively, aristocratic girls like Miss Calpurnia Windlesham were born and raised to marry men like Lord Trevor Montgomery.

Indeed, Callie was but a younger, fresher copy of Laura Bayne; and perhaps where Laura had failed him, Callie, as a malleable eighteen-year-old, would be easy for him to mold into whatever he might want in a wife.

Grace felt her heart turn to lead at the thought, but she refused to indulge the sinking feeling, with Papa's words about the need for a strong new tenant at the Grange ringing in her ears.

Food, crops, money.

If the charming, golden Callie became part of the lure for Lord Trevor to take the Grange, this could be best for everyone, the whole village.

Maybe best for him, as well, after all he'd been through. Grace would not have said it aloud to George, for the Brat would only mock her, but even she was not immune to a bit of feminine sympathy for the ex-spy. Poor man, he had given years of faithful service to his country and risked his life, only to come home and have his hopes of a happy marriage dashed.

At least that explained much of his cold attitude.

He deserved better.

After a moment's consideration, her mind was quite settled on the matter. *Yes.* Lord Trevor should move out to her beloved little Thistleton, buy the Grange, and marry Calpurnia to mend his bruised, if not broken heart.

It wasn't as though *she* could ever win a man like that, anyway. Not if he was used to the likes of Laura Bayne. Besides, as attractive as he was, Grace was not sure she would have wanted him, anyway.

He did not exactly fit her idea of a husband. A man who went around kissing strangers in darkened rooms. A trained assassin, a spy forbidden to tell the truth about his past. Worst of all, he was obviously an expert in brushing people off by calling them "welcome distractions." It still stung.

No, he would never do, not for her. He would make a fine neighbor to live next door to, but it would take more than that to make her abandon Papa, who needed her.

Callie might be perfect for him, however, Grace mused. An exuberant young beauty brimming with life might be just the thing to rejuvenate the cynical, world-weary spy.

She had no doubt he'd be good for Callie, too. Back in the village, the girl was like a younger sister to her, and so she could say without any ill will that the headstrong debutante needed a grown man to take her in hand, not a rakish cub as spoiled as herself.

Dear, silly George wouldn't like losing out to Lord Trevor, of course, but for all his protestations of devotion to Callie, Lord Bratford had a lot of growing up to do before he was anywhere near ready to take a wife.

Yes, this would be best for everyone.

Excellent, Grace concluded, quite pleased with her plan, for George's words earlier this evening had been right. Solving other people's problems was her forte.

It was so much easier than pondering her own.

Then George gestured toward the dance floor as the musicians returned from their break.

Grace smiled back at her rascally young friend and thrust Lord Trevor out of her mind as off-limits, a man destined for another.

Forcing her attention back to her present task of keeping Lord Bratford out of trouble, she took George's offered arm, and off they went off to dance.

CHAPTER 4

Peaceful.

Ten days later, Trevor sat in the middle of a sunny meadow chewing a long blade of grass and staring intently at the Grange.

He was not entirely sure what he was doing here. This had to be the worst time in history to buy a farm, what with the weather all at sixes and sevens.

But at least there was sunshine today, and besides, he was confident that Nature would get back to normal by next year. In the meanwhile, anyone with eyes could see that the country needed food, and he was the sort to attack big problems like that head-on, not run away from them.

This could be a good move, he mused, staring at the building. A cheap one, too, under the circumstances.

At any rate, curiosity had got the best of him, along with a lack of anything useful to do — torture for a man whose every moment in life had had a purpose, goal, and strategy up till now.

He had to admit it was blissful to escape all the prying eyes in London. To be sure, he could not imagine a place farther removed from his whole former existence of intrigue, danger, and betrayal. Miss Kenwood's village was so tiny and quaint, nestled in the English countryside, that it pained him vaguely, like a soldier's dream of home.

It had taken all of sixty seconds to drive through downtown Thistleton, even counting the delay when a shepherd boy had halted their carriage to prod a few straggling sheep across the cobbled lane.

Trevor had studied this unfamiliar world in a quizzical mood as they drove on. They passed a row with all the necessary shops: cobbler, weaver, draper, butcher, baker, blacksmith. On the corner sat the Gaggle Goose Inn that Reverend Kenwood had mentioned, across from the dry goods store with a post office inside.

There were a few simple homes in the village, as well. These were of varying ages, some stone with thatched roofs, others timber-framed. A sturdy guild hall and a large almshouse.

Old men played chess in the shade of a

giant oak tree on the village green across from Reverend Kenwood's church. The white steeple gleamed against the azure sky. Then they were through the village, just like that, and he was glad he hadn't sneezed, or he'd have missed the whole thing.

Leaving downtown Thistleton, or Thimbleton, as he had already renamed it, he drove on with the land agent directing him half a mile north, up a country road.

A lazy river wended its way through patchwork farmlands divided up by hedgerows; this they crossed, rising over the hump of an ancient Roman bridge. They clattered on, until the land agent told him to turn his carriage to the right. There was no gate or marker, but they were now on the property that was for sale.

The agent informed him that the previous owner, one Colonel Avery, had been an eccentric old man who had used his moderate fortune to raise a regiment but never came home from the war. The Grange had sat abandoned ever since.

So here he was.

The wind rippled through the tall meadow grass and whispered through the trees. Birds warbled and chirped, and in the background he could hear the endless babble of the rushing stream, but other than that, it was quiet enough in this place that he could hear the honeybees buzzing from several feet away.

One landed on his surveyor's transit, which he'd set up on its tripod nearby. The insect walked the length of the brass scope, then flew off again.

Having already made his measurements of fields and slopes to compare them against the original survey of the property's three thousand acres, Trevor picked up his pencil and sketched again, looking at the house and envisioning bit by bit what it could be — with, of course, a dashed load of work and a lot of money.

Every line he drew, jotting down his unfolding vision, helped him in ways he could not have put into words.

Swords and guns aside, he was most himself with a drafting pencil in his hand — or a hammer, much to his ducal father's dismay.

He watched the progress of the sun over the property and slowly forgot all about battlefields and assassination missions, making notations on the little maps he had already sketched out. He got up at length and ambled through the untended orchard, and though it had taken a beating from the unusual cold, the apricot trees smelled heavenly in the sunshine.

He sampled the water from the fast-rushing brook, broke the earth of different pastures with a shovel from one of the outbuildings, and crumbled a few handfuls of the rich soil through his fingers. The fields were overgrown. It would take fifty men to get them plowed and ready for new plantings. Then he strolled into the wooded acreage, which was in dire need of husbandry, and saw it held an unsuspected fortune in hardwoods.

At length, he returned to the rambling old pile itself, where he reviewed the records of what few improvements to the property had been done when over the years. It was the house that really interested him.

He knocked on walls, peered up into fireplaces, and stomped up and down staircases, giving the handrails a good shake. Every now and then, he shook his head in concern at what he found, but he had to admit the challenge rather appealed to him. Scanning the musty entrance hall, he could already envision the scaffolding in place.

New casement windows of broad glass to replace the old crown glass would help to make the ancient house warmer. It needed central heating, and if he was going that far, why not modernize completely and put one of the new steam engines in the cellar, to pump heated water to the upper floors, as well?

He was a great lover of gadgets. Modern water closets were going to be a must, and as for the kitchen, it was at least a century behind the times. He was a great believer in the innovative coal-burning Bodley Range over the fireplace-style Rumford Stove.

The place should be wired with a bell rope for communicating with the servants, he thought. And the servant quarters, for that matter, had become a colony of starlings. He'd have to smoke the birds out to make sure the whole flock was out for the season, then seal up the place before the cold returned in earnest this autumn — not that there was much of a summer yet so far this year.

"What do you think, my lord?" the land agent prompted.

"Tempting," he admitted with a rueful smile.

The house had good bones. Strong stone foundations, and the rugged timber framing was still sound despite its venerable age, the best he could tell.

The roof would need replacing, of course, especially in the west wing, where chunks of it were already caving in. That was probably more expense than he had anticipated, still, the Grange's hilltop location had rare, sweeping, gorgeous views and was only four and a half hours from London.

This place could really be something, he thought, looking around, hands planted on his waist.

He was not the most spontaneous man in the world, but he was tempted to buy the place now rather than taking his usual course of mulling it over for the requisite few days.

Aye, why not? The simple life, the country quiet, would probably do him good. Out here, so far from watchful eyes and the unwanted burden of his ridiculous new celebrity, all the people who wanted a piece of him might eventually forget that he existed.

An ideal haven for a man who wanted nothing more than to be left alone.

Perhaps in this peaceful place he could escape what he had become in the course of his service, for he was not proud of everything the Order had made of him.

That was why their sudden fame was so intolerable to him. He felt exposed. He had been so careful all these years to keep certain darker aspects of himself politely hidden from the world at large. Laura. His family. Society. His father's friends at White's.

Only his Order brothers really knew him.

But here in the middle of nowhere, he could simply be himself, with no one looking on to bother him. No one getting too close. And then perhaps all the raw places in his battered soul could begin to heal up from the wear and tear of a long, bloody war.

Eventually, with some room to breathe, he might even figure out who the hell he was going to be now that he was no longer bound to his duty as a trained killer and a spy.

Rebuilding the ramshackle old farm might take a few years, and it would be a serious commitment of time, gold, and effort. Nevertheless, Trevor had a feeling that a project of this magnitude was probably just what he needed.

A worthy challenge.

The price for the Grange was still too high for all the work it needed, but he could always sell it again after he had finished fixing it up. He had never worked on an antique building before. It presented a whole new array of interesting problems, this business of renovating.

The house he'd built for Laura had been

all new construction. He winced at the still-fresh memory of selling it, which he had done in a state of cold rage. At any rate, the money from the sale had just reached his account, so he could buy the Grange whenever he decided.

Damn. He shook his head, still dismayed over the loss of the dream house perhaps even more than by the loss of his anticipated marriage.

That house had been his baby.

It was as different from the Grange as an old, rugged, hay wagon was from a fast, new, sleekly polished curricle.

He had drafted the architectural plans himself for the spectacular white mansion where he had intended to live with his dazzling blond bride and raise their perfect children.

In hindsight, he wondered if he had confused his love for the process of creating something out of nothing with his feelings for the woman who was to have shared it with him. When he had heard the news about *her* change of plans, he had been half-tempted to burn it down in his fury.

Oh, the irony of it all.

Just when he and the dream house were finally ready to deal with the prospect of actually marrying her, making the dream a reality, as it were, she had given him up for dead and moved on with the Major.

Trevor sighed. He had put his heart and soul into the building. But now it, too, was gone.

Scarcely able to bear walking through its empty marble halls, he had sold the white mansion to a very rich, ambitious merchant. He had set the price low just to get rid of it quickly, only recouping the losses of every expensive detail he had lovingly had installed. The chessboard floors of the marble entrance hall. The oak wainscoting. The plastered ceilings hand-painted by the Italians he had personally chosen in Florence.

Gone.

"Do you have any questions, my lord?" the land agent asked, interrupting his thoughts.

"It'd be a bit of a challenge transporting the building materials out here," he said skeptically as he strolled outside again.

The land agent followed. "The canal boats could bring whatever you need to order down from Town. They run almost daily."

Trevor peered through the scope on his transit again, scanning along the tree line. The nearest dwelling was a large and picturesque gray stone cottage past a grove of ash trees. "What's that?"

The land agent glanced at his map, then squinted in the sunshine. "I believe that is the parsonage, my lord."

"Oh, really?" A wry smile twisted his lips as he peered more intently through the transit's telescope.

A blur of pastel motion among the greenery drew his attention.

His smile broadened. *Hullo, neighbor.*

His eagle-eyed stare homed in on the unmistakable figure of Miss Kenwood pulling weeds from her garden.

Instantly, he felt a flutter of pleasure low in his belly, along with a warm surge of masculine interest in rather lower parts.

Didn't think I'd really come, did you, dear lady?

Out here, drenched in sunshine, she was even more alluring than he remembered. He had thought of her more often in the past ten days than he cared to admit.

It might be she was the real reason he had bothered to come out and at least look at the Grange in the first place though he'd have denied it to anyone who suggested such a thing.

A rather more tender smile skimmed his lips as he saw that she had company.

A little girl of maybe four or five stood holding an enormous ginger cat, near the gardening lady. The irked cat wriggled out of her arms and darted away, freed.

On her knees amid her carefully tended vegetables, Miss Kenwood rested her shapely haunches back on her heels, brushed the dirt off hands encased in thick gardening gloves, and laughed at something the little country urchin had just said.

Trevor watched her from the distance in delight and a deepening sense of peace about making this purchase.

After all, he mused, if he took the place, at least he would have amiable neighbors.

Bitsy Nelcott, age four, was glad Miss Grace was listening, but would've probably been just as content telling her story about the duckies in the canal to herself or, at the least, to the cat.

Grace heeded the little girl in amusement, forgetting her dismay over her sad little carrots, puny peas, and sickly radishes.

These were the cold-weather vegetables, and not even they were doing well in this year's malfunctioning weather. She sighed. It was not as though she had any control over that, so why fret? As Papa had insisted, they were just going to have to have a little faith.

Bitsy rambled on. Fluffing out her untidy

brown dress, now covered in cat hair, she spun and twirled slowly over the sun-warmed flagstones beside Grace's garden. "She had five babies following her, but the boat was coming, and I was *so* scared! I thought they were goin' to get squished!"

"Oh, no!" Grace replied. "Did they all get out of the way in time?"

"Yes! The mama duck kept swimming back to push them with her beak. Like this!" Bitsy demonstrated, bobbing her head, arms tucked against her sides like wings.

Grace pressed her lips together to avoid laughing at this very serious show.

Then Bitsy stopped and stared at her with wide, haunted eyes. "They didn't even have a daddy duck to help them," she declared.

Grace paused in her gardening with a pang. "Why didn't they?" she asked tenderly. "What happened to him?"

Bitsy gave her a somber stare. "He flew away."

Grace's eyes nearly welled with tears. "But those baby ducks were safe, though. The mama took care of them," she assured the war orphan.

Bitsy shrugged, then twirled again, but at least she seemed to be getting used to the fact that her father wasn't coming home.

Rot in hell, Colonel Avery, thought Grace.

"Where are your brothers today?" she inquired.

"On a 'venture."

"Again?" Grace exclaimed.

"They go on a 'venture every day, Miss Grace."

The twin nine-year-olds, Kenny and Denny Nelcott, roamed the surrounding farmlands like a wild pair of rough-and-tumble fox cubs, and when they were not getting into trouble, they were pulling pranks. They were loud and merry as only two boys could be, but Grace worried about them now that they, too, were fatherless.

"Do you know where they were going for today's adventure?" she asked dubiously as she pulled a weed, but Bitsy was distracted.

"Look!" She pointed a grubby finger toward the drive. "Someone's coming!"

Someone was, indeed.

Grace got up from her knees beside her plants and pulled off her gardening gloves, turning curiously to find Miss Calpurnia Windlesham thundering up the wooded drive in her one-horse whiskey gig at a breakneck pace.

Grace chuckled to herself. *What now?*

Perhaps she had heard from George. Which was just as well, considering there had been no sign of Lord Trevor Montgomery since the Lievedon Ball, nearly a fortnight past. It seemed he was not really interested after all in the Grange or Thistleton.

Or me.

If he were, they'd have heard from him by now. Perhaps she was a little oversensitive about him — this man who had subjected her to her rather violent first kiss, then called her a "distraction," welcome or not. That was why she had done her best to put him out of her mind.

As for the Grange, it was easy to see in hindsight that he was only being polite when he expressed tepid interest in coming down from Town to have a look at it.

She, meanwhile, had gone and mentally married him off to Calpurnia already, like some sort of meddling mama.

No doubt Callie would end up with George. That was as it should be. The two had been best friends and worst enemies by turns since they were children; as young adults, they made quite a pair, equally headstrong, stubborn, and spoiled. They understood each other, and some might say, deserved each other. Yes, that was likely it.

George and Callie must have finally made up.

It was silly of her to have planned another

fate for Callie, for surely, little Thistleton could never hold as big and bold a soul as Lord Trevor Montgomery, a dark and dangerous adventurer with an eye for blond goddesses . . .

A man like that was practically the stuff of legend, at least in her eyes, while Thistleton was the essence of the everyday world. He would go quite mad of boredom here.

"Grace!" Golden curls bobbing beneath her bonnet, Calpurnia pulled her dappled gray to a halt outside the parsonage and flung down from her pony gig more like a Corinthian than a debutante. "Grace, Grace, Grace!"

"Over here, darling!" She waved to her from the side garden.

The rosy-cheeked belle picked up the hem of her flowered muslin skirts and came barreling over with such a look of crazed joy that Grace suspected they would soon hear wedding bells.

Well, that should make Lady Windlesham happy, anyway.

"What's the news?" she asked with a knowing smile, as Callie skidded to a breathless halt in the gravel.

"See for yourself!" She thrust a pair of opera glasses into Grace's hands.

She furrowed her brow, but Callie had no

patience.

"Look! Lud, woman, haven't you glanced out your window? Hullo, Bitsy," she interrupted herself absently, for the wee girl was a great favorite with both ladies. "Have you been working on your curtsy?"

Bitsy beamed at the attention and showed her, nearly tipping forward.

"Very good!" Callie said.

"What am I looking at?" Grace asked, still puzzled.

"Woman, are you blind?" the girl cried.

"No, I've had my head in the dirt down here in the garden. Why? Have you heard from George, then?"

"Pshaw! George who? Look . . . there." Callie grasped her shoulders and turned her, pointing her toward the Grange. *"Him."*

Grace gasped so hard she nearly choked as she spotted the tall, handsome figure in dun breeches and shirtsleeves strolling idly through a field.

She lost her power of speech momentarily. Her heart was pounding like a drum.

"Do you see him? Eeee! The most beautiful man is walking around the property! I think he's there to buy it!" She let out another eager little shriek, laughing breathlessly.

"When — ?" Grace choked out.

"Mrs. Fiddler saw him drive through town in a *very* nice coach-and-four, and Sally Hopkins came and told me at once — as well she might! Come!" Callie seized her hand. "We've got to go and meet him! You must chaperone me. I'll drive."

"Calpurnia." Grace was suddenly shaking like a dimwit.

"Oh, isn't it wonderful? Finally, someone interesting moving to our stupid little town! Can you imagine how much more lively it's going to be around here with a handsome gentleman taking up residence at the Grange? Oh, and I'll just bet he has lots of handsome friends!"

Grace could not find a single word to say. She stared at Callie and handed her back her opera glasses in shock, as if they had burned her fingers.

"What's wrong with you?" Then Callie rolled her eyes. "You're not going to go into a fit of shyness now, are you? Grace! Of all times —"

"He's busy! He's not going to want us bothering him —"

"Don't be daft," she shot back. "He might have questions! We could tell him all about the village and the local Quality. We have to help him, don't we? Make him feel welcome. You of anyone should know it's our Christian duty to help strangers. Besides, if he's considering the place, this is our chance to influence his decision! I didn't see a lady with him, did you?"

"No," she breathed, her heart pounding. Grace feared she was in a bit of a tizzy and doing her best to hide it.

"Come on, then! Let's go show him how friendly we are around here!" Calpurnia started to pull her toward the gig, but Grace planted her heels, striving to clear her head amid her abject panic — and stunned joy — that he had actually come.

She had given up on him days ago and now here he was! In that moment, she barely knew what to do with herself, and was rather appalled that she was nearly as giddy as Calpurnia over his arrival.

But then she recalled her half-forgotten plan to match him and the bold young debutante. When this scheme suddenly came back to her, it had somehow lost all of its appeal.

Confused, she barely noticed little Bitsy tugging insistently on her apron.

"Hurry up!" Callie urged. "If he leaves while we stand here dawdling, I'm going to throttle you."

"Please, just — let me think for a moment."

"About what?" Callie stared at her in bewildered impatience. "What is wrong with you? Don't be unsociable!" Then she folded her arms across her chest as that look came into her eyes. One that Grace knew quite well, and George knew even better. The spoiled, stubborn, do-as-I-dashed-well-please look. "I am going over there with or without you, Grace," she announced.

"Callie, come. You know that is improper. You don't want to make a poor first impression on him, do you? Let's just give the man a little breathing room —"

"You mean ignore him? But that's beyond rude; why, it's absolutely boorish!"

"Nonsense. He'll come over here and see us when he's ready," she assured her, trying to sound normal.

"Why would he do that?"

Grace cast about guiltily. "Um, well, we'd be his nearest neighbors, and . . ."

Callie arched a brow in suspicion.

"Oh, very well! He's an acquaintance of Papa's," she admitted.

Callie's jaw had dropped. "Your father knows him? Gracie, why didn't you say so?"

"I didn't know if he'd really come. I didn't want to get your hopes up."

Or her own.

Callie bounced and squealed and clapped

her hands. "Oh, but this is perfect! You can introduce us! What's his name? Please? You have to tell me."

"We really must give the man some peace. He's just back from the war —"

She gasped. "A military man?" She clutched her chest with a dreamy stare. "I'll bet he's gorgeous in a uniform."

"Yes, I'm sure he is, but —"

"Is he married?"

"No."

"Excellent! What's his name, then, did you say?"

"Lord Trevor Montgomery," she reluctantly revealed.

"Montgomery . . . as in the Duke of Haverlock?"

She nodded wearily. "Yes, he is a younger son."

Callie stared at her in openmouthed delight, then pivoted and marched back toward her gig. "Come on. We're going."

"Calpurnia, no."

"Oh, don't be like that again!" The blond belle stamped her foot. "You're always such a spoilsport! Why can't I ever have any fun?"

"He's a bachelor! You're not going over there alone."

"Grace. I know you do not care to follow fashion, but you don't understand. I've heard that name before, and I don't mean only in Debrett's," Callie said with a great air of superiority. "I know exactly who Lord Trevor Montgomery is."

"Do you?"

"I saw it in the papers! He's an *Order agent.* A war hero — and a gentleman! He's not going to harm me. Now, are you going to come along and chaperone me or not?"

Grace lifted her chin, prepared to be quite as firm with the girl as she had been with her beau, George. "No. Let the man relax."

Calpurnia's rosy lips pursed with determination. "Fine." She pivoted on her heel and headed back to her gig.

"Callie! What would your mother say?"

" 'Well done, Daughter! But it was very wrong of Miss Kenwood to abandon you!' " The girl did an apt imitation of the terrifying baroness, her mother, and was on the path to becoming equally as fierce. "Now get in the gig!"

"I'm a mess!" Grace gestured down at her gown. "I've been working all morning! I'm covered in dirt!"

"You're rustic. It's charming. You look fine. Well, at least take off your apron. Hurry up!"

"God," she whispered briefly, striving for patience. "You go storming over there like the Golden Horde invading, and you're going to scare him off from buying the place!"

"Scare him off?" She laughed at her none too pleasantly. "That is not the usual effect I have on gentlemen, Grace. Besides, he's a trained warrior! I hardly think he's going to be afraid of little old me. He'll be more fun than you are, anyway!" Callie grabbed hold of her horse's bridle and turned the gig around, then climbed back up in the driver's seat.

"Callie!"

"Hope to see you there!" She flashed a brazen grin and tapped her gray with the whip.

Grace took an angry step after her. "Come back here!"

It was futile. *Maddening little hoyden!*

As Callie drove away at a breakneck pace once more, Grace, in her flustered state, belatedly remembered that Papa had invited Lord Trevor to dine with them at the parsonage. *Good God, I have nothing ready to feed the man!* She flew toward the house, almost forgetting the child.

"Miss Grace!" Bitsy insisted.

"Stay right here, darling," she said absently as she hurried to untie her apron and rushed off. "I'll be right back —"

"But Miss Grace, I gotta pee!"

"Oh — ! Well, then. Very well, come along. Chop-chop."

Bitsy was too little to use the outhouse by herself, so Grace hurried her into the parsonage.

First she rushed to the kitchen to tell Cook to kill one of the good chickens — they'd have a guest. Then she made sure Bitsy got to use the chamber pot in her bedroom.

This was never a simple ordeal, but Grace waited as patiently as possible, still cursing her foolish heart for racing.

They both washed their hands, and when Grace glanced into the mirror, she noted the wild look in her own eyes. *Get a hold of yourself, woman.*

Right. She took a deep breath and slowly let it out. She could not believe the effect this man had on her!

"Now, Bitsy." She bent down before her little friend. "You stay here at the parsonage. I must go after Miss Windlesham."

Bitsy shook her head. "I'm coming with you!"

"No, stay and wait with Cook —" Grace paused, recalling that Cook was about to behead a chicken.

She closed her eyes and strove once more for patience. That bloody business would give the child nightmares, especially after her little story about the duckies. "All right. You can come with me," she relented. "But try to walk fast, like your brothers."

She took Bitsy by the hand and went back outside into the sunshine, then they set off for the neighboring farm. Bitsy walked beside her with a businesslike air, going as fast as her little legs could carry her.

Grace, meanwhile, prayed that Calpurnia did not scare Lord Trevor away — or ruin herself by acting too forward.

But maybe it was for the best that they first met this way, alone.

After all, this could be fate for them both.

Grace's stomach was in knots as she marched toward the Grange, desperate to see how Lord Trevor reacted to Callie. A world-weary spy, a spirited young belle every bit as beautiful as the one he'd lost. A chance to start again — and he deserved that. Callie could be frightfully charming when she put her mind to it.

Anxious to avert any possible calamity — like Callie throwing herself at him — Grace walked as fast as she could without dragging little Bitsy down the road. She reminded herself repeatedly with every dusty step that a match between the handsome ex-spy and the golden belle would be a boon for the whole village.

There was only one problem with that, one she didn't want to admit. If Lord Trevor really did marry Calpurnia, Grace feared a part of her would surely die.

And that was just absurd.

CHAPTER 5

Miss Calpurnia Windlesham clearly found herself adorable. Trevor didn't, quite.

Of course, she was pert and lively, charming, and pretty enough to make a fool of many young men, but she reminded him too much of someone he once knew, and thus set his teeth on edge.

What could have got into the silly chit's head that she should take it upon herself to approach a strange man alone in the middle of nowhere, he could not fathom.

Where were her parents? Didn't she have a governess?

All he knew was that the little schemer was not getting anywhere near him. He kept a safe, respectable distance from her, only half-listening to her youthful prattle and wondering if she was going to be a problem should he decide to take the Grange.

But then, a welcome sight emerged in the distance on the dusty country road. *Here comes Grace.*

That same, odd half smile from before returned to his lips as he watched his pretty friend approach.

Somehow, he knew at once that Miss Kenwood was coming more to rescue him from the girl than the other way round, but the tot walking beside her slowed her progress.

As he watched, the little girl must have asked to be carried, for Grace picked her up and spared the wee one a bit of walking by carrying her on her hip.

Trevor was tempted to go and help her carry the load.

Miss Windlesham turned to see what he was gazing at. She slanted him a smug half smile. "I knew she'd come."

"Who is that?" he asked nonchalantly, unable to help himself. It was second nature to slip back into spy mode, collecting information on persons of interest however he might.

"That's Miss Kenwood," said the blond. Then she wrinkled her too-cute little nose. "It's funny you should ask. She said you've met."

He squinted into the distance. "Miss Kenwood . . . ?"

"The Reverend Kenwood's spinster daughter."

"Spinster?" he asked abruptly, looking at the girl in surprise. But he understood at once. *Why, you're a horrible little thing, aren't you?* Oh yes, he knew her kind all too well: competitive females who didn't hesitate for one moment to stab perceived rivals in the back.

Miss Windlesham nodded, dripping with sympathy. "Poor thing, she's already twenty-five, on the shelf."

That remained to be seen, Trevor thought, annoyed. But the girl might know something useful. Such as *why* Grace had not yet married. "Yes," he murmured cautiously. "We did meet in London briefly, as I recall. I didn't really get much of a chance to talk to her."

Miss Windlesham chuckled, edging closer to his side as she, too, watched the pair approaching. "If you first met Grace in London, then no wonder you didn't remember her. She probably didn't say a word. She hates going to Town, you see. She was never really one for Society."

"Why is that?"

"Because she's boring!" Miss Windlesham said with the merry laugh of a mischievous youngster poking fun at her governess.

"Boring? No," he protested. "I'm sure that cannot be —"

"Well, she's shy," the girl amended. "Don't mistake me, Miss Kenwood is all that's good and kind and dear and wise. She's always reliable. She's just, well, a bit of an old stick!"

"Really." Oddly enough, that was the same taunt Beau and Nick had been lobbing at *him* since they were lads.

Little Miss Too-Cute nodded earnestly. "When I told her I was coming here to welcome you to the village, she said we should leave you alone!"

"Did she, indeed?"

God bless her.

"Yes! Isn't that rude? But I knew she'd follow me," she added with a smirk.

Trevor abandoned his game and gave the chit a piercing look. "I'm glad she did." Then he stepped past her and went to meet Grace halfway.

Wearying of carrying the child, she had put the little one down again as Trevor walked toward them.

Miss Windlesham followed, drifting a few yards behind him.

Even before they were in earshot, Trevor and Grace were walking toward each other with wide, affectionate smiles. She waved to him, then got the little girl to do the same.

He felt his heart climb at the sight of her

118

sun-kissed locks blowing in the breeze.

The light, balmy winds made her pastel skirts swirl around her legs even as it ran hectically through the tall grasses all around and made them dance.

"Well met, Miss Kenwood!" he called as he marched toward the preacher's daughter and her little friend.

"Lord Trevor Montgomery!" she answered gaily, pushing the blowing hair out of her face. "Imagine seeing you here." It might've been just the sun reddening her cheeks, but he thought he detected a trace of breathlessness in her voice as she greeted him.

At last, they came together on the dusty drive below the Grange and stood beaming at each other like old friends.

It was strange how you could meet someone and feel as if you'd known that person all your life. He nodded and put his hands in his pockets, warmed to the core by her presence.

"I wasn't sure you'd come."

"Neither was I. But here I am."

"Well — it's nice to see you again," she said shyly. "We are so sorry to intrude on your deliberations —"

"Not at all. Truthfully, it was a bit of a whim. But your father piqued my curiosity about this place." He shrugged. "Besides, I can only stay in London for so long before the place starts to drive me mad."

"Ah, I know exactly what you mean," she agreed with a small, self-conscious laugh. She sounded nervous to see him again, and Trevor found that entirely endearing.

"Well? What do you think?" she asked, nodding at the rambling old farmhouse behind him.

He glanced over his shoulder at it, then looked deeply into her eyes. "Interesting possibilities," he said.

She held his gaze and seemed to lose her train of thought.

Miss Windlesham did not like being forgotten. "You see, Grace?" the girl taunted as she caught up to him and joined them presently. "Lord Trevor doesn't bite."

"You don't know that for certain," he remarked, and Calpurnia giggled, but the flirtatious remark was meant for Grace.

"I see you've met our beautiful Miss Windlesham, the toast of the county," Grace said without a hint of irony — which startled him.

"Yes." He managed a noncommittal nod at the hoyden, but then smiled at the little ragamuffin. "And who's this little princess?"

Grace and the child, still hand in hand, exchanged a glance. "This is my friend Bitsy

Nelcott. Bitsy, can you give the gentleman a curtsy?"

Bitsy stuck her finger in her mouth and stared imploringly at her minder to be spared this request.

"Go on, it's all right," Grace urged gently. "You wanted to come with me to meet him, didn't you? Well?"

"Show him how you can curtsy, Bits!" Miss Windlesham insisted.

But Bitsy shook her head, finger firmly planted in her mouth.

Trevor grinned and bent down to meet her. "It's all right, Miss Nelcott. I'm not one for standing on formalities. We all get stage fright now and then." He picked a small white daisy and offered it to her. "For you."

She accepted it with a cautious smile.

"What do you say?" Grace prompted.

"Thank you," the little girl mumbled, barely audibly.

"You're welcome." Smiling, Trevor straightened up again.

Miss Kenwood seemed to shake herself out of a trance, gazing at him. "Well! We won't, er, bother you while you're considering the house, Lord Trevor. I just wanted to pay a quick call to remind you, you have a standing invitation to dine with us at the parsonage —"

Before she could finish speaking, Miss Windlesham clapped her hands, cutting her off. "Oh, yes! Excellent idea! You must come to Windlesham Hall for supper, my lord, and Grace, you and your father must come, too, since you're already friends. Gracious, our dining room is bigger than the whole parsonage, so at my house, we can all be together and get to know each other more! It's perfect! Mother will be thrilled. Our man-chef is divine . . ."

While the girl prattled on, Grace and Trevor both looked at her, then exchanged an awkward glance, each trying to think of a tactful way to decline.

For his part, Trevor had no desire whatsoever to meet these Windlesham people, at least not now. Having dinner with the amiable Kenwoods was half the reason he had made the long journey in the first place though he supposed he probably should have written to them first.

"We can tell you all the gossip about the local Quality, because of course, we know everyone —"

"Callie," Grace spoke up tactfully at last, "I'm not sure that's such a good idea." Her diplomatic tone would have impressed his Foreign Office colleagues, Trevor mused.

"Nonsense!" The girl gave Grace an insistent sideways glance that she probably thought Trevor didn't see. "Mother will be distraught if he doesn't dine with us!" Miss Windlesham said through gritted teeth, and when Grace blanched, understanding dawned.

"I don't wish to be any trouble," he interrupted.

He had no desire to land Grace on the enemies' list of the local ruling matron. Every village had one such domineering local queen, and Calpurnia's mother, the lady of Windlesham Hall, must be it here in Thistleton.

He certainly did not wish to cause a rift between Her Ladyship and Grace, or run afoul of the local gentry's pecking order.

"I'm not sure how long my business here will take," he explained in soothing tones of regret. "I brought provisions with me in the carriage, anyway. Soldier's habit. I'll be on my way back to London before dark," he added earnestly. "I can feed myself, but thank you both, ladies. You're more than kind."

"Whatever's easiest for you, my lord." Grace offered a smile that almost hid her disappointment.

But Miss Windlesham pouted.

"Come, Calpurnia. If His Lordship decides to take the Grange, there will be plenty of time for socializing later. Give us a ride back to the parsonage in your gig, won't you? That's a long walk for Bitsy's little feet."

"All right," the debutante grumbled.

"Good day, ladies," Trevor said with a polite nod in farewell, and while the moping chit climbed back onto the driver's seat of her gig, he sent Grace a wink.

She stopped and stared at him in surprise, just as she was about to lift Bitsy up onto the back of the pony cart.

"Let me get her for you." He did the honors, whisking the tot high over his head before floating her down onto the backseat.

Bitsy laughed wildly at this, then Trevor stepped aside and offered Grace a hand up.

Brushing her wind-tossed hair out of her face once more, she turned and hesitated, accepting his offered hand with a tremulous smile. "Sorry about this," she whispered with a slight nod at Calpurnia, who was distracted, gathering up the reins.

"Not your fault." He leaned closer. "I'll see you later. You don't have to feed me, but I do want to stop and pay my respects to your father."

Her eyes were wide as she gazed up at

him, and he was flooded with the luscious memory of kissing her in that darkened room. "All right, then," she forced out barely audibly. "I'll let him know you're coming."

He glanced at her lips as she licked them in innocent self-consciousness. Biting back a moan, he took her elbow and helped her up onto the back of the open carriage.

Grace put her arm around Bitsy to keep the child from falling out. They waved goodbye as Calpurnia tapped her dappled pony with her whip, and the light, two-wheeled carriage set off down the drive.

Trevor watched them go, his arms folded across his chest. Then he pivoted and walked back toward the farmhouse, ready to tell the agent his decision.

"I don't see why he wouldn't come to dinner," Callie fretted, as they drove away. "Mother is not going to be happy."

She never is, Grace thought, beyond annoyed at Calpurnia's interference. Just once, couldn't the bullying Windleshams stay out of it and mind their own business?

The possibility of dinner with Lord Trevor had been the one thing she had been looking forward to ever since she and Papa had returned to their sleepy village.

Nevertheless, good sport that she was, she let out a sigh and attempted to smooth things over. "Callie, you can't just tell a man like that what to do. He's not like George. He knows his own mind."

"He's nothing like George," the girl agreed. "Did you see his muscles? His arms and shoulders are *huge.*"

"Callie, don't talk like that in front of the child."

"She doesn't know what we're saying. Besides, it's true! Hercules himself didn't have so manly a physique!"

"Calpurnia Windlesham!" Grace looked away, red-faced. "I should tell George you said that."

"Do! Lord Trevor Montgomery puts him in the shade, that useless *boy.* Come, Grace. You're a woman — you know he's a dream as well as I do. Did you see how adorable he was with Bitsy? I bet he'll be a wonderful father."

"Callie, if you don't stop, I am going to throw myself off the side of this carriage, I swear."

Bitsy found this threat hilarious.

Callie looked askance at Grace while the tot laughed uproariously. "What is wrong with you?"

"I just — can't believe you did that!"

126

Grace burst out. "Running to him like a hoyden. Why didn't you just fling yourself into his arms?"

"I wish I had," Callie drawled. "Thought about it, truth be told."

"This is not a joke! Don't you ever think about your reputation?"

"Landing the son of a duke would only improve it," she answered with a defiant shrug.

"Oh, landing him?" Grace exclaimed. "You think you could?"

"I don't see why not. I have half a mind to have him for my own," the spoiled debutante declared.

"Really."

"You must be made of stone, Grace. Did you see his eyes? They are gray like storm clouds. He's beautiful."

"Oh, for heaven's sake," she muttered, as Callie waxed poetical. "We'll be lucky if you haven't frightened the man away and ruined yourself in the meanwhile."

Callie lost patience. "You are no fun at all! No wonder you're an old maid!" she snapped.

Grace flinched as if she had been struck, then looked away; she pursed her lips to stop herself from responding in a manner that neither Papa nor his Employer would condone.

It was then, scanning the countryside while avoiding Callie's glance, that Grace spotted Bitsy's twin brothers near the tree line of a meadow belonging to the Grange.

Two little heads were peeking over a thick fallen log.

What are they doing? It seemed the twins' adventure of the day was spying on the spy.

Grace rolled her eyes and all but despaired. *He's going to hate it here even if he does take the place.*

In a village of less than five hundred souls, everyone knew everything about everyone else, or found out eventually. The ex-spy was completely unprepared for the loss of anonymity he was about to experience.

"I don't see why you're making such a fuss over my going to meet him. I was only trying to be friendly."

"You and every other woman on the earth," Grace muttered.

"What's that supposed to mean?"

"Callie, when I saw him in London, the man was under siege from a dozen ladies all making cow eyes at him, much like you were doing today —"

"Was not!"

"And he hated it. When we talked privately, he made fun of them to me. He called them carnivores. Is that how you want him to see you, too?"

"Carnivores?" she exclaimed, but finally a glimmer of understanding about her over-reach seemed to dawn on her, and she began to panic. "But I wasn't throwing myself at him!" she cried.

"That's certainly what it looked like," Grace said evenly.

"You're just jealous because he was paying more attention to me than he was to you!"

Grace glanced at her in surprise. "Couldn't you see you were annoying him?"

"Well, I never!" Callie said with a gasp. "How could you say such a thing to me? For your information, sorry to say, he told me he didn't even remember meeting you!"

Grace paused in shock. "He said that?"

The hurt was swift and terrible — but she looked away, rather stunned, then told herself it was of no consequence.

She had no daft romantic imaginings for herself about Lord Trevor. None that she'd admit to, anyway.

She'd be a fool to expect anything more than the sort of warm, cheerful friendship that she had with George.

Of course, George had never kissed her passionately in a darkened room . . .

Callie cast her a nervous, sideways glance, a trace of guilt in her eyes after her spiteful comments.

Bitsy looked from one lady to the other in concern, then took hold of Grace's hand.

After a moment, Grace found her voice again. "I don't think you understand the situation, Calpurnia. As I'm sure you've noticed from going on the charity calls with me, many of the peasant men around here are out of work. If Lord Trevor takes the Grange and gets the farm operational again, he'll need all sorts of laborers and servants. The poorer families in our village will be able to make a living again. You see? It will be best for all of us.

"That's why I didn't want you scaring him away by acting too forward. We must show more decorum." Grace hesitated but decided to share her heart. "Frankly, Callie, you're our best hope of a man like that settling down in Thistleton. You're the most beautiful girl in the village. If anyone could give him a reason to move here, it would be you. But he's not going to want you if he thinks you're just a cake-head. He's been everywhere, done everything; he's seen it all. He can't be bothered with immaturity. Do you understand?"

With a rare, troubled look, Callie slowed

the carriage, drawing her pony to a halt when they reached the bottom of the shady drive up the parsonage. "I never thought of it like that. That I might have . . . a responsibility."

"I know."

"Do you really think I've ruined it for the whole village already?"

"I honestly don't know."

"But I didn't mean any harm!"

"Of course you didn't. Darling, it's lovely to be friendly, but all I'm saying is that we must not be intrusive. The man's been through a *war.* If he moves into the village, we'll need to respect his privacy, not crowd him. Let him come to us, if and when he's ready. We're going to have to be patient."

Callie winced. They both knew this was not her strong suit. "I *am* sorry; I didn't mean to bother him." She lowered her head with a chastened pout but finally seemed to get the point. "You really think I made a fool of myself?"

Grace said nothing for a moment, letting her draw her own conclusions. Then she shrugged. "Maybe a match is possible between you; maybe it's not. Only time will tell."

The young belle seemed bewildered. "Gentlemen don't usually find me annoying! I'm sure that one little visit from me would not have chased him off, surely."

"I suppose we'll soon find out. What's done is done. Until then, we won't know his decision about the farm until he makes it." Hoping that this small taste of rejection would not simply spur Callie to chase him harder in the future, Grace glanced toward the drive up to the parsonage. "I'll walk from here. Can you take Bitsy home on your way? Her mother will be wondering where she is."

Callie nodded absently, still pondering the error of her ways with a look of distraction.

Grace said good-bye to Bitsy with a gentle half hug around her shoulders. "You go with Miss Callie, little duck. See you tomorrow?"

Bitsy nodded, still twirling the daisy that Lord Trevor had given her.

"Don't drive too fast," Grace instructed as she got down from the gig. "One good bump, and this little one could go flying."

"I *know.*" Calpurnia turned to make sure Bitsy was safe in the back, then hesitated, eyeing Grace reluctantly. "I didn't really mean it when I called you an old maid. You know that, right?"

Grace forced herself to nod as she cupped her hand over her brow to visor her eyes from the sun. "Of course."

A pastor's daughter had no choice but to forgive.

"Good." Callie nodded back, avoiding her gaze, then clucked to her horse. "Well, good-bye, then."

Grace remained standing for a moment in the intersection of the country road and the drive up to the parsonage. She watched them go jaunting away, and after a moment, glanced back at the Grange.

Did he really forget even meeting me?

Every shy, plain, too-tall bone in her body tended to believe it, but her heart argued that such a claim was impossible. *Don't forget, we are dealing with a spy,* she reminded herself. *What he says is not necessarily what he thinks or what he means.*

Which was troubling in itself for a woman who valued honesty. On the other hand, he had been rather forthright with her ever since she had jabbed him with her hairpin.

She smiled at the memory.

Finally starting to recover from the verbal punch in the gut Callie had given her, she certainly didn't think he had acted like a man who had forgotten her.

Indeed, she dared to think he had seemed as happy to see her again as she was him. But maybe that was just vanity on her part, wishful thinking . . .

Grace heaved a sigh, then she turned and started walking up the drive, wondering if he was really about to become her next-door neighbor.

It was going to be agony waiting to hear his decision, but she vowed that whatever happened, she'd wear the mask of her usual decorum, never mind the fact that inwardly, she felt as giddy over his arrival as Callie had outwardly behaved.

CHAPTER 6

Dinner was pushed back as late as possible at the parsonage, and still Lord Trevor did not come.

Grace nearly jumped out of her slippers every time she thought she heard him at the door, but it was only the night breeze. She could not seem to settle down. She tried to quiet her mind by sewing, but nerves made her all thumbs, until she finally cast her needlework aside.

Lud, she hated waiting for a man. It was a lowly, vulnerable feeling. First, she had waited a week and a half for him to appear, and now here she was once more, sitting around wasting time and hoping he'd show up soon.

No wonder his gorgeous ex-fiancée had grown tired of it, Grace mused. *She* had waited years for him, poor woman.

Then Grace wondered uneasily if Lady Laura was still in love with him. Surely a woman that beautiful would only have to snap her fingers to get him back.

Maybe she'd jilt her new fiancé to honor her original betrothal. Maybe they'd reunite.

The thought depressed Grace though she knew it shouldn't. It was really none of her business.

At length, the sky began to darken to a deep rich blue; the chill of evening crept into the air; and the night birds warbled. It was eight in the evening when the two hungry Kenwoods finally gave up on their guest and sat down to dinner.

Mrs. Flynn, their cook and housekeeper, served a fine country meal of roasted chicken with buttered red potatoes and turnips, along with a side helping of string beans sprinkled with delicious-smelling bacon.

Grace masked her disappointment, keeping a smile on her face by dint of will as her father led a quick prayer before the meal.

"Amen."

"Perhaps he feared he'd inconvenience us by coming late," Papa spoke up, "and decided to eat at the Gaggle Goose. I would expect that he's staying the night there."

Grace stopped, startled by this possibility. It promptly wound her stomach in a knot.

Dear God, she thought. *Marianne.*

If his encounter with the bubbly, golden Callie had not been hard enough to watch, Grace did not even want to contemplate him meeting the sultry Marianne, who worked in the tavern at the coaching inn.

The ex–soiled dove had talents, Grace surmised, that no decent woman could compete with. Indeed, she had been the cause of Callie's fight with George.

Grace took a sip of her wine to calm her fleeting, panicked reaction to the likelihood that Marianne was probably waiting on Lord Trevor even at this moment — in whatever capacity.

"Yes," she forced out at last with admirable calm. "You're probably right."

After that, it was easy to becalm herself by simply giving up on him. He wasn't coming, and that was that.

He was probably rolling around in bed with Marianne already.

For her part, it was time to stop acting like another cake-head, Grace thought sternly. Bad enough that a belle of eighteen like Callie should make such a henwit of herself over a handsome neighbor who might or might not be moving in. In her own, older, wiser self, such flutterings were disgraceful.

Inexcusable, really. Yes, he was handsome,

worldly, kind to children, but so what?

And yet, she had to admit, it did seem quite his *style* to leave like a rudesby without even saying good-bye, especially after he had smiled at her so fondly. Of course, he *had* told Callie that he barely remembered meeting her . . .

Grace did not know what to think, but she hated that it mattered so much to her.

Thankfully, her father's soothing presence and ordinary conversation about simple things restored a sense of normality to her overwrought day. After a while, she became herself again in the sheer routine of the evening.

Silly, girlish suspense had nearly robbed her of her appetite, but once she had concluded that the worldly ex-spy had forgotten about two such inconsequential folk as a country pastor and his too-tall daughter, then she made a decision to forget about him, too. Finally, she was able to eat. No man was worth such giddiness when there was such tender, juicy chicken on one's table. He could go hang.

She felt let down, of course, and foolishly neglected, but disappointment was better than nerve-racking obsession over a man she barely knew. His decision about the Grange was his own affair.

Where the wandering ex–Order agent chose to put down roots at last — if he ever did — had nothing to do with her. If he moved in, she would be a good neighbor, but this sort of reaction to him was idiotic on her part and must stop.

Back to her calm, grounded self, she made a point of enjoying the meal she had ordered especially for their absent guest. The food was delicious, and too bad for him that he was missing out. Still, it amazed her that a duke's son should have such shockingly bad manners.

At last, she and Papa finished their meal and repaired to the terrace to enjoy the evening air. They sat in their usual, outdoor, wooden chairs, chatting idly and watching the moths throng the lantern hung nearby on a shepherd's hook.

"I wonder if George is behaving himself after your last lecture," she remarked, and it was at that moment, just when she finally managed to distract herself altogether from the topic of Lord Trevor Montgomery, that, naturally, he arrived.

Grace went rigid and felt her heart give a kick like a mule in her chest at the distant sound of a polite knock on the front door. She gripped the chair arms to stop herself from leaping to her feet and rushing to answer it personally. That would not do. Heart pounding, she reminded herself sternly of her decision to keep her head about her; she also recalled his aversion to overly forward women. Indeed, a decorous cordiality was a more fitting reception for a national hero come to call.

Mrs. Flynn went to answer the door and a moment later, showed their visitor out onto the terrace.

Papa rose to greet him. "Aha, Montgomery! There you are at last! We've been expecting you. Good to see you again, m'boy."

"I'm so sorry to call on you so late, Reverend. I don't wish to disturb you and Miss Kenwood at this hour, but I at least wanted to stop by —"

"Nonsense," Papa cut him off. "No apologies needed. We are happy you could join us. Have you eaten?"

"Actually, no," he admitted ruefully, "I haven't had a chance —"

"Ah, lured in from the darkness by the smell of a good meal," Grace teased with an arch of her brow. "Mrs. Flynn, would you bring our guest his plate?"

"Honestly, I don't wish to be a bother —"

"No trouble at all, sir," the sturdy old woman told him. "Miss Kenwood had me put a plate of food together for you, just in case."

He paused, as though startled to be treated more like family than a guest. "You're too kind," he said to them all with a tentative smile.

"Sit, please." Her father gestured toward the chairs.

Grace had remained seated and inclined her head when Trevor bowed to her. "Miss Kenwood."

"My lord," she answered, fighting for all she was worth against the instant return of her wild overreaction to this man. "Would you like to dine al fresco or shall we return to the dining room?" she asked.

"This is perfect," he replied. "Beautiful night."

"Indeed. Do bring his plate out here, Mrs. Flynn, would you?"

"Aye, Miss." The cook nodded, beaming at their handsome visitor, then she went to get his waiting, covered plate back out of the cold cellar.

Papa returned to his seat again, and Lord Trevor took the chair opposite Grace.

She was grateful that the moonlight hid her usual blush, a pattern that was getting rather tedious by now, yet she was acutely aware of him, his magnetic presence, the broad-shouldered size of him, the warmth that emanated from his big, muscled body. His scent, too. He smelled of sunshine and hard, dusty masculinity.

"Well, young man? Don't keep us in suspense. What is your verdict on the Grange? I fear my daughter will burst if you don't tell us."

"Papa!"

Trevor leaned back in his chair, obscuring his wry smile with his hand for a moment as he held her gaze in amusement. "Will she, indeed?"

"No! I'm sure it's of no consequence to me," Grace averred, but she saw that *he* saw the sparkle in her eyes.

He just looked at her as if he had all the time in the world.

"Oh, come!" she ordered at length.

He grinned. "My friends, you are looking at the new owner of the Grange."

Grace let out a wild gasp, lifted her fingers to her lips, and stared at him in amazement.

"Excellent! Well done, sir!" As Papa rose from his chair to shake his hand and officially welcome him to Thistleton, she felt the very earth tilt on its axis.

It was really happening. She couldn't believe it.

After ten days of waiting and wondering if

she would ever see him again, not to mention the past couple of hours of agonizing anticipation, she could hardly believe that Lord Trevor Montgomery was about to become her next-door neighbor.

To be sure, life in Thistleton would never be the same.

When he turned to her, his brow furrowed in curiosity at her silence, she abruptly found her tongue.

"Congratulations," she forced out calmly.

"Why, thank you, Miss Kenwood." Then he turned to her father. "A few of the old documents we needed were missing. That's what took so long. But I think we've got it all sorted now."

"Old as that property is, I'm not surprised," Papa said. "The Grange needed someone like you, Montgomery. With the energy of youth, adequate resources, and the time for such a project."

"Thanks. The house needs a lot of work, of course, but I'm really looking forward to the challenge. You've got a lovely little village here."

"It is very dear, isn't it?" her father fondly agreed, the lines in his smiling face illumined by the lantern. "Of all the parishes where I've ministered, this one has truly become home to us more than the rest did.

Isn't that right, Grace?"

"Yes, Papa," she said faintly, nodding. But she still could not escape her disbelief. Was this a dream? It felt unreal.

"Now, you know, of course, that anything you need, we're glad to help. We're just across the road. Come over anytime."

"And you, as well, Reverend, and your daughter. In fact, that's part of why I'm here. I'll be heading back to Town to make the arrangements for my move. I wondered if either of you might need anything from London."

"Why, that is terribly thoughtful of you, but I think we are all right. Grace?" her father prompted.

His considerate and highly practical offer snapped her out of her daze. "Er, no. Thank you."

"Well, if anything occurs to you after I leave, you're welcome to write to me. Here is my address in Town."

As he handed her father a small slip of paper from his breast pocket, Grace caught her new neighbor's glance — and held it a little too long.

"Well!" said the reverend. "This calls for a celebration. You both will join me in a glass of wine, won't you?"

"Gladly," Trevor assented.

Grace nodded, and Papa left them alone to fetch the wine.

Trevor turned and smiled at her when they were alone. Naturally, Grace blushed. It was all she ever seemed to do anymore, at least where he was concerned.

"Your father seems the best of men," he informed her.

Grace smiled warmly. "He is."

He sat back in his chair. "I don't usually like most people right away."

"Really?" she countered in amusement. "Well, he loves everyone. Even you."

He gave a small half shrug, lowering his gaze. "I'm not sure he would if he knew what I did on my last mission."

She met his probing glance with a questioning look.

"You do know what I am by now, don't you, Miss Kenwood? You've probably heard. I mean, what I was."

She managed an awkward nod. "George — Lord Brentford — told me."

"Yes." He let out a sigh, staring at his boots with his long legs outstretched before him. "The whole world seems to know the story of my life now, much to my dismay."

Grace chose her words with care. "You must be very brave —"

"Oh God, don't — please."

145

The fleeting hint of desperation in his glance made her pause. "Pardon?"

"I was only doing my duty. And it usually wasn't pretty, to say the least. Don't give me praise I don't deserve."

She studied him, unsure what to make of the man. "Were you really recruited as a boy, like they say?"

"Yes."

It was difficult to imagine. He was staring at her guardedly, his elbow resting on the chair arm, his chin propped on his thumb while his long, manly fingers obscured his lips.

"George said you know nine different ways to kill someone with your bare hands."

He scoffed quietly and looked away.

"Is it true?" she persisted in a low tone.

"I never actually counted," he said dryly.

She furrowed her brow, studying him. "You didn't like working for the Order?"

"Sometimes it was fun." His vigilant gaze scanned the tree line, as if out of habit.

"I see." He was quite fascinating, she had to admit. "So, what did you do on your last mission that would make my father disapprove, dare I ask?"

"Accidentally blew up a church," he replied. "But it was Catholic, if that matters."

Grace looked at him in wry amusement. "At least it was an accident."

"True." He gave her a smile with a flash of relief in his eyes. "Usually, I enjoy the chance to blow things up, but that was most regrettable."

Grace gazed at him in a mix of intrigue and humor. She had never expected to make a friend who enjoyed setting off explosives or had even *one* method of killing a foe with his bare hands.

"What?" he murmured, casting her an intimate smile.

Grace shook her head. "After the sort of adventures that you're used to, I fear you are going to find our quiet country life extremely dull."

He laughed softly, rested his head back against the chair, and gazed at the dark sky. "Miss Kenwood," he replied, "at this point in my life, I'd welcome 'dull' with all my heart."

Before she could work her nerve up to ask him what he had thought of Calpurnia, Papa returned with the wine, passed around their glasses, and offered up a toast. "To the new owner of the Grange!"

"To Thistleton," he answered, then added with a brief glance at Grace, "and new possibilities."

She blushed, of course, and clinked her glass to theirs with a tremulous smile. "Cheers, gentlemen."

"Cheers," they replied.

CHAPTER 7

Trevor was still thinking about Grace when he arrived in London the next morning.

He had stayed for nearly three hours the night before, chatting with the Kenwoods on the terrace. It was midnight when he had finally taken leave, making the drive back to London through the dark. The reverend and his daughter had been alarmed at his undertaking such a "dangerous" journey, but he had assured them he was used to such adventures.

Now that he was back in Town, the clamor, coal dust, and the bustling pace of the city could not have struck a greater contrast from his visit to the countryside. Instead of going home directly, he headed to Mayfair to tell Beauchamp about his purchase.

As he slowed his carriage to a halt before the handsome brick town house that had long been his friend and team leader's bachelor residence, it still felt strange to him to be welcomed in by Beau's new wife.

Sebastian Walker, Viscount Beauchamp, and the petite fey redhead, Carissa, had only been married a few months. Thanks to Nick (bastard), Trevor had missed the wedding.

"There you are!" Carissa pulled him fondly by his arm. "Everyone's been wondering where you were!"

"I thought my days of reporting my whereabouts to the Order were done."

"Never! Come in. He's upstairs."

Trevor followed Lady Beauchamp all the way up to the third floor, where he found his brother warrior in the process of packing his luggage. "Blazes, man, is she already throwing you out?"

Beau glanced over and grinned. "Well, look who it is."

"Going somewhere?"

"I owe my wife a trip to Paris. We leave in the morning."

"Oh, I can't wait!" Carissa flitted over to Beau with childlike excitement. "We're going to have so much fun! You are the best husband in all the world."

"Don't be surprised if I return bankrupt," Beau drawled. "Shopping, don't you know."

"Now, now, you promised me a proper Continental holiday once all this business with the Order was finished," she chided.

"Yes, I did. And you were actually patient, which was most unprecedented."

"I beg your pardon!" she retorted, giving him a pinch.

"There, there, I'm only teasing," he murmured, leaning down to plant a doting kiss on her lips.

Trevor looked away uncomfortably.

Never in all his days could he have imagined that a lothario like Beauchamp would end up an old married man before him.

"So, Trevor, you *are* coming to our bon voyage feast at Max and Daphne's tonight, yes?" Beau asked him.

He hesitated.

"Of course he'll come!" Carissa exclaimed. "He's not going to see us for three months! Besides, Daphne always gives an excellent dinner party. All our set will be there."

Trevor had a galling vision of five happy couples, each madly in love, sitting around the table — and him.

Considering recent events, it sounded excruciating.

Indeed, he'd rather take supper alone with Nick in his dungeon cell.

"Be there at eight. Formal dress is obviously not required." Absently counting the linen shirts his valet had packed in his portmanteau, Beau glanced over and noticed Trevor's taut expression.

A fleeting look of understanding passed across his face, followed by regret. "You know, Jordan's wife, Mara, has a charming widowed friend named Delilah, whom we could invite on short notice to be your dinner companion —"

He scoffed and turned away while Carissa let out a gasp of sympathy. "Oh, Trevor, I'm so sorry! How thoughtless of us all! And here, you should have been with Laura. Yes, do please let us invite Delilah — she is very beautiful and witty — or even my aunt Josephine. She's older than you, of course, but not by much. I wager you'd find her most intriguing."

"See there?" Beau chimed in. "You have your choice of worldly, sophisticated women. So which do you prefer? Or shall we ask them both?"

"Do it, and I'll kill you," he replied.

Beau and Carissa glanced at each other in surprise, then both looked uncertainly at him.

Trevor gritted his teeth at their dismay. He knew they were only trying to help.

Still, it wasn't helping.

"But you must come to our farewell

party," Carissa cajoled him in a soft tone. "What if our ship goes down? What if this is the last time you ever get to see us?"

"Carissa, honestly," Beau muttered.

"Fine, I'll come to the dinner to wish you bon voyage, but don't you dare set me up with some strange woman."

"Fair enough," Beau replied in a tone that warned his bride not to argue. "So where the devil have you been, anyway?"

"Oh, wait!" Carissa interrupted. "Before I forget, we're sending a package to Nick before we leave. We have some gifts for him. Maybe you'd like to include a short note?" Well aware that this was a sensitive subject with Trevor, she brushed a lock of auburn hair behind her ear and waited for his answer with a wide-eyed gaze.

He stared icily at the green-eyed viscountess. "What are you giving him gifts for?"

"Er, to make him more comfortable in prison. Won't you write a line or two?" She offered him an open pad of paper and a pencil from the writing desk nearby. "I know it would mean a lot to him."

"My dear girl, you *do* recall he shot you?" Trevor reminded her.

"Oh, that was an accident. He was aiming at him," she said brightly, nodding at her husband. "Besides, it was only a flesh wound."

Trevor scowled, but to humor her, he took the pad and paper and wrote in large block letters: DEAR NICK, ROT IN HELL, YOU BASTARD. HOPE YOU'RE ENJOYING PRISON. SINCERELY, YOUR HUMAN SHIELD.

He handed it back to her. She read it, tilted her head and gave him a sardonic look, then handed off his message to her husband.

Beau read it and laughed aloud. "Put it in the box," he told her, nodding.

"I'm not sending this to him! The poor man's in prison —"

"He'll love it. Trust me. It's better than icy silence, anyway." Beau gave Trevor a knowing glance as he closed his portmanteau. "You know, Trev, it's not like you to hold a grudge. I thought you already forgave Nick before they took him away."

"That was before I found out the full extent of how he ruined my life."

"Ruined your life?" Carissa exclaimed. "Isn't that rather extreme?"

"He's still blaming Nick for Laura's defection," Beau informed her with a shrewd glance at Trevor.

"Ahh," Carissa said.

Trevor turned away, unwilling to discuss

it, especially not in front of Beau's little "lady of information." Whatever he said, she'd likely tell the world. What sort of spy married a Society gossip, anyway?

Carissa always had her opinions, and once more, she chose to share them presently. "You boys need to make up and play nice again if you ask me."

"I don't think anyone did, Lady Beauchamp." He arched a brow and leaned against the wall, arms folded across his chest.

She frowned. "Come, you all have been friends since you all were children. If I can forgive Nick for grazing me in the head with that bullet, surely you can forgive him for using you as a hostage and locking you in that cellar all those months. It's not as though he did it out of malice. He had no choice! Without you for a bargaining chip, the Order would've had their snipers kill him. You didn't want him to die, did you?"

"Hmm," said Trevor, then he glanced at Beau. "Do you tell her everything?"

"Oh, come," she persisted, "you seem to be forgetting that when you were shot, it was Nick who saved your life."

"And you seem to be ignoring the fact that by disappearing me, Nick cost me my fiancée! Not that it's any of your business

Lady Beauchamp," Trevor clipped out. "but I had a very nice plan for my life all mapped out — oh, never mind. Why are you standing up for that blackguard, anyway?"

"He charmed her," Beau explained.

"Figures."

"Nick's had a hard time!" Carissa insisted. "He doesn't have a nice family or a fortune, like you two. He hasn't been as blessed, you know."

"Nor as wise," Beau interjected.

"Nor as honorable," Trevor agreed.

"Leave the poor fellow alone, Carissa," Beau ordered softly.

Trevor leaned his head back against the wall, considering her words. "In theory, Lady Beauchamp, I could do as you say, I suppose. Forgive and forget and all that. But I think maybe he couldn't stand for me to be happy."

"That's not it at all," Beau scoffed.

"Really? Maybe he just didn't want to be the last one left alone. So he did what he had to do to separate me from the lady I had always intended to marry. What do you say to that?"

"Well, Trev," Beau drawled, "there's 'marry' and then there's 'intended to marry,' and these are two entirely different things."

Trevor cast a baleful eye on the pair of

Beauchamps ganging up on him. "Do you two want to know my news or not?" he demanded, pointedly changing the subject.

"Of course we do! What is it?" Carissa asked.

"I'm moving," he announced.

Beau's eyebrows shot up. "Don't tell me you accepted that position with the Foreign Office?"

"God, no." He shuddered. "I'm never working for the government again. I bought a house in Leicestershire. Actually, a farm."

Beau looked at him in astonishment, but Carissa grinned. "Farmer Montgomery?"

"You bought a farm?" Beau echoed.

"Yes," he said wryly, lifting his chin. "An old, run-down, ramshackle thing. But it'll be quite something, one day, by the time I'm through with it."

"Aha, a new building project," Beau said, looking pleased for him. "To take your mind off . . . other things, I presume?"

Trevor nodded. "I'm really looking forward to it," he admitted. "You two will have to come and see it once you're back from France — though I doubt if I worked round the clock for the whole three months you're gone, I'll have put a dent in it. The house is a good three hundred years old. It needs serious repairs."

157

"Trevor, this sounds perfect for you," Beau said. "Whereabouts in Leicestershire?"

"It's actually near Lord Lievedon's seat. The village of Thimbleton. Er, Thistleton," he corrected himself.

Beau stared at him oddly — the piercing assessment of a fellow spy.

"What is it?" Trevor asked, wondering how much his face might have already given away.

"Any particular reason you chose that place?" Beau asked, almost in suspicion.

Trevor shrugged, but of course, all his thoughts were of Grace. "I just liked it. Lots of fertile acreage. Good views."

"I see." Beau nodded, and though he seemed to sense there were things Trevor wasn't telling him, he did not press. "Well, times have certainly changed, haven't they? I thought Nick's going to prison was a surprise. But your moving out to the country . . ."

"And here you are, married," he countered.

"He's *entirely* married!" Carissa threw her arms around her husband gaily and planted a kiss on his cheek.

"Yes, I see that," Trevor drawled.

"It's not as bad as it looks, really," Beau remarked, at which his lady smacked him.

Beau put his arm around her shoulders and pulled her close, laughing.

"Keep it up, Beauchamp. See what it gets you," she warned him in a whisper.

"That sounds distinctly like a challenge," he replied in a husky murmur.

"On that note, I think I'd better go," Trevor said dryly. "If you're going to force me to come to this dinner with all of you sickening newlyweds, I have to stop at home first. See you at the Rotherstones'."

"Eight o'clock!" Carissa called after him as he turned and headed back out into the hallway to let himself out. "Don't be late!"

"I'm never late," he answered. On his way out, he nodded to Beau's stiff old butler. "Vickers," he greeted him, then he headed home.

His own bachelor lodgings were discreetly located on the third floor of a neat and unobtrusive brick building in Old Bond Street. The ground level housed a fashionable milliner's shop, but his four-room apartment on the third floor was spacious and secure, and quite fine enough for any younger son. It was especially suitable for a man who was so frequently abroad. As a spy, he liked the presence of the shop's customers, too. Their comings and goings helped to mask his own.

When he arrived, Trevor left his carriage in the mews, then walked up the stairs to the door of his rooms. He unlocked it and stepped inside. Closing the door behind him, he looked around, let out a sigh, and tossed his coat onto the nearest chair.

Once he began the work of tallying his belongings, he soon realized there was not as much to do as he had thought. He didn't own all that much, for starters. His nomadic life as an agent had made him frightfully efficient and ingrained in him the habit of traveling light.

Sauntering through the rooms of his apartment, he calculated what he'd need to transport to the Grange. Not the furniture, obviously, but his clothes, his books, especially his architectural tomes, and certainly, his extensive collection of weapons. If trouble in the form of some half-forgotten enemy from his old life followed him out to the country, he meant to be prepared.

Nevertheless, after a brief assessment of his belongings, he believed he could be ready to pick up and move in less than two hours. Of course, there was the dinner party tonight. He wondered what Grace would have thought of his glamorous friends.

Glancing at the clock, he saw he had some time before he had to be at the Rotherstones', so he went back out to the mews. He had long held a lease on a tack room in the old carriage house behind his apartment.

There he stored the large array of construction tools and equipment he'd collected during his last building project. He let himself into his storage room and spent some time refamiliarizing himself with every saw, wrench, and hammer like old friends. Just this simple task was entirely soothing to him, as much as his family might think him a quiz for it.

He smiled, though, musing to recall how his scatterbrained sisters had appreciated his innate tinkering skills back in the old days. Even as a boy, he had been able to fix nearly anything, his younger siblings' broken toys, his mother's broken jewelry, his father's hunting musket, a flintlock that had become hopelessly jammed.

At the tender of twelve, he had left home to attend the Order's school in Scotland, and over time, he had drifted away from his family. He had been through things that they could not begin to relate to, and that was probably for the best. But he felt like a stranger among them.

Nick and Beau and the others had become his true family, but lately, he felt as though he'd somehow lost them, too — Beau to his beautiful new marriage, Nick to the betrayal that had embittered Trevor so.

At last, minding the clock, he went over to the stable and hired the boys there to transfer the contents of the tack room into the back of a utilitarian wagon that the stable had for hire.

Warning them to be careful with his things, he went back up to his apartment to wash up and dress for the evening. But upon opening the door, he froze at the threshold, startled to find a visitor sitting on his couch.

She was alone, her face concealed by a lace veil draped over her bonnet. She pushed it back and rose when he stepped into the room, closing the door warily behind him.

Laura.

"What are you doing here?" he forced out.

"I had to see you." She took a step toward him.

"Does your fiancé know where you are?"

"Of course not. I had to speak to you. Alone."

"Well," he said, moving past her, "I'm busy."

"Oh, Trevor," she said wearily, as he turned his back on her. "You really have terrible timing, you know."

"So it's my fault you ruined our plans?"

"I thought you were dead! What did you want me to do?"

"Oh, I don't know. Mourn a little?" he suggested. He could feel his mood blackening. "Why don't you go before this turns any more unpleasant? There's no point in doing this to ourselves or each other. Just go." He nodded toward the door, but she stared imploringly at him.

"I know you're angry, and you have every right to be, Trevor. But you must know I never meant to hurt you." She ventured closer while he stood there bristling.

"What do you want, Laura?" he asked wearily.

"I know you still care for me, or you wouldn't be so angry. At the very least, you still desire me."

"Who doesn't?" he muttered, flicking a glance over her flawless body.

Holding him in a siren's stare that had mesmerized many, she stepped closer. "Maybe it's not too late for us."

Startled, he lifted his wary gaze to meet hers.

"If you still want to be together," she whispered, "we can. I'd cry off with Hector if you asked me to."

He looked at her in astonishment, but

163

when she reached for him, he jerked his arm away and shook his head. "Right. And when he calls me out for it, and I kill him in a duel, will you be able to live with that? Then again, you probably could. What could be more gratifying to your pride than two worthy suitors killing each other over you? At least it answers one question for me. You don't love that poor bastard any more than you did me."

"How do you know how I feel?" she bit back, her cobalt eyes narrowing. "You never asked. You never wanted to know," she accused him. "You couldn't be bothered with knowing me as a person. You only cared how it enhanced your own reputation to have me on your arm."

"Oh, you want to have this discussion at last? Our first honest talk, darling? Very well. All you ever cared about, Laura, was your own pleasure. Our arrangement suited you well, so don't complain to me about my absence. I know perfectly well what you got out of it."

"And what was that?" she cried, her porcelain face flushed with outrage.

"You could do as you pleased while I was gone!" he nearly shouted. "Flirting and toying with as many fools as you fancied. And if any of them ever got too close, you had only to warn them that I'd tear them limb from limb when I got back if they touched you. You had the best of both worlds — the freedom to entertain yourself with other lovers and the protection of a future husband in case any of them ever got out of control."

"An absent future husband, my lord. What good were you to me on the other side of the Continent when I needed you in my bed?"

He stared at her in icy amusement, a bit surprised by her frankness, but refusing to the rise to the bait. She was only trying to shock him. "Get out."

"Ah, what's wrong? Are only men allowed to admit to feelings of desire? You were always such a prude. The perfect gentleman!" she mocked him. "Why wouldn't you ever take what I offered you? You were afraid of me, weren't you? Afraid of what I made you feel."

He folded his arms across his chest and smiled patiently at her efforts to goad him, remembering the times she had begged him to make love to her. "No. That's not it."

"What then?" she demanded. She never could understand his resistance, but it wasn't virtue that had stopped him. It was mere survival instinct.

Passionate and gorgeous as she was, he

had refused to let her drag him into marriage before he was ready, and marriage would have been the only possible result.

He did not understand himself anymore, why he had not made a firm decision one way or the other about her long ago. Probably because the wrongness of their match, so obvious to his heart, had not made any sense to his head.

Everyone wanted her. She was his for the asking. He had only to find a ring and set the date.

But he didn't love her. He couldn't. Honesty, clarity, finally came at last, now that the Order's work no longer took up the whole of his attention. Beautiful as she was, she was all wrong for him. He saw that now — and maybe he should be thanking God that Nick had "ruined" this for him.

Laura glared at him as though she could read his answer on his face. She shook her head in disgust. "God, I always knew I should've gone for Beauchamp."

Except that Beau saw through you from the start. He told me you'd make me miserable.

Would that I had listened.

But Trevor held back from making these hurtful comments aloud. He shook his head. "Leave, Laura. Go back to your dragoon. He'll make you a countess. You know I can't offer you that. Now, if you'll excuse me, I must get dressed for the evening. I'm expected shortly at the Rotherstones'. There's the door." He gestured toward it. "You can show yourself out."

She eyed him distrustfully but sauntered toward the door, gripping her little fringed reticule with both gloved hands. "Think about my offer, Trevor. Together, we could have Society at our feet."

"We both know you can have that without me."

She reached for the doorknob. "You'll change your mind. You're angry now. I understand that. But don't take too long. Hector grows more ardent every day. I'll marry him if I have to, but you're the one I want."

"Funny, it was Beauchamp you wanted a moment ago."

Her eyes flickered in frustration as she started to open the door, but then, as if she couldn't help herself, she paused. "Who was that tall, plain, dully dressed woman you were dancing with the other night at the Lievedon Ball?"

Trevor lifted his eyebrows. "I'm sorry, I don't recall anyone of that description."

"I heard you looked quite enchanted by her when you were dancing before I arrived.

Someone said they even saw you laugh," she said with a smirk.

"Did they, indeed?"

"You don't have to be embarrassed, Trevor. I'm sure you were only being kind. You always were the most charitable fellow, taking pity on the poor, lonely wallflowers, who never get asked to dance."

Her cruelty toward Grace brought out an edge of cruelty in him. He warned her with a stare. "She's not a wallflower, and I wasn't being charitable."

"Oh, defensive. I see," she said with a tight smile. "You like this plain woman, then? How droll!"

"Not really," he replied. "Few can equal your beauty, of course, but the lady you are referring to has a number of traits you lack, I'm afraid."

"Is that so?"

"Integrity, for example. Loyalty. Generosity. And a little something I like to call a soul."

"I see," she ground out, her crystalline smile in place. "And who is this paragon, exactly?"

Trevor shrugged. "The mother of my future children, possibly."

Her jaw dropped. *"What?"*

"Good-bye, Laura. Be a dear and close

the door behind you when you go, won't you? And give my best to your fiancé."

Rage flickered in her eyes as it apparently sank in that she no longer had any power over him. That there really was someone in the world who could resist her will. Someone she could not control.

That, Trevor saw in a sudden inner flood of revelation, was why she had waited for him so long. Biding her time like a bloody spider waiting to capture her fly.

It was all a game to her — one she now saw she had lost.

She shot him a withering look, then stepped out and slammed the door behind her. Trevor went and locked it.

As he leaned against the door, still rather routed, his heart pounded at the wreck he had nearly made of his own life with that harpy.

Aye . . . maybe bastard Nick deserved his thanks.

He noticed that he felt lighter already, as though someone had lifted a great anvil of responsibility off his back. Crushing duty, gone. It was easier to breathe.

As for his brash remark about marrying Grace Kenwood, he had only said that to infuriate Laura, but now that he'd spoken the words aloud, it didn't sound half-bad.

At least she wasn't the type who would try using everything from her body to her tears to control him.

He pondered a match with Grace for a moment, then shuddered, appalled at himself. God, he must be daft. How could he even think such a thing so soon after that narrow escape? What guarantee would he have that any attempt at love with Grace would end any better than this disaster?

True, Grace was a very different woman than Laura — and the memory of her sweet, innocent kiss still haunted him — but once bitten . . .

With a wordless growl of frustration, Trevor stalked to his bedchamber to get dressed for the night ahead. As he peeled off his shirt and threw it angrily aside, he insisted to himself that buying the farm had nothing to do with Grace or any other blasted female.

The Grange was something, finally, that he had done for himself. Not just to indulge his architectural hobby but to give himself a refuge, where he could escape the world with all its demands and be left alone to heal. Tomorrow morning, first light, he'd be heading back there. Indeed, he could hardly wait to get the hell out of London and start his new life as a solitary hermit in the middle of nowhere, forgotten by the world.

It sounded blissful.

First, however, he would have to get through this hellish dinner party with the five lovesick couples. Trevor lowered his head and sighed.

It was sure to be excruciating.

CHAPTER 8

Peaceful.

Grace's favorite time of day was the first hour of the morning, before the hustle and bustle of everyday life began in earnest.

The new day ahead was still pristine.

One full hour of tranquility before whatever minor madness of the day struck. There in her window seat, however briefly, all was well with the world.

Mrs. Flynn was making breakfast; the air was ripe with the delicious smells of baking muffins and frying bacon. Papa was out taking his constitutional. Every day, the pastor marched down to the village first thing to fetch the morning paper.

As for Grace, she had just finished her daily Bible reading and was sipping her first cup of tea while her cat purred nearby, his paws tucked under his furry chest, the tip of his tail silently tapping in a contentment that she shared.

She gazed happily out the bay window at the shimmering trees cloaked by morning mist, filled with an odd satisfaction at knowing that Lord Trevor had returned to the Grange. His nearby presence pleased her. It was as if she could feel him over there.

Of course, she had no plans to invade his privacy.

He had practically sneaked back into Thistleton in the middle of the night, probably to avoid the whole town's notice. After Calpurnia's welcome, Grace could hardly blame him.

But she had heard his carriage rumbling up the country road, for she had been sleeping lightly ever since she'd met the man. Once the noise had awakened her, and she had confirmed his arrival by the carriage lanterns heading toward the Grange, she could hardly fall back asleep.

Still, she did not intend to bother him. He had been through a lot. He needed to rest, and if they were to be friends, he would come to her when he was ready. Until then, she was content to leave him alone.

Unfortunately, unbeknownst to Grace, the Nelcott twins did not share her sentiments.

Small, urgent whispers emanated from behind a fallen log at the tree line of the

Grange.

"Giant."

"Ogre."

"Giant!"

"Ogre! Maybe a troll. Hard to say."

"Don't really matter, does it? The point is, 'e's taken over our castle. We got to get 'im out!"

"How?" Kenny demanded.

"I don't know yet," Denny grumbled. Older than his twin by forty minutes, he was usually the leader. "We need a closer look. C'mon."

The nine-year-olds sneaked off to investigate the forbidding stranger who had had the audacity to buy the Grange and had thereby ousted them from the place that had long been *their* playground, their sanctuary from the world.

Of course, they were not supposed to be anywhere near the old farmhouse, for some of the ancient outbuildings were in danger of falling down at any moment, to say nothing of the old barn with the ghost of the ruined dairymaid who had hanged herself a hundred years ago.

Ah, but rules were for other boys and girls, not the Nelcott twins, as far as they were concerned. Their father was gone, and they were not about to let anyone else tell them what to do, except occasionally their Sunday school teacher, Miss Grace. But only because she gave them cinnamon-raisin biscuits and never raised her voice to them and also when Denny had busted his knee open once, she had never told a soul how he had cried like his baby sister at the blood.

The boys sneaked off through the meadow, picking their way through the tall grass with admirable stealth.

Approaching the old farmhouse, they listened but did not hear anything, so they sneaked in through the usual window, opening the rusted latch and lowering themselves into the scullery. Climbing down past the great sinks, they tiptoed out of the kitchen, then down the hallway, avoiding those familiar floorboards that squeaked.

Before long, they found the invader, the giant/ogre/ troll-man asleep on the ratty old sofa in the ancient drawing room.

Huddled in the doorway, the brothers exchanged a determined glance. Being twins, they scarcely needed to speak aloud to understand what each other intended. Kenny pointed; Denny nodded.

Then they both crept into the drawing room, neither making a sound. Kenny sneaked over to examine the boxes and cases of books that the big man had unloaded from his wagon when he had arrived. He had sneaked in during the night, but the twins, of course, had seen him. They knew almost everything that went on in the village.

Silently, Kenny opened the boxes and searched the giant's haversack, half-hoping to find something to eat.

Denny, meanwhile, decided to make a closer study of the invader himself.

He had heard what everyone was saying, how this man had been a hero in the war, but the skeptical boy had his doubts. The new owner of the Grange did not look all that heroic to him, sprawled out on the sofa, fast asleep and lightly snoring.

Denny had half a mind to do something annoying, like get a blade of grass and tickle his nose with it to see what he would do.

Still, this did not look like a man a smart lad should cross.

Even sleeping, the ex-spy did not look very relaxed. He was grinding his teeth, his stubbled, square jaw flexing. His closed eyelids twitched restlessly, and the hand resting across his stomach was clenched in a fist even as he slept.

Then Kenny interrupted his scrutiny of the stranger with a "Psst!" summoning his twin over. Denny withdrew silently from his position beside the sleeping giant.

When he reached his brother's side and peered down into the long, black leather case that his twin had opened, the boys exchanged a wide-eyed look.

The black case held a collection of sleek, shiny guns and wonderfully wicked knives, the likes of which the boys had never seen before.

Denny, fascinated, reached to pick one up, but Kenny smacked his hand and gave him an impatient glare.

"What?" Denny whispered. "I can if I want to!"

"Too dangerous! We better get out of here."

"Don't worry, he's sleeping."

"What if he wakes up?"

Trevor only wished he could.

Instead, he was having the most aggravating sort of dream, devoid of logic and full of frustration. In this case, he was reliving the Rotherstones' dinner party from the other night, except that in his dream, everything was off, distorted, like the time years ago when Nick had made him try the opium.

The Rotherstones' scarlet dining room was spinning slowly, and his friends' faces,

177

voices, everything, looked wavy and bizarre.

In the dream, he was sitting with his friends and their beautiful, bejeweled wives around the dinner table. All of them were laughing and talking, eating their fill and drinking the wine, but for some reason, Trevor had been skipped over.

Nobody even seemed to notice. His plate was empty, his cup was dry, and every time he tried to signal one of the liveried foot-men, the servants stoically ignored him.

And so, then, he tried to serve himself, reaching for the fine platter of roasted goose, but just as he nearly got his hands on it — or any other course he reached for — it was whisked away and given to some-body else.

Disappointment threatened to turn to anger. He was hungry!

When he protested or asked for some food, his voice wouldn't work. He lifted his cup to clear his throat with a drink, but it was empty, too. Thirsty and starving in the midst of this feast, every moment at the table had made him angrier.

This was utterly unfair. How was it that none of his so-called friends could even be bothered to notice how he had been denied the portion he deserved? Everyone else had theirs, but not even Beauchamp could be bothered to care.

They were all too busy fawning on their darling wives, too pleased with their good fortune to notice their friend drowning in despair. He was as forgotten here as he'd been in Nick's cellar, being held hostage. In his dream, he had half a mind to leave the table with a curse and storm out of the room.

But then, at last, filtering through the veil of sleep, he became aware of a presence in the room.

Whispers somewhere close . . .

Someone's here.

In an instant, his warrior instincts went on full alert, and years of living under constant threat of death snapped him into battle mode.

Pulling himself up swiftly from the depths of sleep, just a few seconds later, his eyes flicked open.

His hand reached reflexively for his weapon.

His first groggy thought, of course, was that one of the enemies he had made over years of countless missions must have already tracked him down. *Thank you, Prinny.*

He sat up and scanned the room, but the intruder had already fled down the hallway.

He could hear the footsteps but couldn't see him.

Still blinking the sleep from his eyes, he leaped to his feet and bounded off in immediate pursuit, leaping over the pile of boxes and flinging out into the corridor.

He caught only the briefest glimpse of a moving shadow. "Who's there?" he bellowed, but then he heard a sound from his left and looked over.

More than one.

He heard the bang of a door coming from the direction of the entrance hall, while off to his left, a rusty creak hinted at the second intruder slipping out of a ground-floor window. He went after the one who had left by the front door. By God, if it was some leftover Promethean — !

He did not want to have to kill an intruder the first day in his new home. But if it came down to it, he would. Indeed, he wouldn't think twice.

Racing through the entrance hall, he stepped out of the doorway, his heart pounding, and suddenly his eyes narrowed as his gaze homed in on a small, fleeing boy.

He blinked. *What the hell?*

A child?

Understanding dawned. A local.

His reaction changed instantaneously

from wrath to indignation. "Get back here, you brat!" he bellowed. "What are you doing in my house? I want an explanation — and your name! Who are your parents?"

He sheathed his knife and went striding after the young miscreant. The boy looked over his shoulder and ran for his life.

Good. Trevor glowered. "You better not have stolen something from me, you little thief! I'll find out who you are. There will be consequences!"

All of a sudden, something hard struck him in the back. He cursed and spun around and spotted the rock that had hit him, still rolling on the ground.

In utter shock, he raised his gaze from it to the second small person, identical to the first, who had obviously thrown it.

The boy had another at the ready. "Leave my brother alone!" the little ruffian shouted.

Trevor stared at him for a second, then laughed in disbelief.

"What are you doing on my property?" he demanded. "Are you trying to get yourselves killed?"

Instead of answering him, the second one also turned and fled.

Still groggy and not at all amused at this rude awakening by a pair of meddling peasant urchins, he waved them off with a grumble to himself, fairly sure that at least now he'd put the fear of God in them.

But just as he turned around to go back inside, a child's wild, frightened shout rang out from the direction of the rushing river, followed by a loud splash.

Oh, what now? Trevor stopped and turned, frowning.

Two seconds later came the scream.

"Help!"

Cursing under his breath, he sprinted toward the river, which was swollen and fast, thanks to the strange weather of this cold summer. When he saw the old log that had been set up as a footbridge, he understood in a glance what had happened. The fleeing boy, careless with haste, had taken a tumble while trying to get across.

Several feet below the log amid the rushing current, Trevor spotted the boy's head amid the fast, swirling current.

"Bloody hell," he whispered, as the little head disappeared under the water in a section white with foam and churning eddies. Instantly descending the steep, muddy bank, he slid past the leaning trees to the rocks below. He waded into the river until it was up to his waist.

Then he dove in and swam.

■ ■ ■ ■

Still ensconced in her window nook, Grace was finishing her last sip of tea when, all of a sudden, she spotted a small, familiar figure running full tilt up the drive.

She furrowed her brow and looked again. One of the Nelcott twins? It was impossible to say which, but the twins were never seen singly. Her expression darkened. *I hope nothing's happened.* Quickly setting her empty teacup aside, she rose and hurried to the front door in concern.

"Miss Grace! Miss Grace! Help!"

As soon as she opened the door, she saw the panicked look on the boy's face. Grace promptly forgot that she was not yet dressed for the day, still wearing her dressing gown over her night rail, with slippers on her feet and her hair loose and long, flowing over her shoulders. She stepped outside as the boy flung himself toward her.

She gripped his small shoulders to steady him though she still wasn't totally sure which one he was. "What's wrong? Take a breath and tell me what happened."

"He caught us — he caught Denny! He's gonna murder 'im!"

"Who?" she exclaimed.

Kenny grabbed her hand and began pulling her a few steps down the drive. "Come on, you have to stop him! You got to help me save my brother!"

"From what?"

"From the ogre! He's got guns, Miss!"

"Who's got guns? What are you talking about? What ogre?"

"At the Grange!"

Her eyebrows shot up. Then she planted her feet to halt the boy's dragging her. "Kenny," she said darkly, having realized it was the slightly less barbaric twin she had in her grasp. "*What* did you two do?"

He blanched. "No time to explain! Come on, he's got my brother!"

"Kenny."

"Denny and me went to the Grange to spy on him —"

"Oh — !" She bit back a word unsuitable for children's ears. Lud, first Calpurnia, now the twins. "Listen to me." She took the boy's arm sternly. "You mustn't go bothering our new neighbor. He just came back from the war, Kenny. Don't you think he wants some peace and quiet?"

"The Grange is our place!" the boy bellowed back at her. "Me and Denny claimed it first!"

"But he's bought it, darling. Besides, it's

too dangerous for children! You know you're not allowed to play there. Most of those old outbuildings are full of rusty nails and broken ladders. You could fall and break your neck, and no one would ever —"

"That's what I'm trying to tell you! Denny fell! He was running away from *him.*"

Grace paled.

"Are you gonna help me save my brother or not?"

She swallowed hard. "Let me get my shoes." Truly shaken, now that she understood, she dashed back into the house, kicked off her slippers, and pulled on the nearest shoes she could find: her boots.

When she rushed back outside, Kenny was already well ahead of her, racing back toward the Grange rather than waiting around for her. Grace ran after him.

She still wasn't quite sure exactly what had happened, but it sounded like Denny had had some sort of accident. For his brother to have come tearing over to the parsonage seeking adult help, it was obviously an emergency, and she feared it must be serious.

Rather panicked, she ran to the Grange — hoping in the meanwhile that none of her neighbors glimpsed her fleeing across the countryside in her night rail and robe, with no sort of corset that might have helped constrain certain indecorous womanly bouncings.

Arriving at the Grange a few minutes later, she heard thunderous yelling in the distance.

A flash of motion ahead revealed Kenny running through the orchard toward the river, still some distance ahead of her.

Grace followed, and the deep, angry voice grew louder as she neared. Hurrying through the orchard, she spotted Kenny hiding behind a tree to her right. He pointed toward the river with a look of dread.

"Stay here," Grace ordered, passing him. Out of breath, she dropped her pace to a brisk stride, red-faced from her morning jog and trying to catch her breath.

Clearing the orchard's rows of trees, she came out onto the green and immediately saw two figures silhouetted beside the rushing stream.

One was tall and muscular and making all the noise.

The little one was Denny — cowering.

Denny Nelcott never cowered.

"You have no business sneaking around here! You see what happens? You could have been killed, you little menace! I had better never see you or your brother around this farm again. Do you understand me?"

"Yes, sir."

Whatever had happened, the other twin did not look too seriously wounded.

He was, however, soaked to the skin and looking defenseless, chastened, and heart-breakingly pitiful — on purpose, no doubt.

Lord Trevor Montgomery was having none of it.

As Grace marched toward them, as yet unnoticed by either angry male, big or little, she was not sure how she felt about the stern tongue-lashing to which the ex-spy was subjecting the mischievous boy.

For herself, she had been so panicked that serious harm had befallen the child that her instinct would have been to catch him up in her arms and hug him out of sheer relief. Trevor obviously did not share her sentiments.

As she approached, she could see that he was genuinely furious. The scolding wasn't just for show.

Something had clearly happened; the twins had obviously got themselves into mischief. Still, his yelling at the little orphan like this rankled her protective instincts and brought on a whiff of righteous indignation.

As she approached, however, one last emotion tumbled into the already-agitated mix as the sight of the man slammed her with desire.

Trevor was soaking wet, the morning sun gleaming on his skin, his dark hair plastered back sleekly to his head.

His clothes stuck to his muscled body everywhere, hugging every manly line of thigh and bottom. His white linen shirt, hanging open down his chest, had become nearly transparent. Grace swallowed hard, appalled at herself for a fleeting vision of helping him change out of those wet clothes . . .

Her pulse surged, and it had nothing to do with her sprint across the fields. She clenched her teeth, determined to fight temptation, ignoring the tug of shocking lust with a will.

He was still giving Denny Nelcott what-for. "If I ever catch you on my land again —"

"What is going on here?" she interrupted, marching toward them.

Trevor looked over, interrupted in midrant.

Oh, perfect. This was all it needed. An angry Sunday school teacher stomping toward him on the warpath, with an expression on her face like a mother bear about to attack a hunter who had accidentally disturbed her cubs.

Still, Trevor could not help noticing that she looked exceedingly lovely in her state of dishabille. His gaze flicked over her in immediate interest, heating him despite the cold, wet clothes that clung to his body.

Her face was flushed, her blue eyes bright with anger. The V-neck of her banyan robe had parted down her chest and was currently less modest than the spinsterish gown she had worn to the Lievedon Ball.

Indeed, she was rather magnificent at the moment, her hair flowing loose and long over her shoulders, streaked with morning sunshine and billowing in the breeze as she strode toward him with a glare.

Meanwhile, his young captive, noticing that Trevor was distracted, slipped out of his grasp and ran toward his beautiful rescuer.

Trevor let him go. The boy dashed away, squishing with every step in his wet boots. The soggy little miscreant fled behind Grace, joining his identical accomplice.

"What happened here?" she demanded in a clipped tone.

"Why don't you ask them?" Trevor retorted, only to realize belatedly that his answer made him sound more like a third youngster than a man.

Grace arched a brow at him, then turned around to check on the brats huddling behind her. They were hiding from him and making a ploy for her sympathy.

It was working, too, the little monsters.

"Denny, are you all right?"

"He's fine," Trevor grumbled, as she checked the soggy one for cuts or broken bones.

He had already done that, and he was sure he had more medical training than she did.

"He fell into the river trying to walk across it on a log. They both were lucky," Trevor added. "Do you know how easily this could have turned into a tragedy? I woke up from a dead sleep thinking I had a serious intruder. These two broke into my house. It was very stupid of them, too, considering my line of work. People who sneak up on me while I'm asleep don't usually live to tell about it." He glared at them.

"Do you hear that?" Grace said angrily to the children. "Boys, he could have killed you. You don't break into people's houses! Especially not his. Now, apologize!"

Trevor rolled his eyes, for instead of a simple "I'm sorry," the pair of scheming little barbarians resorted next to tears.

Sniffles, trembling chins, sobs worthy of the stage.

To his dismay, it worked on her.

"Don't cry," she said tenderly to each in turn, smoothing their hair, cupping their chubby grubby cheeks. "Look, it's over now. The important thing is, nobody got hurt."

When she hugged them, it was all he could take. "Miss Kenwood, honestly!"

"What? What's the matter with you?"

From behind her, the little devils smiled smugly at him when she turned away.

"Don't baby them!" Trevor said in exasperation. "They're pulling the wool over your eyes, woman! Can't you see that?"

She looked outraged at such a charge against the little cherubs and rose to her full height in maternal indignation. "They're just children!"

"They're a pair of little demons," Trevor muttered. Then he tapped the corner of his eyes and pointed at the brothers. "I'm watching you."

The dry one, the little rock thrower, stuck his tongue out at Trevor from behind Grace.

He narrowed his eyes in response. "Who are their parents? They would not tell me their names, but I mean to have a word with their father about their total lack of discipline."

Grace cast Trevor a warning look and put her arms around the boys. "Don't worry,

I'll deal with it. They will not trouble you again."

"They'd better not, or I'm going to get a big, nasty guard dog and give him orders to eat them next time."

"That will do, my lord. You've made your point. You've terrified them quite enough."

"Terrified them? It was they who terrified me! This one nearly drowned right before my eyes. If you are able to control these rascals, keep them off my property. I bought this place to get some peace and quiet. These boys are not my problem. I will not be responsible for them sneaking around here and getting themselves killed!"

"Fine. Boys — apologize to Lord Trevor. Now." She took them each by an arm and marched them forward. "Go on! Apologize to the great hero for disturbing his precious peace and quiet," she muttered under her breath.

Trevor scowled at her, and Grace scowled back.

The boys mumbled, "Sorry."

"That's better. Good-bye, Lord Trevor. I'll make sure and keep everyone away from you. We'll not disturb you again. Welcome to Thistleton," she added in reproach. Then she turned the pair around and began walking them back toward the parsonage, a hand on each of their shoulders.

Trevor stared after her in exasperation, bewildered at how he had somehow become the villain in all this. "Whoever their parents are, those people should not have the care of a cat, let alone small children!" he yelled after her, unwilling to leave it at that.

At that, Grace stopped walking. For a moment, she stood motionless, her back to him.

The two boys kept going, however; then they, too, paused and turned back to see why their Sunday school teacher had lagged behind.

Trevor blanched as he saw her dainty fists clench by her sides. As though mentally arguing with herself, Grace slowly turned around.

She marched back to him alone. "The reason these two boys go roaming 'round the countryside, Lord Trevor — the reason their parents don't do a better job of minding them — is because their father is dead, and their mother is sickly. She was nearly crushed by grief when her husband died in the war."

Ah, hell, thought Trevor.

She took another step toward him with a look of wrath, an avenging angel in a dressing gown, her eyes shooting sparks of righteous blue fire.

"I'm sorry. I didn't know," he mumbled.

But it seemed the lady could not hold her tongue. "How much did the land agent tell you about Colonel Avery?" she demanded.

"The former owner of the Grange?" He shrugged, on his guard. "Not much. Said he was a cavalry officer, eccentric in his old age."

"Then it's just as I suspected. He left out the most important part." She pinned him in a stare of withering reproach. "Colonel Avery, you see, took it into his head to raise a regiment from around these parts. A hundred men joined him, fifty of them from Thistleton. Ten percent of our young men, and many heads of households."

Trevor closed his eyes, for he could suddenly see it coming.

"Ben Nelcott was among them," she continued, "the father of these boys and of the little girl you gave the flower to. He never came home again. Only a handful of them did. That senile old fool got most of them killed playing soldier. He sold them on 'the good fight' against the Monster, having an adventure, then he all but destroyed this village and countless families with it for miles around, for what? Naught but his own vanity."

"I'm sorry," he mumbled, but she ignored him.

"These boys are orphans," she informed him with devastating clarity, "and if I *ever* hear you roar at a child like that again, you can cross me off your list of friends — permanently."

She pivoted to leave him in the solitude he had thought he craved. Damn it, this day was off to a bad start and just kept getting worse.

It shouldn't matter, but Trevor feared their budding friendship or flirtation or whatever it was, was already doomed. Not wanting it to end this way, yet completely unwilling to grovel after recent events with certain other women, he called after her defiantly — one last question.

"What about you, Miss Kenwood?" His tone came out harsher than he'd meant it to, the result of spending too many years among warriors and men. "Was there some swain of yours who also went off with the colonel and didn't come home? Is that why you still live with your father?"

"Me, love a soldier?" She turned around, visibly outraged by his impertinent question. "Of course not. I could never love someone who made a living killing his fellow man."

The way she looked straight into his eyes when she said it made her point clear: He had no chance with this woman at all.

Not that he had sought one. *Had he?*

Stung, Trevor stiffly dropped his gaze. "Of course not."

Whatever softheaded thoughts he might've had about Grace Kenwood, it was very clear he had just been preemptively rejected on the basis, the very core, of who and what he was. *Well, then.*

She grasped the two boys each by a hand and marched them off down the drive.

As he watched them walk away, leaving him alone — as he had insisted — Trevor dropped his head back and stared at the sky.

So much for that idea. It was stupid, anyway, he told himself. She was not even properly in his class. She would never fit into his world.

Not that he ever quite had, either.

Trevor let out a sigh. Ah, well. He had wanted to be alone.

It looked like his wish had just been well and truly granted.

CHAPTER 9

Still trembling with protective, righteous fury, Grace walked the boys back to the parsonage, where she gave Denny a towel to dry himself. Then she fed the children breakfast. For her part, she was too upset to eat.

What a cad. What a brute . . .

She was glad, of course, that her neighbor had rescued Denny. And he was right. Resilient as the boys were, they were perfectly fine after the morning's escapade.

But Grace was still outraged at Lord Trevor. How dare he comment on her unmarried state! Ask her why she still lived with her father? Such insufferable rudeness! And here she thought he was a gentleman!

Obviously not.

He might as well have called her an old maid to her face. It was not that there had been any "swain" of her own who'd gone to war with Colonel Avery. It was simply none of his business! That, along with the fact, perhaps, that she did not like *anybody's* noticing that she might be a trifle lonely. That her life might not have worked out quite as any young woman might have hoped.

She could break down in tears even now if she dared to think on it. But oh, that cretin, that too-handsome rudesby had had the gall to point it out. As if she owed *him* an explanation!

While the boys shoveled bacon, eggs, and jellied toast into their mouths, Grace stared absently at the bowl of apples in the middle of the table, too incensed to eat a bite.

She wished Papa had never suggested the Grange to him.

How was she supposed to live next door to a former spy, a trained assassin, especially now, when he had seen her looking so ridiculous, crossing the meadows in her night rail, dressing gown, and boots? That was all he needed — more reasons to mock her.

She shook her head to herself in seething silence. By heaven, as a pastor's daughter, she could live with all sorts of deprivations, but if Lord Trevor pitied her for an old maid, no. That was more than her pride could stand. It was not to be borne. Calpurnia could have him, as far as Grace was concerned.

Meanwhile, across the table, the Nelcott boys were laughing at each other's antics, their fright forgotten now that the danger was safely behind them. Indeed, they seemed to regard their brush with disaster as a grand lark and possibly their best adventure yet.

"Denny, did he really save you from drowning?" Grace interrupted, uncharacteristically annoyed by their merriment. "I thought you knew how to swim."

"Aye, I can, Miss —" he started.

"Not as good as me!" his brother interjected.

"Better than you!" Denny shot back, pushing him.

"Can not!"

"Boys! Answer the question!"

"I *can* swim," Denny assured her. "But my foot got caught under a branch or somethin' on the bottom of the creek. I got stuck. Could barely keep my nose above the water."

"So he really did save you?"

"Aye, Miss." Denny grinned. "He was brilliant!"

"For an ogre," Kenny added with a giggle, and Grace scowled to realize the lads had now changed their opinion of the Grange's new owner from villain to hero.

Hmmph.

"Well, you'd better stay away from him. He wants no part of you or any of us. You heard the man. All he wants is to be left alone. So let's respect his wishes, and hopefully, no one will get killed. If I hear about you two sneaking back onto his property, you're going to have to deal with *me.* Understood?"

Identical frowns appeared on their faces, but the mischievous pair finally got the message. The boys lowered their heads, and both mumbled, "Yes, ma'am."

"That's better," she replied, then finally took an irked bite of toast.

Trevor refused to wonder if he had made a big mistake in buying the farm.

Grace Kenwood was not going to ruin this for him.

She had succeeded in making him feel guilty as hell for yelling at a pair of little orphans, but not everyone on earth was a saint like her. Yes, he sometimes raised his voice. Especially when a child's life was at stake. Apparently that made him a cruel brute of some sort.

Or selfish.

Mindful only of what he had himself been through. Forgetting that other people had suffered, too, through this war.

That *did* seem to be what she had been accusing him of.

But how dare she? Well, she could serve that dish, but he wasn't going to eat it.

If she wanted to see selfish, she could look at Nick. Or Beauchamp. He was a saint compared to them.

Strangely, these rationalizations did not make him feel any better — which only vexed him more.

Who did she think she was to take him to task? He was sorry if he did not live up to her standards, but he had saved that boy's life this morning, and he did not deserve to be scolded by some churchman's overly virtuous daughter.

Ah, hell, what did he care what she might think of him? It did not signify.

He was done with women.

Thrusting Miss Holier-Than-Thou out of his mind, he changed into dry clothes, then walked through the house, looking for breach points.

He locked the Grange up tightly as he moved from room to room, and near the end of his tour, he found the rusty window hanging open above the scullery sinks.

Aha. The scullery off the kitchens was sunk fairly low into the earth, which made it an easy climb through the window at ground level; this was apparently where the little devils had been getting in.

Trevor shut the window with a harrumph and turned the latch, then at last set off for town — such as it was. For his first foray into the village, he needed to see if his mail had started arriving from London yet, and the dry goods store served as the local post office.

As he saddled one of his horses, he wondered what sort of reaction he was going to get from the locals. Small, close-knit hamlets like Thistleton did not always welcome outsiders with open arms. Certainly, he did not expect everyone to be as joyous about his arrival as the bubbly Calpurnia Windlesham.

Considering how fast news traveled in little rural communities, he took it for granted that everyone had heard by now about his clash with the pair of pint-sized rascals.

He hoped some of the villagers had first-hand experience with the sort of trouble those two little wild things could cause; otherwise, he feared he was going to be *persona non grata* in his new hometown before noon.

On the other hand, if the locals decided they should be afraid of him, they'd be more likely to leave him alone.

Hmm. He swung up onto his horse, but as he rode off, it occurred to him that Grace's word probably held a lot of weight in this town. She might hold his entire reputation among these people in her hands. He was in her territory, on her turf, he understood quite well, and though her influence here made him feel both sardonic and uneasy, he supposed he'd better watch his step.

Upon arriving at the village, he opted for a neutral expression, unsure of how he'd be received.

He tipped his hat to a cluster of villagers who stared as he rode by, but he did not deign to smile.

Country folk did not trust city dwellers as a rule. Besides, acting too friendly, too approachable, would only invite more intrusions.

Reactions to him seemed mixed as he rode up to the dry goods store and dismounted. But they were obviously curious. Shopkeepers in aprons stepped into the doorways of their establishments as he rode by, no doubt sizing up the value of his purse.

The old men playing chess under the tree

halted their game and watched him warily as he tied his horse to the hitching post, then walked up the few steps to the entrance of the store.

Thankfully, the dry goods dealer was a garrulous man. Trevor introduced himself, collected his mail, and glanced through it; then he wandered the three aisles of the tiny shop, determined to buy a few things whether he needed them or not, as a gesture of goodwill.

This done, he stepped back outside into the village square. Scanning his surroundings, he noted the location of various places of business that he might need in future. Blacksmith, bakery, pub . . .

But it was strange. On his first pass through Thistleton with the land agent, he had merely noticed the general quaintness of the village. Now that Grace had told him about Colonel Avery's misadventure, his searching gaze picked up finer details. A closer look revealed the onset of a creeping shabbiness, a quiet despair that seemed to reflect his own.

Peeling paint, sagging shutters. An air of defeat.

The impact of what Grace had just told him about the old cavalryman's ill-fated regiment sank in.

Fifty dead. Ten percent was a horrendous loss, proportionally speaking. The army had rules about this, but in desperate times, they weren't always followed.

Even worse, the loss had robbed Thistleton of its young men, the muscle of any small farming community. And then the disastrous weather killing the crops on top of that.

Good God, Grace, is this what you're up against?

And he had had the audacity to ask her why she wasn't married?

He hated himself at the thought. He could not believe he had thrown it in her face so irreverently this morning. But he had not understood. Not really. He had merely been a bit jealous and trying to understand. Well, he saw it now, whether he wanted to or not.

This tiny village had suffered a crushing loss of life in a distant war that most of these people probably didn't even understand. Hell, he barely understood it himself, and he had clearance for all sorts of confidential memoranda.

No wonder they were staring at him.

He had *lived.* Survived an ordeal that had robbed them of brothers, husbands, sons. *God.* Fairly tingling with self-consciousness under the villagers' silent scrutiny, he walked back slowly to his horse. *I don't need this.*

Peace and quiet. He hadn't come here for them; he had come here for himself. *Don't look at me like that. You people need to leave me alone.*

He felt like absolute hell, all the more so because neither Grace nor her father had uttered one complaint.

Maybe he was a selfish bastard, just as bad as Nick, but in a different way.

Maybe he needed to open his eyes and look around him, stop focusing so much on himself. If not, he might as well go back and join Laura in a life of preening vanity.

He let out a sigh and lowered his gaze but did not have the heart to go fleeing back to his hermitage, leaving them like this. Indeed, with the morning waning, he was getting hungry, so he decided to try the local pub fare. Walking across the square to the Gaggle Goose Inn, he could still feel everybody staring at him, just like they did in London. Just what he'd come here to escape.

With a sigh, he stepped into the coaching inn. The Reverend Kenwood had said they served decent food.

It was dark inside compared to the June sunshine, but as his eyes adjusted, he glanced around and saw he was the only customer, at least for the moment.

Then he spotted the buxom tavern girl who was leaning on the bar, polishing silver. She straightened up when she saw him, and the way her stare immediately homed in on him, he felt a certain degree of relief.

At least someone here was ready to be friendly to him.

He had long since learned to recognize a professional when he saw one.

Indeed, it was good to know that out here in the middle of nowhere, if he needed female company some night, he wouldn't have to go far to find relief without scandalizing the village. That's what girls like this were here for.

"I'll bet I know who you are," she greeted him as she approached at a slow, hip-swaying saunter. "You're the gentleman that bought the Grange, ain't ye?"

"Guilty," he replied.

"Well! Welcome, then." She smiled broadly, revealing a fetching little gap between her two front teeth. An inviting gleam in her dark eyes, she gestured toward a table. "You just come and sit right down over here — Lord Trevor, ain't it? You're even handsomer than I heard."

He arched a brow.

With a toss of her tousled raven mane, she led him over to a table by the grimy window.

Trevor followed her, bemused. Well, he had already crossed blades today with the town saint. It seemed he was about to make friends with the town sinner.

As he sat down, she set her hand on her waist and stood before the table, letting him look her over. "You can call me Marianne," she said, leaning forward in cozy fashion, making sure he saw her cleavage. "I'm here to get you anything you want," she added softly, her meaning very clear.

"Why, thank you, Miss Marianne. You're very kind," he whispered with an appreciative smile.

Now that's more like it.

CHAPTER 10

By late morning, the day had finally returned to its normal track after the debacle
at dawn.

Still stewing on her fight with her new
neighbor, Grace headed down to the village, carrying a few easy children's books in
a satchel on her shoulder. Three times a
week, she worked with Marianne, teaching
the unfortunate young woman to read.

But after a pleasant walk to the village,
she went up the few steps of the coaching
inn and promptly stopped in her tracks, spying her pupil through the window.

Her heart lurched in her chest. Her stomach instantly twisted into knots. Marianne
was sitting at the window table inside the
pub, polishing silver, laughing, while across
from her, finishing his meal, sat Lord Trevor
Montgomery. He reclined a little, at his
ease, one arm cast across the back of the
empty chair beside him.

Grace snapped her mouth shut. Well, he certainly hadn't wasted any time! Then her heart began to pound.

He said something to Marianne that Grace could not make out, then he listened intently to the answer, which was shocking in itself. Nobody around here except Grace and her father ever actually *listened* to Marianne.

They just stared — women, coldly; men, leering. Trevor was treating her like a person, and Grace had not anticipated that. She wanted to be happy about it, but a curious rush of unpleasant emotions stormed through her at finding them together.

One thing was for certain. She suddenly comprehended in a whole new way why Calpurnia still wasn't speaking to George.

Grace, however, refused to admit that her own reaction could be described as jealousy.

The implications of that were too dark to contemplate, considering she had already assigned him to Callie, at least in her own mind.

Safer to convince herself that, at the moment, all she felt was protectiveness toward her wayward pupil.

Yes. That was it. Marianne had to be protected from that worldly seducer.

Relieved at this conclusion, Grace quickly

recovered her composure. Lifting her chin, she squared her shoulders and noted with relief that Trevor was wiping his mouth with his napkin and paying Marianne for the meal.

She hoped that was *all* he was paying her for.

Not wishing to cause a scene in front of the village, she pushed the pub door open and masked her moral outrage behind a cool stare as she walked in, ready to play the harlot's guardian angel. Somebody had to save poor, misguided Marianne from that devil.

Who better than she? Somebody who had already tasted the sort of temptation he could offer.

Well, here comes the sweets course, Trevor mused as Miss Kenwood came marching into the pub.

He had known, of course, that she was coming.

Marianne had already told him about the scheduled reading lesson. Besides, he had seen Grace from the corner of his eye, gawking in the window with a stricken look.

It was gone now, as she advanced toward their table — on the warpath once again. Indeed, she looked even more furious to find him talking to Marianne than she had been this morning at his *cruel, callous* yelling at the pair of little housebreakers.

The sparks shooting out of Grace's blue eyes didn't have much effect on Trevor but sent a flash of guilt across Marianne's face.

The bold, bawdy tavern girl suddenly turned humble and obedient as her virtuous reading tutor came stomping across the wood-planked floor to stand by their table.

Trevor just looked at her, but Marianne shot to her feet, scrambling to gather up her silverware. "Morning, Miss. I'll be ready in a moment, if ye please. I was just finishin' up my work 'ere — and talkin' with our new neighbor."

"So I see," she answered with a frosty stare at him.

Trevor smiled politely and, hiding his amusement, leaned back in his chair. He gestured to the seat across from him. "Won't you join us, Miss Kenwood?"

He was in no mood to stand at her arrival. Why bother? She had already decided that he was not a gentleman.

"I am here," she said stiffly, "for Marianne's reading lesson."

"Yes, I know."

"I better go put these away, then," the village hussy mumbled.

Grace looked daggers at her. "Yes. Do."

Marianne lowered her head and hurried off with a load of flatware clattering in her apron.

After she had gone, Grace turned to him and, to his amusement, did not even bother trying to find a subtle approach.

It seemed they were past such formalities.

She set her white-gloved hands on the table and leaned closer, glaring into his eyes. "What do you think you're doing?"

"Pardon, dear?"

"You know exactly what I mean."

"I'm sorry, I was just having my breakfast. Can I buy you something to eat? Your father was right. The food here's not half-bad."

"I'm only going to say this once, so hear me well. Stay away from Marianne. Is that clear?"

"As a bell, love." He lifted his eyebrows innocently. Her wrath was too amusing. "But why?"

"That girl has been through more than you can possibly imagine. She's already suffered enough at the hands of cads like you."

"Oh, so I'm a cad now, too? The list of my faults is growing apace."

"Mock me as you like, I'm not going to let you despoil her."

"Despoil her?" He chuckled softly. "Oh, I

213

think it's safe to say someone else did that long before I came along."

"Listen to me. This is not a jest." She glanced over her shoulder to make sure Marianne was not in earshot. "She's trying to change her life, all right? Papa and I found her in a London gutter with two black eyes given to her by her flash man."

Trevor instantly stopped smiling.

"She was penniless and half-starved. Beaten to within inches of her life. Disowned by her family. She had nowhere else to go."

He checked an impulse of rage at this information, maintaining his mask of nonchalance. "Go on."

"We brought her here so she could have a new start, a chance to rebuild her life. If you ruin it for her —"

"I'm not going to ruin it for her. What do you take me for?" he retorted.

"You'd better not, or I will personally come over to the Grange when you're not there, a-and burn your house down as soon as your renovations are complete!"

He raised his eyebrows. "Well, you are even more violent than I suspected. Now you threaten my poor old house with arson, too?"

"I'm warning you. Stay away from her."

He frowned. "Has anyone ever told you that you're a bit of a killjoy?"

"Say what you want of me; just leave Marianne alone."

He lowered his gaze and tried to sound as casual as possible as he asked, "So what's the name of this flash man who beat her?"

"I don't know. She's too frightened of retaliation to tell us."

"Or maybe she's protecting him," he murmured.

"Why would she do that?" Grace asked, keeping her voice down so the tavern girl putting a few things away behind the distant bar wouldn't realize they were discussing her past. "Well?"

Trevor didn't bother trying to explain it. A preacher's daughter would never understand the whore's age-old curse of becoming enthralled with her abuser. "Never mind that. Would you like me to talk to her? I'll get the name."

"Why would she tell you? You only just met her. We've known her for a year, but she won't tell us anything."

"She'll talk to me," he replied. "Just say the word."

Grace shook her head. "Thanks, but I really don't want you getting involved. It's still too soon to press her. She's finally

215

started feeling safe here. She'll tell us when she's ready."

"And you don't want her trusting me."

"Not really, no."

"Because you don't trust me, either?"

She looked at him in hesitation. "I'm not sure, to be honest."

Trevor held her stare. At least he could appreciate her honesty. "If you get a name out of her, you give it to me. Next time I'm in London, I can make sure this man never hurts her or any other woman again."

"More violence? That is your solution?" She sat back and studied him intently. "I should've known."

Trevor paused. "I know you don't like soldiers, Miss Kenwood, but I'm afraid a gun to the head is the only language that certain types of men can understand."

Grace rubbed her brow as though striving for patience with him. "Thank you, my lord. I'm sure you mean well, but please, just stay out of it."

He shrugged, irked. "Only trying to help."

"Then don't go luring her into wickedness! You know what I mean. That's all I ask."

He smiled ruefully at her blush in mentioning such things. "Very well. I'll keep my hands off Marianne. But I hope you don't regret it. For if I get lonely, maybe I'll just have to come to you."

She turned a darker shade of red and fell silent for a second. She looked away. "I wish you wouldn't flirt with me when you're in love with someone else. It may be the custom in London, but —"

"Wait. What? What are you talking about, in love . . . ?"

She tilted her head at him with a knowing stare. "I heard about your broken engagement at the Lievedon Ball."

"Oh, Lord," Trevor muttered, looking away, bristling.

Miss Kenwood shook her head. "Why do you sit here suffering?" she asked in a frank tone devoid of malice. He could tell she was only trying to help, but he wanted to throttle her for bringing it up. "You're like a tiger with a toothache, roaming around ready to bite anybody who comes across your path. If that woman broke your heart, then let her fix it. Go and win her back. You deserve a chance at happiness after all you've been through. Why should you accept this if you love her?"

"Well, thank you for your advice, but my affairs are my own," he answered, rather more coldly than he had intended.

She said nothing, studying him like she

had done with the soggy twin this morning, scanning him for bumps and bruises.

Trevor looked away, his jaw clenched.

"Well, it's true, isn't it?" she persisted after a moment. "I can only conclude that's why you had no interest in all those ladies chasing you at the Lievedon Ball. Why you danced with me that night, I can hardly fathom, but it explains why you couldn't even be bothered with a beauty like Calpurnia. You're still in love with your former fiancée."

"No, I'm really not," he said with cold conviction.

"Look, I'm only trying to help you —"

"Don't! Please. For one thing, you don't know what you're talking about. Laura can go hang for all I care. For another, it's none of your damned business."

"It is my business, actually! The people of Thistleton have already been through enough — including Marianne. Now you come along, a trained killer with a chip on your shoulder the size of Gibraltar. With all due respect, my lord, can't you see that you're, well, a bit of a menace?"

"I am most certainly not!" he said indignantly.

"You are!" she exclaimed. "You're angry at the world. Why don't you go and reconcile with the one you love instead of taking out your bitterness on everyone around you?"

Trevor stared at her, amazed. He'd never been spoken to in this fashion in his life, at least not by a female. By his old handler, Virgil, maybe, but certainly not by some preacher's daughter.

Nonplussed, he swept to his feet and kicked his chair back. "If you'll excuse me, certain tasks require my attention at the Grange." He tossed a few more coins onto the table for Marianne, then turned to go.

"Lord Trevor," she chided, at which he pivoted with a cold stare.

"Sorry, did you have still more advice you wanted to share with me?" he bit out.

"It's not *advice*!" Grace exclaimed, and at least had the decency to blush after all her preaching. "I'm only saying, it's obvious to me that you need to make peace with your *old* life before you're truly ready to start your new one here. Otherwise, your problems will only follow you. That's how it works."

"Ah, so that's how it works, I see. Thank you for enlightening me to life's mysteries. What a great comfort it must be to you, having all the puzzles of existence so thoroughly in hand! How fortunate for me that you're right next door if I should ever need your instructions on *how to put my bloody boots on in the morning*" he bellowed before slamming out.

Slack-jawed with astonishment at his roar, Grace stood staring at the door, still shuddering on its hinges.

Not until today had she ever considered herself capable of murder. But that man just might drive her to it.

Indignation broke forth from her in a torrent when she finally regained the power of speech. "What a barbarian!" she burst out, unable to help herself. "Oh, the sarcasm! The arrogance! I've never met such a thoroughgoing boor!"

She was quite past caring what anybody thought of her, in her outrage.

Marianne returned for their lesson with the tea. "Aw, he's not that bad, Miss," she said with a grin.

"Oh, yes, he is! That cretin needs his head knocked!"

Marianne seemed much too amused by it all. "He was very pleasant to me."

"I'll bet!" Grace fairly spat.

"Fine figure of a man, though, ain't he? A hero, too, so they say."

Grace snorted. "A few minutes in his presence would quickly dispel the illusions of anyone so deceived."

Marianne folded her arms across her chest and studied her in amusement. "You like him, don't you?"

"Me? Don't be absurd!" she exclaimed, though it was pointless to deny the scarlet fire creeping into her cheeks. "He's insulting and intolerable. You try to help some people — !"

But Marianne let out a low, throaty laugh. "The only help that one needs is a woman in his bed," she murmured, much too knowingly.

"For God's sake, Marianne!" Grace plopped into the nearest seat at the ex-harlot's frank declaration. "You know you mustn't talk like that in front of me!"

"Well, it's true." Marianne laughed and pulled out a chair. "Stallion, that one. Poor love, he needs it *bad.*"

Grace looked at her for a moment, at a loss. But as curiosity overcame her, she could not hold back. She leaned closer and whispered fiercely, "Did he proposition you?"

"Never got a chance, Miss, as I'd already propositioned *him.* He's got such big, strong hands . . . Did you notice? You know what they say about that."

"I'm sure I have no idea on this earth

what you might mean." She stared at her disreputable pupil, wondering if a broken heart over his gorgeous former fiancé would drive the blackguard into Marianne's arms — and her bed.

It was all too unspeakable.

"Which do you prefer, love, the couch or the floor?" With a shiver of remembered lust at his kisses in that darkened room at Lievedon House, Grace could still hear the echo of his husky whisper in her memory, could still feel the sensual heat of his big, powerful body against hers.

Indeed, being a strictly virtuous woman, she did not care to count how many times that guilty scene had played out in the theatre of her mind ever since she had made the ruffian's acquaintance — no matter how she tried to banish it. Once she had thought of it right in the middle of church! What was happening to her?

Then she became aware of Marianne regarding her in sardonic amusement, one hand on her hip.

Grace slowly looked over at her.

Worldly and scarred by her experiences as she was, Marianne's dark eyes danced.

"What?" Grace muttered in chagrin, lowering her head.

"So, you's a flesh-and-blood woman after all."

"What are you talking about?"

"You fancy 'im," she teased.

"No, I don't! Don't be absurd! I pity him! I tolerate him . . ." She tried again when Marianne tilted her head and arched a brow. "Oh, very well, he drives me mad. But not in the way that you think! Oh, promise me you'll stay away from him," Grace pleaded, "for your own sake! I'm sure he'll only hurt you. He's a hardened, bitter warrior. A killer and a spy. Bloodshed is second nature to him, and he doesn't care about anyone but himself!"

"If you say so, Miss."

"I only say it for your own good!"

"Oh, right, right, o' course." Marianne nodded, but still looked amused as she picked up her first book. "Don't you worry, Miss. It ain't like with me and George-boy. After all you done for me, I'll keep me distance. That one's all yours."

CHAPTER 11

Still furious, Trevor cantered his horse back to the Grange, his brooding stare fixed on the dusty road ahead.

Devil take her, who did that Kenwood woman think she was, taking him to task like an errant schoolboy — twice in one day? How dare she say such things to him? He barely even knew her!

But by the time he arrived at the farmhouse and flung himself down off his sweatflecked horse, he was beginning to wonder — gallingly — if she might not have a point.

He swore under his breath and shook his head to himself with her words still ringing in his ears.

"You can't begin your new life here until you've made peace with the old one."

What she said made sense, as much as he hated to hear it. But it wasn't Laura he most needed to try to forgive.

With a wordless grumble under his breath,

he gave up fighting the task he had known in his bones that he'd need to do sooner or later. Letting out a disgusted sigh, he unlocked his weathered front door, then stepped inside and marched straight up to his chamber to pack a few things for his trip to Scotland before he changed his mind.

He had no choice.

It'd be a cold day in hell before he ever told her so, but Grace was right. It seemed he'd have no peace here at his new home or anywhere else until this thing was settled. Like it or not, the time had come to go and face Nick.

"Daughter!" The reverend's voice came from his study later that evening. "I would speak with you!"

Grace had just come in from watering her garden and called back, "I'll be right there!" She put her watering can away and wiped her hands on her apron as she headed for her father's study.

It was not uncommon for him to ask her to listen to a section of his sermon for the coming Sunday, to see if it flowed. That was what she had expected when she stepped into his office and found him sitting at his desk, pen in hand, his spectacles perched on his nose.

He looked up. "Ah, there you are. Sit down. Close the door, please, won't you?"

She did, then took her seat on the other side of his desk. "Sermon giving you trouble?"

He furrowed his brow with a thoughtful expression, but did not quite answer the question. "Yes, I wanted to talk to you about . . . the quality of mercy."

She nodded attentively and folded her hands in her lap, wondering which passages of Scripture he would be using for the coming Sunday.

"We must never forget how important it is to forgive others their faults. That is the one thing God requires of us if we wish to be forgiven our own. Likewise, we must take care to ward off falling into pride and wounding charity by judging others we meet on our road. We must never forget what our Lord told the Pharisees was the most important of all the Commandments — to love God, and our neighbor as ourselves."

He fell silent while she considered his message with a shrug. "It's a little dull," she said with a tactful but adoring smile. "Aren't you going to start this week with one of your funny stories?"

He frowned in surprise.

"Daughter, weren't you listening?" he

asked with an arch look.

She furrowed her brow. "Yes. Why? Am I missing something?"

"Grace," he murmured, his tone chiding, but his gaze still fond. "Surely you have learned by now how important it is to make strangers feel welcome in our community."

"Of course —" she started, but then her eyebrows shot upward.

She started forward in her chair as understanding dawned. Her jaw dropped.

"This isn't your Sunday sermon?" she exclaimed.

"Afraid not, my dear. I must say," he offered delicately, looking troubled, "I don't like what I've been hearing about your behavior toward our new neighbor at the Grange."

Grace stared at him in shock.

Her *behavior*?

Oh, no, she suddenly thought. Had Papa found out about the kiss?

But he couldn't have!

Only Lord Trevor and she knew about that, and besides, if he had heard about it somehow, he wouldn't be this calm.

Then what else had she done?

Her thoughts swept over a summary of her recent activities. It only took a few seconds to confirm that she had done absolutely nothing wrong of late. In fact, she was quite offended at the mere suggestion.

Indeed, impeccably behaved as she was every day of her blasted life, her being called to the carpet like this was unprecedented.

"What seems to be the problem? What have you heard — who's been talking about me?" she demanded half in outrage.

He closed his eyes and shook his head serenely. "It does not signify —"

"Oh, yes, it does! If somebody's talking about me around here behind my back —"

"Very well," he relented, then arched a brow at her. "I hear you have been very hard on Lord Trevor. Unforgiving and unkind. Even a little judgmental."

Her jaw dropped for a long moment. "Oh, have you, indeed? And who says so? That barbarian himself?"

He regarded her in surprise. "No, of course not. I thought you got on well with him the other night when he came here, and at the Lievedon Ball. You danced with him, as I recall."

She floundered. "That was before I knew he was a wicked, wicked man — and now we're stuck with him! He's rude, he's arrogant and ornery. And — he's dangerous!"

Her father laughed.

"Papa!"

"My dearest, we must try to be a bit more understanding." He studied her. "I've never seen you have trouble with a newcomer before. Come, nobody's perfect. We are all sinners, aren't we?"

Her jaw dropped as he gazed at her, refusing to soften his frank accusation. She threw up her hands. "Has everyone gone mad?"

"Just try to remember that love is our duty, first and foremost."

"Oh, I see! That's what you'd have me do?" she retorted, folding her arms across her chest. "*Love* a libertine like Lord Trevor Montgomery? And are you speaking as my pastor or my father? Because that is perfectly daft advice for an intelligent man to give his maiden daughter about a former spy!"

"I suppose you are referring to the fact that he is a handsome bachelor, and you are an attractive young lady."

She scoffed, her cheeks coloring.

"Obviously, these factors do not escape my notice," Papa said wryly. "But that doesn't really matter, I'm afraid. He is a human being like any other. I daresay the poor fellow's already been through more than his share of hell on earth. He came here for peace. He has served his country with honor, and I don't want to hear about you making an outcast of him in the village. If you turn the people against him, I'll be holding you responsible. Honestly, Grace, this is most unlike you."

"Papa, I've done nothing of the kind! I'm not turning anyone against him! Whoever told you such a thing is lying! Who have you been talking to? I demand to know — for I assure you, nobody out there knows anything about it!"

He shrugged, relenting. "I went down to the pub today to have a bite to eat and spoke to Marianne."

"Marianne?" Grace shot up out of her chair, paced toward the window and back, then stopped before his desk again, trembling with fury, her hand propped on her waist. "Indeed! And did she mention how he all but propositioned her today?"

She didn't wait for the gentle pastor's answer, bringing her fist down angrily on the edge of his desk. "That man has got to be taught that there are *limits* and boundaries to what he can get away with around here. This isn't Venice, or Paris, or even St. James's for that matter! He can't descend on Thistleton like Attila the Hun and start terrorizing the neighbors, Father!"

She always went from "Papa" to "Father" when she was angry.

"He scared the stuffing out of the Nelcott boys, then made a beeline for the pub, where he tried to lead poor Marianne astray. He is *so* full of himself! What about pride? That's the top deadly sin, as I recall, to say nothing of wrath, murder, lust —"

"Grace!" her father finally interrupted.

"What?"

To her confusion, her father smiled mysteriously. "I see Marianne didn't tell you the substance of their conversation before you arrived for her reading lesson."

"No. I have eyes. I could see for myself —"

"You should not jump to conclusions," he chided, wagging a finger at her in amusement.

She glared at him. "What are you talking about?"

He leaned back in his chair, steepling his fingers as he smiled at her. "According to Marianne, the whole time Lord Trevor was sitting in the pub with her, he was asking questions about *you.*"

CHAPTER 12

It took Trevor three days to reach the remote corner of Scotland where the Order's headquarters lay tucked amid the wild, windswept hills.

He knew he was close when, riding through the forest, he cantered his horse around the bend, and was nearly attacked by a group of rain-tousled, mud-flecked boys, all about fourteen years old.

Though they gave him a startle, he laughed as he realized they were Order youths out on a survival-training stint.

Ah, yes, he remembered those days well.

Like a wild clan of small, young, wiry barbarians, they bristled around him with their handmade weapons. One lad was instantly identifiable as the leader, of course. Slightly older than the others, with an air about him as if he had been born simply knowing what to do, he signaled his "men" with gestures and hard looks and was instantly obeyed.

It was Rotherstone all over again, Trevor thought in amusement as he slowed his horse with a wave of nostalgia and raised his hands until the lads saw he was not a planned part of the training exercise, nor was he a threat.

Having surrounded his horse, they quickly stood down; the young leader clipped out their apologies on the group's behalf. Trevor assured them — in German, just to challenge their language skills — that it was of no consequence.

At this, along with his nonchalant reaction to their ambush, they realized he was an agent returning on some business. Then they were in awe, peppering him with excited questions. Though amused, Trevor did not linger, staying only long enough on the road to offer the ragtag band of young heroes-in-training a few words of encouragement to lift them from the misery of their trek, for he remembered all too well how those adventures used to go.

Of course, the freedom of such independence was delicious to a boy that age, and true, these field exercises had their moments of high adventure, especially when you ran into another group and had to defend your territory. But on the whole, these field exercises involved being lost, hungry, tired, on edge from the obstacle course of dangers and "surprises" the military teachers had planned, all while your body ached from sleeping on the cold, damp ground. The boys had to make their own weapons, catch and cook their own food, and build their own shelters.

Obviously, the ordeal was hardly meant to be a holiday. These excursions were meant to toughen the boys up and unify them as a team.

If they didn't kill each other once the food supply ran low, they might just end up as the sort of cohesive unit the Order wanted, able to think and move as one.

Like Beau and Trevor and Nick . . . though he seemed to be the only one who remembered that these days.

He rode on, stopping at the ancient cemetery for the Order's fallen knights. There he paid his respects at Virgil's grave. This done, he finally arrived at the bustling center square, where various venerable school buildings were arranged across from the great stone Abbey.

Here the life of the Order of Saint Michael the Archangel carried on as it had since the time of the Crusades. He went straight to the administrator's office, and, after a bit of stilted but polite conversation, he received permission to visit Baron Forrester in his cell.

He bowed to his superiors, then took leave of them and headed there at once.

Soon, a heavily armed guard was leading him down into the dank, dim, stone undercroft beneath the Abbey. The man took a torch off the wall.

From there, they went down endless cobwebbed stairs hewn into the stone, then marched through the ancient catacombs.

As the guard showed him into a dark tunnel that stretched even deeper into the mountain, Trevor paused uneasily. This was a place he had certainly never visited before; indeed, he had not known it existed.

"He's down here?" he murmured to the guard a few strides ahead of him.

The man merely gave him a wry glance over his shoulder.

Trevor scowled to find he was starting to feel a bit sorry for Nick. It was not a sentiment he desired to indulge. The bastard deserved it. Nick had done this to himself. It should have given Trevor satisfaction to see that at least this dungeon was worse than the cellar in which Nick had locked *him* when he had served his time as his "life insurance policy."

At any rate, it surely took this severe a punishment to make even a small dent in Nick's impervious bravado.

They passed a few empty cells, then the guard stopped and banged his truncheon on the rusty bars. "Visitor!"

When Trevor stepped into view, Nick and he stared at each other in shock — Trevor, to see his proud, fearless friend in such a place, Nick, to see him there at all.

"Thirty minutes," said the guard.

"Leave us," Trevor ordered.

When the guard had marched off, Trevor and Nick looked at each other warily through the bars.

"Damn," Trevor breathed, taking it all in.

Nick's dungeon cell was only the size of a horse's box stall, maybe ten by ten, one wall sealed with iron bars, the other three of stone.

There was a stool and a small, battered table opposite a sturdy cot. There Trevor spotted the extra blanket and pillow Carissa had been thoughtful enough to send. He saw that the Beauchamps had also sent Nick a supply of extra candles, books, and writing paper to occupy his devious mind, and a tin of candy.

Scanning Nick's dismal accommodations in awkward silence, Trevor felt unexpectedly depressed.

It was a shock to see his brother warrior in prison though maybe it shouldn't have been. The Order was careful about the mix of boys it built into a team. They always wanted a useful blend of skills and personalities. Thus, some fifteen years ago, they had teamed the smooth-talking charmer, Beau, with the steady, logical Trevor.

And then there was Nick.

The bankrupt Baron Forrester's son and heir had wound up with them because nobody else could stand him. Nick was moody and proud, stormy and relentless, prone to sarcasm, difficult and hard. A loner by nature, he was quick to fight and good enough at it that even back then, the older boys had feared him.

He had become fiercely protective of Beau and Trevor once they had befriended him, yet there had always remained an untamed part of Nick that neither of them could reach.

He was a law unto himself, and that was the main reason that Nick could be a pain in the arse to work with. He saw the world differently than everybody else did. His unpredictability was an advantage in their line of work, but it meant his personal life was usually a mess. He had never met a dare he wouldn't take or, as the rebel of the Order, a rule he wouldn't bend.

On second thought, maybe it wasn't surprising at all that he should end up here, Trevor mused as he leaned against the bars. Still, seeing the reality of his fierce, wild friend in a cage, he shook his head, his anger draining away to something sadder. "It might've been me who suffered for your madness, but I never wanted this for you."

"Eh, it's not so bad," he drawled. "They let me out for an hour a day. Two hours next month if I'm a good boy." He shrugged and glanced around his cell. "They've given me some codes to work on for them. Keep me out of trouble."

Trevor did his best to smile.

"Ah, come on, don't look like that," Nick chided. "It would've been the gallows for me if I hadn't had the good fortune to take that bullet for the Regent. In the grand scheme of things, I consider myself lucky."

Trevor finally managed to conceal his dismay. "How is that bullet wound, anyway?"

"Fine, all healed up. Yours?"

Trevor shrugged. Two spies exchanging pleasantries. "Fine. Had good care quick after it happened," he conceded, for when he had got shot in the back in Spain, it was

Nick who had pulled him to safety and saved his life.

That was what had started all the trouble. Seeing Trevor shot, very nearly killed, was what had made Nick snap after all his years of service.

No one was allowed to quit the Order.

Nick had known that as well as anyone, but he had tried.

"And the knee?" the caged agent inquired rather more gingerly.

Trevor arched a brow at him, considering it was Nick who had kicked it out on him in one of their many brawls when he had tried to escape the cellar where the blackguard had made a prisoner of him.

Nick had known that the only way he'd be allowed to leave the Order was if he had leverage in the form of a hostage, namely Trevor, still convalescing from the bullet in the back.

"Well, I'm no longer limping," he replied politely.

"There, you see? I could've kicked it sideways, and you'd have limped for life. I came in straight on purpose, I'll have you know."

"You're practically a saint," Trevor drawled.

Nick let out a low, devilish laugh. "I got

your note in the package from Carissa, by the by. As you can see, I decided to take your advice to rot in hell. Cozy, isn't it?" He glanced around at his cell.

"Hmm." Trevor nodded. "Not as hot as I'd imagined."

Nick shook his head. "I definitely did not expect to see you here."

Trevor shrugged and looked away. "Believe me, I'm as surprised as you."

Nick fell silent, looking around anywhere but at him. He folded his arms across his chest and studied the flagstone at his feet. "I heard about Laura. Trevor, that was never supposed to happen. I really am sorry. You know I never liked her, but for you to end up jilted. Hell, man. If there's anything I can do to help you make it right, I could explain to her that it was my fault you disappeared. I'll write her a letter, apologize —"

"Don't bother," he cut him off. Then he let out a weary sigh. "You and Beau were right about her. I guess I'm better off."

Nick raised his eyebrows.

"But fair warning, if you say, 'I told you so,' I'll throttle you —"

"Wouldn't dare," he said ruefully.

"Still." Trevor gave him a hard look. "If we didn't go back so far, I'd want your blood. But . . . I suppose it's water under the bridge by now. We're both alive, and that is something, after all we've been through. And so I accept your apology," he said.

Nick reached through the bars and offered his hand.

Trevor shook his firmly.

"Thank you," Nick forced out.

Somewhat abashed, Trevor glanced past his friend self-consciously as their handshake ended. "What's that on the wall?" He nodded at the charts and unfurled parchments that Nick had hung up on the stone wall of his cell. Trevor squinted in the torchlight, trying to make it out. "Maps? Of where?"

Nick looked at them, then cast him a roguish smile. "America."

"What? Are you planning a trip to the Colonies when you get out?"

"Not a trip," he murmured in a confidential tone. "I'm thinking of staking a claim there, west of the Alleghenies."

Trevor looked at him in shock. "Leave England? For the frontier? Nick, the bloody wilderness?"

"Why not. I figure the only company I'm fit for anymore is that of wild beasts and savages. I'll fit right in," he said with an easy, hell-raiser's smile.

"And your title?" Trevor asked in astonishment.

"Who gives a damn? The Crown can take it back for all I care. My father left me bankrupt. The old manor house is falling down, and God knows after this" — he glanced around at his cell — "the name of Forrester is permanently blighted."

"That's not true! The rest of the world has no idea where you are. You know the Order always keeps its business private."

"But I know, don't I?" he replied.

Trevor did not know what to say. He did not doubt that behind his stubborn pride, Nick was deeply ashamed of his momentary loss of faith in the cause. "Prison terms, aristocratic titles. The Iroquois and the Cherokee aren't going to care about such things. Mayhap I shall become an Indian trader. Make a mountain of gold off beaver pelts and timber."

"You've completely lost your mind."

"Long ago, my friend. Long ago," Nick answered with a low laugh.

Trevor shook his head, unsure if Nick was serious about his plan or if fantasies of ultimate freedom in the wilderness were just his means of coping with his current incarceration. "You honestly mean to become an American?" He kept his voice down so the guard wouldn't hear. "Never mind they'll lynch you when they hear your accent? You do realize Englishmen are not exactly popular right now on the streets of Boston and Philadelphia? We did burn down their capital."

"So I'll speak French. The Yanks won't bother me. I think I'm beginning to understand those people. Liberty and all that. One gains a keener understanding of the notion when one's locked up in a cage."

"Or a cellar," Trevor agreed in a crisp tone, but they looked at each other, and both began to laugh.

"Nick, Nick, Nicholas," Trevor chided with a sigh, much as their old handler, Virgil, used to say to his problem agent.

Nick shrugged. "I've had enough of the world's corruption. I just want to be left alone, and the frontier beyond those mountains seems the right place to do it."

"The right place to get eaten by a bear," he corrected him, but Nick merely grinned.

"You don't have to come and visit me in my log cabin if you're afraid of the bears, dear lad. But never mind all that. Tell me of the world outside these walls. What's been going on with you?"

Trevor leaned against the bars. "Well, you may be interested to learn that I've bought

243

a farm . . ."

Nick listened intently as Trevor told him all about the Grange. When he saw how hungry his friend was for any news of the outside world, he took pity on him and soon proceeded to regale him with the tale of how he had first encountered Grace Kenwood, kissing the wrong woman in a dark room at the Lievedon Ball.

"She's going to drive me madder than Drake."

"No one could ever be madder than Drake," Nick replied. "A pastor's daughter. She sounds perfect for you."

"That's what Beau said, too. I don't know . . ." He frowned. "We quarreled before I left. I'm fairly sure she hates me at the moment."

"You'd better not muck this up for yourself. Go back to Thimbleton and charm her. Don't end up alone like me."

At that moment, they heard the guard returning to fetch him. It seemed their time was up. Both friends glanced toward the stony tunnel. The guard had not yet appeared, but they could hear his heavy footfalls approaching.

Nick glanced at him through the bars a trifle worriedly. "So are we all right, then?"

"Of course, brother," Trevor murmured,

and offered his hand again. "Of course we are."

Nick shook his hand firm with soulful gratitude in his dark eyes. "Thank you for coming all this way."

"I hate seeing you in here, for what it's worth." Trevor took a slip of paper out of his pocket and jotted down his new address. "Beau's out of the country with Carissa, so if you need anything at all, write to me here. Don't hesitate. This is no time for your stubborn pride. Whatever happens, Nick, you've still got friends."

He dropped his gaze and nodded, taking the piece of paper through the bars with more emotion in his eyes when he glanced up again than his words could have conveyed. "Thanks again."

Trevor gave him a resolute nod as the guard joined them. "It was good to see you. Stay strong," he murmured.

With a farewell nod, Trevor marched out, though leaving his mate in a hellhole like this was one of the hardest things he'd ever had to do.

Satisfied that at least they had resolved their differences, he stalked back outside and soon swung up onto his horse. It was time to head back to Thimbleton.

Thistleton, he corrected himself.

If he was going back to put down roots there, then he'd bloody well better learn the name.

Grace watched and waited, but until the would-be guest of honor returned, plans for the Windleshams' elegant dinner party remained on hold.

Lord Trevor Montgomery had been missing for a week now, an "emergency" over which Lady Windlesham in particular was entirely out of sorts, having already claimed him for her future son-in-law.

Her darling Callie could obviously do better, after all, than a feckless gambling rakehell like George, Lord Brentford. True, Lord Trevor was only a younger son, but his fame as a hero of the Realm made up for the lack of a title in his own right, Her Ladyship declared, and Callie had cheerfully reported back to Grace.

For her part, she was beginning to despair that she had so deeply offended him with her too-frank, self-righteous words that he wasn't coming back.

If she had been wrong enough to earn a rare rebuke from Papa, then indeed, she must have been too hard on him.

She had thought at the time she was right, but maybe she had spoken out of pride or jealousy . . .

Oh, how vexing it was to doubt herself!

So she fretted and frittered away her days, waiting for him to return and trying to convince herself all the while that she was doing nothing of the kind.

With him gone, all she could think about was how very dull it was around here. She didn't want to admit it, but Callie was right.

The great excitement of the week while he was gone was when Farmer Curtis's brindle cow and her calf had escaped their pasture and wandered through the churchyard.

Truly, nothing ever happened around here unless George the Brat came home, got reeling drunk at the Gaggle Goose, sang at the top of his lungs, and fell into the canal.

Grace read a book a day and could not remember what any of the stories were about. She sat by her garden, waiting for weeds to grow so she could yank them out.

Dull, dull, dull.

What had that man done to her life, which heretofore had been so full of country charm, serenity, contentment?

She wanted him to come back so she could strangle him for doing this to her, changing everything. The whole atmosphere of Thistleton had changed — at least for her. And it made her angry at him all over again that he had this much power over her.

Who was this man to come crashing into her life, disturbing her tranquility, making her question all her assumptions and her own correctness?

Her primary assumption, especially, had been that she could never interest a man so handsome, so worldly-wise and accomplished, so firm of will and strong in character.

She had always thought she would end up either alone or with some milquetoast preacher (to be perfectly blunt). Or perhaps, if there was a third possibility, that God might match her up with some wounded bird of a man, some battered soul who needed loving, nurselike care.

None of these possibilities were much inducement to marriage.

But now . . . *Lord Trevor Montgomery* had been asking Marianne about her.

Her.

Plain, boring, steady, sensible Grace Kenwood.

She squeezed her eyes shut with the most delicious, disbelieving wonder, incredulity, and joy.

No. She dared not hope.

There had to be some misunderstanding.

She was too tall and not highborn enough.

A man like that — beautiful, dashing, dangerous, thoroughly capable — always ended up with a Calpurnia in the end.

She looked out the window for the twentieth time that day, and suddenly let out a small shriek.

There!

A flash of motion on the road, a cloud of dust traveling up from town!

The galloping rider disappeared from view behind the trees, but Grace's heart had already leaped up into her throat. Butterflies crashed about inside her stomach.

He's back.

Chapter 13

Now that the guest of honor had returned to Thistleton, the Windleshams' dinner party (or the Win-Din, as Papa had privately dubbed it) could finally proceed.

A couple of nights after she had seen her neighbor thundering up the road on his horse, the grand occasion arrived at last.

Grace was nervous to see Lord Trevor again after their angry parting at the tavern. She was not sure if he would greet her with a smile or a snub, but it would determine how she would receive him, in turn.

Her father fully expected her to be nice to him, and, of course, she'd be gracious, she told herself with some indignation — as if their quarrel were all her fault!

But since she *did* expect a certain degree of hostility from her handsome neighbor after she had behaved so condescendingly to him (though she really hadn't meant to), she kept her expectations low.

She would live up to her father's standards if it killed her. But she wished with all her heart that Lord Trevor might signal a willingness to end their hostilities and enter into a truce.

Only time would tell. But at least she wouldn't have long to wait.

Windlesham Hall was quite the finest baronial manner for miles around, save only the grand ancestral pile of the Marquess of Lievedon. As the Kenwoods rode up in their carriage, they found the long, stately drive up to the house illuminated with lanterns.

Pulling up to the entrance, they saw the front pillars swathed in gauzy lengths of fabric. Massive urns teemed with mounds of flowers whose parti-colored blooms and trailing tendrils waved in the breeze.

A row of liveried footmen stood by to assist the arriving guests. One whisked Grace's Paisley shawl away from her when she and Papa walked into the entrance.

The impressive space was hung with garlands and bunches of grapes, and the British flag was proudly displayed, draped over the upper railing of the grand staircase. All very suitable for the occasion of welcoming a conquering war hero to a dinner party held in his honor, Grace thought rather dryly.

She and Papa exchanged a glance.

"Quite a show, even for the Windleshams," he said under his breath, as they waited for the lady of the house to receive them.

Grace took a deep breath and squared her shoulders, mentally battening down the hatches as Lady Windlesham sailed toward them.

"Reverend! Miss Kenwood!"

Greetings were exchanged, the expected compliments offered, then the Kenwoods were assigned to their respective groups.

Of course, Papa had a longer leash than she did. He got away with lingering in the entrance hall for a while longer, talking to a couple of the other gentlemen about some sporting news, while Grace was politely ordered upstairs to the drawing room, where the other ladies and the more obedient gentlemen awaited Lord Trevor's imminent arrival.

"He has not yet come?"

"No. Listen — my dear." Lady Windlesham grasped Grace's forearm to command her full attention while she walked her up the staircase to the drawing room. "There is a matter I wish to discuss with you."

I'll bet. "Yes, my lady?"

"I was shocked, Miss Kenwood, shocked, I say, to hear that you let my daughter go rushing over to the Grange unchaperoned."

Grace blinked in astonishment at this rebuke. Oh, this was going to be a wonderful evening.

"Fortunately, however," the baroness conceded with a sly half smile, "I believe it worked in her favor. He had no choice but to notice her. Still, it could have been a disaster."

"I tried to tell her so, my lady. But she wouldn't listen to me."

"Of course she wouldn't listen to you!" Calpurnia's doting mother exclaimed. "She is eighteen! She doesn't listen to anyone, not even her own father. I just would have thought that you would have managed to go with her there! Not to trouble you," she said in reproach, "but you have always been so solicitous toward her ever since she was a child. I'm sure you don't want to see her ruin herself any more than I do."

Grace hated how the woman had made her stammer. "I-I'm afraid Miss Windlesham dashed off so quickly that day — well, I followed as fast as I could."

"I understand," Her Ladyship said with lavish condescension. "I just hope you will be faster if such a thing should happen again. In the meanwhile, I have talked to her. She understands now that if she intends to win a man of the world like our new neighbor, she is going to have to cool her heels and not chase him about like she's riding to the hounds. Oh, Miss Kenwood. You were there." Lady Windlesham stopped near the top step and pulled Grace to a halt, turning to her with a hint of shame. "By the time you caught up to her, what did you see? Did my daughter make a fool of herself? As her mother, I really should know, and, of course, Calpurnia would never admit to any mistake. But if she disgraced herself in any small way, it will help me determine how to treat my guest. Are apologies in order, or —"

"No, no, not at all, my lady," Grace assured her. "I believe Lord Trevor was charmed, and simply saw her as an innocent girl full of youthful exuberance."

The baroness pressed a hand to her heart. "Oh, I am so relieved to hear it. Thank you, Miss Kenwood, you have put my mind at ease. I know you would not lie to me."

"Never, ma'am."

"Well!" Lady Windlesham took another commanding grip of Grace's elbow and resumed steering her up the stairs and into the upper hallway. "Tonight I am determined that Lord Trevor should see my daughter as a possible future bride."

"I'm sure he will, ma'am. Look at her," Grace said fondly, as they stepped into the drawing room. "She looks like an angel that fluttered down to earth."

"If only she would act the part," her mother quipped. "If you'll excuse me, I must go and gather the rest of our guests. I am glad we understand each other," she added, giving Grace a conspiratorial nod before she bustled off.

Turning to face the drawing room, Grace offered the gathered company there a curtsy.

"Grace!" Calpurnia exclaimed from the striped sofa, where she sat on display like a doll in a fancy toy shop.

Grace smiled at her with the loving admiration of a proud elder sister as the girl popped up out of her seat and flounced over to her in a whoosh of the pale yellow satin skirts. "I'm so glad you're here!"

"I'm glad to be here."

Calpurnia took hold of her and steered her away from the others before she could do more than exchange a few smiles and nods with the assembly of their more genteel neighbors. "What is it, dearest?"

"I'm so nervous to see Lord Trevor!" the girl confessed in a giddy whisper. "I'm so afraid I'm going to make a cake-head of myself again!"

"Oh, no, I'm sure you won't. Just be your-self."

"Pshaw, that's not going to work. I already tried that, and everyone scolded me. Including you! But now Mother's told me what to do. Might as well try it," she said with a wide-eyed shrug.

Grace looked at her uneasily. "What did your mother advise?"

"Less is more," Callie quoted. She then proceeded to elaborate in hushed tones on the advice the baroness had given her. " 'Do you remember when you were a little girl and you were enchanted with your father's fancy pigeons?' she asked me, and I did. I was a toddler back then. How I loved those beautiful birds with their shaggy, tufted legs! I always wanted to pick them up and hug them. 'But every time you'd go tripping toward them,' Mother said, 'you'd scare them away, and then you'd scream bloody murder until somebody handed one to you.' She said it's the same with men."

"Really?"

" 'You must let Lord Trevor come to you in his own time, or he will flee you like the pigeons.' I suppose she's right. Ladies have been probably trying to snare him ever since he came of age. After all, he is the son of a duke. So —" Calpurnia let out a sigh. "I will bide my time and restrain myself somehow. Then he will think I'm demure and biddable, then, once I've married him, I can go back to being myself!" she finished brightly.

"Ahh," Grace echoed with a mystified nod. Beyond that, she was speechless at these machinations.

As Calpurnia bounded off again to answer a question from Lady De Geoffrey, Grace was left wondering if she should be a little insulted that it did not even occur to Lady Windlesham — let alone her daughter — that she herself might have an interest in their new neighbor.

Or that he might be interested in her.

She supposed it seemed unlikely. Although Marianne had told Papa that Lord Trevor had been asking questions about her, that didn't necessarily mean he was interested in any romantic sense. He could have been simply gathering information about life in the village. At this point, Grace wasn't even sure if she was really interested in *him.* So what did it signify?

She had not liked the way he had yelled at the Nelcott boys, and she had not at all approved of how quickly he had found his way to Marianne. But thinking back to that darkened parlor in Lievedon House, she had to admit that she certainly liked the way he kissed.

Just then, a commotion and a loud cheer from the entrance hall below could be heard all the way up in the drawing room.

The fat, jolly countess Lady Stokes flew across the room with startling speed for a woman in her sixties. She pushed aside the drape and peered out the window overlooking the courtyard. "He's here! Man alive, no false calves on those legs, I wager. Ha!"

At this, the pinched, gray Lady De Geoffrey, her nemesis, nearly fainted dead away into the fireplace.

Grace lowered her head and pressed her fingertips to her brow, letting out a sigh. Hero or not, Lord Trevor had no idea what he was in for tonight at the Win-Din. Hopefully his spy training in how to endure interrogation and detect others' hidden agendas would stand him in good stead.

When Papa and Lord Windlesham showed him into the drawing room a few minutes later, the ladies stared for a second in awed silence.

He was devastating in formal black and white, larger-than-life, his broad shoulders hugged by an excellently cut tailcoat. Smooth black trousers hugged the long expanse of his legs — and Lady Stokes was right. No false padding there.

His starched cravat was snowy white, his silk waistcoat a pin-striped silver shade that brought out the gray of his eyes.

Grace was loath to admire him, all things considered, but even she was slightly breathless by the magnificence of their new neighbor.

He bowed to the assembly, and as he straightened up again, he had the most beautiful posture she had ever seen. His chin high, his shoulders back, chest out; he carried himself with an almost princely air. But his tone was one of humility, and his attitude most warm and gentlemanly as he turned his attention to their hostess.

Every lady there seemed to be fighting not to swoon, but Lady Windlesham snapped out of her study of him.

He appeared to meet with her approval right away, except for his long hair. But that, she no doubt told herself, was an easy fix in a future son-in-law.

She went gusting toward him, grasped his arm with a proprietary air, and led him around the room like a prize stallion she had just bought at auction.

Her first stop, of course, was Calpurnia, who dimpled at him and blushed and looked like the perfect doll on the sofa again.

He seemed charmed. "Nice to see you again, Miss Windlesham."

"My lord." She bowed her head demurely.

From there, the baroness brought him around, introducing him to all the other guests in order of precedence.

Precedence was everything with Lady Windlesham.

"Now then. You must meet Lord and Lady Stokes."

"Jolly good!" said the earl, a man as jovial and rotund as his wife, and every bit as vulgar.

The high-ranking pair unashamedly enjoyed shocking their more decorous neighbors, especially Sir Phillip and Lady De Geoffrey, who came next.

"Sir Phillip was knighted after years as a judge of the King's Court in London. Before that, he was a barrister."

Lord Trevor bowed. "Pleased to meet you, Sir Phillip, Lady De Geoffrey."

The stately pair, gray-haired and angular, greeted him politely.

"*Now* Sir Phillip serves as our local magistrate, or justice of the peace," Lady Windlesham rattled on, as if none of her prized guests could speak for themselves. "The Marquess of Lievedon himself appointed him — you do know Lord Lievedon is lord lieutenant of the county, don't you?"

"I do now," he replied with a smile, and Grace thought he'd better be careful around Sir Phillip. The justice had been complaining of late that they needed a new constable, and the war hero might just find himself tapped for this honorary post, just one of the many little duties of local life.

It was supposed to be no more than a yearlong commitment that rotated among the leading male citizens of the community, but somehow, old Clive Reese, their leading local chess player, had insisted on carrying the burden of the office for many years now, never mind that he was entering his eighties. Fortunately, there was never anyone in Thistleton to arrest.

Beaming with pride in her assembly, Lady Windlesham tugged her guest of honor along. "Now, then, this is our dear Dr. Bowen-Hill and his wife, Mariah. He is not just our local physician but a great writer of books on health advice. He invented Dr. Bowen-Hill's Mint and Lavender Tonic for the Sore Throat. Perhaps you've heard of it?"

"Er, it certainly sounds familiar," he answered, obviously lying, Grace thought, but his smile was charming. "Pleased to meet you both."

"And, of course, you already know our dear Reverend Kenwood and his daughter."

Lord Trevor stopped in front of Grace and met her gaze warily, then bowed. "Miss Kenwood."

"My lord." She offered a modest curtsy in reply, her heart pounding, but he was impossible to read.

His gray eyes were mirrors, revealing nothing of his sentiments toward her, neither warm nor cold, but carefully guarded. She did not know what to make of it, but she was soon forgotten, for everyone had a million questions for him, and moments later, it was time to go down to dine.

Not even a blind man could have missed the true purpose of the dinner party as everyone was paired up like the animals in Noah's Ark for the procession down to the dining room.

Lady Windlesham, as hostess, took the arm of Earl Stokes, the highest-ranking male. Lord Windlesham, a perennially annoyed man, escorted the laughing Lady Stokes down the stairs with a stoic look on his face though he never quite managed to hide his general irritation.

Lord Trevor was directed toward Calpurnia, to the surprise of none. Sir Phillip and Lady De Geoffrey were absorbed in conversation with Dr. and Mrs. Bowen-Hill, and since they lingered, Grace took her father's offered arm.

They exchanged a wry look and proceeded down the stairs.

Strictly speaking, the couples had fallen out of the correct order of precedence. Fortunately, Lady Windlesham did not notice this infringement of protocol, busily telling the gourmand Lord Stokes about the grand meal ahead. In any case, since the Kenwoods had fallen in behind Calpurnia and the hero of the evening, Grace found herself privy to their exchange whether she liked it or not.

She didn't.

Indeed, what she heard made her eyes widen. Good God! Surely this was not part of Calpurnia's plan to "play it cool."

It seemed the girl could not restrain her exuberant nature. "Please don't think that I'm one to listen to gossip, my lord, but I couldn't help overhearing how you've suffered a recent disappointment. Please — don't be alarmed," she assured him. "I don't mean to intrude. It's just that I, too, have experienced a broken engagement to a young man. I *know* from personal experience how painful it can be. So I just wanted to tell you, if you ever need to talk . . ."

Grace closed her eyes, mortified for her feckless young friend. Papa coughed to hold back a laugh.

Lord Trevor looked at the girl as if she had sprouted two heads.

"You can call on me at any time," Callie vowed with all earnestness. "I'm a good listener, and I know what you're going through."

The poor man managed a smile.

Perhaps he was merely touched by an artless young dunce. Perhaps he was attracted to her or merely amused. Grace did not dare not venture a guess, but listening over his shoulder she heard his answer, smooth as velvet. "Miss Windlesham, you are as kind as you are lovely. Fortunately, such things are in the past. I'm sorry to hear about your own misfortune. But we all must realize when it's time to move on, don't you think?"

"Oh, definitely, sir." Calpurnia stared earnestly into his eyes, no doubt reading more into his answer than she ought. "We must share our own toast this evening — a toast to moving on to better things!"

"Yes," he said cautiously. "Just so."

Even from her angle behind him, Grace could tell his smile was forced. He gave Callie a polite but extremely uncomfortable nod.

She beamed at him, in turn.

Looking over his shoulder, Grace couldn't help but feel somewhat amused at his discomfiture. In truth, she would not have been surprised if the Grange were back on the market again by tomorrow morning after this.

It was going to be an interesting night.

CHAPTER 14

As the guests all filed into the resplendent dining room and found their seats, liveried footmen in powdered wigs pulled out their chairs for them and pushed them in again.

Grace was surprised to find herself seated beside Lord Trevor. Then she saw that Calpurnia had been placed across from him, no doubt so that the guest of honor could keep his full attention fixed on their hosts' beautiful daughter throughout the meal.

Ah. Grace quickly grasped why she had been situated in this post. From here, she could help Calpurnia along in conversation, smoothing over any youthful gaffes. After all, the girl's mother was seated far away, down at the foot of the table, where she could do little to help, while Calpurnia's father presided at the head.

As Grace kept her smile fixed in place and set her napkin on her lap, she wondered if she should start sending the Windleshams a bill for all the work she did as an unofficial governess to the headstrong aristocratic chit.

Trevor looked askance at her as he took his seat.

Grace met his glance warily. Lud, she had no idea how she was to smooth over any awkwardness between him and Calpurnia when the air between herself and the ex-spy was charged with more awkwardness than she could endure.

The guest of honor cleared his throat quietly, whisking his napkin into place. Grace's heart pounded as they both stared down at the name cards on their plates written in beautifully scrawled calligraphy.

After another excruciating thirty seconds or so, they exchanged a hesitant glance, followed by an impeccably polite nod.

Grace still couldn't read him; he studied her, in turn, as though trying to do the same.

But to her satisfaction, it seemed that not even his spy skills could penetrate her own training: She wore her pastor's-daughter mask of unshakable tranquility.

God knew it had everybody else fooled.

After that, they must have both mentally dismissed each other as they proceeded to act like everything was normal between them. The only other person at the table who knew about their quarrel was her father, after all, and he could always be trusted to remain discreet.

With that, Lady Windlesham rang the bell, and so the meal began.

Bloody hell. The woman was a wall. And behind that wall, Trevor was fairly sure Miss Kenwood hated him.

This was going to be harder than he had thought.

Or not.

What did he care, anyway? Hadn't he had enough of females ruining his life?

He decided to ignore her and turned his attention to the other guests instead. There *were* other neighbors in Thimbleton, after all.

Trevor was genuinely touched by the lengths to which Lady Windlesham had gone to welcome him to the village and into local life.

On the other hand, as the meal wore on, and her daughter stared at him and all but sighed every time he spoke, he was slightly apprehensive about what he might have got himself into.

He had moved here because he liked the house and wanted to put his own stamp on the Grange as a gentleman-architect. Beyond that, he was not at all sure about what other plans the local Quality might have in store for him. But he detected all sorts of worrisome notions floating around the room concerning his future.

Still, he was truly grateful that the Windleshams had gone to all this fuss on his account, and so he paid the baroness the greatest compliment he could think of, and since he was quite familiar with her type, he knew exactly what to say. "On my honor, Lady Windlesham, my mother herself could not have feted her guests more lavishly than this feast you've set before us all tonight."

He was pleased with the results of his offering. Lady Windlesham's ambitious eyes nearly welled with doting tears. "Oh, my dear young man, how kind of you! We are more than pleased to do it. And if Her Grace should ever come to Thistleton to see your new home, it would be such an honor to make her acquaintance."

"I'm sure," he responded, raising his glass to her. "To our hostess."

As the others joined him in this toast, he was rather sure Lady Windlesham now forgave him for his long hair.

Which was a good thing because although he didn't really care what anybody thought, he had no intention of cutting it. Why should he?

He had done the dutiful thing all his life, and his usual short-cropped hair seemed to sum it all up, that good boy in the mirror. He had gone where they told him to go, killed whom they told him to kill, followed his orders and never complained. And what the hell had it got him?

His hair had started getting overlong when he was locked in solitary confinement as Nick's captive. Now he was a free man — not just free from Nick, but free from the Order. Free from Laura, for that matter, who had liked him to look a certain way.

Rather than cutting his hair, he had let it grow long as a defiant symbol of his liberty. Anyone who didn't like it could jolly well hang.

Then, from the corner of his eye, he caught Grace Kenwood giving him a cynical little smirk after his compliment to the baroness. It seemed to say: *You are so full of shit, my lord.* Though, of course, the virgin saint would never use such naughty words.

He turned his head and smiled charmingly at her. "Miss Kenwood, may I refill your wine? Oh, you've hardly touched it," he observed. "Perhaps you should."

Might loosen you up a bit, no?

She narrowed her eyes at him, understanding perfectly. "How kind of you, my lord. But I can fend for myself. Perhaps Miss Windlesham could use a bit more, though." She lifted her wineglass and took a defiant little sip.

"That's all right," Calpurnia assured him, waving off this pointless suggestion. "Miss Kenwood, he'd have to reach through the candelabra to help me!"

"Well, we wouldn't want him to catch his arm on fire," she answered in a tone that said she'd find that prospect terribly amusing.

Harrumph. Trevor set out to ignore her once again and turned his attention to the food for a while.

A silver tureen of lobster soup sat in the center of the table. Around it, symmetrically arrayed, were platters of boiled trout opposite veal cutlets; chicken pie opposite orange pudding; bright green blanched asparagus across from Jerusalem artichokes.

And that was only the first course.

In due time, the second was brought out, fresh with springtime specialties: roasted duck across from rabbit fricassee; lamb tails opposite a ham. There were green peas and carrots from the fields outside, and roasted sweetbreads sat opposite steaming, buttered crab.

"You really will spoil us, my lady," Reverend Kenwood said warmly to their hostess.

The mention of people being spoiled must have reminded Lady Windlesham to bring her daughter to the fore. "Calpurnia and I have been wondering what sort of plans you may have for the Grange, my lord. We hear you are thinking of improvements."

He nodded and took a swallow of wine before he replied. "Certain repairs need to be done. I have a shipment of supplies coming soon on the canal boat. Timber and roofing slates and such."

"Really?"

"A lot of work needs to be done. Part of the roof over the north wing has already caved in, unfortunately. But the walls are sound there, so I was thinking of replacing the roof with a glass one. It would be a fine place for an orangery, I should think."

"An orangery!" Calpurnia exclaimed. "Oh, how elegant!"

"Indeed," her mother agreed in approval. "If you need advice on your interior decorations, do not hesitate to call on me, my lord. As you can see, I can boast a certain skill in making a residence beautiful."

Miss Kenwood stifled a cough at the frank boast. Likewise, Trevor hid his surprise. "Quite so, my lady."

"More importantly," the baroness said with a knowing smile, "I have passed on my abilities to my daughter. It is imperative that a young lady of Quality learn all those subtle enhancements that turn a house into a home before she marries, don't you think?"

He nodded politely, but from what he'd seen so far, he found it hard to believe that Miss Calpurnia was the domestic sort. Then he asked Dr. Bowen-Hill about his medical books in order to escape being the subject of scrutiny for a while.

The mild-mannered physician modestly described his latest tome of remedies that could be made at home from ingredients either grown in the kitchen garden or easily acquired. He credited his wife, however, with having authored the recipes for ladies' beauty potions that ran alongside those for his health concoctions.

"So much knowledge in one couple! Do you have children?" Trevor asked politely, then he wished he had not, for he saw Mrs. Bowen-Hill wince.

"No, my lord."

"Oh, we are frightfully proud of our local doctor," Lord Stokes chimed in, adding a testimonial. "One of my tenants' children broke an arm last summer falling off the hay wagon. Ghastly! You could see the bone. Fortunately, Bowen-Hill was there in a trice to save the day. The child didn't even have to lose the arm. We were all sure he was going to die. You are quite the miracle worker, sir!" Lord Stokes toasted the physician, who colored with modesty.

"The young mend quickly," Dr. Bowen-Hill murmured.

The third course arrived, another well-balanced dance of flavors in season. Over roasted venison, broiled salmon, forced cucumbers, French beans, and a charming addition of apricot puffs, somebody finally got around to asking him about his career as a spy.

Trevor was ready. He figured it was coming sooner or later. Might as well get it over with, now that the company was well lubricated with wine.

Since they had gone to such great lengths to welcome him, he conceded to regale them with certain stories, each carefully edited for just such occasions into harmless picaresque tales.

He started with a funny one about how he had been sent off to the Peninsula disguised as an army captain, his mission, to figure out which aide-de-camp of a certain British general had been tipping off the French of future troop movements in order to fatten his own purse.

"The task required me to pose as a captain of the regulars. As part of my role, of course, I had to carry out the normal duties of a man in that position. Well, one day I was sent out as a scout to do some reconnaissance of the terrain ahead.

"Unbeknownst to me," he continued, "the Spanish field through which I was so stealthily passing was home to an enormous black bull, a champion of the local bullring. The beast took one look at my red uniform — and charged."

As the guests gasped, Trevor shook his head and laughed. "My friends, any foolish rumors you may have heard about me being some brave hero must be quickly dispelled if you could have heard me scream. The next thing I knew, the bull flipped me over his horns and tried to trample me to death. Fortunately, I avoided being gored."

"*Olé!*" said Lord Stokes.

Trevor chuckled. "Indeed."

"How ever did you escape the beast?" Calpurnia asked, wide-eyed.

"Some of the farmer's field hands saw me getting attacked and waved the brute away. As it happened, one of them had a tip for me about the aide-de-camp's corruption, so it all worked out for the best."

When they pressed him for more, he moved from humor to intrigue.

"A colleague and I managed to intercept a code being used to signal three American privateer ships out of New Orleans that we learned were bringing supplies to the French. We got to the cliff side above the harbor where the ship was expected and were able to signal him with lanterns not to come in. If that ship had succeeded in unloading fresh materiéls, who knows how long that particular battle might have gone on? Instead, the French surrendered two days later."

"Bravo," Lord Windlesham murmured.

"Oh, do please tell us more," Lady De Geoffrey insisted.

He was ready once again, moving back to the safe ground of humor. "I suppose I can't do any harm now if I tell you about how we rescued the opera diva from Naples."

"Not the great Benesini?" Lord Stokes gasped.

"The same," Trevor answered gravely, allowing them their awe at so famous a star. "Though Napoleon had made his brother King of Naples by that time, La Benesini remained loyal to the Bourbons. In fact, she was a personal friend of Queen Maria

Carolina, who, being a sister to Marie Antoinette, hated everything having to do with the French Revolution and Napoleon, as well. Unfortunately, she was not among the royal party as they fled from Naples when the French troops arrived. She was left behind when power changed hands.

"The opera singer's great talent and her fame shielded her from the usual fate suffered by the Bourbons' more prominent friends. She was invited in, to become an ornament of Joseph Bonaparte's court, just as she had been under King Ferdinand.

"Now, this cannot leave this room," he warned them half in jest, "but she accepted, and given her position in the court, it wasn't long before Madame Benesini had collected a considerable amount of information on the new rulers of Naples. She was prepared to share that intelligence with us in exchange for safe passage out of Italy. So we went in and got her."

Murmurs of admiration at the nerve of such a rescue passed around the table. Even Miss Kenwood looked a little impressed in spite of herself.

But he truly did not want them thinking he was a hero.

He didn't deserve it. Virgil had been a hero. He was just an ordinary chap doing his job — though he took some pride in doing it well.

"Gentlemen, if any of you ever thought you've dealt with a difficult lady, I challenge you to conduct a covert rescue of an opera diva. The Regent's wife herself could not have been more demanding." He laughed as he recounted the tale, though, to be sure, it had not been very funny at the time.

"The woman was incapable of keeping her voice down, and her list of demands on how she must be treated exceeded anything that I have ever seen. She had a little wee dog that she carried around in a velvet purse. The dog took precedence over everything. But that was just the beginning. She had to have a certain kind of soap in her stateroom on the ship — lavender with a hint of orange. I'll never forget it. And if anyone woke her up at the wrong time — even by accident! — well, I daresay La Benesini could've turned even King Henry VIII into a meek, docile husband. If he had disobeyed her, he was the one who would've lost his head. Frankly, I was glad to escape with my own."

Everyone was laughing.

"Was she able to go and sing elsewhere, Lord Trevor?"

"Yes, did La Benesini find her way to a

new stage?"

"The last I heard, she was dazzling audiences in Saint Petersburg. I'm sure she'll make her way to London on her tour soon. And when she does, remember — you didn't hear it from me."

"Well, Lord Trevor, you make it all sound like a grand lark," Lady Stokes remarked, "but I'm sure you must have seen your share of tragedy and danger."

He gave a slight shrug. "I cannot deny it, madam."

She leaned closer, narrowing her eyes as if to goad him. "No doubt you have been placed in the position of having to take an enemy's life."

"Antonia!" Lady De Geoffrey exclaimed.

"What, it is a reasonable question, is it not? I for one am always fascinated by our officers' experiences at the war."

"She likes those gothic tales of the macabre, too," Lady De Geoffrey chided in disapproval, but Trevor merely smiled.

"I was not technically an officer, my lady."

"Yes, but you know what it's like to kill," the large, ruddy countess intoned in an ominous voice.

"Madam, honestly," Sir Phillip chimed in.

Trevor did not wish to be the cause of animosity among his neighbors. "It is unavoidable in war, you're quite correct, Lady Stokes. But still, I prefer saving lives to taking them." He strove to turn the conversation. "Did I mention that my fellow agents and I were given extensive training in battlefield medicine? Perhaps Dr. Bowen-Hill and I might discuss it some time."

Young Calpurnia was having none of it.

"I think what Lady Stokes is trying to ask, Lord Trevor — well, what we're *all* really wondering after all they wrote about you in the papers is — how many men have you killed?"

"Ha!" Lady Stokes burst out, as if not even she had dared ask this but very much wanted to know.

At the same moment, while Trevor stared at the debutante, frozen — indeed, cornered — all of a sudden, Miss Kenwood seated beside him went into a burst of violent coughing.

He turned to her in distraction, still wishing he could be anywhere but here.

Then his eyes widened as he realized she was choking.

"Good God!" Pushing back his chair, he leaped to his feet with alacrity, smacking her soundly on the back once, twice.

"Can't — breathe!" she wheezed, pounding herself on the chest.

"Grace!" her father shouted in alarm.

"She's turning red! Doctor, do something!" their hostess cried.

Dr. Bowen-Hill was already scrambling out of his chair and starting to race around the table. Reverend Kenwood was on the verge of bursting out in prayer, while Calpurnia shouted at her to breathe.

"Oh — dear!"

Suddenly she was all right again, on her feet now, gasping for breath. She clutched Trevor's arm as he steadied her.

"Good heavens," she gasped out, catching her breath again. "I'm so sorry, everyone."

Lady Windlesham was outraged at the disruption at her table. "Miss Kenwood, you must be more careful! You gave us such a fright!"

"Y-yes, Your Ladyship. I-I think it was a cucumber seed." She sank back down apologetically into her chair, then Trevor pushed it in for her, frowning. "It must have gone down the wrong pipe."

"I daresay," Lord Stokes said with a knowing twinkle in his eyes.

His pulse pounding, protective instincts still on high alert, Trevor handed Grace her wineglass, this time without sarcasm.

She took a swallow to clear her throat. "Thank you so much," she murmured, avoiding his gaze.

But as he took his seat again, he realized it was he who should thank her, for the topic of how many men he might have killed and how he felt about having done so was blessedly forgotten.

He looked askance at her as Sir Phillip steered them into a safe new conversation about the soiree he and his wife would be having soon, when his friends and fellow judges on the circuit court passed through on their way to the Assizes.

"You'll all be invited," Lady De Geoffrey said with a decorous smile, but Trevor wasn't listening.

If there was any doubt that Grace had choked on purpose, or rather, faked it from the start to rescue him, she removed it when she gave him a good kick under the table.

As if to say, *"You owe me."*

He hid his faint smile behind the brim of his wine-glass as he took another sip. *Indeed, I do, my dear.*

Maybe "hate" was too strong a word.

Hope yet remained.

CHAPTER 15

"Now, Miss Kenwood, my mind is quite made up!" Lady Windlesham dragged her aside as soon as the women had retreated to the drawing room, leaving the men to their brandy and cigars. "Now that I've had a chance to meet this charming man for myself, I am quite resolved. Lord Trevor must marry my daughter. Heaven knows the stubborn gel will have nothing more to do with poor Lord Brentford. She cannot abide even to hear his name spoken — and we all know why *that* match didn't work out," the baroness reminded her with an accusing huff. "Thankfully, you have another chance to make it up to me, and pay for what you've done to this family by bringing that unspeakable woman here. I shall be counting on you to help me secure Lord Trevor for Calpurnia."

Grace pressed her mouth shut, her lips tightly sealed.

She would have liked to tell the baroness where she could put her plans, but how did one refuse a favor, however outrageous, to a hostess who had just treated one to a grand feast?

She did not always do well in awkward situations. The choking trick was unlikely to work but once a night. While she hesitated, debating how to reply, Lady Windlesham took her silence for agreement.

"Good, then. I knew I could count on you. Still, it is all such a bother. She and George always seemed so perfectly matched — and he will be a marquess! But what he did was unforgivable." Her Ladyship let out a vexed sigh as she scanned her drawing room, making sure the other ladies were content. She shook her head. "If he had kept his dalliances out of sight in London, we could have turned a blind eye. But to do it right here, under our noses! He humiliated all of us with his flagrant indiscretion. He should be ashamed."

"He is, my lady. He is very sorry."

"Well, it's not enough," she murmured. "At least not for Calpurnia. I'm a practical woman. I would happily forgive him, but she's the one who'll have to live with him, and she's not having it."

"But she has received his apologies?"

"Oh, several. She burns them. I imagine our dear George will soon have cause to feel even sorrier still. Maybe then he'll learn his lesson."

At that moment, over by the fireplace where the other ladies sat on the small, striped sofas, Lady Stokes passed wind loud enough to be heard in the next county.

"Good God!" Lady Windlesham muttered while the others fought not to react. "If she weren't a countess, I wouldn't allow that woman to mop my floors."

Mrs. Bowen-Hill quickly supplied a polite new topic, while Calpurnia looked ready to fall on the floor with the agony of holding in hilarity.

Grace did not dare meet her young friend's insistent stare as she knew that the debutante would lose that battle.

"Now, then. I will work to arrange some sort of outing for us all again, so that our new neighbor will have another chance to appreciate my daughter's charms."

"Um, my lady, what if it becomes plain at some future point that Lord Trevor and she are not well suited?"

"Nonsense. Any man can be made to suit any woman as long as their match is appropriate."

"Yes, but what if he has reconciled with

285

his former fiancée?"

Lady Windlesham turned to her in suspicion. "Why should he do that?"

"Oh, I don't know," Grace said rather guiltily. *Because I told him to?*

"They, um, they were engaged for a long time, I believe."

"Not anymore!" the baroness said with a gleam in her eyes. "I hardly think that is going to happen. Think on it! That fool Laura Bayne humiliated Lord Trevor as badly as Lord Brentford did Calpurnia. You see? It gives them all the more reason to be drawn to each other.

"Who better to understand what the other has been through? Might not suit, indeed. Leave the planning to me, Miss Kenwood," she chided. "All I want from you is a little assistance in managing Calpurnia. Nicely done at dinner, by the way. I thought I'd choke, myself, when she asked that horrid question. To hear any daughter of mine say such a thing! Believe you me, I intend to scald her ears about that. Thankfully, you saved the day, as always."

With this astounding rare compliment, Lady Windlesham gave Grace a conspiratorial smirk, then sailed off again to join her lady guests in taking after-dinner tea.

Lord, help me. That woman scares me to

death. Grace frowned after their hostess, unhappy with her own inability to stand up to Her Ladyship.

The iron-willed baroness seemed to think she could control everyone around her if she exerted sufficient effort. Grace rather doubted that Lord Trevor Montgomery was the sort of man to bend to the ruling matron's wishes.

But if somehow he should take a liking to Calpurnia, maybe he'd be happy to go along with her mother's scheme.

More likely, he had already taken the obvious advice Grace had given him during their quarrel and made up with his frosty golden goddess from the Lievedon ballroom.

Grace supposed if that were the case, she would have to answer to Lady Windlesham for her role in giving him such traitorous advice.

Either way, Grace thought, it seemed so foolish of her now to have dreamed even for a brief few minutes that he might somehow end up with *her.*

But what would she do with a hardened warrior, really?

That's what he was, she thought, but nobody else around here seemed to see it. They were all fixated on what he could do for them, but Grace had seen the awful guilt, the pain, that had flashed across his handsome, chiseled face when he had been asked how many men he had killed.

It pained her to think of what he must live with, the burdens he must carry, even if he was only her friend, or neighbor, or whatever he was to her.

Surely he would rather marry someone who could not see into his secrets but took his adventure tales at face value and let him play the idle gentleman-architect, as he preferred.

Once more tamping down any foolish notions of winning him for herself, as if she'd want him, Grace went and joined the other ladies at tea, and before long, the gentleman entered the room.

Then it was time for the evening's entertainment, which chiefly consisted of admiring Calpurnia's accomplishments.

Of these, she had many. Everyone gathered around to hear the young belle of the county charm their ears with her repertoire of songs. Mrs. Bowen-Hill played the pianoforte for their songstress, as she often did. Indeed, the good doctor's wife often volunteered of a Sunday to play the organ in church.

Grace listened from the back of the room, leaning against the wall. She looked over warily as Lord Trevor sauntered over and joined her, lowering his head to whisper in her ear so as not to disrupt the musical performance.

"Pardon me, Miss Kenwood, but if Miss Windlesham ever finishes singing, I was wondering if we might be treated to a second performance of your acting skills."

She fought a smile. "I don't know what you're talking about," she murmured. "What about your talents as a storyteller? Will we get another chance to hear more?"

"Not if I can help it," he replied, smiling in amusement.

"Those stories of yours were marvelous — but rather well rehearsed."

"I save them for special occasions."

"Ah. State secrets or cock-and-bull tales?"

"A little of both."

"I notice you didn't mention the one you told me, about blowing up the Spanish church."

"Accidentally," he reminded her with a glimmer of mischief in his eyes that made her knees go weak.

"Accidentally, of course," she conceded, slipping him an arch smile in answer.

He nodded toward the room. "I wanted to thank you for that. Back there."

"Nonsense. They had no right to ask you

such appalling questions. Calpurnia's just young. She doesn't understand. I hope you won't hold it against her."

"For your sake, I won't."

She wasn't sure how to take that, or his steady, searching gaze.

She swallowed hard. "As for Lady Stokes, you'll just have to get used to her. She and her husband both love shocking people. Still, to bring up such topics. 'Twas altogether barbarous."

"I get those questions all the time, actually."

"Really? I had no idea people were so rude. Well, you shouldn't have to answer."

"It's a good thing I didn't have to, or I fear I'd have set the whole table to choking."

So many? She glanced at him in surprise.

He gazed into her eyes with a complicated mix of emotions in his own. Because the answer was there, nakedly, no longer in disguise.

Yes. That many.

She wasn't sure what to say.

Years of sitting in her father's church had the words "Thou shalt not kill" and "Blessed are the peacemakers" positively ringing in her ears.

"Well" — she finally managed a hesitant

word of comfort — "I'm sure you were only doing your duty."

"Yes. I wasn't sure if you'd see it that way after what you said about soldiers. Or maybe now you're just being kind?"

She stared at him as it fully sank in: His face, those fierce gray eyes, had been the last image some men had seen on this earth.

Her gaze trailed down to the strong, elegant fingers idly hefting his brandy snifter. Fingers that could pull the trigger when the moment came. Hands trained to wield a knife.

She trembled and edged away from him a bit, her heart in her throat. She couldn't help it.

He cast her a wan, knowing smile. "I won't hurt you," he murmured in a velvet tone. "I told you that the night we met."

Grace swallowed hard, her heart pounding. The last thing she needed reminding of right now was the kiss they had shared in that darkened room. God, she wanted him.

She looked away, wishing he would get away from her and go back to playing the nice guest.

Instead, he was ever so subtly seducing her while Calpurnia warbled on.

"How was your trip?" she forced out, changing the subject and cringing to feel the flames in her cheeks. "I wasn't sure if you'd be coming back."

"Why? I just bought a house here, didn't I?"

"I thought you were regretting it." She hesitated. "Because of me."

"Ah, you won't get rid of me that easily. Did I miss anything exciting while I was gone?"

"Farmer Curtis's cow got out of the pasture with her calf. High drama."

"I can't believe I missed it!"

Grace could not look away as she and the man Lady Windlesham had branded as Calpurnia's future husband stood gazing at each other.

It took a moment for her to find her voice. "Did you accomplish what you set out to do?"

"Hmm?"

She braced herself. "Did you reconcile with your lady?"

"My lady?" he echoed, furrowing his brow.

"The woman you had planned to marry."

"Oh, that's not where I went," he said with a dismissive wave of his hand.

She nearly coughed with shock. "It's not?"

"No, no, all that's over. I went to see my gambling friend in jail."

"Your friend?"

"Yes. You were right, Miss Kenwood. It was better to make peace. We've been like brothers for too long for me to go on holding a grudge against him. What's done is done."

She stared at him in astonishment.

"Is something the matter?"

"I thought — I thought you were getting back together with your fiancée!"

"She wishes," he said flatly.

"But — I was half-certain you'd be bringing her back to the Grange with you!"

He laughed. "Laura Bayne at the Grange? No. Not in a million years. My dear, she wouldn't last a day. All that is over between us, and frankly, I am glad. Nick was right about that much — my friend in jail," he explained. "Laura would have made me a most unhappy man." He glanced over at Calpurnia and added, "Believe you me, I don't intend to make that mistake twice."

He looked at her again, as if to make sure she got the point.

Grace gulped, staring at him, wide-eyed.

"I see," she said faintly after a moment though she didn't, and in fact was very sure she was mistaken.

He couldn't be talking about . . . her?

Half-strangled with awkwardness and suddenly struck with dread at the prospect of

Lady Windlesham's wrath if she ruined this match, too, Grace cleared her throat. "Calpurnia sings beautifully, does she not?"

"An admirable singer," he replied with a gentlemanly nod, then they both redirected their attention to their host's daughter for a moment.

Grace sneaked a sideways glance at the tall, dark man beside her and had to stifle an idiotic sigh at the nobility of his profile.

"Miss Kenwood," he remarked, keeping his voice low as he continued staring straight ahead. "It is very important to me that you realize I have no ill intentions toward your friend Marianne. I don't want you to think—"

"I'm sure it's none of my business," she interrupted hotly, cheeks flushing with embarrassment.

"But it is. You were right on that point, too. Marianne depends on you; as for her, I daresay there is more to her than meets the eye. She's got a strength about her."

"Yes. She's had to endure a lot. It's made her tough."

"She told me what a tremendous help you've been to her. She calls you her guardian angel, did you know that?"

Grace lowered her head with a smile.

"I'd never jeopardize Marianne's progress

or ruin all your work. I just wanted you to know that."

"Oh — well — thank you." She was so out of sorts at his admiring gaze that she attempted to defuse the charged atmosphere between them with humor once again. "Of course, you should never mention 'that woman' by name around here. She is persona non grata with the Windleshams. And naturally, I am to blame for it," she added, "since I'm the one who brought her to Thistleton. They blame me equally with her for breaking up Callie's match with the son of the Marquess of Lievedon."

"Young Brentford?"

She nodded.

"Hmm, too bad. They seem a good match. By the way, how are the little intruders?" he asked before she could quite interpret his idle remark about Callie and George. "I've been wondering if the one who fell in the river took ill later from his dowsing. That water was very cold."

"It's kind of you to ask, but no worries, Denny's just fine."

"Denny, eh? You never did tell me their names."

"Kenny and Denny Nelcott."

"I'm sorry about their father. It must be very difficult for them."

"Indeed. Mrs. Nelcott has four children: the twins; Bitsy, the little girl you gave the flower to; and an eighteen-month-old baby at home."

"And no husband to support them all?" He shook his head. "That is hard."

She nodded in regret.

"I have a thought," he said after a moment as the song ended, and they all applauded Calpurnia, who curtsied like the picture of demure eligibility.

"What's that?" Grace asked.

"Why don't you send the boys over to the Grange tomorrow afternoon? I could use a couple of assistants. I'll give them some chores so they might earn a few coins to help their mother. And learn a little discipline," he added pointedly. "Unless, of course, they are too scared of me now, after I yelled at them —"

"Scared of you? I hardly think so. Those two aren't scared of anything. That's half the problem with the pair of little savages. As for you, sir, you might be interested to know you went from being an invading ogre to a knight-errant in their eyes when you saved Denny's life — which, by the way, I never did get to say thank you for that. I can't imagine what his mother would have done if she had lost her son so soon after her husband."

His eyes glowed with modest pleasure at her praise. "Glad to be of service." Then he nodded. "If Mrs. Nelcott gives her boys permission, send them over to me, and I'll have them help me with some simple tasks."

"No sharp objects, I assume? And by the way, make sure your weapons are locked up. I know you had just moved in and hardly started unpacking, and you certainly weren't expecting to have your house broken into by a pair of mischievous nine-year-olds, but I don't want them getting hold of any dangerous weapons —"

"Consider it done," he said firmly.

"Very well, then. I'll bring them over myself to do the introductions. Believe it or not, they can get very shy around grown-ups."

"If I get to see you, that's all the better." He gave her an arch look askance. "So, we are friends again, then?"

"Indeed," she answered heartily.

"Excellent." He lifted his glass to clink it against hers, his eyes aglow. "Miss Kenwood." He sketched a polite bow. "I'd better take my leave of you before we start a scandal."

"My lord," she fairly purred, and when he

sauntered off to mingle with the other guests, Grace couldn't take her eyes off him.

CHAPTER 16

"Now, remember," Grace said to Kenny and Denny the next morning. "You're not going over there to play, so no misbehaving. If you do a good job, you'll earn a little money to buy something nice, and your mother will be proud."

"Yes, ma'am," they said in unison.

"Good, then! Into the carriage with you now. Quickly. One should never be late to work."

The twins raced across the drive and went leaping up onto her carriage like a pair of small highwaymen springing up onto their mark. She raised her eyebrows, startled at how eager the boys were to start their first day of gainful employment.

She followed them into the carriage and picked up the reins, wondering what sort of chores Lord Trevor had in mind for his two small helpers this day.

As she had expected, the twins who had

started out so boisterously from the parsonage grew shy the closer they drew to their
destination.

By the time they reached the Grange, the
pair were silent, wide-eyed, and uncertain.
They always drifted closer together whenever they were nervous; presently, they were
shoulder to shoulder.

Grace herded her passengers down from
the carriage as the master of the place
walked out of the old farmhouse, wiping his
hands on a rag.

The grin he flashed at them dazzled her
like the morning sun. "Thank goodness,
help has arrived! I sure need it." He smiled
broadly to put the boys at ease.

"I know," Grace answered encouragingly,
"you'd be very lonely working here today
all by yourself, wouldn't you?"

"Yes, I have a lot of work to do. Man's
work," he added with a stalwart glance at
the twins. "I trust you gentlemen have
brought your muscles?"

The scrawny nine-year-olds assured him
that they had, and preceded to flex their
arms to see which of them had the bigger
biceps. Grace rolled her eyes in amusement
and shook her head. Trevor met her glance,
his eyes twinkling.

"So what will you have them doing today?" she inquired.

"I've got to clear a space for the delivery I have coming tomorrow. My men are bringing timber and other materials on the canal boats. They need to be stored out of the weather, or the wood will rot, and the tools will rust, and we can't have that, can we, boys?"

"No, sir!" the twins agreed.

Then he showed all of them into the house. Grace glanced around as Lord Trevor pointed out the cluttered area in a corner of the old ballroom, where junk would have to be cleared away to make room for the building supplies.

"A simple matter of moving this stuff from here to there," he explained.

"Make sure they don't try to pick up anything too heavy for a child," she warned. "Don't let them hurt themselves."

"Honestly, Miss Kenwood, I'm not entirely ignorant of how to manage children. I was a boy once myself, as it happens. Though I will take any tips you care to give me on what to do if they start acting like the little monsters I originally met."

"Oh, they won't, believe me. But if they do" — she gave the boys a warning stare — "let me know, Lord Trevor, and I will deal with them myself, hm?"

The twins edged back from her a little, as though she were a witch with a cauldron easily big enough to fit two small, naughty boys. "Understood?"

"Yes, ma'am," they said.

Lord Trevor was trying to conceal his smile of amusement behind his hand when Grace turned to him. "They're all yours."

He clapped his hands briskly. "Come, men! Let's get started. The morning's wasting. We've got much work to accomplish before sundown."

"Sundown?" Grace exclaimed. "My dear fellow, you do realize they are nine? I'm coming back for them in two, three hours at the most."

"Oh! Right. Of course. That's plenty of work for two small boys, you're quite right, Miss Kenwood. We'll see how much we can get done before you return. Unless you care to join us? I pay well," he teased.

"Not on your life," she said with a chuckle. "I have enough chores of my own to do today."

"Like what?" he asked as he followed her back out to her carriage.

"I always make my poor calls on Mondays and visiting the sick."

"Admirable."

"Not really," she said, as he handed her

up onto the driver's seat. "You had your duty; I have mine. Have fun. And above all, remember," she teased him in a whisper, "never show fear."

"Begone, woman. You're scaring me."

"Good-bye, boys!" Grace waved to them as they emerged from the house. "I'll want to hear all about your morning when I come back to fetch you."

"Bye, Miss Grace!" Kenny waved back, but Denny was instantly absorbed in trying to catch a grasshopper.

Grace was still smiling when she was home in her kitchen, helping Cook to make the soup and bake the fresh rolls for the poor.

As she went through her list of items that various families had donated for the parish poor: extra blankets, a coat, two pairs of still-usable old shoes, and tonics and medicines contributed by the Bowen-Hills.

It felt good in a way she could not put into words to know that Lord Trevor was just across the way, working with the children.

If only she had Calpurnia's opera glasses! She would have loved to catch a glimpse of him and his assistants to see how they were faring.

At that moment, as if the mere thought

had conjured her, the debutante herself came barreling up the drive once more in her pony gig.

Grace paused at the window, surprised to see the carriage clattering up in front of the parsonage. *What now?* With the unpredictable Callie, it was always impossible to guess.

Moments later, the eighteen-year-old came whooshing in, her usual whirlwind self, all bouncing golden curls and rosy cheeks. "Oh, Grace, isn't he divine? I had to see you!"

"My dear, what's going on? You seem all at sixes and sevens. Is something wrong?"

"No, Grace, everything's wonderful!" she said breathlessly. "It's just that I'm so desperately in love!"

She blinked. "What?"

"Wasn't last night wonderful?" Callie twirled into the parlor. "I never met a finer man! Do you think he likes me, too? I mean, could you tell? I couldn't tell — but then, his being a spy and all, you know, I'm sure he must be awfully good at hiding his feelings. Don't you think?"

"Yes, probably . . ." she mumbled in shock.

"Exactly! That's just what I suspected! With other gentlemen, not so — but with a former spy, well, just because he didn't really give a sign he likes me doesn't mean he isn't interested. Did he say anything to you? I saw you talking to him in the back of the room while I was singing. I didn't mind, as long as he said something nice about me?"

"Um, he said you sing very well."

"Oh, la! Anything else?"

"I, er, no — nothing, to my recollection."

Callie grasped Grace's hands and sighed, leading her into the window seat. "Mother and I are in earnest agreement that he's simply perfect! Well, of course, Mother doesn't like his hair, but that is easily remedied. Personally, I rather like it — but it does not signify. The important thing is, I've found my one true love!"

Good heavens.

Grace was routed. "Are you . . . very sure of that?" she asked gingerly.

This was all much worse than she had imagined.

Callie waved off the question. "Is anyone ever really sure, in matters of the heart? I thought I loved George, too, but . . . well. Never mind him." She looked away at the thought of her former suitor, then brushed off his memory and grabbed Grace by the wrist. "Come, let's go spy on him again! I

305

brought by opera glasses!"

The girl proceeded to drag her outside onto the terrace, but when this did not afford a clear view, Callie cajoled her back inside and up onto the landing of the stairs to look out the window there.

"Who's there with him? The Nelcott twins? They're carrying crates or something . . ."

Grace was forced to explain the whole story. Meanwhile, she was mortified as Callie continued peering through the trees, waiting to catch whatever glimpse she could of their new neighbor.

"You better hope he doesn't see you," Grace advised, folding her arms across her bosom.

"How could he see me? We're too far away."

"I should think spies are trained to sense when someone's watching them."

"Well, he should take it as a compliment," she declared. "Even Father says we'll make a very handsome couple. And Grace, I'm so grateful to you!" Callie tore herself away from spying on Lord Trevor, turning earnestly to her. "Mother told me how you promised to help make Lord Trevor fall in love with me."

"What? Good Lord, Callie, I never promised anything like that!"

"You didn't?"

"No! Whether or not he falls in love with you, that is entirely up to him, not to me!"

"Oh, of course! That's not what I meant." Her cheeks colored a bit with a rare glow of embarrassment. "I know a gentleman can't be *forced* to fall in love. Obviously! All I meant was that I appreciate your agreeing to chaperone me around him. Now we just have to come up with a few ways that we can be together," she finished, beaming anew.

Grace stared at her in dismay.

It was hard to be angry with Calpurnia when she looked like a wayward angel late for choir practice, tousled and golden, with her sky blue eyes full of hopeful innocence.

On the other hand, it was impossible not to be angry with the chit, for always thinking only of herself.

But with such a mother, where would she have left it?

"Dearest," she said at length, striving for patience as she took her young friend gently by the arm and steered her away from the window. "As you are aware, Lord Trevor has suffered a recent heartbreak."

"I know. It's so sad! But frankly, I'm happy. Is that wrong? What an idiot that woman is for letting him slip through her fingers!"

Grace ignored all this. "My point is, you must take it slowly. After what happened, I doubt that he will be ready to begin a new romance for quite some time."

"Ohh. I see."

With any luck, Callie would lose interest within a few weeks.

"I suppose you're right. I don't want to go throwing myself at him, like you said. First, we must be friends." Callie lifted her eyebrows in question, as though waiting for Grace to approve this strategy.

As if a spinster of five-and-twenty knew the first thing about snaring an eligible man.

Nevertheless, Grace patted her hand. "I think that's very wise." In truth, her main concern was shielding Lord Trevor from being shoved into something he obviously didn't want.

Or so she told herself.

Far be it from the pastor's daughter ever to do or say something absolutely selfish.

She coaxed Callie back to the kitchen with a promise of one of the rolls she had just finished baking, along with sweet strawberry jam.

But as the clock ticked on, she could delay no more. She wiped her hands on her house apron, untied it behind her back, then took it off and hung it on the door peg. "I'm afraid I have to go."

"To fetch the twins?" Callie leaped out of her chair. "I'm coming with you!"

"Calpurnia," she started, but it was no use.

The baron's daughter refused to be denied. "You can't leave me out of this, Grace! It's the perfect opportunity for me to see him again, however briefly. Please, don't be cruel. You don't understand how much I love him!"

"Oh, Lud."

"Please, please, let me come with you —"

"Hush, girl! There is no need to whine. I'll make you a bargain. Come with me on my poor calls today —"

"Grace!" she protested.

"I have a lot to carry!"

"But it's *so* depressing!"

"I know. Believe me! That's why I'd like you to come along. You're very good at being cheerful when you choose. Wouldn't it be nice to brighten up the day for these poor, unfortunate souls?"

"But they *smell.*"

"I wonder if a brave, gallant war hero like Lord Trevor Montgomery would ever marry a girl who doesn't care about the poor."

Callie heaved a long-suffering sigh and rolled her eyes. "Very well."

Grace laughed at her air of martyrdom. "The things we do for love! Now help me load my carriage."

Having the boys' help turned out to cost instead of save time, but Trevor did not particularly mind. The high-spirited lads were two of the most amusing individuals he had met in many years. They regaled him with tall tales, pausing often to act out the high points of their stories in the process of carrying clutter from point A to point B.

In addition, they were happy to share their opinions on a wide range of topics.

Including their Sunday school teacher, which greatly took his interest.

"She's the best lady ever," Kenny–or was it Denny? — informed him.

Trevor still couldn't tell them apart.

"Why's that?"

"She knows how to do *everything*. She never forgets our birthday. And she makes good biscuits."

"Herself?" he asked in surprise, but he never got an answer, for he was suddenly under interrogation.

"Why do you want to know about Miss Grace?" Denny demanded, eyeing him in suspicion, while Trevor was still trying to imagine Laura baking anything. 'Twas impossible. And if she had, it likely would have been inedible.

"Do you like her or something?" the boy persisted.

"Of course I like her," he said casually, fighting back a sneeze as he hefted another dusty old trunk up onto his shoulder and carried it to the other end of the room.

Meanwhile, to his surprise, the twins went slightly insane at his admission, running around in circles, whooping and howling like feral children raised by wolves.

He set the trunk down and looked at them in wonder.

They stopped, one on either side of him. Denny folded his arms across his chest, and Kenny followed suit.

"What are your attentions on our teacher, sir?"

"Pardon?"

"What are your attentions to Miss Grace?"

"My intentions?" he asked abruptly, then laughed. "Where did you learn that expression?"

"We *know* things," Kenny said sagely.

"Miss Grace told Miss Windlesham when she was crying that a gentl'man has to declare his attentions toward a lady."

"But they weren't talking about you. They were talking about Lord Brentford."

"You know Lord Brentford?" Trevor asked.

"Of course. He's a jolly fellow!"

"So I hear," Trevor murmured.

"Everybody's mad at him, except for us."

"And Miss Grace. She never gets mad at anyone."

"Oh, she gets mad at me," he assured them.

"Are you sure she ain't just pretending? She makes a face when she wants you to think she's cross, but she's really not. Like this." He screwed up his face into a scowl. His brother joined the effort in imitating Grace.

Trevor eyed them in amusement. "I'll remember that. But I'm pretty sure she meant it when she got mad at me. Believe me, I won't risk that again."

"Why not? Do you love her?" they teased.

"Are you goin' to marry and have babies?"

"Good God!" Trevor said.

They laughed uproariously, and Kenny added, "Babies smell!"

"Because they poop on everything!"

"Enough! No one wants to hear that kind of talk," he scolded, but thankfully, they were interrupted by the sound of a carriage arriving outside. "There's Miss Kenwood now," he said in relief. "And you'd better not let her hear you talk like that. Come on."

They followed him outside. Trevor hoped that soon, once he was rid of the pair, he might actually be able to get something done.

But admittedly, the boys had not been too great a bother. He had rather enjoyed the change of pace.

"Now, listen," he murmured as her carriage neared. "You two had better not say anything silly about me to her, or I'll hang you off the chandeliers by your suspenders and leave you dangling there. Got it?"

They grinned at his threat.

"Do you think she'll bring some biscuits after all our work?" Kenny said.

"What work?" Trevor muttered.

"I'll bet she does!" Denny replied.

Then Trevor smiled broadly as the lady drove up to the house in her father's work wagon; he raised a brow, however, when he spotted Calpurnia Windlesham following Grace's lumbering cart in her jaunty pony gig. With her bonnet ribbons trailing gaily in the breeze, Miss Windlesham waved to him as if she had learned the gesture from the royals. "Oh, Lord," he said under his breath.

Then he went to help Grace down from her carriage.

"Well, how did we do?" she asked, gathering her skirts in one hand as she accepted his help in climbing down.

"Did you bring biscuits?" Kenny cried.

"Subtle," Trevor drawled to his young assistant.

" 'Course I did. Hard work deserves to be rewarded," she declared as she pulled back the cloth covering her basket and revealed freshly baked biscuits.

She picked one out for Denny, then paused before rewarding him and glanced at Trevor. "Any misbehavior to report, my lord?"

"No," Trevor said fondly. "We didn't get much work done, I admit. But they're very entertaining."

"Aren't they, though?"

The twins were hopping in place with excitement.

"Hm, would you say that they deserve a biscuit?" Grace inquired.

"Mmm," he debated.

"Please, please!"

He chuckled. "They were grand. They can have it."

"I am so pleased to hear it! Here you are, boys. One for you, and one for you." She gave each child his treat, then she offered one to Trevor while, a short distance away, Miss Windlesham pulled her carriage to a halt.

Trevor held Grace's gaze in warm amusement. "I confess I have heard rave reports about your baking, Miss Kenwood. Don't mind if I do." He accepted the biscuit more from curiosity than hunger, but when he bit into it, he was instantly addicted.

"Hullo!" Calpurnia cried brightly as she came striding over to where the rest of them stood.

Grace offered her a biscuit, too, but she waved it off. "I have to watch my figure." She smiled proudly at Trevor, but he refused to take the bait and supply the expected compliment.

It was Laura all over again.

"Miss Windlesham," he greeted her with cordiality, "this is a surprise."

She flashed her dimples and slipped her arm through the crook of Grace's elbow. "I thought I'd follow Miss Kenwood over to see you! We're on our way to visit the *poor,* don't you know."

"But first," Grace interrupted, "we have to take these two rascals home. We really

315

should be going. Come along, boys."

"Wait, I haven't paid them."

"Not the full sum, if they didn't complete their work," she reminded him as he reached into his vest pocket for a few coins.

"That was my fault. We kept finding interesting things among the clutter — in fact, that reminds me. I came across some items that I think the boys' mother might be able to use for the children."

"Oh?"

He nodded. "There are a few pieces of sturdy children's furniture and the like. It all seems to be in good repair. If she can use it, I'd be glad."

"Are you sure you can spare them?"

"I have no use for them," he said with a shrug. "She's welcome to have them, and if she can't use them, she can always break them up for firewood. If you want to wait here, I'll go and get them."

"Thank you!"

He proceeded to carry the children's furniture out of the house. There was a crib and a high chair, plus two small desks. It was old, but still good quality.

"I'm guessing Colonel Avery had his servants move these things down from the old nursery once the roof over that part of the house started going bad," Trevor told her when he had carried out the last piece.

"Are you sure you won't need these things?" she asked. "You don't have children now, but you might in the future."

"I'll cross that bridge when I come to it. These lads could use these items now. Especially the desks," he added, giving the wayward pair an arch look.

Then he loaded it all into the back of her cart, noting as he did so the rows of baskets of bread and lidded crocks of soup, the repaired old clothes and shoes, and folded blankets that she had assembled for the poor of the parish. Trevor gazed a moment longer at all the supplies she had brought. Then turned to her abruptly.

"Maybe I had better come with you."

"It's all right, I can manage —"

"No, do!" Calpurnia interrupted. "How perfectly gallant! As you say, my lord, it's good-quality furniture. Much too heavy for ladies to carry! It would be ever so nice if you could come along and bring the heavy things in for Mrs. Nelcott."

"Calpurnia, he's got work to do. I'm sure we can manage by ourselves," Grace said, but Trevor had already made up his mind.

"It can wait. I'd like to meet Mrs. Nelcott anyway," he said. "Tell her what an excellent job her sons did today."

Grace glanced at him in grateful surprise. "Well, it would be a rare thing for her to hear compliments about them. Usually it's people complaining of their mischief. Honestly, I think it would do her good to hear it."

"Then let's go," he said amiably, and with that he lifted each of the twins up into the back of Grace's cart.

The boys picked their way past the new desks and chairs and the sturdy crib for the baby, each finding a spot to sit.

"Don't you two raid my baskets," Grace warned. "You can have more biscuits, but the bread is for other people."

"Yes, ma'am."

"Would you like me to drive?" Trevor offered when Grace turned back to him.

She gave him a quizzical look. "No. Why?"

He looked at her in trepidation.

Miss Windlesham let out a pert laugh. "Oh, Grace, don't you know gentlemen always prefer to take the reins? Ride with me, my lord. I don't mind if you drive!"

"Er, I'm afraid that would not be proper, Miss Windlesham. I wouldn't want people to talk. I'd better stay in the cart so I, er, can chaperone the boys."

"Oh. Of course. I suppose you're right. How considerate of you to think of my reputation! Very well, then! I'll see you all there!" She went skipping back to her pony gig and bounded up to take the reins again.

Trevor and Grace exchanged a glance as they, too, settled into their seats.

"Should I be worried?" he asked discreetly.

"Most definitely," she answered in amusement.

The cart lurched into motion. Trevor glanced back to make sure the boys and all the supplies Grace had prepared were secure. He caught Denny starting to reach into one of the bread baskets, but the boy froze when he saw Trevor's stare and drew his empty hand back guiltily onto his lap.

Calpurnia came from behind and drove past them like a Corinthian, waving as she urged her pony faster.

"Race you!"

Trevor shook his head at the girl with a rueful smile, but after Calpurnia had pulled ahead of them, laughing, Grace looked askance at him.

"You see? She may win you over yet. Most gentlemen find her irresistible."

"Miss Kenwood, for shame," he chided softly as he looked into her eyes, remembering their kiss.

Grace blushed a little, and he was pleased.

She looked away self-consciously, keeping her gaze fixed on the dusty road ahead. "Unfortunately, if you fail to fall in love with Miss Windlesham, I'm going to be the villainess in her mother's eyes."

"You? Whatever for? You have no control over who I fall in love with. On second thought," he countered, "maybe you do."

She cast him a wide-eyed glance, but could not seem to come up with any answer.

And you think Callie's irresistible? he mused, laughing softly when she clapped the reins over the horses' backs, as if his nearness made her long to arrive at their destination.

Trevor relished being with her, but when he glanced back to check on their passengers, both boys wore knowing grins on their grubby little faces.

Egads, had those two curious imps been listening the whole time and watching his attempts to flirt with their teacher?

Trevor glowered at the pair of wee spies, lest they breathe a word to Miss Grace about their conversation earlier. *Humph.*

Marry her, indeed.

CHAPTER 17

The Nelcott family cottage was in a sufficient state of disrepair as to alarm Trevor about the welfare of the children who dwelled therein. It was a humble affair of wattle and daub, surrounded by a ramshackle fence and a small yard overgrown with weeds.

As Grace slowed her cart before the waist-high front gate, Trevor spotted a little face peering out the dust-caked window. He recognized the wee girl Bitsy, who had been with Grace on the afternoon that he had bought the Grange.

Then, before the cart had scarcely stopped, the twins were already leaping off the back, racing to the gate.

"Mama! We're back! Lord Trevor's come, and Miss Grace, too, and Miss Windlesham!"

The cottage door opened and a weary-looking country woman, thin and haggard, stepped into the doorway with a baby on her hip. It seemed to take all of her energy to summon up a smile.

The boys barreled into the yard, one holding the gate open so the furniture could be brought in, while the other answered the greeting of the family dog, a floppy, oversized retriever.

Trevor wondered how they kept it fed.

When Calpurnia had joined them after tying her pony to the fence, Grace presented Trevor to Mrs. Nelcott. He bowed to the woman, but the air of depression that hung over their humble home seemed almost contagious. He could feel his own spirit sinking in the heaviness that surrounded the widow.

Then Bitsy came running out to show him her little corncob doll, but she was struck shy again a few feet away from him and stopped abruptly.

She hugged her doll and hung back, staring at him.

Trevor chuckled in amusement while Grace explained to the children's mother about the furniture from the old Grange nursery.

"Oh, I'm sure we could never accept —"

"Nonsense, it's perfect!" Grace said cheerfully.

"Please do take it, Mrs. Nelcott, if you would," Trevor spoke up. "You'd be doing me a favor since I have nowhere to put it now. It seems awfully good quality. I'd be pleased if the boys and your little ones could use it.

"Your sons did very well today," he added. "These boys are not afraid of work. If you could've seen them, I'm sure you'd have been proud."

She stared at him in shock. "Really?"

The twins flocked proudly to their mother, one on each side, hanging on her. "Look, Mama!" they said, showing her their coins. "We carried junk from one room into the other! It was fun!"

"Yes, and it was *really hard* work!"

"Well, it wasn't too hard, 'cause we got strong muscles."

"I didn't say it was too hard!"

"Enough," their mother chided. "Sir, I hope they weren't any trouble?"

"Not at all. They were very helpful."

"Will you be needing them again tomorrow? Shall I send them over?"

"Actually, no, but thank you. Tomorrow I have a large delivery coming — building supplies for repairing the Grange. I have some men coming out to help me, and I expect we'll be spending most of the day

323

unloading the canal boats. I expect it will be a bit too dangerous for two small boys, but they're welcome to come and watch."

"Oh, can we, Mama?"

"Can we watch them work the crane?"

"What's a crane?" Bitsy asked.

"A machine that lets you pick up heavy things," Denny informed her.

"Speaking of heavy things, I'll bring in the furniture," Trevor said.

"And I will get the soup," Grace chimed in, following him toward the door.

"Miss Kenwood, you shouldn't have!" Mrs. Nelcott protested.

"Oh, I misjudged my quantities again and ended up making far more than Papa and I could possibly eat ourselves, so I brought you some. It smelled delicious while it was cooking. You at least have to try it."

"You are too kind."

"Not at all! It's my pleasure; besides, you've got your hands full with the baby. How's she been? Hullo, darling!" Grace greeted the baby, who babbled and flapped her arms in excitement to see her.

Cooing over the tot, Grace put her hands out to see if the baby would come to her. Trevor smiled as the tot reached for her. Grace lifted the baby out of her mother's arms and cuddled her. "Ah, you are getting so big so fast!"

"How old is the child?" Trevor asked.

"Eighteen months," Mrs. Nelcott answered with the first sign of life in her eyes.

"This is Miss Mary Nelcott," Grace introduced her, giving her downy head a kiss.

"A fine child," Trevor complimented the mother.

"Thank you, sir." The widow let out a sigh. "She's already startin' to toddle about the place, makin' mischief like the others."

"Mrs. Nelcott has the loveliest children in Thistleton," Grace declared. "But you'd better not tell any of our other neighbors I said so."

Color was finally started to come into Mrs. Nelcott's pallid face.

"Miss Windlesham, would you mind bringing in the soup for me?" Grace addressed her young friend. "It's the one in the blue crock, and don't forget the bread."

The debutante nodded to Grace, looking grateful to be given a task. She had been mysteriously silent so far, standing out of the way. Clearly, the presence of the peasant woman's suffering made her uncomfortable.

Then she followed Trevor out of the cottage and back to Grace's wagon.

"Sad, isn't it?" Callie whispered to him as

he handed her the blue crock of soup and the bread basket next to it.

He nodded, then started lifting the various pieces of furniture off the back of the cart.

As Callie brought the food into the cottage, she called to the twins to hold the gate for him. Trevor still wasn't entirely sure which boy it was who came out in answer to the summons.

"Which one are you?" he mumbled as he carried three small chairs through the gate.

"I'm not tellin'!" the twin answered merrily.

"Hmmph."

Grace held the baby so Mrs. Nelcott could eat some of the soup. Callie helped dole it out into bowls for the three other children, while Trevor took a wet cloth and cleaned up the furniture that he had brought.

The child-sized chairs were a particular delight to Bitsy, and when Grace carefully set Mary in the high chair, it was the perfect size for the tot, at least for now.

Their visit lasted another half an hour, and while they seemed to have cheered up Mrs. Nelcott considerably by the time they left, Trevor felt as though he and Grace and Callie had all absorbed a little of her depression somehow in exchange. Even Grace showed signs of looking a little peaked and pale when they finally took their leave.

"What's next?" he asked the ladies as they returned to the carriages.

Grace smiled at him, but her cheerfulness seemed a little forced. "I have more visits to make."

"I'm exhausted," Callie moaned.

Trevor turned to Grace and searched her blue eyes. "Perhaps I should come with you."

"Oh, not at all! We can manage perfectly well from here."

"Don't you want me to come?"

"Yes, do!" Callie cried.

"He has a lot to do. My lord, you've already been more than helpful."

"Yes, but sometimes there are little jobs the poor need us to do for them that we're hardly strong enough to accomplish!" Callie interjected.

Trevor wasn't sure if Grace was trying to get rid of him. "I don't want to get in the way, but I really think I should come with you."

"Why?"

He frowned. Something about the Nelcott woman haunted him. "Colonel Avery got her husband killed, didn't he? And now I have his house. I . . . I just feel I ought to do something."

"It's not like you're responsible for his actions."

"No." He couldn't explain it, but a foreboding feeling had taken hold. "Will you permit me to escort you? I'd like to come."

Grace looked surprised but pleased. "Of course, if you wish. We'd be glad to have you along. Then I could introduce you around to everyone. Most of Thistleton is still dying to meet you. There are lots of other neighbors who weren't at the Windleshams' dinner party," she added with a rueful twinkle in her eyes.

He took her meaning at once. Lady Windlesham was hardly the sort to invite the poor into her splendid home.

"Good! Then let us be under way," he said.

Callie grabbed hold of his arm. "Hurrah! I'll come in your carriage, Grace. I'm sure Mrs. Nelcott won't mind if I leave my pony here. I've tied her in the shade, and we'll just be a couple of hours, right?"

Grace nodded, and Trevor realized it would be more respectable to travel as three rather than two — Callie in her carriage, and him alone with Grace in the other.

They all climbed in, Trevor handing the ladies up onto the driver's seat.

"Where are you going to sit, my lord?" Callie asked in concern.

"In the back."

"Grace, shouldn't you let him drive? He's the man."

"He doesn't know where he's going," she replied.

"I'm quite comfortable, Miss Windlesham," Trevor assured her as he vaulted into the back and casually took a seat on the wooden ledge behind the driver's box. Back-to-back with the ladies, all he had to do was turn a little to converse with them.

Grace clucked to the horses, and her cart rumbled off.

Callie turned to beam at him as they headed for town. "We'll give you a tour of the village along the way!" Her usual vivacity was back after the draining visit with Mrs. Nelcott. Indeed, she could hardly seem to contain herself. "I'll point out all the important sights."

"Are there any?"

"I beg your pardon!" Grace retorted, shooting him a playful scowl over her shoulder.

He flashed a teasing grin. "Please, I am most eager to learn all about Thimbleton, and meet all my fellow Thimbletonians."

"Thimbleton?" the ladies cried, but they

laughed despite their indignation.

As Grace drove through the village, with Callie gaily pointing out various points of interest to Lord Trevor, she had no doubt that everyone who saw them pass assumed that she was merely playing chaperone, and that their handsome new neighbor was paying court to Miss Windlesham.

She did not know why, but this thought put her in an uncharacteristically sour mood.

She did her best to fight it. After all, visiting the poor in their squalor was dismal enough without silly jealousy and self-consciousness added to the mix.

Grace did her best to brush it off and turned her horses onto the road to the extraordinarily cluttered home of an elderly couple called the Pottfords.

Mr. and Mrs. Pottford were both tiny and frail, extremely opinionated, and mostly deaf.

Mr. Pottford, who had once owned a shop, tended to hoard odds and ends for some strange reason, and so the entire property was littered with stacks and stacks of junk. It wasn't worth anything; all it did was attract mice and worse creatures, but Mr. Pottford could not be persuaded to part with any piece of his trash.

Grace half feared that someday, one of the precarious towers of junk piled in every room would come crashing down on one of the elderly residents.

When Trevor caught his first glimpse down the dim, narrow pathway inside the Pottfords' cramped, stinking home, he glanced at Grace in shock.

"You wanted to come along," she reminded him under her breath, but she gave his arm an encouraging squeeze before she headed inside.

Grace opened the front door and called out cheerfully to her aged neighbors.

"Come in, dear!" a thin, quavery voice answered from the back room.

Relief filled her when she heard the response. She always feared that one day she'd come to visit and find one or the other dead.

She was sure that having each other was the one thing that kept them going. But she dismissed her grim thoughts and gave her helpers a quick smile over her shoulder. "Follow me. And watch your step."

Callie gave Trevor a dire glance as he held the door for the ladies, then they went in single file.

Grace found Mrs. Pottford just where she had expected her: in the one clear refuge the old woman had amid her husband's endless clutter, a shabby armchair by the fireplace with a plant stand next to it for a table.

Mrs. Pottford grasped her cane and started to rise, but Grace bade her not to bother as she brought in the soup, her smile pasted into place.

Again she gave the same story about having accidentally made too much. "It would be a great favor to me if you would take it. Otherwise, it'll just go to waste."

"Bless you, child. You're always so thoughtful."

"Pish-posh," said Grace. Then Mr. Pottford wandered in, and she introduced Lord Trevor to the ancient pair.

He was asked if he would not mind taking down a particular item from atop one of the precarious junk towers — a particular book that Mr. Pottford said he had been meaning to read again for weeks.

Trevor reached up and found the title, shaking dust and mouse droppings off the cover with a grimace as he brought it down and handed it to the old man.

The glance he sent Grace said he thought the whole place ought to be burned down and a new home built from the ground up for the exasperating yet endearing pair.

Callie, meanwhile, stood to the side with her handkerchief pressed over her mouth and nose. She lowered it to answer direct questions asked of her, but her eyes darted around continuously, as if she expected some giant rat to jump out at her from among the piles of junk.

Come to think of it, that would not have been overly surprising, Grace mused.

"How can people live like that?" the girl muttered when they finally returned to the carriage.

"Why won't they throw anything away?" he asked.

"I hardly know," Grace said with a sigh. "Some sort of mania on his part. I've tried to get him to part with a few things, but Mr. Pottford always says that whenever you throw something out, you always need it the next day. He gets very upset whenever someone tries to help him. He calls it robbery and starts shouting for the constable."

"Well, one stray spark, and that place goes up in flames," Lord Trevor warned. "And them with it."

"I know, but what can I do? If you have any ideas, I'm all ears, believe me."

He brooded on the problem of the Pottfords all the way to the next stop on Grace's route, the tidy little home of Miss Hayes.

The blind woman lived on one of the quaint, cobbled, side streets of the village. She was not poor or needy like the Nelcotts, or infirm like the Pottfords, but the sweet soul was quite alone in the world.

Miss Hayes never failed to twist Grace's heart with poignancy at her endless gratitude for any small kindness shown her. Again, Grace delivered the soup along with a small bunch of flowers from her garden, and Miss Hayes praised her beyond all bounds.

"Oh, come, Clara," Grace teased her, blushing, "it's just some soup, not a pot of gold!"

"It might as well be, to me. Each week, I wonder if you'll forget me, but you never do."

Grace clasped the woman's hands between her own. "And I never will. Now then, we've brought someone new to meet you today. Our new neighbor, Lord Trevor Montgomery."

He stepped closer and bowed to her, though she could not see him. "Miss Hayes, a pleasure."

"How kind of you to come, sir! You're the one who bought the Grange?"

"I am," he said firmly, smiling.

She let out an almost mischievous giggle

and leaned toward Grace with a stage whisper. "Everyone says he's very hand-some."

"It's true!" Callie piped up gaily.

"Pshaw," the man in question scoffed.

"I suppose he's not half-bad," Grace conceded, eyeing him in amusement.

He smirked at her.

"Do you mind if I judge for myself?" Miss Hayes ventured.

Grace glanced at Trevor. "Miss Hayes can tell what a person looks like if you'll let her touch your face."

"If you don't mind, of course. I wouldn't want to make you uncomfortable —"

"I don't mind at all," he assured her in a breezy tone as he sat down on a nearby stool. "Just don't get your hopes up," he added dryly. "I assure you, Miss Hayes, I am altogether ordinary."

"Pshaw," said Grace, echoing his earlier denial.

He crooked a brow at her, surprised at her compliment, but she smiled fondly at him, filled with gratitude. His gentleness with the old Pottfords and the young Nel-cotts, and his patience as he let Miss Hayes explore the contours of his face made Grace find him handsomer than ever.

He really was a rather wonderful man.

"What strong features you have, Lord Trevor," Miss Hayes said admiringly as she molded her fingers against the shape of his brow, over the angle of his nose, and the chiseled line of his jaw. Once more, she lowered her hands demurely to her lap. "I'm afraid the gossip is true, my lord. You have a noble face."

"And a black heart," he teased. Then he noticed the pianoforte by the wall. "Are you a lady of musical talents, Miss Hayes?"

"She plays beautifully," Grace spoke up on her friend's behalf.

"Not as well as Mrs. Bowen-Hill," Miss Hayes started.

"Yes, you do! My father has even asked her to play in church now and then, but she's too shy to risk it in front of the whole congregation."

"Too many people!"

"I wonder if we could persuade you to play something for us now, Miss Hayes?" Trevor asked. "That would be most diverting."

Grace could hear it in his voice that he was going out of his way to be friendly to her, and she was touched.

"Certainly," Miss Hayes responded, then she echoed his own teasing words back to him. "As long as you don't get your hopes up too high."

"I will take that under advisement," he replied. Then he assisted her in rising from her seat, offering a gentlemanly hand as he would to any lady.

Clara Hayes was fully capable of making her way around her home independently, but no doubt, she appreciated the gallant gesture. A moment later, she settled herself before her pianoforte.

When she began to play a familiar tune by Bach, Trevor winced; Grace sent him a sideways look, for although Miss Hayes was a talented player, her pianoforte was hor- ribly out of tune.

Considering that her music was her one consolation in a life that could not be easy, Trevor looked outraged at the injustice of the dear woman having to play on such an ill-tuned instrument.

Grace wondered what he thought of it all as they returned to the carriage. "Well?"

He sent her a troubled frown. "She's very ladylike. What's her story?"

"She was born blind. Her father was a gentleman though he wasn't rich. Her parents left her a modest inheritance, but unfortunately, she's had a lot of unexpected bills from various physicians."

"Is she sick?"

"No, she took a bad fall a few years ago during the winter. Slipped on the ice and badly hurt her back. It was a difficult recovery, and, I'm afraid, quite drained her resources. Thankfully, she's finally out of pain, but what's left of her inheritance has got to last her the rest of her days, so she must make economies, as do we all."

"I suppose tuning her pianoforte isn't the priority, then."

"No, I wouldn't think so."

"She's a real inspiration, isn't she?"

Grace nodded. "She doesn't let her blindness slow her down a bit."

"Do you think if a piano tuner could be found, she'd permit me to hire him for her as a gift? It's sad enough that she can't see. The woman deserves at least to be able to hear a decent melody in tune."

"That's very kind of you, but I don't think she would accept. She was raised a gentlewoman, and that would not be proper. And what about her pride?"

"Well, I can understand that." He shrugged. "But she wouldn't have to know it was from me. We could say it was your father's idea, so that she could practice more and play in church, as he requested."

"Hmm." Grace considered the notion, impressed with his thoughtfulness. "I suppose we could tell her that Mrs. Bowen-Hill might want a break every now and then, instead of having to play *every* Sunday . . . She might just go along with that."

He tapped her on the nose. "Good! Now all we have to find is a piano tuner. Where to next?"

There were three more calls on Grace's weekly list, but before the last one, she drove Callie back to her pony gig waiting at the Nelcotts'.

The final stop was not one in which Callie could participate.

"Why is that?" Lord Trevor asked.

"Because she's off to see Tom Moody," the girl informed him.

"Who's that?"

"The town drunk. A most unsavory fellow," Callie added sardonically. "My parents have forbidden me to go near him."

"Indeed? And our Miss Kenwood goes to visit him alone?"

"Every week," said Calpurnia.

He turned to Grace, scowling.

"Oh, he's harmless! He goes on a drunken rant every now and then, curses the world, and screams at anyone in sight. But other than that —"

"I see." He glowered at her in lordly displeasure.

"Don't worry," she insisted. "If I thought he was a danger to me, I wouldn't go. I'm not stupid."

"No, but you're too nice," Callie interjected. "Mother says some people aren't worthy of our charity."

Trevor glanced at her, considering this.

"I appreciate your concern," Grace said, "but you should let Callie drive you back up to the Grange."

"I'd be happy to!" the girl said brightly.

"Absolutely not. I'm going with you," he told Grace.

"There's no need! Honestly," she assured him, amused and a little taken aback by his protectiveness. "You have a lot to do, and you've already been such a great help today. I don't want to take up any more of your time."

"Your safety is more important."

She blushed. "That's very sweet, but really, I-I only go and spend ten minutes checking to make sure he's still alive. He wouldn't dare aim his wrath at me. I'm the only person in town besides Papa who treats the poor beggar with any dignity."

Trevor just stared at her, making no move to get out of the carriage. "Good day, Miss Windlesham."

"You're serious?" Grace exclaimed.

340

He glared at her, and Callie chuckled.

"I, for one, am glad he's going with you," the girl said. "I expected nothing less from a genuine hero!"

He sent her an irked frown, for Callie had not yet realized, as Grace had, that he hated being called that.

Callie jumped down from the cart and strode back to her pony, untying it from the Nelcotts' fence.

"Last chance to escape a tedious duty," Grace advised him.

He shook his head stubbornly. She shrugged and urged her horses into motion.

Callie waved good-bye as they pulled away. Lord Trevor stepped up from the back of the cart and sat himself down in the driver's seat beside her.

Grace looked askance at him; he gave her a dirty look.

"What?" she insisted.

"I took you for a woman of sense."

"I beg your pardon!"

"Visiting an angry drunk alone in the middle of nowhere? Has he ever been violent?"

She shifted uncomfortably on her seat. "Not to me."

He cursed softly in a language she didn't know, possibly Italian.

"You don't have to insult me!"

"I don't care how unfortunate he is! If he ever harms you — no, if he ever merely scares you — I will most assuredly cut his throat."

His violent utterance took her aback. She looked at him, startled, and drove on, frowning uneasily.

"I don't like violence," she informed him after a moment.

"I don't care," he answered matter-of-factly.

"There's no need to growl at me! I've been doing this long before you moved into town. Do you think I enjoy going to see him? Believe me, I find Mr. Moody as revolting as everybody else does, other than his poor, long-suffering, little dog."

"But you don't let that stop you."

"The dog is nice," she replied, feeling defensive but trying to sound reasonable as they rolled along the dusty road. "I just think of it as if I'm going to visit Nelson. A very sweet little Brittany spaniel."

Lord Trevor scoffed and huffed at her attempt to placate his protective ire.

"Come," she cajoled him, then she attempted to explain her reasoning because she was so flattered by his concern for her safety. Besides, she didn't want him to think she was foolish. "It's easy to be generous to the Nelcotts, adorable as they are, and to Miss Hayes, who is so good and gentle and asks the world for nothing. But our Lord went among the lepers, didn't he? It's with people like Tom Moody where the true test lies."

He scoffed. "Test of what?"

"Love," she answered.

"Grace, it's dangerous."

"So? Your duty for the Order was dangerous, too, wasn't it? But that didn't stop you. Well, this is mine. My duty. Why should it be any different for me? In our separate spheres, we're not so different, you and I."

Trevor stared at her, nonplussed.

He had never heard such talk from a female before in his life. He was equal parts annoyed and awed at the woman.

He scarcely knew what to think.

Perhaps she fancied that a lightning bolt from the Almighty would come down and protect her, strike this Moody fellow dead if the vermin ever sought to harm her.

Bloody blind faith!

And yet, she was totally committed to her principles, and that, he could not help but respect.

"Very well," he muttered at length, noting

343

her worried glance in his direction. "I'll go and see the *dog* with you, then. But next time, you come and get me first before you visit this 'unfortunate soul.' Understand?"

She smiled fondly but made him no such promise. Looking almost amused at his protectiveness, she returned her gaze to the road ahead and simply drove on.

CHAPTER 18

Tom Moody lived on the edge of the woods in a hovel far worse than anything they had seen so far today. In fact, it was near the farthest border of the Grange property, and Trevor was panic-stricken to think of the two Nelcott boys playing by themselves so near the haunt of a man of such low, uncertain character.

As they neared the old shed where the "unfortunate soul" lived, before Grace had even halted the carriage, they could hear furious yelling and raucous noise coming from inside. *What the hell?*

"Is this normal for him?" Trevor murmured, scanning the place on full alert.

"No." Grace grasped his arm and glanced at him in concern.

Wails and incoherent shouts, crashes and bangs emanated from the shed. "Nelson! Nelson?" howled a male voice, slurred and full of anguish.

"Nelson's the dog?" Trevor murmured.

Grace nodded, fear stamped across her face. She halted the cart, threw the brake, and immediately jumped down from the box.

"Hey, wait! Not so fast!" He leaped down after her and, in a few swift strides, caught her by the elbow. "You don't want to surprise a man in his condition."

"Let me go! I know what I'm doing! He sounds like he's hurt."

Trevor did not release her. "Is he likely to be armed? I want to know what I'm walking into."

She glanced at the hovel in distress. "I don't think so." It seemed to cost her a great effort to tear her attention away from the noises of rage. "Maybe a knife. If he ever owned a gun, he'd have traded it long ago for drink."

To Trevor's frustration, she tore her arm free of his hold and rushed to the door. "Mr. Moody? Tom! It's Grace Kenwood! What's going on in there? Are you all right?"

She pounded on the unpainted door.

It suddenly banged open, and a face emerged from the shadows: dirty, weathered, streaked with wild tears.

Trevor was taken aback at the sight of a grown man sobbing. He had not seen that kind of raw pain on a man's face since the battlefield, and it instantly brought back of flood of memories he had no desire to recall. All of a sudden, he felt physically ill.

"Oh, Miss Grace! Thank God you've come!"

"What's happened?" She approached him without fear.

"It's Nelson," he wrenched out. "I think he's hurt."

"What?"

Trevor strode toward them, but foxed as he was, Tom Moody had not yet noticed him.

"What happened?" Grace asked quickly.

"I don't know! It wasn't my fault," the dirty-faced man slurred. "He jumped up like he always does and knocked everything over, and I —"

"What did you do, Tom?"

"I kicked the damn thing! All right? And now he's run off into the woods! He won't came back. I think I might of broke his ribs. I didn't mean to, ma'am, I swear. You know I love that dog. He's all I got. But now he's gone. I keep callin'. He won't come back. Won't you please help me find him?"

Grace was saying soothing things, trying to get control of the situation, but Trevor just stood there, numb. Frozen. The man's despair had turned his blood to ice water in his veins.

When he saw the peg leg that probably explained why the town drunk could not get very far in searching the woods himself for the dog, the realization sank in that this man was probably a veteran. He had an instant, sickening suspicion that Tom Moody was one of the few survivors from Colonel Avery's regiment.

He lowered his gaze, fighting against an unwanted sense of kinship to this broken man, this lost soul.

But for the grace of God.

Suddenly, Trevor felt a million miles away, jarred into a cold, detached frame of mind that he'd not had occasion to use in the past several months. A dark, emotionless state that was all about simply getting the job done, whatever it was.

Grace glanced twice at him, her soothing words to Moody breaking off midsentence. "Trevor?"

"How long has the dog been gone?" he heard himself ask in a clipped staccato.

"Who's this?" Tom Moody asked Grace, dragging his tear-filled gaze away from her to Trevor.

"Our new neighbor, Lord Trevor Montgomery. He bought the Grange."

"Can ye help me find my dog, sir? He's a good dog."

"Which way did he go?" he asked in a deadened tone.

Moody gestured toward a path that opened into the woods. "That way."

"How long ago?"

"Only about ten minutes or so."

Trevor nodded, but he had to get away from this man, right now. As if Tom's brokenness was catching.

It was as though, deep in the back of his mind, he could hear a hurricane howling in the night black distance, and he knew it was coming for him.

Perhaps that was why he had never married Laura. Perhaps he'd always known that when the storm in him broke, it would blow her away. Blow his perfect house down. Ruin everything. And then he would have been trapped under the ruins for the rest of his life.

"Trevor?" Grace asked softly, searching his face. "Are you all right?"

"Of course. Stay here." He glanced warily at Grace. "I'll be back." With that, he pivoted and headed for the woods, every muscle in him taut and bristling.

"I'm coming with you!"

He could hear her following but did not

look back. "Please don't."

"Trevor, what's wrong?" Grace demanded, striding after him toward the path into the woods.

He knew it was no use denying that he was out of sorts, but there was no way in hell he was telling her the truth. He stared straight ahead. "I don't like people that hurt animals."

"It's more than that."

"Go and wait in the carriage. If the dog is too badly hurt, I may have to kill it. You don't want to see that."

She fell behind in dismay, watching him march off like a wooden soldier.

Grace had never seen that look on his face before.

Anxious as she was about the dog, she was more worried at the moment about Trevor. Something about this situation had obviously struck a nerve.

If the drunkard had indeed accidentally killed his dog, she did not know how she was going to stop Trevor from killing *him*.

From the direction of the woods, she could hear him calling the dog's name. They said that animals could sense a human's emotions; even if Nelson were able to move, Grace doubted the dog would be eager to risk coming out to face another angry man.

On the other hand, the smell of food might help to lure the frightened animal out of hiding. Picking up the hem of her skirts, she hurried back to the cart and fetched the last jar of soup. She had, of course, brought it for Tom, but the best way to help the weeping drunkard at the moment was to locate his dog. The poor man was inconsolable.

Praying they would not find the lovable little spaniel too badly injured, Grace carried the jar of soup into the woods. Keeping to the path, she followed the sound of Trevor's voice through the green, leafy shadows.

"Nelson! Here boy!"

Grace was not sure what was going on inside his mind, but clearly, their visit here had affected him deeply. When she caught up to him, he sent her a dark glance, but she lifted the jar of soup to show him she had brought it to lure the dog.

He gave a begrudging nod and moved on.

She followed him through the woods while he continued using his tracking skills to find the animal. Leaves crackled underfoot, twigs snapping as they forged a path through the underbrush, following little more than a deer path. "Nelson!" They both kept on calling the dog.

Trevor held a branch aside for her; Grace picked her way along behind him over the uneven ground, no easy feat in long skirts.

"I wonder if we should spread out?"

"No need." He stopped. "He's in there." He pointed to a low, horizontal crevice like a fox's den in the little rocky hillside. "Nelson?"

Trevor took the soup from Grace and even as he approached, calling the animal's name, she saw a black-and-pink-speckled nose poking nervously out of the den.

"Here, Nelson. Good boy," he greeted the dog in a gentle tone, slowly setting the soup on the ground in front of the little cave. He pried off the lid and the odor floated into the air. "Come out and see us, boy," he coaxed the frightened animal. "How are you doing in there? Let us have a look at you. Come on, now."

Grace scaled the steep angle of the little hill. "Here, Nelson. Remember me? Come out, boy. We're here to help you." She approached quietly and crouched by Trevor's side outside the mouth of the miniature cave.

From within, Nelson let out a small whine.

"I know, boy. It's cruel," Trevor said softly,

putting out his hand so the dog could smell him.

They still couldn't see the dog's body as Nelson cowered in his hiding place. Grace waited with a cold knot of fear in the pit of her stomach for the dog to emerge so they could learn the extent of his injuries.

"Good boy, it's all right now," Trevor was soothing him.

"How can someone do this? All the creature wanted was to be his friend," Grace whispered, tears welling up unexpectedly in her eyes.

Trevor shook his head, mute.

Then the brown-and-white spaniel came slinking out of the fox's den with another pitiful whine, his head low, his feathered tail wagging nervously.

But his head was hung low with visible canine sorrow, and he only took a few steps, hunched with either pain or fear, before dropping submissively at Trevor's feet.

He licked his nose anxiously and, with his great, brown, soulful eyes, stared at them as if waiting for them to explain why this had been done to him.

"He's hurt," Grace whispered, knowing Tom's fear was confirmed.

"It's all right, boy. Let me check you now," Trevor forced out.

Grace petted the dog's head to calm and comfort him while Trevor ran his hands over the animal, searching for any broken bones. It rather surprised her that the dog allowed him to do this, though Nelson nosed his hand away when Trevor touched his rib cage.

"Hold his head more firmly," he instructed her. "If his ribs are broken, he might've punctured a lung."

"Be careful, don't hurt him." Half-blinded by tears, Grace captured the dog's head gently between her hands. She distracted Nelson, giving him a tender scratch under his floppy ears, while Trevor examined his rib cage more closely.

The dog obviously didn't like it, but at least he didn't yelp or whine or try to nip either of them.

"You're a good dog," she whispered over and over, but Trevor was silent, concentrating on his task.

She could not think of anyone with whom she'd have rather faced this nerve-racking moment. Trevor had clearly been upset before, but then when it came down to the moment, he seemed to take the crisis in his stride.

Grace was just the opposite. She had been fine before, but now that she saw the gentle, innocent dog cowering in pain, she felt like she was falling apart inwardly, trying to hold back tears and losing the battle after all the pointless suffering that she had seen today.

Why did life have to hurt so much? Why was there so much ugliness, and what was the point in trying to go against it? The darkness was too deep. Surely, she was a fool to waste her life in a losing battle. A tear fell from her eye onto the dog's head.

Thankfully, Trevor didn't notice. He ran his hands carefully over the dog's spine and down each leg, then he finally let out a sigh of relief.

"No breaks that I can feel," he finally announced in a low tone. "Poor little fellow, he's been pretty well beaten up, but I think he's going to be all right. No guarantee a few of the ribs aren't cracked. They obviously hurt him, but maybe they're just bruised. Been there myself, boy. Not very comfortable, is it?" he murmured, stroking the dog's head. "No blood on him. But if Moody kicked him in the belly, we'll have to keep an eye on him to see if there's any organ damage."

Grace was so grateful for this news, she couldn't get a word out. She wasn't entirely sure why she was so overcome, but her voice was blocked by the lump in her throat. She pressed her lips together, holding back a stupid sob. What on earth was wrong with her?

Trevor still hadn't noticed her discomposure, fortunately. She was, after all, supposed to be the strong one.

Always.

Without fail.

She was Grace bloody Kenwood.

"Poor Nelson. Let's hope he lives up to his namesake — Grace?" Trevor asked abruptly as a pair of tears dripped from her eyes without warning and fell onto his hand as he was petting the dog.

At the same moment that a small sob wrenched past her lips.

"Grace," he said wonderingly.

She turned away and covered her mouth with the back of her hand, but it was no use. She simply crumbled.

Trevor stared at her, taken aback. The woman he knew as a tower of strength was weeping uncontrollably.

Her shoulders shook; she kept herself turned away, as though trying to hide the obvious from him. She took her fist off her mouth for a gulp of air amid a tangled sob, but still refused to turn to him.

His brow furrowed in bewilderment,

Trevor laid his hand gently on her shoulder. "Grace, Nelson's going to be all right."

"It's not that. Please — never mind me," she choked out. "I'll be fine in a moment, really —"

"Tell me what's the matter," he said softly.

She looked at him in bewilderment. "I just d-don't understand. Why does there have to be so much pain a-and brutality? First all those people we saw today, and now this. The suffering, it's endless," she wrenched out. "I mean, if a man can do that to a poor innocent dog, a dog that loves him, what hope is there for any of us?"

"Come here," he whispered, pulling her into his arms.

The green woods whispered around them as they knelt in the dirt, embracing. Trevor shut his eyes, firmly cradling her head with his hand while she soaked his shoulder with her tears. "Shh, it's all right. I know," he whispered. "You've been strong for everyone for so long, haven't you? I'm here now. You go ahead and cry."

Grace scarcely knew what had come over her.

This sudden storm of emotion was totally unlike her, but as she clung to him, still haunted by the pain on all those faces, the ex-assassin comforted her with the utmost tenderness, stroking her hair and her back, hushing her and speaking soft nonsense in soothing tones, while the sobs racked her.

She was well aware that he knew the darkness of this world all too well. Indeed, it had touched him, marked him, as she had seen for herself by the hatred in his eyes on the night of the Lievedon Ball, and his willingness to use her that night as a plaything. She also recalled what George had said, about how Order agents knew several ways to kill with their bare hands.

God only knew what all he had done in his years abroad. It unsettled her to lean so heavily in her moment of weakness on a man so expert in dealing out death, a man who had looked pure evil in the face, even unto the horrors of war. But yet, his battles against it had made him strong, while she felt boneless, melting into his embrace, devoid of strength.

Nor did she take any thought of the compromising position they were in, alone in the woods in each other's arms. It wasn't like that . . .

At least not until his embrace began to quiet her sobs and then, as though he couldn't help himself, he bent his head closer and began slowly, gently kissing the salty tears from her cheeks.

The kiss, though pleasant, caught her off guard, called her attention to the very masculine hardness of his strong arms around her. Her awareness moved to the solid architecture of his broad shoulders and his muscled chest.

He caressed her hair and, still holding her, glanced at her face. He cupped her cheek in the palm of his hand and wiped her tears away with his thumb.

"That's better," he whispered.

She slowly lifted her gaze to his, her lashes starred with tears. He looked into her eyes, then his gaze drifted down to her lips, swollen from her crying, and his pale eyes filled with anguished want. "You're so beautiful, Grace." His low, shaky whisper seemed to escape without his permission. "Your heart is so pure. So beautiful," he breathed.

Grace went very still as he lowered his head. When he pressed his lips to hers, she closed her eyes in wonder, the shock of it reverberating silently through her world.

His kiss was exquisitely gentle, a silken caress of his mouth on hers.

It intoxicated her as well as brought her solace.

He paused with an anguished gaze into her eyes.

Grace thought she ought to say something, but her mind was a blank. She felt emptied of all the bottled-up grief she had been holding back for far too long.

Emptied . . . and she longed to be filled with him.

She dug her fingers into his broad shoulders as her lips parted. Trevor kissed her more deeply with a moan, his hand cupping her other cheek.

She felt the passion in him instantly ignite, just like it had that night in the darkened room at Lievedon House. His tongue glided in her mouth, and his fingers burned like fire.

Dizzied with longing, she quivered as he ran his fingers down her neck; his chest heaved against hers. She let out a small sigh as his lips left hers, however.

Somehow, he forced himself back a small space, as though he did not trust himself to continue. Pressing one last, lingering kiss to her brow, he released her. She came back gradually to her senses as he eased off to a safer distance.

She dragged her eyes open and stared at him as she realized that here was something beautiful and good that could make the darkness of this world bearable.

He lowered his gaze, looking as routed as she felt.

He swallowed hard. "We should get the dog back to the village," he said after a moment. "Perhaps Dr. Bowen-Hill would take a look at him."

"Yes," she whispered, still dazed.

Trevor paused and sent her a probing glance full of swirling, complicated emotion. Need glittered in his pale eyes, and wariness, along with too much defiance to speak some chivalrous apology that would have been a lie.

It struck her absolutely speechless to realize this man *wanted* her. *Her.* Not some Society golden girl.

He dropped his hungry gaze and looked away; with another low clearing of his throat, he turned his attention back to Nelson, whose snout was now buried in the soup jar.

Trevor took it away from him with a rueful smile.

Meanwhile, Grace fought her way back to sanity after her strange crying spell and that brief but mind-melting kiss. She brushed the last of her tears away as Trevor pushed to his feet.

But when he offered Grace his hand to help her up, and she clasped his fingers, his touch nearly lost the battle for her again. She had a decadent vision of pulling him down on top of her. *Forget about the dog.* Instead, she accepted his help and stood up, her legs still shaking beneath her.

He studied her with a sharp eye. "You all right?" he murmured.

"Fine," she managed.

He nodded, staring at her for a moment longer.

Grace couldn't believe it. Never did she dream a man would look at her like that, call her beautiful, and certainly not a man like Lord Trevor Montgomery.

Trying to clear away the sense of unreality, she smoothed her hair while he bent down and carefully picked up the dog.

It dawned on her belatedly to be helpful. She quickly put the lid back on the soup jar — no easy task with the way her hands were trembling. Then they returned to the path and walked back without another word between them.

When they stepped back out into the clear, Tom Moody came hobbling toward them at once. "You found him! Oh, Nelson! How is he? Is it bad?"

"We're not sure," she answered. "We're taking him to Dr. Bowen-Hill."

"I'll come with you —"

"No." Trevor marched past the man and went to place the dog in the back of Grace's wagon.

The soup had cheered Nelson up considerably, but the presence of his harsh master made him fidget and whine nervously again.

There was one blanket left in the back of the wagon. Grace had meant to give it to Tom, but Trevor wrapped the dog in it instead.

Tom frowned. "He's my dog. You have no right to take him! At least let me see him first —"

"I'd like a word with you," Trevor cut him off, turning to him. "Stay with the dog, Grace."

"Trevor?" she asked worriedly.

He ignored her, his big, muscled frame bristling as he approached the drunkard.

Tom backed away. "Now hold on right there. What do you want with me —"

Slam!

Grace gasped as Trevor drove Tom back hard against the wall of his hovel, his forearm across the man's throat.

With his back to her, she could not hear the low-toned words Trevor had for him, but at length, he released the drunkard roughly. "You either clean up your act or get out of Thistleton. You understand me?"

"Y-yes, sir," he stammered, ashen-faced.

"Good. Remember this warning. It's the only one you're going to get." Trevor pivoted and stalked back to the cart with an icy stare.

Tom rubbed his throat, gazing after him in terrified astonishment.

Nelson wagged his tail as the ex-spy approached, but Grace gaped at him, astonished at what she had just witnessed.

"I'll drive this time," he said in a dark tone.

She did not see fit to argue.

CHAPTER 19

They rode to the Bowen-Hills' in silence, Trevor alone in the driver's seat, Grace riding in the back to hold the injured dog steady. The spaniel seemed to be improving from the mere knowledge that they had rescued him from his abusive master, if a dog could know such a thing.

Grace, meanwhile, still couldn't decide what to think about Trevor's threatening Tom Moody. Perhaps the drunkard deserved the harsh warning, but seeing Trevor go after him like that was an unsettling reminder of the violence in which her new neighbor was so expert.

Petting the dog as much to soothe her own rattled nerves as to comfort the animal, she glanced again toward the driver's seat at the tall, rugged figure of the man silhouetted against the evening sky.

What a mystery he was.

She was at a loss for what to make of the

man, and yet everything in her wanted to be closer to him.

At length, she put Nelson off her lap before she lost her nerve, tucking him into his blanket. With a sense of daring, she climbed up onto the driver's seat.

Trevor glanced back in surprise. He quickly offered her a strong, capable hand, steadying her as she stepped up from the back. At the risk of baring an ankle most scandalously, she sat down and took her place beside him.

As she settled into her seat, he gave her a smile. The sunset lit the mellow glow in his eyes.

She smiled back. With hardly any hesitation, she slipped her hand through the crook of his arm, a far bolder move on her part than he probably suspected.

"Something on your mind, Miss Kenwood?" His husky murmur, along with the intoxicating feel of his muscled flesh beneath her fingers, made her tingle all over again.

"Not really."

"You're smiling."

She paused for a moment. "I think everything's going to be all right," she answered slowly.

"Ah, now you've done it," he drawled, but he flashed a rueful grin.

She chuckled.

They passed another warm, delicious minute or so in companionable silence before she spoke again — wistfully, caressing his arm in spite of herself. "This town has long needed someone like you, you know."

And I have long needed someone like you, Trevor thought, glancing cautiously at her. Of course, he dared not say it aloud.

He did not want to push his luck, considering all she had let him get away with so far today.

"What is it?" she asked, watching him with a fond half smile, her blue eyes shining.

He shrugged. "I'm just surprised you haven't scolded me, that's all."

"For what?"

"Threatening Moody, first off."

"I understand why you did it."

"Good." It was difficult to watch the road when he could barely take his eyes off her. "I noticed you didn't scold me for kissing you, either."

"No, I didn't," she admitted. "There didn't seem much point," she added with a teasing look askance.

"Careful, I may take that as encouragement."

"Maybe it is." When she bit her lip coyly, blushing in the twilight, he shuddered at the reminder of how those plump lips tasted.

He shook his head and dragged his gaze away. "Don't do that, Grace. You don't know what you do to me."

"Lord Trevor," she rebuked him in a playful whisper.

"Drop the title, please. We are surely on a first-name basis by now."

"Very well. But don't tell the neighbors."

"In that case." He leaned close and stole another soft kiss. "You're addictive," he whispered.

"Trevor? You wouldn't toy with me, would you?" she asked shyly after a moment.

"Good God, no. Why would you ask such a thing?"

"Because . . . things like this don't generally happen to women like me," she said.

"Things like what?"

"You." She dropped her gaze demurely. "You seem almost — too good to be true."

"I'm true. And do you know what?"

She lifted her eyes to his in question.

"I'm going to prove it to you," he told her.

"How?"

"You'll see." He smiled and left her to ponder this, for just then, they reached the doctor's residence.

Trevor drew the carriage to a halt as sunset faded into night.

Grace suggested he stay with the dog while she climbed down to go explain the situation to the doctor and his wife. He agreed, and she headed for the door.

It opened before she reached it.

Mrs. Bowen-Hill peered out into the darkness. "I thought I heard someone!" For a man of medicine, a visitor at this hour could only mean one thing. "Miss Kenwood?" she exclaimed.

Grace quickly explained the situation.

"A dog?" the doctor's wife echoed. "Well, of course, bring him in. I'll fetch my husband." As she rushed off, Grace beckoned to Trevor to bring Nelson inside.

Soon, the village physician was examining the dog on the table usually reserved for human patients. "Poor little fellow. But I agree with your assessment, Lord Trevor. I don't believe he has any broken bones. Still, he's going to need a bit more considerate care than Tom Moody is able to provide, at least for a while."

"This dog's not going back there," Trevor replied.

"Well, someone's got to look after him. Any ideas?"

Grace and Trevor glanced at each other.

"Don't look at me!" she said. "My cat would never stand for it."

Trevor glanced back wryly at the doctor. "Looks like I've got myself a dog."

"Congratulations," Dr. Bowen-Hill answered with a chuckle.

"Would it be possible for me to leave Nelson with you for a few days for monitoring? The evidence of further injuries may yet emerge, but I'm not going to be at home much to watch him as my deliveries come in."

"I'll watch him for you." Mrs. Bowen-Hill had been standing at the head of the table in her usual role of nurse to her husband's patients, stroking Nelson's head and keeping him calm while the doctor probed him. "You may leave him here — but only temporarily! He's too adorable, poor puppy."

"My thanks, madam. I'll take him home when he's mended enough not to need constant care. And if Tom Moody doesn't like it," he added, "he can come and discuss it personally with me. But I have a feeling we won't be seeing him around here much longer."

Grace looked at him in surprise, then she gave the Bowen-Hills the blanket in which Trevor had wrapped the dog for transport.

Nelson was soon settled into a clean pallet in a corner of the kindhearted couple's kitchen.

Trevor said his good-byes to the dog he had just spoken for, then Grace and he took their leave.

"That dog really got to you, didn't he?" she remarked as they strolled back outside into the balmy, blowing night. Full darkness had descended.

Trevor slid his hands into his pockets with an almost boyish air. "I always wanted a dog, but the life I've had, always on the move —" He shrugged and shook his head. "It just wasn't practical."

She smiled. "Well, he'll be much better off with you, that's for certain. Come on, neighbor, I'll drive you home."

"Wait." He reached for her wrist as she started to walk away, drawing her back gently to him. "I'm not going back to the Grange just yet."

"You're not? It's getting late. Why don't you have supper with us again tonight at the parsonage?"

"Thanks, but there are some people I need to talk to down in the village. Those old men should still be playing chess, no?"

"You mean old Clive Reese and Mr. Johnston? Gracious, by this hour, they're usually done with chess and should be on to drinking games and cock-and-bull tales," she answered archly. "Why do you ask? What do you want with our esteemed village elders?"

"I'm going to need some information. Especially from you."

"Oh?" She tilted your head. "Very well, ask away."

"What I've seen today has changed my mind about the Grange."

His words sent her stomach plummeting down to her feet. Did he already regret moving here? "W-what do you mean?"

"There are more serious needs at hand than my remodeling plans."

"What are you saying?"

"That I want to help."

She stared at him in astonishment.

"You know this place better than anyone. You're the heart of this village, Grace. I saw the proof of that today with my own eyes. So, tell me, if money were no obstacle, where would you begin?"

She went slightly dizzy at the question and leaned against the carriage. He waited patiently, his chiseled face limned in silver moonlight.

"Trevor, are you sure about this? You haven't even moved in properly yet. I mean, it's terribly generous of you, but —"

"I'm sure. This place is my home now, too, Grace. I'm not the richest man in the world — I'm just a younger son — but after all I've seen today, well, I don't exactly need marble columns or crystal chandeliers quite yet. Not when I see some of these poor families going hungry. They're my neighbors, too, now, after all, and what's happened to them is not their fault."

She stared at him in amazement. "That's very kind of you."

"It's your doing," he shot back with a fond smile. "You woke me up today once again, Miss Kenwood. Just like you did with your hairpin at the Lievedon Ball, when I couldn't stop kissing you. You do remember that, I trust?"

"Yes." She blushed at the reminder; his smile broadened as he held her gaze.

"I'm a well-meaning fellow, but sometimes I need a good kick to get my mind off myself — or a jab in the arm with a hairpin, as the case may be. So tell me where we start."

She barely knew how to answer. "I might need a little time to think about it, but off the top of my head, I'd say . . ." She shook her head, her mind racing.

"Yes?" he coaxed her.

"Are you serious about this?" she exclaimed.

He nodded firmly, then furrowed his brow. "Why do you look so surprised? The Kenwoods aren't the only people in Leicestershire who care about their fellow man. Besides, I'm beginning to think I was sent to this place for a reason."

"So do I!" she blurted out, then snapped her mouth shut as he arched a brow.

He *was* rather an answer to a prayer, but she wanted to hear more, and she sensed that he needed to tell it.

She leaned warily against the wagon beside him. "Any idea of what the reason might be?"

"Well . . ." He let out a sigh and dragged his hand through his hair, then absently pulled away the leather cord holding back his queue, as though it were too tight and had begun to bother him.

As his dark mane fell free around his shoulders, Grace stared in admiration. He looked more like a pirate than ever. "I suppose I've always had one main, overarching purpose for my life ever since I was a lad. Train as hard as you can. Prepare for the next mission. Kill the enemy." He shrugged. "Repeat." Then he lowered his head. "Now it's done. And the plans I had set up for after the war didn't quite work out — thank

God. So here I am."

"Here you are," she echoed softly.

"Fixing up the Grange in itself was not so much the point, Grace. It was finding something useful to do, that's all. I don't feel right," he said slowly, "unless I have some worthwhile objective to accomplish. And by the night you found me at the Lievedon Ball, God, I was in such a state I barely knew what to do with myself. Angry at the world. Hating everyone, especially women." He looked askance at her. "I probably shouldn't admit that to you, should I?"

She smiled. "I was there. I remember. I saw you with my own two eyes, and I must say I agree. You were not a happy fellow."

"Not exactly." His roguish grin flashed white in the darkness. "But then I met you. So decent and so sane," he teased softly. "And your father, too. When he suggested I look at the Grange, I decided out of boredom that I might as well, since I had nothing better to do. Then I arrived, and some beautiful, blue-eyed lady charmed me into buying the old wreck."

She paused, wanting to assume he was talking about her, but Calpurnia also had blue eyes and had certainly tried harder than she to coax him into buying the Grange.

She gave a stilted nod, but had to test the waters. "Calpurnia's very taken with you, you know."

He furrowed his brow. "What? Who cares? My God, woman, can you be such a dunce?" he exclaimed mildly when she started to voice a flimsy denial. "I don't like little girls," he informed her. Challenge glinted in his eyes as he narrowed them, scrutinizing her. "Why do you pretend not to notice how I feel about you?"

Grace nearly choked with shock at the frank question.

"I-I'm not pretending anything — and I have no idea how you feel!" she insisted with a gulp.

"So you didn't notice me kissing you at any point today?" he drawled.

"Well — yes, but — I just thought you were being — nice. B-because I was crying."

"I'm not that nice," he informed her.

She looked anywhere but at him, her cheeks scarlet, her pulse ticking in her throat like the second hand on a fob watch.

He laughed softly after a moment, as if he saw through her just as much as she had him on the night of the Windleshams' dinner party, when he'd gone on, telling all his colorful tales. As if the truth were not much bloodier, darker, more deadly.

"Please don't laugh at me, I'm shy," she admitted in chagrin after a moment, still red-cheeked.

"Yes, you are. And it's adorable." Turning to face her, he leaned one shoulder against the cart and tapped her on the nose. "Yet you frustrate me. Are you frightened of my desire for you?" he whispered.

She could not tear her gaze from his, could hardly get the words out, but at least they were honest: "A little."

"You needn't be. I'd never hurt you. Surely you know that."

"Yes."

"Maybe it's your desire that scares you most of all."

Without a doubt, she realized.

"Can we stop talking about this, please?" she begged him, equal parts mortified and aroused. "Was there something else you wished to discuss with me — about the village — my lord?"

He visibly stopped himself from protesting, and with a knowing smile full of patience, trailed a fond, sardonic gaze over her. "My lord, again. All right, very well, Miss Kenwood," he said in sardonic formality, "I want you to tell me how I can help. Where do we start?"

It was not easy to tear her gaze away from his earnest, businesslike stare, when longing for the man had flooded her body with the most bewildering sensations.

She managed to look away and took the further precaution of folding her arms across her chest to avoid hurling herself into his embrace. *Hullo?* She called mentally to herself. *Answer the question, Grace.*

Where . . . should they start?

A stray thought of how he'd looked the day he had rescued Denny from the river flashed through her mind. She could still see him soaked to the skin, his white shirt near transparent, clinging to his sculpted chest.

She closed her eyes, trying to rout the picture from her mind. *Sane and decent.*

Right.

Do you really think I'm beautiful? she nearly blurted out. *Me?* He must need his eyes checked. "Yes, ahem. Let's see . . ." She forced herself to focus on the rare opportunity at hand.

He was offering his help, and all of Thistleton needed it. Fortunately, sanity returned while he waited, studying her with a curious look.

"First and foremost, I suppose — if it were up to me, I would start with making sure we get whatever late-season crops into the ground that could be sown now — to be harvested this autumn."

"So we'll need workers."

"And livestock," she said with a nod. "Chickens, for the eggs. We might restock the old dovecote on the Grange, as well. Goats, sheep. A few cows if possible." Her ideas came faster, flying off the list she had been making for so long in her head without any hope of ever really seeing it come to pass.

Oh, ye of little faith, Papa had so often teased her. Yet here was the answer to their prayers — oddly enough, in the form of a consummate sinner.

"Repairs to the worst homes should be made before the cold sets in, and coal stores and kindling bundled for the winter. But my main concern is food," she told him. "You see the prices now, and with the weather all out of sorts, if it's this cold in June, how bad will it be in January? Nobody's ready."

"This will pass, you know," he assured her softly, lifting his big, warm hand to cup her cheek. "We're going to get through it, don't you fret."

She nearly melted at his reassuring touch. "That's what they say. And yet I feel like

I've been telling myself for years that things will get better, but nothing ever changes."

"It's changed now," he said firmly as he held her gaze. "You're not alone in this anymore. That's what I've been trying to tell you. I'm here now, and I'm not going to let you shoulder all the problems of this village on your own anymore." He took her hand between his own and lifted it to his lips, pressing a kiss to her knuckles.

She watched him, overwhelmed.

"Come along now." Keeping her fingers snug in his warm grasp, he handed her up to the driver's box. "It's late, and you've had a long day. You should be getting home to your father before he starts to worry." Then he went around to climb up easily onto the passenger side.

She was still in a bit of a daze as they drove back to the village with nary a word between them.

"Good night," he said when she let him off in the main square to go speak to the old men and Farmer Curtis.

"Good night, Lord Trevor," she answered faintly.

In tremulous silence, she watched him walk away, then she drove on home through the darkness. The way was familiar, but moonlight dusted the countryside with a snow of powdered pearl.

She still could not believe all that had happened today, and yet, with every yard of ground her weary horses covered, the higher her heart soared.

By the time she reached the parsonage, she feared that she was dizzyingly, dangerously smitten.

Quite possibly in love.

"There you are! I was just beginning to worry." Papa looked up from his studies as she floated by the open door to his office.

Grace returned and leaned dreamily in the doorway, still barely knowing what to think of all that had transpired.

Her father furrowed his brow and studied her from over the rims of his spectacles. "What is it, daughter? I can see the wheels turning even from here. What's happened?"

"I'm not quite sure, actually . . ."

"Are you all right?"

"Oh, yes!"

He arched a brow, scrutinizing her. "Anything I should know about?"

"Well, it's Lord Trevor," she said abruptly, and could hear the lingering amazement in her own voice.

"What about him?" Her father studied her face from across the room.

"I invited him to come along with Calpurnia and me on our charity calls today."

"Really? That was very clever of you. And did we learn his mettle?"

"Oh, yes. It would seem so, Papa."

"Well?"

She shook her head at her father, marveling. "He says he's going to help."

Papa studied her keenly from over the rims of his spectacles. "Indeed?"

CHAPTER 20

Three times throughout the night, Grace was jolted awake by a dream of falling. Each time the dream woke her, she lay there for an hour, unable to fall back asleep — her blood astir, her mind awhirl with thoughts of Trevor — and with contemplating the mystery of what was happening between them.

How could anyone sleep in such a state of flying exhilaration? Happiness . . . confusion . . . and a lingering disbelief that a bona fide hero could have taken any such notice of her. He might hate being called that, but she knew now that was what he was. It wasn't just idle gossip in the papers.

He was the genuine article.

Perhaps she was too trusting, but it didn't even cross her mind to doubt he'd do what he said. She put her faith in him.

By the time she finally drifted off again, the world beyond her window had lightened to a predawn gray, and the dewy air was thick with birdsong.

As morning crept over the countryside, she slept on, her cat curled on the opposite pillow, until, gradually, high-pitched voices invaded her slumber.

They were calling her name.

"Miss Grace! Miss Grace! We need to see you!"

"It's important!"

Her lashes fluttered in irritation.

"Miss Grace!"

She lifted her head off her pillow and furrowed her brow, recognizing the familiar voices of the Nelcott twins.

When she heard them banging on the front door of the parsonage just below her bedroom window, she suddenly sat bolt upright as the memory of the last time Kenny had come pounding on her door came flooding back.

What now?

The cat jumped aside indignantly as Grace climbed out of bed and rushed to the bay window, still in her night rail. When she opened the casement, a rush of bracing wind blasted her in the face and woke her up entirely. "Kenny? Denny? I'm up here!" she called down to them. "What's the matter?"

The boys backed away from the front door and came into view.

Denny grinned. "There you are!"

"Miss Grace, come quick! You have to come down to the village!" his twin hollered.

"What's wrong?"

"Nothing's wrong!" Denny answered merrily. "Miss Callie gave us a shilling to come fetch you!"

"Why?" she exclaimed.

"Lord Trevor's men brought loads of neat things to Thistleton on the canal boats! Everyone's there! You have to come and see! Lord Trevor's taking charge of everything!"

She blinked. "He is?"

"Hurry!" Kenny insisted. "You're goin' to miss his speech!"

"Speech?" she echoed in wonder.

"C'mon," Denny urged his brother. "Let's go back and watch them work the crane!"

Having carried out their mission to bring her the message, the boys dashed off again. Obviously, the twins did not intend to miss out on all the excitement.

And neither did she!

Grace pulled the window shut, rather dazed. She could hardly wait to see what was going on down in the village.

"Nine thirty!" she mumbled when she saw

the clock. *Oh, blast.* All her tossing and turning last night had made her oversleep. Her heart pounding with anticipation, she scrambled to wash up for the day and get dressed.

She quickly donned a beige walking dress with dark blue embroidery.

Mrs. Flynn looked up from scrubbing the floor as Grace ducked into the kitchen to snatch a piece of bread. "Morning," she said absently, then poked her head back into the kitchen before rushing off to get her bonnet. "Have you seen my father?"

"He went out on his morning walk, Miss."

"Oh — thank you!" Was she the last person in Thistleton to find out about the excitement of the day? Yet she had helped to plan it — well, at least a little.

It was a quarter till ten when she finished downing a few hasty swallows of tea and finally strode out onto the drive, still pulling on her gloves.

She shook her head over her late start. Walking briskly into town, the gusty wind buffeted the brim of her bonnet so she had to stop and retie her ribbons on the way.

The day was overcast, gray clouds like puzzle pieces with silver sun shining behind them.

The moody sky flung down a brief sprinkling of raindrops as she spotted the crowd gathered on the edge of the village around the canal boats' little dock.

For most of its journey, their branch of the Great Midlands Canal wended its way peacefully through the green fields of the countryside on its way to the next large town; but at Thistleton and countless other villages along the route, barges could stop to load or unload goods. Their rural dock, like so many others, was nothing elaborate: just a plain stone wharf area about thirty feet wide, with a sturdy iron crane to do the lifting.

A gentle, curving lane led down to the water's edge, its mild grade meant to make the arrival and departure of heavily laden wagons easier. Grace looked on, mystified, to find the lane and the open wharf area thronged with the citizens of Thistleton, all come to watch the great unloading.

The twins had not exaggerated. Half the village had turned out this morning. How had they all known to come? she wondered. Well, word had got out somehow. There was a festival atmosphere, and no wonder. This was the most excitement they'd had in Thistleton in many years.

Gracious, what all had been happening while she had been asleep? she thought, perplexed and a little put off by her lack of awareness, let alone any say, into whatever new business was afoot in *her* village. But one thing was clear.

Trevor had obviously been busy overnight.

She could only conclude that his meetings with the village elders had been fruitful. As she reached the back of the crowd, she realized how smart it had been of him to go to the old men first with ideas about how to help the village. This show of respect from a newcomer would earn him their acceptance.

Greeting her friends and neighbors here and there, she started weaving her way toward the water's edge and gradually got a better view of the proceedings.

Three plow horses lumbering along the towpath alongside the canal had pulled three long, low barges to a halt near the rusty iron crane.

The canal boats were laden with mysterious tools and crates and barrels, pallets of lumber and neat stacks of bricks.

Grace caught her breath when she saw Trevor aboard the first one, giving orders to several men who apparently had also arrived on the boats.

She gazed dreamily at him for a second, enjoying the fleeting sunlight on his shoulders, the wind riffling through his long hair, and the chill in the air rousing a ruddiness in his cheeks.

Then she spotted Callie waving to her from over by the towpath, up at the front of the gawking crowd. The debutante beckoned to her eagerly.

Grace went and joined her.

"Where've you been?" Callie exclaimed. "You've been holding up everything!"

"I have?"

"He wouldn't start without you. Good thing I sent the boys to fetch you, isn't it?" Callie waved to Trevor. "Lord Trevor, she's here!" she called. "He's going to address the village."

"About what?"

"I don't know for certain. Isn't he gorgeous?" she interrupted herself with girlish glee when he turned in answer to her call and waved, flashing a handsome smile, indeed.

Grace waved back, lifting a gloved hand, but though she could not help blushing, she refused to stare.

"He's got something up his sleeve," Callie continued. "I heard him tell your father he'll be counting on you to help organize the people — though I'm not sure what he has in mind."

"You've seen Papa?"

"He's over there." Callie nodded toward the crowd.

Grace followed her gaze and spotted her father conversing with Emily Nelcott. A gruff, weathered stranger was with them; he had an honest face, hard-hewn like a very battle-axe. Yet as Grace watched, baby Mary bouncing on her mother's hip charmed the rugged warrior. He cracked a smile at the babe's antics, seemingly in spite of himself, and whatever he said to Mrs. Nelcott, the long-grieving widow beamed, to Grace's shock.

"Who are all these men?" she asked Callie.

"Former soldiers. They work for Lord Trevor or his Order or something. The one there, talking to Mrs. Nelcott, he's their leader. Sergeant Parker. Lord Trevor told us Sergeant Parker has served as a bodyguard to many important people, even some of the Order agents' wives. He is their most trusted man."

"Really," she murmured, staring as Kenny and Denny appeared on either side of their mother and instantly started peppering Sergeant Parker with their usual barrage of questions.

Grace shook her head to herself. Had Trevor imported a crop of husbands into Thistleton among all his building supplies?

Bemused, she glanced again toward the canal boat. This time, Trevor caught her gaze and sent her a wink.

A little sigh escaped her. Thankfully, Callie didn't notice. Little did the man know he had spent half the night waltzing with her in her dreams.

A moment later, he jumped up onto a pallet of bricks and lifted his arm to signal for the crowd's attention.

"Ladies and gentlemen, thank you all for coming out to meet me and to hear what I have to say. For those I haven't met personally yet, my name is Lord Trevor Montgomery. As you probably know by now, I'm the one who bought the Grange. I'm very keen to get the farm producing again. So if you know anyone who's looking for work, please send them to me. I'll need at least fifty good laborers."

As Grace stared at him, lips parted in amazement, she was sure this had to be another dream.

The man was carrying out, nay, exceeding her father's original intentions when the reverend had invited him to come out to Thistleton. This was more than either of the Kenwoods had ever hoped for. Jobs for the able-bodied. Some genuine hope for the future that they wouldn't run out of food.

An infusion of money into the town meant livelihoods.

Dignity.

"I've been told by wiser heads than my own" — he gestured toward Farmer Curtis and the old chess-players — "that it's still possible to get a good crop of rye into the ground for the autumn harvest. That should be hardy enough to withstand the cold. But we're running short on time.

"Therefore," he announced in a deep, strong voice, "anyone who's willing to work hard with me now to get the crops in quickly will be entitled to wages as well as a one-percent share in the proceeds from the sale of this harvest, beyond what is put aside for the needs of the village."

A murmur of astonishment ran through the crowd.

"If you're interested, give your name to Sergeant Parker. He'll put you on the list and figure out where we can best use you.

"Also," he continued, "I seem to have ordered more lumber and other supplies than are necessary for my own repairs to the farmhouse. Since we have so much extra, and since you've all been so kind in welcoming me to your fine village, let me make a neighborly gesture in return and of-fer my men's services and my own to help my new friends with any pressing repairs to your houses or shops you need done before winter."

The whole town stared at him shock.

"Why would you do such a thing?" one of Lord Lievedon's ill-used tenants yelled out.

"Fair question," he replied, "and the answer's simple. I've been traveling abroad for the past several years. Now that I'm back in England, Miss Kenwood pointed out — I trust you all know the rector's daughter?"

Grace went motionless as everyone turned and smiled fondly at her. Two hundred faces, and she knew them all as well as she knew her own.

Nevertheless, all the attention suddenly struck her shy again. She wished she would've taken a little more than five minutes to get ready before running out of the house.

She saw Trevor smiling as though he, too, could feel the town's affection for her and was, indeed, relying on it.

"Miss Kenwood pointed out that if the weather's this cold now, we'd all do well to ready for winter early this year. Make sure our homes are warm, sufficient stores in our larders to get us through till spring."

"Easier said than done," one of the shopkeepers muttered loudly.

"I know, believe me," Trevor answered to the whole assembly. "All of England is enduring hardships right now. The past decade has been difficult on all of us. We've lost many friends, family members. These are not easy times. But if we pull together, I believe we can make good strides and make sure our neighbors are ready for winter before the cold sets in. So is anybody with me?"

"I am!" cried Calpurnia, shooting her hand straight upward to volunteer, which brought a doting chuckle from the populace, who had watched their little local princess grow up from an adorable child into a beautiful girl.

"Us, too!" the Nelcott twins whooped, jumping in place.

"And I!" the Reverend Kenwood called in his best Sunday sermon voice, sonorous and rolling.

And that was all that anyone needed to hear.

There was no higher authority in a country village than the word of a sensible pastor. The Marquess of Lievedon himself did not truly outrank Papa, at least in the eyes of these folk.

With his declaration of support, the matter was settled. Grace watched in fascination, realizing that her father had just publicly placed the trust of the entire village — and thus his own good name — in Lord Trevor's hands.

It was Papa, after all, who had summoned the hero to Thistleton.

Maybe he was shrewder than she gave him credit for, considering how he was always misplacing his spectacles . . .

Trevor nodded back to Reverend Kenwood in dutiful respect, as though accepting the mantle, and from that day on, all of Thistleton rallied around the new owner of the Grange.

The next two weeks brought a buzz of activity the likes of which the village had not seen since Colonel Avery had readied the menfolk to go to war.

Trevor deployed his army of civilians to attack the challenges of peacetime, dividing them up into squadrons and bringing in new recruits in the form of farm helpers.

These were never easy to find at this time of year, when proper farms were in the height of their haymaking, the busiest time of year on any English farm. All the most experienced hands were already working for others, so Trevor had to go to the nearest large town, Melton Mowbry, to hire men.

The workers he brought back told of decimated crops at so many farms where so much of the hay had been destroyed, there was precious little to harvest.

It was clear that feeding the animals, especially horses, over the winter, was going to get even more expensive. Fortunately, Farmer Curtis had advised that they reserve a few fields to grow mangel-wurzels, beetroots, as forage for the livestock. These were even hardier than the cold-weather rye intended for the humans.

With the farmhands ready to work, the fields needed dressing before the crops could be sown. The soil had rested during its fallow years and was sure to be fertile, but it had become hard-packed over time. Trevor set a first crew of laborers to breaking it up, turning the soil and aerating it, while a second crew dug out irrigation channels.

When these were cleared, he had them tend to the old fishing pond, which would be restocked with several varieties of edible fish.

He set another half dozen men to fixing fences and cleaning out the old dovecote to prepare for the animals and birds he would soon purchase. Repairs were also done on the large sheds where the sheep would be sheltered in winter — the usual time for the ewes to bear their young. By spring, the meadows would be full of frolicking lambs.

Meanwhile, the Nelcott boys led a contingent of village children on a mission into the wooded acreage of the Grange to gather twigs and fallen branches to be bundled up and laid aside for kindling. Papa walked through the forest with the children, making sure they stayed out of harm's way, especially when they neared Tom Moody's ramshackle cabin on the far edge of Trevor's property.

Papa reported that when he knocked on Mr. Moody's door, the place had been abandoned. Apparently, the troublesome drunkard had deemed it prudent to move on.

More canal boats came laden with supplies. One brought a great mound of coal, which was divided up among the residents — a gift to the village from the fat, jolly Earl and Countess Stokes, who were amused at Trevor's project.

Sir Phillip and Lady De Geoffrey were not to be outdone. When another barge arrived carrying roof tiles, bricks and mortar, paint and brushes enough for all the men to use, just as the work on the fields was finishing up, Sir Phillip took it upon himself to supervise the massive effort to repair the exterior of various villagers' homes.

Lord Windlesham looked on with his usual detachment, sitting astride his horse and idly smoking his pipe while Sir Phillip minded his tidy list of repairs to designated houses with the careful attention of a former law clerk.

Lady De Geoffrey and even Lady Windlesham joined in the community's effort, shamed, perhaps, into casting aside their complacency. No longer was it possible simply to sit by, judging and complaining, fretfully waiting for somebody else to solve the village's problems.

Their Ladyships now joined in the general effort with gusto, commanding a joint army of their own female servants to help sort out the dark, moldy, chaotic interior of the elderly Pottfords' home.

As it turned out, the only thing strong enough to stand up to Mr. Pottford's hoarding impulse was the iron will of Lady Windlesham herself.

Grace had to give her credit. The busybody baroness succeeded where everyone else had failed. On Her Ladyship's unyielding orders, the ancient Mr. Pottford finally parted with many square yards of his horrid, rotting junk.

Most of it was duly burned, the army of marching maids carrying it out by the armload, and throwing it onto the fire. When Grace came to view their progress after three days, she was amazed to see floor space and light coming through the windows, which the tireless maids were now washing.

She also called on Miss Hayes but had to let herself in, for her knocks went unheard over the loud piano scherzo coming from the parlor. "Hullo?" She found her blind friend seated at her newly tuned instrument, playing a duet with a smiling bald man who turned out to be the piano tuner.

He seemed charmed by Miss Hayes, and Grace was most intrigued to hear that it was his third visit to her house in a fortnight. Well, well, she thought.

Leaving the musical pair alone, she returned to her main task of coordinating the various groups, smoothing out conflicts, and making sure everyone had what they needed. Shortfalls were brought to the attention of the commander, but other than brief meetings, she saw little of Lord Trevor.

Her own time was divided between keeping the village children out of the way while their homes were being fixed, or drying their tears after Dr. Bowen-Hill had lined them up to give them their smallpox inoculations.

She also spent many hours lending her own needle to the women's sewing campaign. While the men readied the farm and fixed the houses, the women mended curtains to help keep winter drafts out of windows and whipped up new sets of warm clothes for those whose garments had grown threadbare.

At last came a day of celebration, when the fences were ready and the animals arrived on the canal boat. With them came great burlap sacks of seeds — rye and beetroot. The whole village marched in triumph to the Grange, Trevor at the head of them, laughing and leading one of the cows; his dog Nelson was ever at his heels, as was Calpurnia, which Grace tried to ignore.

The doves were released into their round stone turret and thirty chickens into their coop, along with their brightly plumaged rooster. The sheep and goats skipped into their new pasture ahead of twenty lumbering cows. Everyone cheered, astonished at the progress they had made in such a short time.

As Grace looked around, scanning the faces, she saw hope, so long absent, shining on each familiar countenance.

God bless you, Trevor Montgomery, she thought with a lump in her throat.

And finally, the time had come for planting.

She watched him walking through his fields among the people, personally making sure that the seeds they had worked so hard for were safely tucked into the waiting ground.

The women had prepared a few straw scarecrows, each one humorously made to resemble certain villagers, including Papa. Amid much laughter, these were staked into the fields to keep the birds away.

Grace shook her head to herself. Thistleton was hardly the same place. It looked better, tidier, the storefronts sparkled with bright windows and fresh paint, roofs everywhere freshly thatched or newly shingled.

A new vitality had infused the entire village.

People greeted each other with a vigor and cheer no one had seen for years. When Sergeant Parker announced he was marrying Mrs. Nelcott, Trevor threw the pair a party at the Grange.

The daylong celebration had the air of a church picnic, with music, games for the children, and each family bringing a favorite food. Farmer Curtis's contribution was a barrel of his homemade whiskey, which was tapped at dusk.

Grace and Callie watched as he handed off cups of it to Marianne to pass out to Sergeant Parker and his men.

"What is she doing here?" Callie mumbled.

Grace shrugged. "Maybe she'll find a husband, too," she replied, noting that every one of Sergeant Parker's soldiers seemed eager to volunteer.

Then again, it probably wasn't marriage that the soldiers had in mind.

"Look at her, preening. She loves the attention," Callie said.

Grace raised an eyebrow, hearing this particular accusation from the lovely blonde who had to be the center of attention at all times.

Nevertheless, she had to admit that the raven-haired Marianne did seem to be in her element, surrounded by men. She tossed her head, her dark eyes flashing, and made no-doubt-scandalous remarks as she passed out cups of liquor to the soldiers.

"Maybe some women are just meant to be whores."

"Callie!" Grace exclaimed.

"Well, it's true! You want to pretend

everyone's good at heart, Grace, but they're not. Her for instance. She's a harlot. Fortunately, she has no effect at all on Lord Trevor," Callie added in satisfaction, nodding at their host.

Grace said nothing of the conversation she had had with Marianne on that very topic.

"He's all yours," Marianne had teased her.

Unfortunately, Calpurnia seemed to have other ideas about who he was destined to belong to. "It's not fair," the girl remarked, still staring at Trevor. "Why is it all right for the likes of Marianne to do all sorts of unspeakable things with any of those men, when decent ladies like us are not even allowed to give a worthy gentleman a kiss?"

Grace clenched her teeth. It did not take any sort of genius to know which gentleman Callie was thinking of.

She dropped her gaze, struggling over whether or not to say something. No words of wisdom came.

Though she loved the girl like a sister, she could not deny that the sense of rivalry between her and Callie was growing ever keener — at least in her own mind.

Indeed, Grace did not like herself very much for the resentment she had begun to feel toward the vain but bubbly innocent. Jealousy did not comport at all with her notion of who she *was.*

Certainly, she did not want to be angry at Callie. But how could the girl be so vain and selfish as to assume straightaway that Trevor was hers for the taking? That what she wanted she *must* have, no matter how anyone else felt?

Ultimately, however, Grace kept her mouth shut because she didn't want to fight, especially not at a party.

Oblivious to all but her own desires as usual, Callie suddenly elbowed her with a chuckle. "Look at him over there. Isn't he darling?"

And, of course, he was.

Trevor was coughing and laughing after sampling Farmer Curtis's famous firewater. "God, that's strong!" He thumped himself in the chest with his fist.

"Then you'd best have some more!" Farmer Curtis replied.

The men laughed heartily, and Grace smiled, but Callie turned away from the sight of Marianne twirling from man to man. "How jealous George would be if he could see his little harlot with all of Sergeant Parker's men!" she said with a scowl.

Grace seized upon the girl's mention of her former beau; it was the first time in weeks that Callie had brought up that particular topic. She chose her words with care. "I wonder what George would have to say about all that's been happening," she ventured with a probing, sideways glance.

Callie snorted in disdain. "It's his own fault for missing it. By all rights, George should've been the one to start all this work long ago. He *is* the heir of the highest-ranking local lord, after all. He could have easily taken it on himself. Instead, Lord Trevor's done his work for him. But that just goes to show that Lord Trevor is a man. George is just a boy."

"Trevor does have ten years on him, to be fair," Grace pointed out. "That's a lot of life experience, not to mention all sorts of training in leadership."

"Precisely. But how long does it take a man to grow up? I'm tired of waiting."

Grace couldn't argue with that; indeed, Callie's words reminded her of the beautiful Laura Bayne, who had given up waiting for Trevor after being betrothed to him for a few years.

Before she could think of anything wise or comforting to say, she saw her father beckoning her over to welcome the Pottfords to the party. The ancient pair would no doubt need a little help getting situated, so Grace took leave of Callie and went to greet them.

She was eager to find out how they were adjusting to their newly uncluttered home.

Callie remained sitting alone beneath the big old oak tree, watching the maids light the paper lanterns strung up around the party as twilight fell.

Soon, Grace was fetching chairs and plates of food for the Pottfords, but in the midst of assisting them, she happened to glance over toward the oak tree, only to spy Calpurnia walking briskly toward the farmhouse by herself.

Something in the girl's posture made Grace instantly sense trouble.

Her words trailed off in midsentence; she swept the surrounding grounds with a quick, curious glance.

She noticed that Lord Trevor was no longer in sight, drinking with the men. She did not see him anywhere.

Of course, it was growing dark, but he was not among the villagers sitting around the bonfire; he was not among the people dancing or clapping in time with the music; nor did the glowing paper lanterns reveal his muscled silhouette anywhere on the green.

He must have gone inside, she thought. And when Calpurnia also disappeared into the house, a dire suspicion suddenly bloomed.

Good God! Bold Calpurnia was about to make her move! If Lord Trevor was discovered alone in a room with the brazen debutante — even if he behaved like a perfect gentleman — he'd have no choice except to marry her.

Grace blanched. "Would you excuse me?" she blurted out, already on her way to try to avert a disaster.

"Something wrong?" Papa called after her with a frown.

"No, no, I-I'll be right back." She rushed off, shocked at her own raw jealousy, but still, she was not about to let that bratty girl rope Trevor into marriage.

After all he'd done for the town, at least he deserved to choose his own wife.

But Callie was so infatuated with him, and had been from the start, that Grace would not put it past the headstrong belle to try to snare him in a compromising situation, just so she might win him for her own.

Something had to be done, and right away.

"Kenny! Denny! Quickly! Would you boys please come over here and help me with something?"

The twins heard her call and came bounding over. She leaned down to give them their instructions in a confidential murmur, then sent them running off into the house: her little spies.

Heart pounding, Grace folded her arms across her chest and waited in a nervous state of guilt for exactly two minutes before she followed the boys into the house.

Marching inside, she felt like a liar but wore what she hoped looked like an innocent expression on her face.

"Kenny? Denny?" she called, feigning ignorance as she stepped into the house.

"Up here, Miss Grace!" one twin yelled down the steps after a moment. She glanced up the staircase as the boy waved to her over the railing, not from the second but the third floor. "We're up here!"

Grace nearly choked on a sudden rush of fury. This was worse than she had thought! The third floor was usually where the bedchambers were located.

Exactly which room were they in? What on earth did Callie think she was doing? Lifting the hem of her skirts, Grace dashed up the steps, her heart pounding in dread at what she might find. She followed the cheerful sounds of the children's endless questions. "What's this for? What are you going to build in here? How long will it take? Can I help?"

When she stepped into the doorway, she found all four of them. Her little spies seemed to have had no trouble locating their quarry. On the floor, Kenny was jabbering on while playing with the Brittany spaniel's floppy ears. Denny was carefully tapping a nail into a scrap of wood with Trevor's hammer, and Calpurnia had cornered Trevor by the wall.

Though a neophyte, she was flirting with him for all she was worth, laughing and playfully running her fingers over his lapel.

Grace bristled at the sight, but Trevor cast her a long-suffering glance over the girl's head, a silent plea for help. "Ah, Miss Kenwood!" he greeted her in relief.

Callie whipped her wandering hand back down to her side and spun around to face her with a guilty, wide-eyed blink.

"There you are!" Grace forced out with a smile. "Boys, they're about to serve the cake — oh, and Miss Windlesham, your mother's asking for you."

"Me?"

Grace managed a friendly nod, while Trevor rolled his eyes in exasperation as soon as the girl's back was turned.

Faced with the reminder of her mother's wrath, for not even Lady Windlesham would sanction such behavior in the interests of landing a husband, Callie lost her nerve.

Thank God, thought Grace.

"Well, I guess I'd better go see what she wants," the girl mumbled in disappointment. But she stole another fawning glance at Trevor as the Nelcott twins stepped in to carry out the task Grace had previously arranged with them; each youngster grabbed one of Callie's hands and dragged her out of the room, telling her to come and get the cake.

Trevor let out a huff of exasperation when they were alone. "Thank you for the rescue," he muttered when at last they were alone. "That was close."

Grace was overjoyed at his annoyance with the girl but resisted the urge to gloat, smiling ruefully at him.

Turning to make sure the three had indeed gone, she rubbed the back of her neck, trying to seem casual despite her self-consciousness. "I had help." Then she paused, acutely aware that she was now the one alone with him in an empty room, in the same compromising position she would have forbidden Callie.

Well, now she was a hypocrite as well as a jealous fiend. Her veneer of virtue was wearing away fast.

"I'm going to have to have a talk with her," he remarked with a glum look, then let out a sigh.

"Maybe it's time I wrote to George," Grace suggested.

"Brentford, Miss Windlesham's former suitor? That's a brilliant idea."

"I'll see if I can get them to reconcile. Heaven knows George is still in love with her."

"Please do, by all means."

She grinned. "I'll send a letter first thing tomorrow. Hopefully, he'll be able to take her off your hands."

"I would be grateful." Hands in pockets, Trevor leaned against the wall and smiled fondly at her. Grace smiled back. "Are you enjoying the festivities?"

"Oh, yes, my lord. You're an excellent host. Are you enjoying yourself, too?"

"I am now."

"Charmer," she chided softly.

His smile broadened. "I have some news."

"Oh?" She tilted her head in curiosity.

"Sir Phillip has just made me the new constable."

She laughed aloud. "Are you serious?"

"I am. You knew it was coming, didn't you?"

"I suspected."

"Well, it's soon to be official. So don't do anything naughty, or I may have to arrest you."

"Me? Naughty?" she retorted.

"Oh, yes," he answered evenly, narrowing his eyes as he fixed her with a wicked half smile. "Come, Miss Kenwood, you may fool the rest of the world with your all-conquering niceness, but I have firsthand experience of your naughty side from a certain night in Lievedon House, remember? And cue the blush," he added with a sardonic laugh.

She folded her arms across her chest as, indeed, her face turned scarlet. "You obviously have me confused with someone else. I am Grace Kenwood. I am practically a saint. Ask anyone."

"Right," he whispered. "Why don't you come over here and let me see about that?"

"Are you trying to tempt me?" She bit her lower lip, enthralled by his searing stare.

"Is it working?" He put out his hand. "Come here," he ordered softly.

She swallowed hard and took a cautious step closer. "You'd better not try to kiss me," she breathed, though that was precisely what she longed for him to do.

"Never." He reached out and captured her wrist, tugging her nearer. "It's just that I haven't seen much of you lately, with all the work going on. I've been missing my pretty friend. Missing our talks."

"Talks?" she asked with an arch smile as he gathered her into his arms.

"Aye, just talking," he assured her in a whisper. He took hold of her waist and drew her up against his chest.

Grace quivered when his hand pressed gently into the small of her back, a slow, sensual caress that focused her fevered attention on how perfectly their bodies fit together.

"So how've you been?" he whispered, but she never got the chance to answer the playfully casual question, for he tipped her head back with his fingertips and claimed her mouth.

His kiss deepened as she opened her mouth wider for his questing tongue. As she wrapped her arms restlessly around him, clinging to his shoulders, weak-kneed with desire, Trevor turned her with a smooth motion, bracing her back against the wall.

He kissed her harder, faster, driving his body against hers. She moaned in pleasure and confusion. Trevor threaded his fingers through hers, lifting her hands above her head to pin her to the wall. He kissed her again and again and did not stop until she was panting.

But voices from downstairs warned them not to get any more carried away than they already were.

It would have been so easy to do. Grace couldn't stop touching him, exploring his chiseled jaw with her knuckle, twining her fingers through his long, dark hair, rubbing the muscled expanse of his chest.

She wanted him — and he knew it.

He closed his eyes and licked his lips with a small moan as though he couldn't get enough of her caresses. But when the noises from downstairs grew louder, after a moment, he captured her hand and kissed it, bringing her explorations to a halt. "Come to me whenever you're ready," he whispered in her ear. "I'll be here, waiting for you." He kissed her chin softly where his day's beard had chafed her skin, then he nuzzled her cheek and skimmed his lips along her throat. She tilted her head back to cradle his face against her neck, her fingers threading through his long, dark hair.

But when he lifted his head again and braced his hands on the wall on either side of her, Grace looked up to meet his stare and saw the hungry smolder in his eyes.

He needs it bad, Marianne had opined, and Grace was beginning to think that she did, too.

"Whenever you want me," he repeated in a searing whisper, and it was all suddenly more than she could bear.

She dropped her gaze, her blood on fire, her cheeks burning. He let her escape with a patient, knowing gaze full of hunger; her pulse pounding in her ears, she ducked beneath his muscled arm and fled.

CHAPTER 21

"You look different," George said to Grace when he arrived a few days later in answer to her urgent summons.

They went out onto the terrace and sat down on the chairs.

George stretched out his long legs and crossed one champagne-polished bootheel over the other. "This whole place seems different, actually. What's happened around here?"

"Lord Trevor Montgomery, that's what happened."

He furrowed his brow. "The Order agent?"

"He bought the Grange, haven't you heard?"

At first, George received this news with a curious smile, but then he shot up from his chair, his face draining of color. "Has Callie met him?"

"Yes," Grace answered darkly. "That's why I wrote to you."

416

George stared at her for a long moment with a stricken look, no doubt remembering all those ladies mobbing Trevor on the night of the ball at Lievedon House.

"Very well, don't try to spare my feelings," he said as he slowly lowered himself back into his chair. "Is she in love with him?"

"Maybe a little," Grace admitted gingerly, "but we both know Callie belongs with you! George, listen to me," she insisted when he cursed. "If you're ever going to sort out this bad blood between Callie and you, you're going to have to stop being so passive. Take responsibility for your relationship with her and for your own actions. That's what a man must do."

"I had a feeling you were going to say that." He shook his head uneasily. "I don't know if I'm ready for this."

"Well, it's either that or lose her." She paused. "I know you love her, George. You and Callie belong together. You have to make her see that. The time has come for you to win her, whatever it takes, as I said in my letter — or this time, I fear you may lose her for good."

"But, Grace, I'm an idiot! A scoundrel!"

"Excuses."

"Facts! I'm a happy-go-lucky rake. How can I ever compete with a hero of the Realm like an Order agent, especially when he looks like a bloody demigod like Montgomery? Ugh, I think I'm going to be sick."

"George," she soothed with a sympathetic frown.

"I'll die if I lose her! I'll die if she marries someone else! She's probably already forgotten I exist."

"No she hasn't. She mentioned you just the other night."

"She did?"

"Yes. Now get ahold of yourself," Grace scolded. "You don't have to worry about Lord Trevor and Callie."

"Why?"

"Because he's —" She stopped abruptly. It seemed too bold, too grandiose to claim that he was in love with her. "That is," she cast about, "Lord Trevor and I —"

George's eyebrow slowly rose. "Yes?" he prompted.

Grace stared at him, tongue-tied.

"What? How now, Miss Kenwood? Are you telling me . . . you and the Order agent?"

She closed her eyes and nodded fervently as her cheeks turned radish red.

George let out a short, loud, and very roguish laugh. "Jove's braces! Well how do you like that."

"Oh, George, I love him terribly." The words slipped out in spite of her modesty. "If I had any idea what agony it is to fall in love — but I didn't mean to!"

"There, there, my dear. I know. I sympathize, believe me. But are your affections returned? They'd better be, for if he breaks your heart, I'll run the bleeder through. Even if he murders me before I have the chance to draw my sword."

"Ah, there's no need for that," she said with a tremulous laugh. "For, yes, I have reason to believe that he cares for me, as well."

"Well, dash my wig," George murmured, gazing at her. "Somebody finally got to you."

"It's not so strange, is it? I am a woman. I do have a heart."

"One so diligently turned to love of fellow man that I wasn't sure you were capable of the Cupid sort."

"Not capable?" she protested.

He shrugged.

"Well, the little bounder obviously had an arrow with my name on it hidden away in his quiver," she said. "I suppose it was only a matter of time."

George chuckled and leaned in his chair. "I'm so proud of myself! I feel absurdly responsible for this somehow. After all, you

419

were at *my* house when you first saw him."

She shot him a dubious look. "And I recall your saying you told your father's secretary not to invite him."

"And you were the one cringing in terror that 'the assassin' was going to kill everyone in the ballroom!" he retorted, and Grace giggled.

"Well, he hasn't killed anyone since he arrived here, so I think we'll be all right."

"I'm glad you have amended your opinion of our celebrity guest."

She paused. "Are they still talking about him in London?"

"A bit. Not as much, though, now that his former fiancée has married her new beau." He looked askance at her. "Do you think he knows about that?"

"No." She puzzled over this. "I don't think so."

"From the sound of things, it doesn't seem like he's going to care."

"I hope not. He's already been hurt enough." She sighed. "I can't believe that after his involvement with such a dazzling beauty, that he'd ever look on me —"

"Oh, don't be a cake-head!" George cut her off with lordly indignation. "Honestly! What are you, fishing for compliments?"

"No!"

420

"You're as lovely as any other woman out there, Grace. You just try to hide it, for some strange reason. I've no idea why."

"Vanity is wrong," she said after pondering it briefly. "One oughtn't parade oneself."

"Why not? Everybody else does! You'd like to blend into the furniture if given a chance."

"Not anymore," she replied.

George studied her intently. "I see. Well, if that is the case, then this fellow is good for you, and therefore, I approve." He bowed his head.

She laughed.

"As happy as I am for you, and for him, frankly I am happiest for myself. This really means he has no designs on Callie?"

"None whatsoever," she replied, mimicking his slouching pose with a one-shouldered shrug. "He sees her as little more than a child. He's nearly twice her age, after all. He's tried to drop the hint, but you know Callie. Once she makes her mind up, she's not one to take no for an answer."

"Ho, believe me, I know it," George answered with a snort.

"I don't want her to make a fool of herself, and I really don't want her to be hurt. You must help me. At this point, to be honest, you are my only hope. Otherwise, war might break out in the village. At least between the Kenwoods and the Windleshams."

"I see . . . What exactly shall I do?"

"Simple. Go and make up with her and save her from heartbreak. You're the only one who can prevent a lot of sorrow around here if you can persuade her that she belongs with you, not Trevor. I'm worried, George. I don't want to lose her friendship any more than you want to lose her love. I just want everything to be peaceful."

"Do you really think she's in a frame of mind to forgive me?"

"I'm not saying it will be easy," she admitted, watching the birds flit from tree to tree. "But most ladies can't resist a man who's genuinely sorry, especially if he is willing to grovel to be given another chance."

"Grovel?" He shot her a skeptical frown. "I am a future marquess."

Grace shrugged. "You either love her or you don't. Besides, you know full well that even a marquess can be miserable if he lets love slip through his fingers."

"Hmm." George slouched again and scanned the cloudy sky. "Very well," he said judiciously at length. "I will do this thing, no matter how she rails."

"Callie loves you, deep down."

"Very deep," he said wryly.

"I firmly believe she doesn't have any intention of ever marrying anyone else but you. Her interest in Lord Trevor is but a fleeting infatuation. I think she longs for a serious love in her life. You just have to show her that you're the one she's meant for and that you're ready."

George was silent for a moment, pondering her words. Then he reached into his waistcoat pocket. "Do you think this might convince her?" He pulled out something that glinted in the light.

When he held it up between his fingers, Grace marveled. A diamond ring! "Well done, Georgie-boy," she murmured in astonishment. "That's the spirit!"

"I had a feeling you were going to say these sorts of things to me. I brought it just in case you thought she might finally be receptive." He grinned and tucked the engagement ring safely back into his waistcoat pocket. Then he shook his head and took a deep breath. "As they say, I shall either come back *with* my shield or *on* it."

Laughing, Grace reached over and squeezed his hand in affection. "Now, George, that's what the Romans said to a young man going off to war, not one setting out to win the hand of his lady."

"Love, war, same thing. Either one, you bleed for."

"When did you become a philosopher?" she asked in amusement, as he rose to undertake his mission.

"All gamblers are philosophers, poppet. Hard-won wisdom. It's the one thing you have left after you lose your shirt."

"Bosh. Now then," she said, rising to see him off, "I want to be the first to hear the news of how you fare! And remember, the bit about Trevor and me is still a secret, all right?"

"She's going to find out eventually, isn't she?"

"Yes, but not until the two of you make up. After that, she shouldn't mind so much that Trevor and I want to be together. Nor will her mother," Grace added pointedly.

"Such scheming, Miss Kenwood!" he taunted in mock disapproval.

"I have no choice. If it goes badly, Lady Windlesham is sure to paint me as the villainess of the county."

"So you had devious motives for summoning me here all along."

"I can't help it, George! I love him so much, my heart could burst."

"Well, we can't have that, can we? Fear not, dear lady." He laid his finger to the side of his nose and gave her a wink. "I can be as secretive and sneaky as a spy when the occasion calls."

"Good luck, George," she answered in affection.

He leaned down and gave her a brotherly kiss on the cheek. "Same to you, my dear. Now go get 'im." He elbowed her in teasing affection before striding off to his carriage.

She watched him spring up into his phaeton. Instead of waving farewell, the jester made the sign of the cross over himself. "Wish me luck! Better yet, get your father to start praying because this is probably going to take a miracle."

"You'll do fine. Just don't lose your temper. And remember to grovel!"

He sent her a dubious wave, then drove off.

Grace stood there for a long moment, watching his elegant phaeton zooming away down the drive behind his prancing horses. In truth, she was nervous for him. She prayed that Callie was in a good mood today.

She knew the debutante was at home. Hopefully, Lady Windlesham would not spoil everything by a gushing overreaction when her original, hoped-for son-in-law appeared at the front door.

Lady Windlesham had always been George's greatest campaigner with her daughter. Perhaps that was part of why the teenaged girl had dug her heels in — not just to punish George for cheating but to defy her overbearing mother.

Then Grace's restless thoughts about her neighbors and everything else faded as she cast her gaze out beyond the trees toward the Grange.

All her focus — mind, body, and emotions — homed in on the prospect of taking Trevor up on his scandalous invitation.

A shiver of desire moved through her. She closed her eyes and lowered her head, losing the battle against temptation. How long had she been fighting it?

She did not want to fight anymore.

She took a deep breath and stared at the ground, then tilted her head back and looked up at the sky.

Everything in her longed for him. Suddenly, she gave up trying to resist. Surrendered to her need. She left the doorway of her father's house without a backward glance and started walking down the drive.

Her pulse thrumming, she refused to think of anything except the next step over the graveled ground, the next and the next, until she was on his doorstep, rapping on the door with a hand that shook, her heart pounding.

And when he came to the door, opened it, and saw her, she took an uncertain step forward, then she was in his arms.

He did not make her talk, did not ask her to explain.

She launched herself into his embrace and kissed him passionately. He pulled her into the house with an arm hooked round her waist.

She heard the door bang as he pushed it shut, but she paid no mind, enthralled in the fevered stroking of his open mouth on hers. She clung to him, trembling. Then he swept her off her feet and carried her upstairs to his bed.

Joy and lust surged through his veins, a heady, potent brew spiked with startled relief that she had come at last. That this was finally, actually happening. Intoxicated by her fiery onslaught, Trevor felt like the lad who'd kicked the beehive: Instead of stings, she swarmed him with delightful kisses all over his face and neck and chest.

He knocked his chamber door shut behind him and set her on her feet. She drove him back against the closed door and came at him again, her hands planted on his chest like she meant to have her way with him.

Trevor didn't know whether to groan or laugh at her ardor. Surely, she did not want him to take her all the way quite yet? Didn't she want him to marry her first?

It was all the same to him. He cupped her face between her hands and plunged his tongue more deeply into her delicious mouth.

She moaned and curled her fingers round his nape beneath his queue. Perhaps it was convenient that she had found him in a casual state of dress. Expecting to do a hundred tasks at home today, he had not bothered with waistcoat or cravat. She was already pulling his loose white shirt free from the waist of his trousers.

An echo of memory from the first time he had got his hands on her echoed through his mind. *Floor or the couch, chérie?* "I guess you finally know what you want," he whispered, panting, when she let him up for air.

She gave him a seductive half smile that rather shocked him, coming from her. Blazes, what had he got himself into? he wondered in delight.

"You," she answered, then she clutched the crisp lawn of his shirt. "Take this off, Montgomery."

"Yes, ma'am." He lifted his shirt off over

his head and dropped it on the ground — which made the massive bulge in his trousers all the more obvious, but what could he do?

His battle-ready cock was as hard and proud as any granite obelisk erected by the pharaohs.

A monument to how very well behaved he'd been with her.

She looked at it, then let her gaze climb over his bare torso. Her fingers followed; he twitched with want as they trailed lightly up his belly and over his solar plexus.

He swallowed hard, his chest heaving. Whatever she wanted, he thought as he stared at her in hunger.

"What is this?" she murmured as her fingers stopped on one of his scars.

He glanced down at it. "Beauty mark."

"It looks like an old bullet wound to me."

"Or that." Unable to hold back, he captured her by her elbows and drew her closer. "I'm sure I'll tell you all my war stories one day, darling. But not now." Kissing her again, he started undressing her, gently pulling the white fichu away from the neckline of her gown.

He untied the sash around her waist while she stood dreamily, letting him. Leaning closer, he lipped her earlobe, and whispered,

"Off with your dress."

Her lashes flicked upward; she looked uncertainly into his eyes, then visibly remembered that she trusted him.

She made her decision, and as she took off her dress, Trevor went mute with awe at her virginal trust.

Trust, not gold, not silver nor platinum was the rarest commodity on earth. He should know, having tasted betrayal by those who had once mattered most.

Grace turned away and went to drape her walking dress demurely over the back of a nearby chair so it wouldn't get wrinkled, and watching her, his very heart clenched.

So sweet. So innocent. So good.

Then she turned around shyly, and his eyes glazed over, his mouth watering.

Gorgeous, heavenly tits.

"Good God, Miss Kenwood," he purred. "What a body you've been hiding under those prim gowns."

"I beg your pardon, my lord?" she cried, turning redder than she'd ever done before.

Trevor flashed a rueful grin. "Sorry. But . . . it's true," he added, raking her curves with his dazed stare. Then he met her gaze, and said quietly: "Get over here."

She approached him warily, her stockinged feet silent over the dusty, hardwood floor.

430

The sunlight teased him, making her chemise slightly transparent as she padded toward him with wide eyes full of nervous desire.

She was devastating, really, he thought, and he could only shake his head in amazement at his sheer luck in finding her. Maybe he should start taking Nick's place at the gaming tables because he was obviously a son of fortune.

"You are ogling me," Grace said.

"You deserve to be ogled," he replied as he took her hand and pulled her closer. "Leered at. Drooled over. Absolutely lusted for. But only by me."

Then she smiled and brought the very heavens down into his room.

"You're rather lovely yourself."

"For an old hunk of Swiss cheese."

She chuckled. "I get it. Because of the holes."

He laughed softly. "It's so nice to be understood." But he could not stop staring at her chest. "My God, Grace, honestly."

She frowned at him in self-conscious confusion, but he skimmed the creamy expanse of her chest with one knuckle, taking it slowly. Her firm, round breasts were plumped up on display, lifted for his perusal by the corset that hugged her rib cage and her waist.

But looking was not going to be enough for him. Trevor wanted to taste. So he took her in his arms and kissed her with re-assuring protectiveness, while his fingers roamed behind her back and delicately plucked away the lacings of her stays.

When he had freed her from the corset and dropped it on the floor, a very curious thing happened. It was as though by losing that strict, binding garment, the wanton in her was fully unleashed.

He felt the change in her posture, in her touch, in the way she sighed and ran her hands down his biceps while he, in turn, kissed his way down her shoulder. His heart pounded with anticipation as he lowered her chemise on one side, to bare one rip-ened, beautiful breast.

He went slowly to his knees, his arms around her, as he took her nipple into his mouth. She tipped her head back weakly and let out a groan while he sucked and savored her like she was made of marzipan.

She melted accordingly, stroking his hair, letting him play. "You are absolutely stun-ning . . . delicious," he rasped hoarsely as he moved to the other breast.

The moments became a sensual blur of want and bliss and heightened awareness.

The next thing he knew, he had her on her back in his bed and was caressing her through her chemise. Her hips and her stomach entranced him almost as much as her wonderful, addictive bosoms.

She held him in her arms as he lay beside her, but when she bent her knee restlessly, he took that as his cue to let his fingertips venture underneath her shift.

Gliding his hand up her thigh, he felt the honeyed cascade of the dew dripping from her core and trembled with need. Somehow, he held himself back, pleasuring her with his hand until she was writhing — but he wanted blindly to devour her. Moving over her with a wholly possessive intent, he swept downward over her silken body to receive her first orgasm on his tongue.

Her clit was swollen, rigid, as his tongue played and stroked, his fingers gliding in and out, her light garment bunched up above her waist.

Grace's hands rested atop his head, her fingers twining through his hair as he brought her to a silent, heaving climax. He could hear her panting and smiled against her tenderest flesh as he surmised she was biting back a wild shriek. "It's all right," he whispered against her belly. "You can scream. Nobody will hear you."

"But, y-you'll think I'm a harlot," she whispered, gasping to catch her breath.

"You silly girl, I could never think that of you. And even if I did, it would be our little secret," he promised, flicking his tongue into her navel. "Let's try that again, shall we?"

"Oh, God, Trevor!" she wrenched out as he returned lower and softly kissed her ripe and ready womanhood to the next level of delight. Her hips moved with his open-mouthed kiss though he supposed she had never even imagined that such naughty pleasure was possible. Oh, she had much to learn, and he could not wait to teach her. He knew he had been born to love her, in every sense of the word.

No wonder he hadn't died on his many missions, he thought as he licked and sucked her quivering mound. He knew now that he was meant to die in her arms.

On her second climax, she raked her nails into his shoulders, her head thrashing on his pillow like that of a woman fighting to survive some unbearable tropic fever.

I have got to fuck you soon, he thought, feeling his own control slipping. "Need a break?"

"No."

"Good girl," he purred in devilish approval, abandoning his southward post. She

434

trailed her fingers over his still-wet chin as he rose over her. Trevor dipped his head to capture her fingertip in his mouth. She groaned again as he sucked her fingers one by one and slowly lay between her legs.

Though he wanted her like he'd never longed for any woman before, he still did not *seriously* mean to deflower the pastor's daughter . . . until she said his name in that particular way.

"Trevor."

It was the most seductive sound he'd ever heard in his life. Breathless wonder. Innocence. Womanly need.

And love.

He heard it in her voice. And he knew that she, of all people, Grace Kenwood, the tower of virtue, would not be here with him in his bed unless she truly loved him.

Struggling with unbearable temptation, he could feel himself losing the battle as he glided his hands down the hourglass curves of her body, then grasped her juicy buttocks when he reached her hips. God, he could explode just from touching her. *You are almost too much for me.*

"Please, Trevor," she begged him in tremulous whisper. "I want this just as much as you do."

He shut his eyes, shaken by her "please,"

and promptly lost the war.

Raw want, rough and primal, flooded into his veins, flowing in from some far deeper reservoir of need than any woman had ever tapped in him before.

"Take me," she panted, grasping his waist.

"You'll marry me," he ground out.

"Yes, yes, of course — just, please . . . make love to me. I've needed you forever." She smoothed her palms down the small of his back, pushing his unbuttoned trousers down over his hips. When she grasped his buttocks, his conscience vanished, his will buckled. So much for good intentions.

This virgin had seduced him. As his lips lingered at her sweat-misted brow, he guided his pulsating member to the teeming threshold of her passage.

She sighed in restless satisfaction as he slowly penetrated her. The velvet welcome of her body made him gasp. Lots of women had wanted him over the years, but never an angel giving herself to him as his innocent bride.

"Oh, Trevor," she groaned his name again. "I thought it was going to hurt. But it's wonderful. It's so deep."

"I told you I'd never hurt you," he whispered, and he was glad then that he had taken the time to make her fully ready, kissing away every last inhibition. Now that she was open to him in every regard — her lush body, her sharp mind, and her honorable, compassionate heart — he was glad for every day, every hour that he had restrained himself with her. It had been so deliciously worth it.

She wrapped her legs around him with an instinctual knowing and chafed his chest, up and down, maddeningly with her palm. Her touch made him have to fight not to go insane. *Patience, patience.* She seemed game for whatever he wanted to do, but nevertheless, it was only her first time.

He cast about for some way to hold back, his chest heaving. How easily she could have made him lose control.

Somehow, he held himself in check and kissed her over and over again as he rocked her tenderly, making her utterly his own. He fondled her thigh and slipped his middle finger into the top of her stocking when he came to it. Grace hugged him with her legs and draped her arms around him drunkenly, perhaps intoxicated by pleasure.

They moved in unison, as naturally attuned to each other as they had been from the first night they had danced together at the Lievedon Ball. She hugged him hard in her embrace; he knew she was close and fought for all his worth to hold back just a little longer.

A crazed cry broke from her lips. When she came again, with his cock buried deep inside her, it was more than he could bear. She had barely finished screaming out when the storm broke from him, so long and carefully pent up.

He took her like a wild man, forgetting all his thoughts about patience, holding back. He was swept away by blind, raging hunger that only she could fill. Braced on his hands above her, his hair falling in his face, he ravished her in a blaze of savage pleasure, deaf to the slams of his bed frame pounding on the wall.

All he could hear were her sharp, crazed moans of delight.

A low shout of release tore from his lips, as well, and when he finally stopped, he was shaking and covered in sweat.

Careful not to crush her with his weight, he shuddered with a belated throb of sensation as he withdrew from her body and eased back a bit. He lay atop her.

"Oh, *Trevor.*"

"Oh, Grace." He smiled drunkenly, then kissed his way up her throat, rounding the angle of her chin. When he looked down into her eyes, they were sparkling like a thousand stars above the sea.

She bit her lip against a shy, girlish grin.

Trevor stared down at her, utterly in love.

She wrapped her arms around him. "Are you all right? What is it, darling?"

"Nothing. Well — actually, I have a confession to make."

"You do?" she whispered tenderly, caressing his bare back in long, slow, languorous strokes.

"Everything I did in this town," he told her softly, "it was for you. But surely you already knew that."

Joy misted her blue eyes. "I suppose I had my suspicions, but I never would presume. I just thought since you're a hero — it's true, you are — and that's what heroes do."

He looked at her with a rueful smile, uncomfortable with that term.

"You're *my* hero," she amended, seeing his hesitation. She cupped her hand against his cheek. "And I'm going to love you more than any other woman ever could."

"I trust you, Grace," he whispered, holding her gaze.

It was the biggest compliment he knew how to give.

She took his face gently between her hands. "I will never betray that trust. I'll never hurt you, either, darling. I've waited all my life for you."

Words failed him at her earnest stare. He couldn't speak, so he merely nodded, then smoothed her hair and kissed her once again.

When she smiled at him so warmly, so intimately, Trevor was amazed to realize that at last, he had truly found the place where he belonged. Whatever he'd done for this village, it was nothing compared to what she'd given him. Love, acceptance.

And a home.

CHAPTER 22

Meanwhile, on the other side of town, alas, things were not working out half so well for George.

He flinched as Callie Windlesham laughed in his face.

"Marry *you*? After what you did to me? You must be joking. Go away with your boyish games. I'm tired of them and tired of you!"

He strove for patience and humility, though heaven knew neither were his forte. "Callie, I made a mistake. I admit that. I was wrong, and I am very, very sorry."

"That's not nearly good enough!"

"Please! Can't you see I'm trying to grovel here?"

"As well you should! Listen to me and listen well, Lord Brentford: You are a very bad young man."

"I thought that was just part of my charm," he muttered under his breath.

But Callie stalked across the drawing room toward him, counting off his failings on her dainty fingers. "You are addicted to gambling. You chase after inappropriate women. All you care about is yourself, your own pleasures. Having fun!"

"We could have fun together, don't you see?" he attempted.

"There's more to life than that! Aren't you ever going to grow up? If you weren't so distracted with all your pleasures, you might have noticed that you are needed here in Thistleton — but I suppose you are too spoiled and selfish to care."

"Oh, *I'm* spoiled and selfish?" he shot back, stung sharply enough to retaliate. "Are you sure you aren't talking about yourself, little princess?"

"Don't come into my house and insult me."

"It's not an insult if it's the truth," he retorted.

She folded her arms across her chest and glared at him, but George scowled back.

"Stop trying to act like you're so perfect. You just merrily assume that everyone else's world revolves around you, including mine!"

"It ought to if you loved me."

"God, give me patience!" He dragged a hand through his hair, fighting the urge to throttle her. "What do you want from me, Callie? What is it going to take?"

She looked at him for a long moment, thinking it over, apparently. "That's a good question. Frankly, you deserve to suffer, George. You cheated on me with a harlot —"

"Here we go again," he huffed, dropping his head back.

But his lapse in groveling clearly enraged her.

"You had my heart, and you threw it away! I loved you —"

"You did?" he asked in astonishment.

"But not anymore!" she bellowed loudly enough to be heard in the next county.

George felt his heart crumple. "Oh, Callie, please don't say that. I didn't know how much you cared at the time. You hid it!"

"I had to! That's how a young lady is trained!" she wailed. "She has no choice but to be coy until the ring is on her stupid finger!" Tears flooded her eyes. "God, I hate you! Why did you come here, just to rub salt in the wound?"

"You know why I came here. Because I love you." Gathering up the full measure of his courage, he suddenly dropped to one knee in front of her and tried again to take her hand. "Callie, I'm telling you, that night with Marianne meant nothing to me. How do you think a young gentleman is trained? When you have — certain feelings, you go to a girl like Marianne. Not a lady! Not your future wife. It isn't proper! Should I have come to you instead? Your father would've shot me, and I'd have ruined you."

"Humph!" She turned away, pivoting on her heel and pouting at the wall, arms crossed.

"Humph, what?" he asked, bewildered. Then it dawned on George that she wanted his kisses.

And possibly more.

He was so shocked he could have fallen over.

"You must think I'm an empty-headed fool."

"O-of course I don't think that," he sputtered, still trying to wrap his mind around the fact that Callie's rage at him might actually be born of passion.

"Yes, you do. You must think I'm a nitwit if you're actually trying to claim you only slept with her to protect me from your — manly impulses."

He rose again, still dazed. "Every member of White's has got a mistress, married or not," he mumbled.

"Well, I will never have that kind of marriage, George. Never, ever, ever, *ever*! It's awful and it's wrong. And what about your gambling? Have you got excuses for that today, as well?"

"Callie, I'm not addicted to gambling. It's just something to do! I have no talents. How do you want me to entertain myself? I'm an heir to a marquisate. I'm not allowed to do anything useful, remember?"

"You could have helped your father's tenants. He doesn't even notice the sort of shape they're in, as long as their rents are paid —"

"Believe me, you won't get any argument from me that Father has all the warmth of an iceberg, darling."

She turned, eyes narrowed. "And you're too much of a coward to stand up to him."

George froze as though she had just slapped him across the face. "What did you say?"

"It's not an insult if it's the truth, isn't that what you said?"

"I am not afraid of my father. You know it's just that I have to dance to his tune, or he'll cut me off."

"Exactly. You're a child. Not a man."

He stared at her in shock, insulted to the core.

"As selfish as you are, George, you see,

that's not even your worst fault," she mused aloud, gloating at him. "You could have helped the villagers. In fact, it should have been you, and that's why I'll never love you again, because *you don't care* about anyone else."

"Yes, I do."

"You don't even notice that other people exist. You're too much of a *coward* to let yourself care."

George drew in his breath and turned away. If a man had dared to call him that most unacceptable of names, the one label that spelled destruction to any gentleman's honor, it would have meant bloodshed.

But since she was a lady, he could do nothing but stand there, futilely, impotently, and take it.

So the girl he loved thought he was a coward.

It went against everything in him, but he tried to grovel one last time, just to prove her wrong, recklessly putting his heart on the line to a degree he never thought he would've dared. "Callie, I do care. Why else would I be here?" He swallowed hard. "I'm in love with you."

"Well, you're too late," she said in cold satisfaction, reveling in her moment of

446

revenge. "I've found someone better than you."

George went motionless, frozen to the core.

"Someone brave, kind, strong, noble, and unselfish. A man, George. Not a boy like you."

"Have you, indeed?" he forced out, scoffing outwardly to hide the fact that, inside, he was crushed.

"Yes, I have," she flung out, lifting her chin. "And there's nothing you can do about it! All I have to do is bring him up to scratch."

"Please, tell me his name, by all means. Who is this paragon of manhood?" he bit out, already suspecting.

And there it was.

"Lord Trevor Montgomery!" she answered with a flourish, and then it was George's turn to laugh.

Coldly.

Callie furrowed her brow. "Why are you laughing? You look down on him because he's a younger son?"

"I'm not laughing at him, my dear. I'm laughing at you."

"What? Why?"

George didn't even try to fight it. All he wanted was to hurt her in some small measure, just like she had hurt him. "He has no interest in you. He's in love with someone else. Someone far more deserving, actually."

Callie looked shocked for a second, then scoffed with indignant denial. "You don't know what you're talking about."

"Oh, yes, I do. I suspect they are together even now. I'm sorry, does that hurt your precious feelings?" He ignored a twinge of conscience; after all, he hadn't mentioned Grace's name.

Callie gave him a withering look. "Honestly, George, for all your many flaws, at least you've never been a liar until now."

A liar and a coward? he thought, stiffening. It was not to be borne. "Fine, don't believe me. I wasn't supposed to tell you, anyway. If you'll excuse me, Miss Windlesham, I'll take my leave of you and don't worry, I won't darken your doorstep again. *Adieu.*"

"George!" she snapped after him as he walked toward the doorway.

"What?" he growled, pivoting.

She studied him in suspicion. "Surely you weren't referring to Grace Kenwood?"

He could not resist goading her. "Hmm?" he asked innocently.

Her eyes narrowed to fiery blue slashes.

448

"That's ridiculous! Lord Trevor cannot possibly prefer a plain, boring spinster over me!"

"Ouch," he said with a wince. "You really can be quite a harpy, Callie dear. If that's how your treat your friends, no wonder my life's been hell being your enemy. Thank God I don't care anymore, as of this moment. But, consider this: Maybe it takes a paragon to love a paragon, and a sinner to appreciate a sinner. Which reminds me. I think I'll go and visit Marianne."

"Oh! You'll never change! Fine! Go! I still know you're lying!" she yelled out the door after him.

"Am I?" he called back easily as he jumped up into his phaeton.

With a final cold glance at her, swallowed up in defeat, George slapped the reins over his horses' rumps and left.

"Vermin!" Callie said under her breath after he had driven off. *Well!* she thought. *I'm going to get to the bottom of this.*

Then she yelled at the groom to ready her pony gig and soon went barreling off to get some answers for herself. With her carriage wheels throwing up a furious dust cloud behind her, Callie headed for the Grange like a young Athena in her chariot, off to war.

■ ■ ■ ■

Grace lay in Trevor's arms, savoring their
closeness, though by this point, they had
put on at least some of their clothes again.
With their passion spent for now to a state
of peaceful, warm contentment, it seemed
as good a time as any to tell him what she
had heard.

"Trevor?" she spoke up uncertainly.

"Hmm?"

"I have some news from London that I
think you'll want to know. But it might
upset you . . . unless, of course, you've
already heard. But I don't think you have."

Lying on his side, his cheek propped on
his right first, he paused in drawing little
circles on her chest with his fingertip and
frowned. "What is it?"

She hesitated, scanning his face. The hard
planes and angles of his countenance had
softened with tenderness after their love-
making. She did not want this intimacy
between them to be strained, but she had to
give him the news. "George told me your
former fiancée has now married her new
beau."

"Oh, that," he said absently, to her relief.

"I'm sorry," she offered.

"I'm not," he replied.

Grace was pleased but did her best to be sympathetic. "It must have been difficult to lose her."

"Ah, I think I came out all right in the end." He stole a kiss.

"It really doesn't bother you?"

"No. In a way, it's a relief."

She looked at him in puzzlement.

"Grace —" He struggled visibly for how to put it. "I was never as close to her as I am to you. Perhaps you find that hard to believe, given all the time we were officially a courting couple. But I'm afraid our failed alliance had more to do with ego than affection."

"Really?" she asked in surprise.

"Mm-hmm. I'm afraid we saw each other as an enviable catch with which to impress our friends. And our families approved, as well."

"So you didn't ever really love her?"

He gave an idle, one-shouldered shrug. "I thought I did at the time. But now, in hindsight, I think that simply knowing I had picked out a wife and had my future plans all sorted out made it easier for me to put that part of my life in a box — mentally speaking — and set it aside, so I could concentrate on my missions for the Order."

"Ah," Grace nodded, contemplating this. "Did you tell her about the Order?"

"A bit. Given the risks, I didn't expect her to go into it blindly. That wouldn't be fair to anyone. I never shared specifics, but I at least wanted her to have an idea of what she was getting into."

"What did she think about it?" she asked as she ran her hand lovingly over the broad angle of his shoulder and traced the hard sinews of his arm.

"Oddly enough, she wasn't really curious."

Her roaming hand stopped its explorations as she looked at him in astonishment. "Not curious!"

"I don't think she really cared, to be honest with you." He hesitated. "Truth is, I don't think she ever really cared that much about *me*. She fancied my friend, Beauchamp."

She shook her head. "Then why on earth get engaged to her?"

"Eh, every woman wants Beauchamp. You probably will, too, when you meet him."

"No, I won't!" she said indignantly, but he just chuckled.

"The point is, Beau saw through her, while I was dazzled by her looks. She was a trophy that other men would envy, that is all. I'm not proud of my motives. But her shallowness, her superficial attachment to me, her lack of curiosity, indifference — all of it actually made my life much easier, and there it is."

"I see. So you could have your cake and eat it, too?"

He nodded. "A suitable betrothed by my side when I had need of her for family occasions and the like, then I could set her aside and simply go about my business. Damned cold of me, wasn't it," he stated.

She gave him a rueful half smile, but she wasn't about to convict him, considering that Lady Laura's loss had been her own most splendid gain.

Trevor sighed and rolled onto his back, gazing at the ceiling for a moment. "Well, I hope she will be happy with the dragoon. Because I intend to be very happy with you."

With that, he pulled her on top of him and began kissing her with renewed intent. Grace laughed breathlessly between kisses as she felt his body respond beneath her as she straddled him.

But then, all of a sudden, the sound of Nelson's barking outside alerted them to the arrival of some visitor.

"Oh, be quiet, you silly mongrel!" an

angry voice outside yelled at the dog.

Grace and Trevor looked at each other in sudden shock, recognizing that voice.

"Calpurnia!" Grace whispered, leaping guiltily out of Trevor's bed.

"Shite. What is she doing here?" Trevor muttered, then he, too, was on his feet, pulling on his shirt, hastily tucking it in.

"George must have said something he shouldn't. Blast that foolish churl! He promised!"

"Don't worry, I'll take care of this," he said, as an angry rapping sounded on the door below.

"Lord Trevor! I know you're in there! Is Miss Kenwood with you? I need to speak to her!"

Grace shut her eyes and pressed her fingertips to her forehead, feeling a trifle dizzy. "What a debacle. I'm going to wring George's neck."

Callie banged on his front door. "Come down here and face me, you two! I deserve an explanation!"

"No, she doesn't," Trevor said quizzically. "What is she talking about?"

"She's in love with you!" Grace exclaimed.

He rolled his eyes. "I've tried to drop the hint — and now she's breaking in," he said dryly when they heard the door fly open downstairs.

A heartbeat later, it slammed behind her. "Lord Trevor! Grace?"

"I'll go talk to her." He left the bedroom with a scowl, but Grace knew she couldn't leave all the unpleasantness to him. Especially when most of this was her fault. She had to face Calpurnia herself, as painful as that was going to be for both of them.

She hastened to finish getting dressed, though the shaking of her hands slowed her progress fastening her buttons. To be sure, the sweet languor of the past hour in Trevor's arms dissolved as she faced the full brunt of her mistake. If only she had been honest!

But she had not wanted to be cast in the role of villainess, getting in the way of Callie's dreams. Guilt flooded into her mind as she saw she had also been a coward, too scared to risk crossing Lady Windlesham.

Most of all, she had lacked the faith, and indeed, the confidence in herself to believe that someone like Trevor could actually love her, that she might have a right to her own dreams and happiness.

The whole time she had thought she was being unselfish, trying to deny her attraction to him, in truth, she had been trying simply to shield herself from disappointment in a hope that seemed too good ever to come true for her. What she had called virtue had merely been a lack of guts.

Thankfully, Trevor had that in spades, but even so, she couldn't leave him to face the music alone over what had happened here today.

"I can't believe it," Callie was saying in a withering tone to Trevor. "You led me on."

"That's a lie," he bit out. "If you really believe that, it was not I but your own vanity that deceived you. How many times did I pull away from you when you threw yourself at me?"

"I did not!"

"Oh yes, you did. I didn't want it to come to this, Callie — you're just a child. I hoped you'd take the hint. I'm sorry. I'm not interested. You are too young for me, and my affections are elsewhere engaged."

"So I see." Callie's eyes narrowed as Grace came uncertainly down the stairs. "You! Traitorous witch! So it's true, then, what George said. You *are* Lord Trevor's mistress!"

"Well, I wouldn't say I'm his *mistress,* exactly —"

"And here I thought we were friends!" she shouted, tears rushing into her eyes.

"Oh, Callie, I didn't mean to hurt you."

456

Grace started forward.

"Stay away from me, you strumpet! Hypocrite!" she accused her in a shrill tone. "You go around acting like you're better than everyone else — so virtuous! — but you're no better than that, that harlot, Marianne! No wonder you're friends with her. The two of you are just a pair of man-stealing whores!"

Grace dropped her jaw as Callie ran out crying.

Trevor glanced at her, an eyebrow arched.

"This is terrible," Grace uttered when she finally found her voice. "She's going to go running home to her mother, and it's going to be a scandal."

"How can it be a scandal when I'm going to marry you?"

"My father is a minister! Oh God, how could I do this? I've hurt everyone," she said abruptly, as her stomach knotted up. "Callie's heart is broken, and my father's reputation will be tarnished —"

"Calm down," he interrupted gently. "Listen to me. Here's what we're going to do. I'll go speak to your father right now. You take my carriage and catch up with Callie before she reaches the village. Try to calm her down. Tell her it's all my fault — say I seduced you if you want. I don't care

457

if you blame it on me. At least then she might not try to ruin your reputation. In the meanwhile, I'll go ask your father for your hand. Don't worry, everything will be well."

As panicked as she was, his words temporarily captured her full attention and made her heart clench. Turning to him with a melting look, she leaned toward his solid frame. "We're really going to get married?"

"I'm not foolish enough to let you get away," he replied, bending down to kiss her with a handsome smile.

Moments later, however, they parted ways, dashing off on their separate missions.

Grace wasn't sure how things were going for him at the parsonage, but to her dismay, she failed to catch up to Callie before the girl reached the village.

"Oh, Lud," she mumbled under her breath when she saw Callie's pony gig parked outside the Gaggle Goose Inn behind George's fancy phaeton.

Jumping down from the driver's seat of Trevor's carriage, Grace quickly tied his horse to the hitching rail. Well aware that her own appearance was still nowhere near up to her usual prim standards, but guiltily tousled and flushed, she picked up the hem of her skirts and ran into the tavern to see what was going on.

Even before she opened the door, she could hear Calpurnia screeching in girlish fury. The piercing shriek that escaped through the pub's doorway when Grace arrived spooked the horses tied up outside.

Calpurnia stood in the middle of the tavern, her back to the door, her fists balled at her sides.

Before her, sprawled in a chair at one of the tables was George, cravat undone, a bottle of whiskey in his hand — and Marianne seated proudly on his knee.

None of them had noticed Grace's entrance just yet, in the sheer volume of Calpurnia's rage.

For a moment, Grace feared the girl would attack the tavern maid.

George's deliberate taunting was not helping matters.

"What do you care, Callie? You just told me in no uncertain terms that you want nothing more to do with me. Well, I give up. I promised not to trouble you anymore, so why did you even bother coming in here? Is it because you finally realized the great Lord Trevor is out of your reach? Pretty little fool! Well, don't come crawling back to me —"

"In your dreams!"

"Because you're out of luck. Now Marianne here, she knows how to treat a fellow. Don't you, love?" George gave her an amiable slap on the thigh. "Come on, girl, let's get out of here."

Marianne stood up with a languid motion though she kept her hand on George's shoulder with a proprietary air, her chin high as she sent Callie a gloating smirk. The ex-harlot was clearly loving the chance to gloat at Callie's loss, but Marianne faltered when she saw Grace come in.

"What is going on here?" Grace exclaimed, as George stood and tucked the ex-harlot's hand into the crook of his elbow.

Calpurnia spun around and glared at her. "What are *you* doing here? Somehow managed to pull yourself out of Lord Trevor's bed?"

Marianne gasped at this revelation.

"Egads," said George. "Well done, Grace. I expect you'll soon be married. Felicitations. Fortunately, I myself escaped that fate. Come along, Marianne. Let's get back to London."

"Marianne, where are you going?" Grace cried, as the raven-haired woman let him lead her by the hand toward the door. Callie fairly hissed when she brushed by her.

"Back to London," Marianne replied.

"But why?" Grace exclaimed. "You've got a whole new life for yourself here! You've been doing so well!"

"Sorry, Miss," Marianne replied. "I'm grateful for all you've done for me, but I'm never goin' to fit in here. Especially now," she added, with a withering look at Callie. "I might as well go. A girl's got to make a living. Besides, I'm sick o' this place, and Lord Brentford just offered me his carte blanche."

"George!" Grace uttered in shocked reproach.

He gave a boyish shrug, then swaggered off, taking his new plaything with him. "*Au revoir,* Miss Windlesham. I hope you have a nice life and find just the sort of husband you deserve."

"Marianne, please, you don't have to do this!" Grace insisted, following her as George led her out to his phaeton. "You can't go back to that old existence. You've come so far! Don't throw it all away!"

"Virtue don't keep a lass warm in the winter, Miss Grace, beggin' your pardon. Enjoy Lord Trevor," she added with a cheeky wink. "Better you should have 'im than little Miss Toplofty."

"Oh!" Calpurnia uttered, looking her over in withering indignation.

Grace glared at George as he jumped up onto the driver's seat. "I thought I swore you to secrecy."

"I'm sorry, couldn't help it. Well, the truth had to come out sometime! And as for Calpurnia, she's going to have to live with her choice because I won't be back."

He sent his former idol a cold look, then drove off without saying good-bye.

Grace turned to Callie in despair. "Can we talk, please? I didn't mean to hurt you —"

"Stay away from me! I hate George, and I hate you!" she wailed, then she ran out bawling and fled home to her mother.

Good God, Lady Windlesham! She had temporarily forgotten about the baroness. Grace shut her eyes and knew she'd better batten down the hatches for the full fury of the coming storm.

Meanwhile at the parsonage, Trevor also braced himself, for Reverend Kenwood was seriously displeased by the news of their fornication.

For all his spy skills as a trained liar, Trevor respected her father too much to dissemble when the old man asked what was their hurry.

Trevor stammered his way through a

euphemism about their being together and how Calpurnia had walked in.

Then the good minister sat in stunned silence, too furious to speak for a long moment. He glared at the floor, nodding slowly, and tapped his cheek with his finger, one hand obscuring his mouth, as though to stop himself from bellowing with fatherly outrage.

"Let me see if I have this right," he said at length. "As of this moment, my daughter is a fallen woman. You seduced her. And the whole village is about to know it."

"Uh, yes. More or less. But I-I do love her, sir, very much. And you have my word I will take excellent care of her for the rest of her life."

"I see."

The reverend eventually got his ire under control and grumbled that of course they had his permission, but he was not happy.

Not one bit.

And no wonder, Trevor thought. In his own way, her father was as selfish as George, quite content to let his daughter use up all the years of her youth taking care of him instead of establishing her own life.

Well, no more.

They were going to have a life and a family of their own just next door. This last fact was the only point that mollified the old man when Trevor pointed it out. "She won't be far from you, sir. You'll still get to see her every day."

Reverend Kenwood grumbled, but he gave Trevor a piece of paper to fill out to apply for the marriage license, and that very Sunday from the pulpit, he read the first of three weeks' banns announcing their upcoming nuptials.

The old tradition gave anyone a chance who objected to the match to come forward and state why a couple could not marry.

Of course, no one did. Not even Lady Windlesham.

Still, Trevor doubted that Grace and he would ever be invited back for another lavish Win-Din at the Hall.

It was a few days later in London when Marianne awoke to a loud knock on the front door of George's bachelor lodgings.

She lifted her head from the pillow; beside, her, George slept on. The banging came again.

Marianne furrowed her brow. She sat up quietly in his gilded bed, glanced at her sleeping keeper, and slid her mercenary gaze toward the door.

The Wedgwood clock on the mahogany

side table informed her it was nearly noon, so of course, George was not awake yet. For her part, she was not yet dressed, still tousled and scantily clad in the new silk peignoir that her doting protector had given her. Depending on who was at the door, however, this might be perfectly appropriate attire . . .

Especially if it was one of his rich, young, aristocratic, fellow rakehells.

She rolled out of George's bed and set her bare feet on the floor. Pulling on the matching silk robe, she padded out of the bedchamber and down the little hallway to the sitting room at the front of George's fashionable apartment.

Beside the front door, an elegant pier glass hung on the wall above a slender console table.

Marianne paused and glanced at her reflection, fluffing up her hair a bit and licking her lips to make them shine. She hoped with all her might that it was one of George's pretty fellows coming to call on their fashionable comrade. It was important for her survival that his rich friends get a good look at her wares, for she had a feeling that although George was fond of her, he would not be keeping her for long. He was too humiliated by the fact that his man parts hadn't worked with her again last night. Whatever that Windlesham wench had done to him this time, it had affected him in a most distressing way.

Marianne, with all her tricks, had been astonished at how his formerly randy member had refused to cooperate.

Honestly, a girl could be insulted.

She had assured the poor lad it wasn't his fault, but nevertheless, George had proceeded to get drunk and curse Callie Windlesham for this shocking new affliction.

All Marianne knew was better safe than sorry.

She straightened her posture, opened her robe just enough to give a glimpse of her cleavage, then continued languidly to the door.

When she opened it, however, and saw who was standing there, she gasped in horror and immediately tried to slam it shut.

"Hullo, love. Miss me?" Jimmy Lynch planted one tattooed hand on the door. His eyes glinted with cruelty as he smiled, one foot thrust in the doorway, clad in his usual snakeskin boots.

"What are you doing here?"

"Oh, I'm sure you already know." He forced the door open a little wider as his greedy gaze trailed over her. "Well, look at you. Lookin' finer than ever. Where you been, Stella?"

"Go away," she uttered, instantly starting to shake from head to toe.

"Come, now, you weren't goin' to cut me out of your windfall, were you, love? I always knew you'd do well for yourself, and now, look at you. A proper high-class courtesan."

"Get out of here," she whispered fiercely, trying to hide her dread of him. "I don't want to see your face ever again."

"Wot, after all we been through? I'm hurt. News just hit the rookery you're back. I don't know where you've been hidin', but the boys told me they saw you ridin' in some rich man's carriage in Hyde Park. So I did some askin' around. Heard some young lord has given you carte blanche. Is he here?" the infamous flash man asked, glancing past her into George's fine apartment. "Because if he is, he needs to pay."

"You don't own me," she vowed. "Whatever I earn, the money's mine."

"Now darlin', you know better than that."

"You'd better get out of here before he hears you. Believe me, you don't want to tangle with him," she warned, but he saw through her bluff and snickered.

"I've missed your sass." He cupped her cheek; she smacked his hand away.

"Don't touch me!"

"I'm sure he doesn't give it to you like I do," Jimmy whispered. "You do look mighty fine in that gown."

"I say, what is going on here?" George came shuffling out in his long drawers, bare-chested, his hair sticking out in all directions, his eyes full of sleepers. "Who is this?"

"My, my, is this the lucky fellow? Lord Brentford, ain't it?"

"That's right," George said proudly, glancing from Marianne to their cutthroat visitor in the purple coat. "Who are you and what are you doing here?"

"Name's Lynch. I'm our lovely Stella's business partner."

"Stella?" he echoed.

Marianne dropped her gaze. That was the old stage name Jimmy had given her when she had first got started in the business of taking off her clothes for an audience.

"Sir, whatever your business here," George said in a tone of aristocratic hauteur, "this is not the hour to conduct it. I can't even think how you got past the guards at the gate. Marianne will have to see you later. For now, I'm afraid you have to leave."

"Marianne?" Jimmy echoed with a smirk,

making no move to go. He looked askance at her. "Why, he must mean a lot to you if you let 'im use your real name."

George frowned. As sleep and the groggy aftereffects of too much drink the night before began to clear, he noticed the stranger's flamboyant yet shabby clothes, tattoos, and snakeskin boots, and it dawned on him what manner of man this was.

And suddenly he was outraged.

How dare this low piece of filth come to his very doorstep?

Keeping an admirable check on his fury, George sauntered over to the wall and casually picked up his dress sword. "Leave. Now," he advised as he stalked toward the door. "You have no business here."

"My business is standin' right in front you, milord." Lynch gestured at Marianne.

"George," she cautioned. "Jimmy controls a gang in Seven Dials, called the Rooks."

"I don't give a damn," George replied. "Begone now and don't come back."

"If you want my merchandise, you going to have to pay for it."

"Of course I'm going to pay her," George replied through gritted teeth. "It's none of your affair."

"No, you horse's arse, you pay *me.* Now, we either need to come to terms, or she's comin' home with me. Where she belongs," Lynch added coldly.

Marianne whimpered when the flash man grabbed her arm and started to pull her outside.

"Take your hands off my mistress!" George roared with Callie's accusation ringing in his ears.

"You're a coward."

He'd show her.

"Unhand her or die!" he ordered, bringing the tip of his sword up to Lynch's throat.

The whoremonger instantly reached into his waistcoat for his pistol. Marianne screamed and George reacted with his blade, slicing downward at Lynch's right forearm.

Lynch dropped the gun with a furious yelp of pain. The pistol fell and slid across the polished parquet floor of George's apartment. Marianne lunged after it and picked it up in shaking hands, aiming it at her longtime tormentor.

Whose arm was bleeding profusely.

"You little bastard," Lynch said to George. "You're a dead man!"

"Jimmy, wait," Marianne started, lowering the pistol as her former flash man turned away from the door.

"Look what he's done to me!" he bellowed. Then he headed back to his carriage, throwing George a glare over his shoulder. "I'll be back soon, milord. Don't doubt me. I know where you live!"

"Jimmy, please! Let me come with you. I can bind the wound —"

"Are you mad?" George stopped her when she started to follow him. "Let him go!"

"You don't understand!" She turned to him with terror in her eyes. "Jimmy doesn't make idle threats, George! You need to get out of London before he comes back here with an army — probably tonight. I've seen this too many times, George, please. You need to get out of Town and hide! I'll try to talk to him. Maybe I can calm him down. Otherwise, believe me, you've insulted the wrong man; for his reputation's sake, he won't rest until you're dead." She handed Lynch's gun to George, then rushed out the door.

CHAPTER 23

Dinner at the Kenwoods' that night held an atmosphere of forced cheer. All three of them — Papa, Trevor, and she — were trying very hard to put things back to normal.

Nobody spoke of it aloud at the table, but Callie had made sure to tell the entire village about finding Lord Trevor and the rector's daughter *en flagrante delicto* at the Grange. And no wonder. It was the biggest scandal to hit Thistleton in decades.

Grace barely knew what to do with herself. She had never been the subject of gossip before, did not know how to feel with so many people disapproving of her.

Lady Windlesham was the angriest, of course. Her Ladyship had taken time out of her busy day to track Grace down and give her a memorable tongue-lashing.

Lady De Geoffrey had pursed her lips in prim disapproval when she saw Grace at church. Even Mrs. Bowen-Hill had seemed pained to greet her.

Most devastating of all were Papa's stern private words about sin and carnality and having raised her better than that. Could she not have waited until marriage? he had thundered. Thankfully, it was a rhetorical question, one too humiliating to answer.

In any case, she had no reply. It was not the sort of thing she could explain, especially to her clergyman sire.

With so many people disappointed in her — a bewildering state of affairs after having been universally admired for her virtue — it certainly caused her to see herself in a new light. True, she had failed miserably in her role as a good example to others.

But Grace Kenwood: passionate? Scandalous?

Disapproval seemed absurd when loving Trevor came so naturally.

All she knew was that no amount of public censure could truly make her regret what she had done.

If anything, it was oddly liberating. One thing was certain — being painted as a scarlet woman gave her a whole new respect for her failed "project," Marianne.

She understood now more than ever how much courage it took for a woman to hold her head up when the whole world disapproved. To be sure, the fear of that disapproval had been a large part of what had held her back from going to Trevor sooner.

Whatever happened, he was worth it.

Fortunately, a lifetime of service and good behavior coupled with Trevor's extraordinary efforts to help the village meant that Thistleton's disapproval did not equal banishment.

Anyone could see that as a couple, they were very well matched. Most people were happy for them, just not entirely pleased with how they had gone about it.

Not that it was anybody's business.

Callie, however, sadly showed no signs that she'd be forgiving her anytime soon. Grace felt awful that Callie had been hurt, though she was hurt, as well, by the girl's determined effort to ruin her reputation and turn the village against her.

As for George, well, Grace was angry at him, too, for revealing her secret against her specific instructions.

She could only blame herself for trusting an immature rake in the first place. She had been a fool to pin her hopes on the idle wish that somehow George's actions, reconciling with Callie, could magically solve her problem for her.

Instead, it had only made everything worse.

In any case, with all of the tears and painful reproaches of the past few days behind them, at last, the village, and especially Papa, seemed ready to let her and Trevor look ahead.

They had a wedding to plan, after all.

Only Trevor himself had taken everything in stride this week. The ex-spy was unflappable.

Indeed, she thought, the man was a rock. She supposed that when you had spent years of your life with enemies trying to kill you, a little disapproval from the local villagers was nothing to make a gentleman sweat. Dirty looks and whispers were easier to shrug off than bullets. He truly didn't care what anybody thought. It was inspiring to her, actually.

At length, Mrs. Flynn brought out the roast beef that had been cooking for hours in the oven and filling the parsonage with wonderful smells.

The dog, Nelson, followed at her heels, and ignored Trevor when he ordered him to sit.

The dog went everywhere with him now, which Grace's cat did not at all appreciate. The oversized red tabby was hiding under

Grace's bed upstairs behind the closed door of her bedroom.

When Mrs. Flynn retreated to the kitchen, the reverend said a prayer over the meal. Though their heads were bowed, Trevor and Grace gazed at each other across the table with a sparkle of impropriety in their eyes.

"So, how long is the guest list these days?" her father inquired a little while later, as they dug into the meal.

"Well, we have a bit of a dilemma," Trevor answered. "I have brothers, sisters, and all their families with them, and my fellow agents from the Order, and there's nowhere to put them all. The village inn isn't nearly large enough, and even if it were, I'm afraid some of my siblings would not consider it fine enough for them."

"Well, I don't think we can count on the Windleshams opening up their home to offer hospitality, even for the family of a duke," Grace drawled. "Pity."

"Nor Lord Lievedon, considering George's role in all this," her father added wryly.

"Maybe it would be easier if we just eloped to Gretna Green," Trevor said, then he took a large bite of beef.

"Certainly not!" her father said with a scowl of indignation. "I'll not have my daughter married by some Scottish black-smith."

Trevor sent his bride-to-be a wink.

"Humph," said Papa, but Grace just gazed at her intended with an adoring blush.

Just then, Nelson growled, perking up from where he had curled in the corner awaiting a handout that was sure to come. The spaniel suddenly jumped to his feet and trotted toward the front door to investigate. Then a bark exploded from him.

"Stop that racket!" the pastor scolded.

Trevor rose to restrain his pet, waving off Mrs. Flynn, who came hurrying out to assist with a dish towel over her shoulder. "Someone at the door, sir?"

"I'll get it," Trevor said casually. They heard him a moment later ordering his dog to be quiet. Nelson obeyed, and when the door creaked, Grace could hear Trevor talking to someone. "You'd better wait here for a moment," he said to their visitor before coming back into the dining room.

"It's your friend George, Lord Brentford," he said, bracing his hands on his waist. He gave Grace a probing look. "Do you want to see him or not?"

"Of course, send him in," her father said, though for Grace, the decision was a bit more complicated. Still, it was her father's house, and she knew that it was wrong to hold a grudge. She nodded to Trevor and decided to be cordial to the bounder.

A moment later, George came into the room, looking chastened. Her father stood and shook their visitor's hand.

"Of course you can come in," he told the prodigal warmly. "You're always welcome here, m'boy."

George lowered his head, then glanced uncertainly at Grace. "Thank you, sir. Miss Kenwood," he added a bit more gingerly.

"Join us," her father invited him, gesturing toward the empty chair. "Have you eaten? Please, help yourself. Mrs. Flynn," he called to the housekeeper. "Would you set a place for Lord Brentford?"

"Oh, that's all right. I'm not hungry —"

"Nonsense. A healthy young man will never turn down a good meal, in my experience."

George smiled sheepishly. "Thank you, sir, you're very kind," he mumbled, offering the housekeeper a smile that signaled his willingness to be fed, after all.

"What brings you to Thistleton, Brentford?" Trevor asked in a mild tone edged with skepticism. He took a drink of his wine while his dog returned to his spot in the corner.

"Oh, nothing." George swallowed hard.

Grace furrowed her brow and looked askance at him.

"Let me guess," Trevor said. "You came to try again with Miss Windlesham. I do admire your persistence."

"Oh, but if that's the case, I fear you are too late," Papa spoke up. "The Windleshams left today for Brighton. They find themselves with an urgent wish to escape our fair village for a while. And no wonder that, with the spectacle Her Ladyship made of herself, screaming at my daughter. I fear you have just missed them."

"Actually, no, sir," Mrs. Flynn interjected with a cautious glance as she returned to lay out a place setting on the table for their guest.

"Oh?" George perked up, no doubt in spite of himself.

"Aye. I heard from Sally they got a late start. Trouble fittin' all the luggage the ladies wanted to bring along onto the carriage," she said with an arch look. "So perhaps His Lordship won't be staying for supper, after all?" the old housekeeper inquired, glancing at George.

Papa looked at him, as well. "You might still catch them if you hurry."

George shook his head wearily. "I didn't

come here for Callie. She's made her feelings abundantly clear. No, the real reason I came is to apologize to you," he said, turning to Grace.

She could have choked on her food. George the brat apologize?

"You asked me to use discretion, and I promised you I would. But I lost my temper at some of the cruel things Callie said, and I revealed news that wasn't mine to tell. Frankly, I threw it in her face. I wanted to hurt her," he admitted, "but I never wanted to hurt you. You're one of the best friends I ever had, Grace. Losing Callie is bad enough. I don't know what I'll do with myself if you should hate me, too."

Grace felt her anger melt away in an instant at his little speech, his eyes wide and earnest. "Oh, George, you are so dear," she said in spite of herself, reaching over to squeeze his forearm. Tears welled in her eyes. "Of course you haven't lost my friendship. You're like the little brother I never had. I'm so sorry it didn't work out between you and Callie. You always seemed so perfect for each other. I don't know what the girl was thinking. And I wish you hadn't told her, so I could have handled it more delicately.

"But — then again," she continued with a

shrug, "I also have to thank you. Because when I saw you take the chance, risking your heart to go to her, it gave me the courage, in turn, to tell Trevor how I felt about him. If not for that moment of inspiration you gave me, the truth is, I might've stayed a blushing, tongue-tied spinster forever."

"You really think I would've let that happen?" Trevor drawled, his sardonic tone lightening the mood.

After a moment's laughter, George turned to her again.

"As long as you forgive me. That's all I care about. I should be crushed if I were disinvited to the wedding."

"Of course you're invited to the wedding, George," Grace said.

"Good. You'd better take care of her," he added, wagging a finger at Trevor.

The bridegroom-to-be bowed his head. "You have my word as a gentleman. Miss Kenwood will be treated like a jewel in a velvet box when she is my wife."

"Here, here," Papa said, "I'll drink to that." He raised his glass, and the rest of them did the same.

Mrs. Flynn quickly filled George's glass, then at Grace's insistence, poured one for herself, as well, to join in their toast to Grace and Trevor's happiness.

It was a bit later, as they were finishing the meal, that Grace finally worked up her nerve enough to broach the subject of George's new mistress.

She looked askance at him, and still could have wrung his neck about leading Marianne back into her old life, but it wasn't as though he had put a gun to her head.

Marianne had made the decision herself, and there was only so much you could do for someone.

"So how is Marianne?" she asked.

George looked at her like a startled hare.

Trevor's eyes narrowed. He studied him intently. "You seem nervous tonight, Brentford."

"What, me?" He faltered.

"Is everything all right?"

Suddenly, they heard voices outside, but Nelson's instant outburst drowned them out.

The dog launched himself toward the front door, barking more viciously than they had ever heard.

"Oh, God." George's face was turning ashen. "They've found me."

"Brentford." Trevor stared at him in ominous, brooding calm. "What have you got yourself into?"

But George couldn't even speak, his gaze

482

darting around the room. When he spotted the back door out the kitchen, he swept to his feet. "I've got to get out of here. They must've seen my carriage."

Trevor grabbed his arm. "Who?"

George blanched. "Marianne's former flash man, Jimmy Lynch," he admitted in a shaky whisper. "He came to see me in London. We had — words. I'm afraid I-I, well, I-I rather stabbed him."

Grace gasped.

"Sliced open his arm. Well, he was pointing a pistol at me!" he hastily explained. "But apparently that wasn't the end of it. The rookery bastard vowed he'd kill me for the insult." Staring at the door as though he expected Lynch to come bursting through it at any minute, George swallowed hard and tried to smile. "Dashed if he didn't also turn out to be the leader of a gang. Just my luck."

"So you led them here?" Trevor answered, while Nelson continued barking up a frenzy at the front door.

"I didn't think he'd follow me out to the country, let alone the parsonage! I meant to hide at Lievedon Hall, but when I got there, I couldn't stand being alone in that big, empty house. That's why I came here. I didn't mean any harm! I just didn't want to be alone. I can't believe they tracked me here to Thistleton! Poor Marianne," he said suddenly, his face darkening. "She wouldn't have told Lynch where I went unless he did something awful to her, I'm sure."

"Oh, no," Grace breathed, her heart pounding. "Trevor, I think this is the man who used to beat her."

George glanced from Grace to Trevor and nodded. "Judging by how I saw him treat her, I'd assume so," he whispered, ashen-faced.

Trevor glanced coolly toward the door. A peculiar icy gleam had come into his eyes. "All of you, remain calm. Sit still. I'll handle this."

"What are you going to do?" Grace asked quickly.

"Just talk to them." He threw his napkin down onto the table. "George, it would probably be best if you stay out of sight unless I call for you."

"Gladly."

"Do they want money?" Trevor asked.

"Not anymore," he forced out. "I think now Lynch just wants my blood."

Trevor considered this with a nod, then he stalked out of the dining room and went to the front door of the parsonage.

Grace stared after him with her heart in

her throat. She did not insult his intelligence by warning him to be careful, but exchanging a frightened glance with her father, she fought to keep the threat of panic under control.

George, however, was losing that battle. "They're going to kill me."

"Now, now, if Trevor says he can handle this, he can," she assured him with more conviction than she felt. "You're the one who told me he knows all those ways to kill someone with his bare hands, remember?"

"I remember you were appalled."

"Well, maybe I was wrong to be. I'm sure he's faced much worse than some lowly rookery vermin. Don't worry, he'll have it all sorted soon." She hesitated. "Do you think we should hide you somewhere in the house, George?"

"No point. If they saw my carriage outside, they know I'm here. Montgomery can try reasoning with them, but I don't think they're going to be satisfied until I go out there myself to pay the piper. I'm certainly not going to let them do anything to hurt the rest of you," he added in grim resolve.

"Give Trevor a few minutes first. Let's see if he can reason with them," Grace insisted, though her heart pounded with sickening dread.

George looked terrified, but it was the fear on her father's face that rattled her most of all.

"Papa, don't," she said in a taut voice when he rose to his feet.

"I should go out and stand with him. If God be for us, who can be against —"

"They have guns," George said.

"Trevor told us to stay here. If we stray from his orders, we might only make things worse. It's a delicate situation. Besides, we need to stay with George."

The young dandy stared in the direction of the doorway. "Rev," he said, "now might be an excellent time to pray."

Trevor walked out slowly into the night, counting four scruffy-looking cutthroats riding around the parsonage on horseback, obviously trying to get a look inside the building and possibly assessing it for possible points of entry.

There was no way he would let that happen. They weren't getting past him.

He checked his fury as they spotted him standing in the front courtyard in a casual pose; he propped his fists on his waist so they could see he was not armed.

They urged their horses over toward him,

halting in the lanternlight outside the front door.

"Evening," he greeted the strangers in a pleasant but guarded tone, while his dog continued barking wildly in the front bay window. "Can I help you boys with something?"

"This your house?"

"Who's asking?" he replied.

"That's none of your affair." The young, bearded rider on his left dismounted and stepped toward him aggressively.

Trevor just looked at him, unimpressed.

"Take it easy, Jonesey," the one in the purple coat ordered, still sitting astride his horse.

The bandage on his arm confirmed that this was the man George had wounded — the leader, Jimmy Lynch, Marianne's former flash man. "We're here for Lord Brentford, and we're not leavin' till you hand 'im over."

"He's not here," Trevor answered serenely, glancing from man to man, noting the weapons each one carried. "We don't get many strangers out here. I didn't catch your names?"

"Don't you worry about that," sneered the scar-faced horseman on Lynch's right. "You either hand over that snot-nosed brat, or we'll come in and get 'im ourselves."

"What's all this about?"

"Stay out of it, hayseed! Our business is with him. Just hand him over, and we'll be on our way. No one else gets hurt. If you refuse, you're not going to like what happens."

"It's not wise to threaten me."

Lynch shrugged. "Give him up, or we'll burn your village to the ground, it's that simple."

Trevor felt the readiness for battle rushing hard into his veins, familiar, terrible, and bracing. His heart pumped with martial eagerness, but with civilians just inside the house, the most important civilians in his life, he had to be cautious, given the odds were four to one and the enemy had the advantage of height astride their horses.

"I don't take kindly to strangers coming into my town making threats."

They laughed at him, arrogant and careless.

"Friend, I'm going to give you one last chance to hand over that little strutting coxcomb before we come in and get him ourselves," Lynch said.

"I'd like to see you try it."

Lynch laughed harder, his voice as harsh as gravel. "You think this is a game?" he demanded. "Maybe this will convince you we're not playing around. Jonesey, shut that fucking dog up."

To Trevor's left, the bearded man who had dismounted raised his pistol at Nelson, who was still barking through the window pane.

Trevor attacked, swinging his arm down with a clubbing blow to Jones's forearm; Jones's firing arm dropped, and when he pitched forward a little, knocked off-balance, Trevor drove his elbow back and nailed him in the throat.

Jones dropped his gun to clutch his damaged windpipe, gagging in shock; Trevor bent and picked up the weapon, turned, and fired on the middle rider, who was reaching for his gun. The man pitched off his horse with a garbled cry.

Less than five seconds had passed as Trevor strode toward the third man and pulled him off his horse, turning to use the blackguard's body as a shield when Lynch fired at him.

"Son of a bitch!" the gang leader cursed, but he did not waste time apologizing to his friend for shooting him.

Instead, Lynch wheeled his horse around and fled, galloping off down the drive.

"Too easy," Trevor mumbled to himself, his chest heaving.

Grace came running out. "Are you all

right? We heard shooting!"

"Fine. Get back in the house."

"Trevor, what are you doing?" she cried, when he swung up onto one of their horses.

"I've got to catch the leader. Brentford!" he bellowed, gathering the reins as the young earl and the pastor followed her out. "Deal with these three."

"Good God," Kenwood uttered.

"Blazes, you're efficient, man!" George exclaimed.

Grace glanced around at the three dead or dying men, then lifted her head and looked at Trevor in shock.

The horror in her eyes unsettled him far more than the quick skirmish he had just fought. Indeed, to him, this was merely business as usual, but the shock on her face took him off guard. He found himself arrested by a sudden cold wash of dread that he might have just ruined his own life. Cut down all the promise of their future together when he'd put down this threat.

"I could never love a soldier." With his casualties lying at his feet, her words from weeks ago suddenly rang in his ears and hung in the air between them like a fog, for how could a pastor's daughter ever love a man trained as an assassin? She served the cause of love while he was an abomination.

It was a role he'd learned to live with, as long as the world at large — his family, those close to him — never quite figured out how it really was, not the asinine hero tales in the papers.

Only his Order brothers, who'd made the same sacrifice of their humanity, could ever fully understand.

Grace never would. This would be the barrier between them, he saw now, the limit of how far she could go with him. In truth, she should never have to face such things.

Trevor looked away, bitter, shaken, and confused, feeling as though this hoped-for future was about to be snatched away from him, too. He knew he couldn't afford to get rattled right now, but he was suddenly more afraid of her reaction to his naked savagery than he'd ever be of any number of enemies coming at him. As the two separate pieces of his existence, past and present, clashed like iron double gates slamming closed, he cursed himself as a fool for ever getting so close to her in the first place. Surely, he was headed for a fall, because this kind of happiness couldn't be trusted.

Too late now. He was unmasked; the moment of truth had come. He quite expected to discover that, like she had once worried, what they had found together was too good to be true. Now that she saw the awful proof of his abilities, she would turn her back on him, abandon him, just like Laura had. Another major loss, and this one, damn, he'd never seen it coming.

Maybe some men were simply meant to be alone.

He clenched his jaw and looked away from her with a pang of odd, angry shame, telling himself all that mattered was that she was safe. She and her father, and George, too, and even the dog. As for himself, he could not afford to falter, could not let doubt creep in. That was how men in his profession got themselves killed.

His work tonight wasn't finished yet. The leader had escaped. With a low curse under his breath, he squeezed the horse's sides and raced off into the darkness to catch the last would-be intruder.

Grace was still standing there in shock, her hand covering her mouth.

Wide-eyed and slightly queasy, she couldn't stop staring at the three corpses outside her front door.

I think I'm going to be sick.

Her father rushed from man to man to see if any of the fallen were still alive, but two had the gore of crimson bullet holes gaping open on their chests, and the third had apparently suffocated from a crushed windpipe.

God, it was too horrible.

To be sure, he had protected them and himself. But was all this really necessary?

"Nothing more to be done for these three," her father grimly announced.

"I'm going after him." George ran to get his phaeton. "Lynch threatened my life, and besides, that blackguard needs to answer for all he's done to Marianne."

"I'm coming with you!" Grace called in a taut voice. If anything went wrong — if anything happened to Trevor — she had to be there to help him.

Her father tried in vain to dissuade her, but she refused to listen and stepped up into George's carriage. In the next moment, Papa decided to come with them, but his goal was to try to prevent any further violence.

"Let's go!" George slapped the reins over the horses' rumps and sent them barreling down the drive.

"There he is!" the lad exclaimed a few minutes later as soon as they turned onto the country road.

Grace no sooner looked ahead than she spotted Trevor galloping through the moonlight. Then he disappeared from view around the bend. "They're heading toward the village!"

"Lynch will have to cross the bridge to get back onto the main road to London," George remarked.

"Don't get too close. I don't want us getting anywhere near the line of fire," her father warned, though as fast as Trevor was riding, it seemed unlikely they'd be able to catch up until the two enemies had stopped.

His borrowed horse slowed its jolting gait a little when they went from the packed earth of the road to the cobblestone street at the edge of the village.

Lynch wasn't far ahead.

Trevor cursed to himself for not having caught the bastard before they reached the town: The presence of civilians was always a complicating factor. But he bade himself be patient. Once they were through the village and over the bridge, then he'd close in and put an end to this.

Riding for his life, Lynch turned the corner ahead, thundering into the village square. Trevor was only seconds behind him, but as he swept around the corner and charged into the square, he suddenly swore.

Ahead of him, Lynch roared at the rest of

his gang, waiting for him at the tavern.

Son of a bitch. The blackguard had brought an army with him. Trevor pulled the horse to a skidding halt, but in seconds, he was surrounded, a dozen guns pointed at him. One of the gang members grabbed the bridle of Trevor's borrowed horse and pulled it to a halt.

He had no choice but to lift his hands in surrender.

But he immediately noticed he wasn't the only one who had run afoul of the visiting gang. Lynch's minions had also cornered the Windleshams, apparently on their way through the village to leave for their Brighton holiday.

Several gang members had taken hold of the Windleshams' carriage horses. Others had pushed the coachman and grooms to the ground and wouldn't let them get up. Amid the gang's mocking laughter and shouted abuses, Trevor could hear Callie screeching in fright, Lord Windlesham bellowing in futile indignation, and Lady Windlesham protesting shrilly from inside the fine coach as the gang harassed them.

Presently, the gang members paused in their sport, turning to see what was happening in front of the pub.

"Get off that horse," Lynch ordered

Trevor, breathing hard. When he did not move fast enough for them, Lynch's nearest henchmen pulled him down from the saddle.

"Put your hands were we can see them!"

"On your knees." The gun Lynch thrust against his temple persuaded Trevor to obey. He lowered himself slowly to his knees, his hands in the air, but he was already scanning for an opportunity to turn the tables on them.

"Where are the others?" somebody asked the gang leader.

"This bastard killed them," Lynch ground out, then he punched Trevor in the face.

He absorbed the blow, shaking his head to clear it. Lynch poked him in the cheek with the pistol. "Who are you?" he snarled.

"Nobody in particular," Trevor replied with a mild wince.

"Answer me! Where'd you learn to fight like that? He killed them right in front of me like it was nothing," Lynch told his men.

Trevor just stared at him.

Lynch sneered. "Very well, it's all the same to me. You can die as easily as they did." He cocked his pistol, and Trevor shut his eyes.

"Jimmy! Don't you dare!"

Trevor flicked his eyes open in surprise

and glanced in the direction of the woman's voice.

Marianne.

"Let him go."

To his surprise, Marianne was holding a shotgun. He recalled her saying something once about the fowling piece that Old Abe, the innkeeper, kept behind the bar for protection.

She aimed it at her former flash man, but as she stepped closer to the lantern on the wall, Trevor saw that her face was covered in bruises. Still, the tenacious ex-harlot showed no sign of backing down. "He's got nothing to do with this. Leave him alone."

"You know him?" Lynch barked at her.

She nodded. "Trust me, he's got connections. You don't need that kind of trouble. Just let him go."

"The hell I will! He killed three of my mates."

"You'll get a lot worse if you don't leave him alone. I'm trying to protect you, you idiot! He's the constable!"

"Oh, really?" Lynch let out a harsh laugh. "I see. Are you goin' to try to arrest me?" he taunted.

"It's just an honorary post," Trevor said modestly, but his eyes glinted as he waited for an opening to launch his counterattack.

"You have the look of a soldier to me. You seen some action in the war?"

"I'm just a farmer," he replied.

"Let him go!" a voice called from some distance behind him. "It's me you want!"

Lynch looked past him. "Well, well, if it isn't our young lordling. You come to give yourself up, Lord Brentford?"

Trevor glanced over his shoulder, appalled to see that George had just arrived in his phaeton. Worse, Grace and her father were with him, and all three of them looked as horrified to find him in this situation as he was to see them arriving. George stepped down from his carriage.

"Bring him," Lynch ordered his men.

Just then, Callie poked her head out of the carriage. "George? George! What do they want with him? Leave him alone!"

She began screaming when George was also shoved down onto his knees beside Trevor.

Trevor scowled at him. "What the hell do you think you're doing?" he growled under his breath.

"This wasn't your fight, Montgomery," he answered. "You saved my life. I'm not going to let them murder you."

"George!" Callie kept screaming his name in a panic, until Jimmy's nearest henchman gave her a rough shove.

"Shut up, you barmy hen!"

Her parents erupted in fury inside the coach.

Trevor felt the situation spinning out of control as the Reverend Kenwood next attempted to insert himself into this debacle. "Please, people! Listen to me, I beg of you! Everyone needs to calm down!"

The old man walked cautiously toward the ruffians surrounding the front of the tavern. "There is no need for all of this. Please!"

"Who are you?" Lynch demanded.

"I'm the pastor here. Surely whatever has happened here, we can sit down and talk about this like civilized men —"

"Don't make me laugh! Stay out of this, priest. You get in my way, don't think I won't shoot you. Now, back off!"

The Reverend Kenwood faltered, but Trevor's stomach clenched when he saw Grace come forward cautiously.

Get out of here, he begged her mentally, to no avail.

"Marianne? Please, Mr. Lynch, may I speak to Marianne for a moment?" she asked in a tone of unquestioning respect. It was wise of her to let Lynch feel that he was in charge, Trevor thought, though he suspected she must be seething, knowing who and what this brute was. Nevertheless, he'd wring her neck for putting herself in danger.

"Grace, get back!" her father started, but she ignored him, too.

"What do you want with the wench?" Lynch demanded.

"I'm her friend. I only want to know if she's all right." As Grace pushed her way to the front of the crowd, Trevor watched in mingled horror and admiration.

How calm she looked! He was ridiculously proud of her in that moment. Apparently, she had enough experience in dealing with the downtrodden and sorry souls like Tom Moody not to be intimidated by the likes of Jimmy Lynch and his gang.

Trevor also noted she did not even glance over at *him.* He realized that she couldn't, not when he had a gun to his head, or she'd lose control of her emotions. It sank in that she was trying to help him, perhaps buy him time by redirecting the flash man's attention to his former mistress.

"I'm over here, Miss Grace," Marianne called in a shaken voice from the stoop outside the tavern, still clutching her shotgun.

The iron lantern above the pub's door

made Marianne's shadow loom large over them all. Grace stepped closer, turning away from Trevor. "Marianne, what's happened?" she asked wonderingly. Then she went very still when she saw the bruises on her face. "My God," she breathed, "what's he done to you?"

"Grace," Trevor warned, but she ignored him or maybe did not hear.

"Hoy! Missy! Get the hell away from her," Lynch ordered, clapping his hand down on Grace's shoulder to spin her to face him. "I bet I know who you are. You're the preacher's daughter that caused all this trouble in the first place!"

Grace's eyes widened and filled with righteous fury.

Oh, no, thought Trevor. He knew that look firsthand.

"Bloody do-gooder!" Lynch spat, looking her over. "You're the one that brought her here to try to hide her from me, eh? Thought you'd steal my property?"

Lynch was surprised, but Trevor was not when Grace suddenly went on the attack. "You monster! Get out of our village! Leave her alone! Who do you think you are? Some kind of a tough man, beating up a woman? You're lower than a dog!" she flung in his face.

"Well, every dog gets his day, don't he?" he taunted. "Maybe you should come along with us. Try a little whorin' yourself. You might like it. I can arrange that, you know."

As he grabbed Grace by the arm, her father yelled, but Trevor leaped to his feet and lunged at the gang leader. He tackled Lynch, slamming him down onto the cobblestones.

In the next instant, although he had his hand around Lynch's throat, he was surrounded by a bristling phalanx of weapons. "You keep her out of this," he snarled at Lynch in rage.

"Oh, she means somethin' to you, does she?" he mocked him, panting. "Well, that settles it, then. She's comin' with us."

Trevor squeezed harder and would have killed Lynch on the spot if not for the fact that one of the gang members suddenly put a gun to Reverend Kenwood's head. "Do it, and I kill the old man, eh?"

"Papa!" Grace yelled in terror.

Trevor considered his options and knew he could not take the chance.

He let go of Lynch and raised his hands and ignored Grace's cries of distress as they spent the next several minutes punishing him for his attack on their leader.

Fortunately, the Order taught their agents

how to endure this sort of brutal gauntlet. Not that he had ever really expected to have to *use* his training in quaint, sleepy Thistleton. But at last, when Lynch was satisfied that the gang had beaten out of him any thought of trying that again, Trevor was thrown into the Windleshams' carriage, the baron's family having been tossed out into the street.

Trevor was a little woozy from having his head slammed on the ground. And with six or eight men thrashing him, he realized he must have lost consciousness briefly, for he could not quite remember the moment they had manacled his wrists. He tested the handcuffs in groggy confusion, but winced as Callie's piercing shrieks filled the square.

"George! George! No!"

Her voice made his head throb worse.

"It's all right!" the young lord called back bravely, though he looked terrified as the ruffians shoved him into the coach beside Trevor. He, too, was handcuffed. "I'll be fine!"

"No, you won't, you piece of shit. I'm goin' put a bullet in your head," Lynch informed him. "Just like I promised." Then he laughed.

Grace whispered something to her father just as Lynch grabbed her by the arm.

"Come along, poppet! We wouldn't dream of leavin' without you!"

"Grace!" her father shouted.

"Jimmy!" Marianne protested.

"Shut up, bitch. Get up on the driver's box," he ordered Marianne as he made his followers handcuff Grace. She was not fighting them nearly hard enough for Trevor's liking, almost as if she wanted to be taken captive with him. Then Lynch pushed her into the coach and slammed the door. "Let's get out of here."

"Where are they taking us?" George whispered as the Windleshams' carriage lurched into motion seconds later.

"Trevor?" Grace asked softly. "Are you all right?"

"Never better. I'm going to wring your neck," he grumbled at her. "You had no business butting in. Why didn't you run when you had the chance?"

"They didn't give me much of a choice," she retorted. "Besides, when you quit fighting back, I knew I couldn't leave you. Even an Order agent can't defend himself when he's unconscious."

Trevor scowled that she had seen him that way. "How long was I out?"

"Maybe thirty seconds. I couldn't tell how badly you were hurt. Is anything broken, sweeting?"

"I don't think so."

"Poor thing." She leaned closer, lifting her bound hands to touch his swollen face tenderly with her fingertips. He flinched a bit at the contact, but even now, her touch felt heavenly.

What a baffling creature she was. One minute he thought he'd lost her love; the next, her actions proved she'd rather risk dying with him than be left behind to live without him.

Then she leaned closer and kissed him on the cheek, pausing to whisper in his ear: "I told Papa to fetch Sergeant Parker and his men."

Trevor received this news with a wave of relief. He gave her a canny half smile and nodded. "Clever girl."

"I'm so sorry," George uttered, sounding near tears. "Now all three of us are going to die, and it's all my fault."

"The hell we are," Trevor answered, willing himself back fully into the land of the living.

"We're not?" George asked, wide-eyed with fear as he sat across from Trevor and Grace in the darkened coach.

"Of course not," Trevor promised in a hard tone. "Don't worry. I've been in much worse situations than this. Just do as I tell you and give me a moment to figure out our next move."

"You see?" Grace whispered to George. "I told you he can handle whatever comes. We just have to work together, and Trevor will get us out of this."

Her blind faith in him made him ache. Blazes, hadn't she learned by now that he was trained to lie?

Think, he told himself, as the coach clattered on at top speed through the night.

CHAPTER 24

About an hour later, they pulled off the road and turned in at a wooded drive. Through the trees, Grace saw a dim, orange light shining like a baleful eye.

"Where are they taking us?" George asked anxiously.

"I don't know, but we'll soon find out," she murmured, staring out the carriage window as she sat beside Trevor.

When the woods cleared about a hundred yards up the drive, she saw that the light was actually a window in a small, gloomy, stone house surrounded by several acres of fields.

A ramshackle barn sat languishing amid one overgrown pasture, and although the light in the window of the house seemed evidence that somebody must live here, the small farmstead had an eerie, abandoned atmosphere, hidden from the world by its remote location and the woods that screened it from the road.

"What is this place?" Grace whispered to Trevor. "Some sort of hideaway for Lynch's gang?"

He nodded, scanning out the carriage window. "If I were to venture a guess, I'd say they probably use it for a safe house when they have trouble in Town. Maybe a way station for moving stolen goods out of the city, as well. That barn could serve as a warehouse for storing their contraband until they can carry it out to be sold in other parts of England."

"And a place to hide the bodies," George said dryly.

"Lovely."

"Lord Brentford, don't be a coward," Trevor said in a cool monotone.

George scowled at him in return.

As the carriage rolled to a halt, Grace's heart pounded with dread and an ominous uncertainty. She had a bad feeling about this place. George was probably right.

The three of them were probably going to end up in shallow graves in one of these pastures.

Then Lynch's hard-eyed henchmen opened the carriage door. The three prisoners were ordered out and taken into the ill-kept cottage, and herded into a back room.

Here they were thrust down into wooden chairs set back-to-back.

Trevor and George had their ankles tied to the chair legs, but at least the ruffians spared Grace this indignity. She scowled at the man with the rope as he reached to grab her ankle. "Don't you dare," she warned.

"Leave her alone," Marianne pleaded, following them into the back room. "Jimmy, please! Don't be cruel to 'er! She's a lady!"

"Eh, never mind the wench," he told his henchmen, ordering them out with a nod toward the door. "Leave us. Shut the door behind you, Stella."

Marianne withdrew with a worried frown.

Then Lynch studied them, pacing slowly around all three of them tied up in a ring back-to-back. Grace refused to cower with Trevor by her side. She could feel his fury as he watched Lynch pass with an icy stare.

The criminal stopped in front of George.

"Ow!" George muttered.

Grace looked over her shoulder and saw Lynch reaching down to wrench the signet ring off George's finger. "What do you want that for?" her friend demanded in a shaky tone.

"Well, Your Lordship, y'see, I had some time to think on the drive here. Funny how things come into perspective. I wanted to kill you before for slicin' up my arm, but it's not as if you killed three o' my men." He slanted an evil glance toward Trevor. "You're a pain in the arse, to be sure, but I'm thinkin' you're worth more to me alive. Lord Lievedon's son, aren't you? This ring should inspire your father to cooperate. As for you, *Constable . . .*" Lynch sauntered around to sneer at Trevor. "You're another story. You're not leavin' here alive. I'll let you ponder that a while, and you can think about what I'm going to do your lady here before I put you out of your misery. But don't worry, you'll get to watch the whole thing."

Grace felt her blood run cold, but she refused to let her terror show on her face. Instead, she reminded herself that there was a big difference between making a threat and carrying it out. Still, the man was a monster.

Just then, one of his henchmen poked his head in the door. "Hey, Jimmy, you better get out here. Trouble outside. I think we might've been followed."

"What's this? A rescue attempt from the hayseeds?" He scoffed. "You better hope your little farmer friends don't try anything stupid." As soon as he stalked out of the room, George nearly started hyperventilating.

"Oh, my God, how can this be happening —"

"Be quiet!" Trevor clipped out in a low tone. "That'll be Parker and his men. We don't have much time. Grace, did they tie your feet?"

"No."

"Good. Listen carefully. I want you to stand up, then step through your hands. Just bend down, bring your arms as low as you can, and step one leg through, then the other. Once you get your hands in front of you, come around to me and untie the ropes round my ankles. I'll get us out of here, I promise."

Shaking with fear, she did as he said, though it was an extremely awkward motion, especially in long skirts. "I better stop baking all those lemon biscuits," she muttered, trying to make light of the fact that she wasn't sure if she'd be able to squeeze her rear end through the circle of her bound arms.

"You can do it," he encouraged her.

At last, she succeeded in stepping one foot, then the other, through the circle of her bound wrists. When her manacled hands were in front of her, she hurried around to the front of Trevor and knelt, plucking at the knots tied around his ankles.

Trevor gazed lovingly at her while she finished untying his feet.

"There you are." All of a sudden, she heard him gasp. She glanced up at him in alarm.

"What is it?"

"You have a hairpin!" He was staring at her topknot.

"Well, yes —" she started.

"Give it to me! Hurry!" he whispered.

He stood up, freed from his chair, as she quickly slid it out of her hair — the same pearl-tipped hairpin she had poked him with on the night of the Lievedon Ball.

He stepped through the circle of his bound hands, just like he had ordered her to do, then Grace gave him the hairpin. "Untie George's feet," he ordered, hastily using her hairpin to pick the lock on the manacles around his wrists.

"How did you do that?" she exclaimed in a whisper.

"Just a trick I learned at school. Come here, I'll get yours, too."

"Where did you go to school?" she asked dubiously as she hurried over to Trevor so he could free her hands, as well.

"Long story. There's a lot I still have to

tell you about myself, Grace, someday, if you want to hear it."

"I'll hold you to that," she whispered.

He nodded, holding her gaze deeply for a moment, then he glanced at George. "Brentford, go lock the door, then get over here, and I'll get those off you."

All three of them were quickly freed, but Trevor hushed them, reminding them to be silent despite their jubilation at their progress.

Silently whisking a chair over to the wall, he stepped up to have a quick look out of the room's only window. It was small and narrow and set unusually high in the wall, probably as a security measure.

Fortunately, they were on the ground floor. It would be an easy drop. They would come out at the back of the house, but then they'd have to make a sprint across the back field to the woods.

He knew Lynch's men were outside checking the property. He spotted a couple roaming here and there off by the drive where the carriages were parked, but they seemed distracted.

As Trevor stood on the chair scanning the tree line, he saw motion in the dark woods. Sergeant Parker stepped out stealthily into the moonlight, rifle in hand; Trevor waved from the window; Parker beckoned, hurriedly signaling that it was safe to come.

"We need to go. Now." Trevor jerked the window open, tilting it as wide as it would go. "Parker's out there with his men. George, you first. Then help her down." He moved aside so George could climb out.

"As soon as you hit the ground, stand flat against the wall and wait for Grace and me. It's important that you not draw attention to yourself," he whispered. "Parker will send a few of his lads to distract Lynch's men, and when their attention is drawn elsewhere, we'll head for the tree line. Stay low. Hopefully those blackguards won't see us, but if they do, just keep moving forward. Parker and his men will give us cover. Got that?"

George nodded and practically dove through the window.

Grace was next, as soon as George whispered, "Ready!" from outside. She turned and gazed at Trevor with big blue eyes full of distress.

"Go on, it's all right," he urged her, cupping her cheek gently.

"Trevor, if we don't make it —"

"Don't talk nonsense!" His heart clenched with protectiveness; at the same time, he wanted to tear Lynch apart for scaring her.

"I'm not going to let anything happen to you. Now get the hell out of here."

She forced a brave smile and nodded with nervous resolve, then reached up for the windowsill. Trevor gave her a boost, steadying her by her hips as she climbed up. Brentford was waiting for her on the other side.

She braced her hands on his shoulders, but as the young earl grasped her by her waist to help her down, somebody tried the door.

Eyes narrowed, Trevor glanced over his shoulder, instantly ready to fight. He could hear the gang members puzzling over the locked door.

"What the 'ell? Did Jimmy lock it?"

"Where's the key?"

"There is no key! This one only locks from the inside!"

"Get in there!" one of them yelled, realizing.

They began kicking the door.

It jumped on its hinges.

"Hurry!" Grace cried in a frantic whisper.

But Trevor knew it was too late.

Lynch's men would be through that door in a moment and would shoot them in the back before they had reached the woods. There was only one option. He had to stay and fight. "Get her out of here," he ordered Brentford. "I'll hold them off."

"Trevor, no, you have come with us!" Grace insisted. "They'll kill you!"

He looked at her in searing anguish. "Go." He nodded toward the woods, where Parker was waiting impatiently. Two of his soldiers emerged from the shadows with rifles drawn, ready to give them cover.

Brentford was already pulling her away by her wrist.

"You come back to me, or I'll never forgive you," she vowed over her shoulder.

"I'll always come back to you, Grace. Now, go."

Brentford had to drag her another few steps, but she finally started running willingly. As the pair of them sprinted away from the gang's hideout toward the woods, Trevor watched them for another heartbeat, but he dared not linger. He knew he had only seconds to brace for the enemy's arrival.

He turned back to face the room and scanned it for anything useful. Lifting the chair he had been tied to, he smashed it on the floor, breaking off one of the legs to use as a bat. He got into position beside the doorway, his back to the wall and waited, every muscle tensed, wild instinct filling his veins.

When the door crashed inward off its hinges, the first gang member through the doorway got a shattering whack to the face.

Trevor used his bat to block the fist of the next one who swung at him, then knocked him out with a left hook to the temple.

Lynch must have heard the commotion, for he also came running. "Get in here! They're escaping!" the gang leader bellowed from the corridor outside the room. "Split up!" he barked at several others behind him. "Go kill the other two! This one's mine."

Trevor knew he needed to buy more time for Grace and George to get farther away by taking out as many of Lynch's men as possible.

The next drew a gun on him; Trevor counterattacked with a circular block and a step behind him, grabbing the man's weapon arm and twisting it backwards to wrench the son of a bitch forward from the hips.

It was as natural as breathing to extend the twisted arm and break it over his knee. A garbled cry escaped the man as he fell to the floor.

Trevor stooped down and had the man's dropped pistol in his hand in a heartbeat.

The next thing anyone knew, he slammed Jimmy back against the wall, one hand clamped around windpipe, the other holding the pistol to the gang leader's cheek.

"Anyone moves, he dies," Trevor warned, panting.

Jimmy cursed, and outside they could hear the sharp report of shots fired, but in the room, the remaining two men backed off; they had to step over the one with the broken arm, who had just passed out from pain.

Trevor was filled with battle frenzy, nearly tasting blood. Everything in him wanted to rid the world of this slimy underworld snake. It would be so very easy.

Lynch must have seen the spark of madness in his eyes. He wilted back against the wall. "No hard feelings, man. It's just business."

"Call them off." He squeezed his windpipe just a little.

Lynch gagged, and Trevor relented, allowing him to nod at his men. "Tell 'em to stand down," Lynch ordered.

The other two ran off to do his bidding, leaving Trevor alone in the room with the gang leader.

No witnesses to whatever might happen.

Lynch realized it, too.

518

"Now, what was that threat you made to my fiancée?" he asked softly.

Lynch gulped. "You c-can't kill me, man. Y-you have to obey the law. I thought you were the constable?"

The criminal's insistence that *he* obey the law outraged him all over again, but hearing that one term, "constable," Trevor was abruptly reminded of his new life.

Grace.

The Grange, the village. All those people counting on him.

No longer roaming through the shadows, one of the Order's dark angels of vengeance. In that existence, he would have taken pleasure in killing this vicious parasite.

But that wasn't his life anymore.

And Grace would never understand if he finished the job here, the way he might have done with one of the Order's enemies. He had seen her face when she had discovered his handiwork outside the parsonage, like he was something from a nightmare.

He could not bear for her to look at him like that ever again even though he deserved it. No, if he truly wanted to be with her, it ended here. It was time to let go of his old life.

He was a civilian now.

"You have no idea how lucky you are," he

whispered, still trembling with rage as Parker stepped into the room.

"Lord Trevor! You all right, sir?"

"Take over with this one before I do something I'll regret," he ground out, shoving Lynch against the wall one last time for good measure.

"Aye, sir." Parker switched places with him.

"Grace?"

"Safe as houses, sir." Glancing round at the men strewn about the room. "Well, you've been busy," he offered wryly. "Hand me those manacles, would you? We got eight more under arrest outside."

"This one's the leader. Three more up at the parsonage. Dead."

"I heard," Parker said with a grim look as Trevor retrieved the manacles. "Rev told us when he came to fetch us. Guess you haven't lost your touch."

"Not yet," he answered guardedly.

Then Parker slammed the manacles on Jimmy Lynch's wrists. "I can take it from here, my lord. I figure you've probably had enough fun for one night."

"To be sure."

"There's a lady outside waiting to see you," Parker added, then he called for two of his soldiers to come and escort the gang leader off to wait facedown in the field with his followers.

Lynch scowled as Parker's men marched in and took him by his arms. They proceeded to show him out, but when they passed Marianne, who had just stepped out of hiding to curse at Lynch, the soldiers stopped in their tracks, seeing the bruises on the face of their favorite tavern girl.

"He did this to you?" one demanded.

She put her head down in shame.

"Right. You're comin' with us, lad," the other soldier said to the gang leader in a hard tone. "We got a little something special for you out back before we put you with the others."

"What? Hey!" Lynch began resisting.

"I think you deserve a taste of your own medicine."

"Hey! You can't do this! I have my rights! Constable?!"

"I don't hear anything, do you?" Trevor asked Marianne in a casual tone.

"Crickets," she replied, folding her arms across her chest. "Such a pleasant summer night."

"Hey! Let me go! Get your hands off me!"

They took him away.

Marianne gave Trevor a taut, wry smile. "He always was a coward at heart."

"Bullies usually are." Trevor studied her. "You all right?"

She gave him a stoic nod, then offered a smile of sympathy. "You look about as good as I do. Anything broken?"

"Nah. Come on, let's go see Grace."

Marianne stayed planted. "I don't think I can face her," she forced out.

"What?" Trevor turned to her, setting his hands on his waist. "Why?"

She lowered her gaze. "After all she did to help me, I threw it away when George invited me to London, and look what happened. Look at what I brought upon everyone. This is all my fault. You could've been killed, and George and even dear Miss Kenwood. I'm such a fool. How many chances does someone deserve?"

"As many as it takes, I hope." He paused. "Marianne, Grace isn't angry at you. Lucky for us both, we're dealing with a preacher's daughter."

"Montgomery! There you are!" George rushed through the door at that moment. "Are you all right?" he asked, crossing the room to them.

"No worries. You did well tonight," he encouraged the shaken young man. "Thanks for getting Grace out of harm's way for me."

"Thanks for saving my life!" he countered.

"She's outside, by the way — staying put, just where Parker told her."

Trevor smiled wistfully. "Good girl."

George turned to Marianne and took her hands in his own with a pained look. "I am so sorry —"

"Rubbish, I'm the one responsible for all this —"

"That's not what I mean," he interrupted. "I . . . I'm sorry that I treated you like a whore, Marianne."

She blinked. "I am a whore, George," she said.

"No, you're not. I mean, you're so much more than that! You should give yourself more credit. Look at you! You nearly gave your life to save mine. And I can guess why Lynch beat you — to make you tell where I had gone."

She lowered her head. "I tried not to break."

Trevor took a deep breath and looked away, fighting the dire temptation to go outside behind the house and join Parker's men in punishing the bastard, or better yet, finishing him off entirely like his fiercer instincts still longed to do.

"I'm all right," Marianne assured them, gathering herself and lifting her head again. "I've had worse."

George looked at her admiringly for a moment, then reached into his pocket and took out his billfold. "Here. Lynch stole this out of my pocket earlier, but Parker got it back for me. It's yours." He took the whole thick wad of folded paper bills and pressed it into her hand. "Take this and start a new life for yourself."

"George! This is a lot of money."

"It's the least I can do after what Lynch did to you on account of me. Please — I won't accept it back!"

"There's three thousand pounds here!" she said in shock.

"I know. I thought I'd have to hide out, you know, go incognito for a while with that barbaric tribe out for my blood. But I don't need it now. Take it, please, I'll only gamble it away. I want you to have it instead."

"It's too much. I could buy the pub with this much money!"

"Why don't you?" Trevor replied, arching a brow. "With the way you've charmed Parker's men, I know you'd have at least a dozen loyal customers, and believe me, the boys know how to run up a tab."

"Buy the Goose?" she echoed. "That's an interestin' idea. At least I could keep the books since I can read now." She tilted her head, warming to the notion. "Aye, maybe I could."

Trevor smiled fondly.

"Just one problem," Marianne said with a sigh after a moment. "Nobody wants me in Thistleton. Especially now."

"Yes, we do," a familiar voice said from the doorway.

George turned in amazement. "Callie!"

Calpurnia Windlesham stood in the doorway with her fists balled at her sides, her golden curls run riot, her heart-shaped face stained with tears. "I'm glad all three of you are here."

She glanced from George to Trevor to the ex-harlot. "I know I've been horrible to everyone lately, but I want you all to be my witness. Marianne, if you want to stay in Thistleton, I won't let Mama make your life miserable anymore, and I won't, either. We might never be friends, but I heard how you saved George's life. You're a very brave person, and I-I wanted to thank you for helping him a-and to apologize for being mean to you."

George stared at her in shock.

Even Trevor was impressed.

Both men glanced at Marianne, who looked like a feather might have knocked her over. "Well, of course," she blurted out, but beyond that, she appeared too dumb-founded by the belle's contrition to say another word.

"Callie, what are you doing here?" George burst out in a wondering tone, taking a few steps toward her.

"I just arrived with Pastor Kenwood," she explained, glancing over her shoulder toward the drive. "He was obviously distraught over their taking his daughter, so we followed Sergeant Parker's riders at a safe distance to find out what was happening . . . and if you all were still alive." She swallowed hard, clearly still shaken up by the night's events. "My parents tried to make me stay behind with them, but I had to see you for myself.

"Oh, George, if anything had happened to you — !" she burst out. "I mean, it's one thing for *me* to torture you, but no one else is allowed to do it! When I saw them point a gun at you —" Her words broke off in a sob, and she ran to him as tears flooded her eyes, launching herself into the astonished fellow's arms.

Marianne looked askance at Trevor, who watched in mystified amusement as Callie covered George's face in adoring, girlish pecks. "I don't want to fight with you anymore! Haven't you figured it out yet, you blockhead? I'm in love with you and always have been."

"Oh, Callie . . ."

Trevor and Marianne exchanged a smile of furtive humor as they turned away to give the couple their privacy.

"It would seem all is forgiven," he remarked to her under his breath, as they stepped out into the night.

"Not everyone," Marianne murmured, narrowing her eyes in the direction from which Lynch's occasional shouts of pain were coming. "My dear Lord Trevor, would you think ill of me if I took this opportunity to tell Mr. Lynch what I really think of him?"

"Tell him?" Trevor frowned. "I always feel that actions speak louder than words."

"Hmm," she agreed, slanting him a sly look. "I like the way you think, sir."

"Enjoy it. And don't worry, he's going to jail for a long time."

"In that case . . ." She sauntered off around the back of the building to revel in watching the soldiers trashing her tormentor. At their invitation, she did not pass up the chance to knee him in the groin. And when he cursed her for it, called her a whore, her soldier friends took umbrage, and poor Jimmy Lynch only made it worse for himself.

Meanwhile, Trevor walked across the open field near the edge of the woods at the drive, where Grace was trying to comfort her weeping father. "Honestly, I'm all right, Papa, I promise. I'm quite unscathed."

"Oh, my dearest child." He hugged her harder. "If I have to lose you, let it be for the sake of your happiness, not the violence of murderous brigands!"

"You're not going to lose me, Papa! I'll just be next door, I'll see you every day. You know I'll never abandon you. Look," she interrupted him, "here comes my fiancé."

Trevor smiled and did his future father-in-law the courtesy of ignoring his distraught paternal tears. "I thought being a country constable was supposed to be a quiet duty. Don't worry, they said. Nothing ever happens."

"Well, it didn't — until you came along." The Reverend extended his hand to Trevor, and when he took it, the old man pulled him in for a fatherly hug. "Thank you for saving my daughter," he whispered, seeming near tears again. "If there's anything I could possibly do to repay you."

"Nonsense. I'm just sorry you both had to go through all that."

"Thank God, it's over now. Sweet heaven,

I never prayed so hard in my life," the pastor said.

Marianne walked toward them through the darkness, having enjoyed her taste of revenge. "Oh, you come with me, Reverend!" she called, taking his arm as she joined them. "You look like you could use a drink."

He let out a wordless exclamation of agreement, then polished the tears off his spectacles.

"Come on, you. Let's leave these two alone." Marianne chuckled and led him toward the carriage.

At last, Grace and Trevor turned to face each other and were promptly lost in each other's gaze.

Trevor rested his forearms on her shoulders and smoothed her hair gently behind her ears. God help him, he wasn't sure where to start. He was wary, his defenses already braced against the pain of judgment, rejection. He'd already lost one fiancée, after all, because of his dealings with the Order. If he lost Grace, too, he did not know where he'd go, what he would do, or if he would ever find the courage, or even the ability, to love again. *Please don't turn me away.*

After all the chaos of this night, the last

thing he wanted to do was call attention to the savage side she'd seen tonight. No doubt the details of it were emblazoned in her mind, but now that they came down to it, he did not know what to say for himself.

He shook his head. "You never pressed about my secrets," he forced out. "Now you know."

"Dearest," she breathed, laying her hand on his chest. Her blue eyes searched his face, caked with dried sweat and streaked with blood.

He looked away and dropped his gaze. "I had to protect you," he answered barely audibly.

"And you did," she choked out, suddenly stepping into his arms. She threw her own around him and held him tightly, pressing her cheek to his chest. "You nearly gave your life for me."

He could feel her shaking as he wrapped his arms around her.

"God, Trevor, I'm so ashamed of myself that I ever judged you," she whispered in a voice half-strangled with emotion. "I realize now I've never even *seen* the kind of evil you've been fighting all your life."

"I don't ever want you to see it. You shouldn't have to. That's the whole point of what I do. Used to do," he corrected himself in a low tone, still amazed at her reaction.

She pulled back to fix him with an earnest, artless gaze. "You are a hero, Trevor, whether you like the term or not."

He stared at her. "If you say so." Then he hesitated. The answer to his only question seemed obvious, but he had to hear it out loud for himself. "You can . . . accept me, then?"

"I adore you!" she answered vehemently. Then she reached up and cupped his cheek with anguished tenderness. "Oh, my love, thank you for all you've done. Not just for me, tonight. But for all of us."

That simple whisper coming from her meant more to him than all the pomp and circumstance the Regent had forced on the Order at Westminster Abbey a few months ago.

Here and now, it all meant something, finally. With Grace in his arms.

She wiped a fleck of dried blood off his face with the pad of her thumb. "You can rest now, my warrior," she whispered. "You've done your duty. Now let me take you home."

His eyes misted at the beauty of those words. He shut them and held her closer. Did she have any idea, he wondered, how much he needed her?

For the first time since the war's end, he began to think that maybe he wouldn't have to hide at all. At least not with her. He cupped her sweet head against his chest, still marveling that she didn't run from him after all she'd seen him do. When she sighed with contentment in his embrace, nestling against him, he held on to her a little more tightly, rather like a shipwrecked man clinging to a solid rock in a cold, stormy sea.

It was so strange after the savagery of this night to be flooded with tenderness. From love to hate and back again, from darkness into light.

"You're a beacon in the night to me, Grace," he whispered. "Never change. You've given me more than you will ever know."

A place to belong.

"I'll always be here for you, Trevor. I love you." She glanced up and met his gaze in artless honesty. "With all my heart, I love you," she repeated, as if she knew how much his scarred soul needed to hear it.

Trevor held his breath, then he said the words he had never thought he'd be able to say, because he wouldn't lie. "I love you, Grace. So very much, my darling." He bowed his head to claim her lips and kissed her with a tenderness that blazed in him in equal measure as his fury did when it came to protecting what he loved.

This woman most of all. His woman. All he wanted as her lips yielded beneath his kiss was to take her home and lay her down.

She must have sensed the onslaught of the passion gathering in his blood, for she ended the kiss and pulled back with a knowing little smile. Flirtation sparkled in her eyes. "Ahem." She cleared her throat and glanced around at the soldiers milling about, minding their prisoners.

"So I trust you've got this spot of bother sorted out, then?" she asked in a business-like tone, smoothing his lapels.

"I have," he answered in wary amusement, vastly reassured by the arch humor in her voice.

"Well done, then. In truth, I expected no less," she said with a brisk nod. "That's our Lord Trevor. Do something well and thoroughly or not at all."

Trevor was bemused. He furrowed his brow and shook his head, studying her. No tears? No fainting? So soon she found the ability to joke with him? He really was impressed. "You handled yourself well back there."

"Only because you were beside me." She shrugged. "I knew you'd rescue us. It's what you *do.*"

He stared at her. "Grace, that's the biggest compliment you could ever pay me. Thank you. I mean it."

"Well, it's true. You're like a great stone pillar that holds up the sky, Lord Trevor Montgomery. You and your fellow agents. Strong. Solid," she added, giving his biceps a playful squeeze. "I'm proud to call such a man my own. Shocked about it, really. Wallflower like me."

"Wallflower?" he exclaimed, finally relaxing enough to tease her back. "From what *I* hear, you are the new scarlet woman of the village."

"Yes, but only for you."

"Ow," he said when she pressed up onto tiptoes and kissed him on the jaw where he had been punched several times earlier this evening.

"Oh, you poor thing! Come with me," she ordered. "Time to clean up all your mean old bumps and bruises." She took his hand, tugging him along as if he were one of the Nelcott children with a scraped knee. "I trust Sergeant Parker can manage things from here."

"Grace, you don't have to baby me."

"Excuse me, you're mine, and I can do whatever I please with you," she shot back, casting him a deliciously wicked half smile over her shoulder.

It startled him. "Well!" he said, pleasantly surprised. "If you put it that way." And he went with her most willingly. "Parker!" he called. "You're in charge here! I've got to, er, take care of something at home."

"If we make it that far," she whispered under her breath.

Parker sent him an amiable wave. Lord knew the man had plenty of experience in sweeping up the aftermath of the Order agents' many dangerous quests.

Frankly, they couldn't do it without him. But Trevor put all the bloody business of this night out of his mind, focusing his attention on the alluring prospect of spending the hours until dawn with his fiancée. He yelled to Parker that he was taking one of the horses, then he helped Grace mount up and swung into the saddle behind her.

As he took the reins, steadying her against his body, he had visions of tumbling the luscious creature straight into his bed. One place where he would quite enjoy receiving a hero's welcome.

Suddenly, he couldn't wait to get home.

"Ready?" he murmured, sliding one arm around her waist.

"For anything," she vowed. "As long as

we're together."

"That, my love, is a given," he whispered at her ear. She laid her head back happily on his shoulder. Then Trevor urged the horse into motion, and they went cantering off together down the moonlight-silvered road.

EPILOGUE

Six Weeks Later

"Grace, hurry up, we need to go! Darling, I know you're feeling queasy, but you're going to miss the biggest wedding Thistleton's ever seen. Come on, sweeting. Callie will be a wreck without you."

"You did this to me," she replied as she stepped out from behind the corner screen after being sick again, as she did most mornings these days.

Not that she minded one bit, in truth.

If marrying Trevor had been a dream come true, then having his baby, a child of her own to love at last, was worlds beyond any joy she ever could have envisioned.

Let the morning sickness come.

But today, she really wanted to feel at least somewhat human, so she accepted the tepid ginger tea he'd brought her and took a sip. He tucked a lock of hair behind her ear and felt her forehead to see if she was feverish though, of course, she wasn't.

"All right. I'm ready to go."

"That's my girl. I love you," he added, bending to give her a boyish kiss on her cheek.

"In sickness and in health, eh?"

"Always." He kissed her hand, then tugged her along. "Hurry. You look beautiful," he added when she lingered before the mirror.

Gazing at herself in the glass, Grace saw a woman transformed by the changes in her body, and indeed, in her life. She was glowing. Then from the corner of her eye, she noticed Trevor watching her, arrested.

"Radiant," he whispered. "Absolutely luscious, and all mine."

She cast him a tremulous smile.

"Now stop dawdling," he ordered, grabbing her hand. He tugged her toward the door and outside, past all the reconstruction work under way inside the house.

This morning, Papa would be marrying George and Callie, and the festivities were sure to last for days to come. But it was just as well that Grace's morning sickness delayed their exit from the Grange, for if they had left on time, they would have missed the messenger who came galloping up the drive.

"Lord Trevor Montgomery?" the courier called.

"Yes?" he answered, as they walked outside.

"Delivery for you, sir!"

"Good timing." Trevor took the letter and quickly paid for it.

"Who's it from?" Grace asked, as he helped her up into his finest carriage, newly brought down from London.

"The Beauchamps." Joining her in the coach, he absently ordered Nelson to stay but told his coachman to hurry. At last, they were on their way to the wedding. Trevor cracked the waxen seal and unfolded the letter.

She waited while he skimmed a few lines in curiosity.

"Are they back in London?"

"No, this came all the way from France. They're still on holiday."

"It must be rather urgent. What's the big news?"

Trevor lowered the letter with a stunned look. "Why, that sneaky old Scot! I can't believe it. He always said he had no family . . ."

"What is it?" Grace touched his arm and looked at him in concern. "Not bad news, I hope?"

"No, no. Nothing like that . . ." He shook his head to clear it. "Seems Beau caught a whiff of information in Paris and decided to follow the trail."

"But he's on holiday!"

"Once a spy, my love," he said absently. "And I'm sure Carissa insisted on 'helping.' "

"Aha," she murmured. "So what did he find out? Or can't you tell me?"

"Well, confidentially — it's about our old Scottish handler, Virgil Banks."

"Oh, yes, you've mentioned him before. How he was like a father to you all, and how difficult it was for you when he was murdered." The grim subject took some of the glow out of the day before them.

"Well, as it turns out, the old Scot was even more of a mystery than we suspected." He shook his head in wonder. "I can't believe he never told us!"

"Told you what?" she exclaimed impatiently.

He shook his head in wonder. "Virgil had a daughter."

Grace frowned, seeing that his full attention had gone off on this astonishing news. She plucked the letter out of his hand. "No spy business today!"

"But you don't understand. We never

540

knew he had any family!"

"Husband, we are on our way to a wedding! This is a day for love, not intrigue. Please?"

He paused, then smiled ruefully. "You're right." As stunned as he was by the news, he did his best to put it aside and drew her into his arms. "I want everyone in the world to be as happy as we are."

"Even Callie and George," she agreed.

"Now that they're both ready." When he looked at her, she saw the love and husbandly concern in his gray-blue eyes and felt her heart lift again. "You all right?" he murmured.

"Never better," she whispered, giving way to a warm smile, which he reflected back to her.

Then he bent his head and kissed her, and once more, the day, indeed, their entire future glowed.

As long as they were one.

AUTHOR'S NOTE

Lovers of nineteenth-century literature may recognize Grace Kenwood, the heroine of this story, as an homage to those most famous of preacher's daughters: Jane Austen and the Brontë sisters. The Reverend George Austen was the vicar of Steventon and Deane in Hampshire for more than thirty years, while the Reverend Patrick Brontë, born in County Down, Ireland, became the Anglican incumbent at Haworth in Yorkshire in 1820 and served there till his death in 1861.

Another research topic that I thought readers might like to know more about is the massive eruption of Mount Tambora, which turned 1816 into the infamous "year without a summer." Located in Indonesia along the Pacific "Ring of Fire," mighty Mount Tambora was a fourteen-thousand-foot-high mountain before it woke up from its five-thousand-year nap to spew columns of ash and steam some twenty-six miles into the stratosphere.

It was this great height to which the ash cloud flew that enabled it to spread so effectively, encircling the globe. Veiling the sun, it dropped global temperatures an average of five degrees Fahrenheit over the next year or so, until it finally dispersed.

The volume of material that Tambora blasted into the atmosphere is hard to imagine. It is estimated to have been 10 times greater than Italy's Mt. Vesuvius (which buried Pompeii) and 150 times greater than the Mt. Saint Helens' eruption of 1980. Even Indonesia's gigantic Krakatoa, which erupted in the 1880s, is estimated to have been the equivalent of twenty Hiroshima bombs going off simultaneously. Yet Mount Tambora was one order of magnitude on the VEI (Volcanic Explosivity Index) greater than that!

Considering that it hit in April 1815, while the Congress of Vienna was under way on the other side of the world, it was spectacularly bad timing for war-weary Europe. The exhausted armies of both the Allies and the Napoleonic forces alike were finally marching home after twenty years of war. Economies and infrastructure were already in shambles when the ash clouds rolled in and killed the crops. For a still mostly agrarian world, where new, scientific agricultural "improvements" were only just being implemented by the more foresighted landlords, this spelled disaster not just for the human population but for the horses they relied on for transportation and for the farm animals that provided food. With dire Malthusian warnings of overpopulation and starvation ringing in their ears, the people of the nineteenth century wondered if the end of the world was at hand as they watched the snow fall in July and August.

In France, the wine grapes died on the vine, while in Germany, the skyrocketing cost of fuel (i.e. oats for horses) became such a problem than an enterprising nobleman and gentleman-inventor, Baron Karl von Drais, invented the first bicycle. "The Running Machine" (later dubbed the velocipede) didn't have pedals or brakes: You sat on the equestrian-inspired saddle and pushed along the ground with your feet. Throughout the world, weird-colored sunsets were the norm. Across the Pond in President Madison's America, pioneers whose crops had been ruined by the snows pushed farther west into the wilderness, hoping to find areas unaffected by the malfunctioning weather. Up in Canada,

Quebec City got a foot of snow in the middle of June. Because of the food shortages, there were frequent riots and looting in many places, and when populations are weakened by famine, they soon become vulnerable to disease. Eastern and Southern Europe were especially hard hit by typhus. It sounds like I'm describing the setting for a dystopian novel rather than the "glittering" Regency period, doesn't it? But such is history. Personally, I find it encouraging in our uncertain times to hear about how our forebears dealt with times of severe adversity like the "year without a summer."

Thanks again for reading, and I hope you'll look for Nick's story, the next (and final!) installment of the Inferno Club series, coming sometime next year.

Best wishes,
Gaelen

The employees of Thorndike Press hope you have enjoyed this Large Print book. All our Thorndike, Wheeler, and Kennebec Large Print titles are designed for easy reading, and all our books are made to last. Other Thorndike Press Large Print books are available at your library, through selected bookstores, or directly from us.

For information about titles, please call:
  (800) 223-1244

or visit our Web site at:
  http://gale.cengage.com/thorndike

To share your comments, please write:
  Publisher
  Thorndike Press
  10 Water St., Suite 310
  Waterville, ME 04901